FL-28-.

★　　★　　★　　★

IF MEN
WERE ANGELS

IF MEN WERE ANGELS

REED KARAIM

W. W. NORTON & COMPANY
NEW YORK · LONDON

For Aurelie

165648924

Copyright © 1999 by Reed Karaim

While some historical events depicted in this novel are factual, as are certain locales and persons and organizations in the public view, this is a work of fiction whose characters and their actions are a product of the author's imagination. Any resemblance to actual persons, living or dead, organizations, or events is entirely coincidental and not intended by the author, nor does the author pretend to have private information about such individuals.

For information about permission to reproduce selections from this book, write to Permissions, W. W. Norton & Company, Inc., 500 Fifth Avenue, New York, NY 10110

The text of this book is composed in Minion Display, with the display set in Trajan Bold
Desktop composition by Ekim Knowles
Manufacturing by Quebecor Printing, Fairfield, Inc.
Book design by Ekim Knowles

Library of Congress Cataloging-in-Publication Data

Karaim, Reed.
    If men were angels / Reed Karaim.
        p.   cm.
    ISBN 0–393–04780–6
    I. Title.
PS3561.A5745I36   1999
813'.54—dc21   98–51838
                                                                     CIP

W. W. Norton & Company, Inc., 500 Fifth Avenue, New York, N.Y. 10110
http://www.wwnorton.com

W. W. Norton & Company Ltd., 10 Coptic Street, London WC1A 1PU

1 2 3 4 5 6 7 8 9 0

What is government itself, but the greatest
of all reflections on human nature?
If men were angels, no government would be necessary.

—JAMES MADISON

★ ★ ★ ★

IF MEN
WERE ANGELS

★ ★ ★ ★

BOOK ONE

I.

THE ROAD is narrow and rolls up and down in hesitant, not-quite hills that capture all the half-hearted defeat I once saw at the heart of this country. I park on the edge of town. There is no one here who would welcome me. I sit in the car, watching snow slant across the hills and the sad little town, and after a while a strange thing happens. I am looking at a field, the gaunt figures of bent cornstalks leaning together into the gray distance, and it comes alive.

The world of my memories is lined with the faces of strangers, and now they rise pale and attenuated in the wintry light, pale but hopeful, raised and always hopeful, as if the most delicate of all emotions has gathered substance in the flesh. We were, in the end, just another road show, another carnival in a world jaded by spectacle, but in the beginning there came these moments when the crowds gathered in the summer twilight and you felt it out there. You could hold out your hand and feel it against your palm.

There was a night when we arrived late at a small southern town in a state I have long forgotten. They had been waiting for five hours and the noise started even before we left the buses. We walked through the crowd and they were cheering us for no reason, leaning across the rope and clapping, slapping us on our backs, and soon we were all running, running in this narrow space between thousands, carried along by the sound, flying through the darkness until we came out into the space reserved for us and we saw the courthouse brilliantly illuminated, a Georgian wedding cake, white as a bridal gown, curved pillars suspended in the air by light.

He was standing on the porch with his wife, swaying to the music, and their shadows were thrown up huge and black against the wall. It was August but a girl in an Easter dress, her black hair in a white bow, walked up to the microphone and sang "The Star Spangled Banner" in a voice so guileless you had to close your eyes, and the crowd fell into a hush, and before he even spoke, you could feel it gathering and you knew that there is nothing ephemeral about hope; gathered, it is a force like the wind that bends trees and blows rooftops into the sea.

Then he spoke. He took off his jacket and it wasn't long before he sweated through his blue shirt. He went through all he would do in his gentle midwestern voice, that voice in which the words each did their business and got out of the way. I won't let you down, he said. I won't fail you. I will be there. There has been enough blame. There is a time for trust. There is a time to believe in each other. There is a time to say we have forgiven and we will move forward. There is a time for hope. He stood with his shadow swinging back and forth across the courthouse and when you looked into the crowd you saw their faces raised to his and you could feel everything they wanted to believe pounding like a rush of blood into your temples. When they cheered the sound seemed dragged up from the earth itself.

That night I believed he would do it. I knew I wanted him to, despite all my protestations of neutrality, and I thought he would. I thought he would be the next president of the United States and I thought he would be a good one.

I want you to know that I too believed. I want you to know that I shared your hope, maybe more than most. I want you to know I too could see it, the kingdom of the wish coming alive.

I want you to know so you'll understand that I ruined him for something else.

I told myself once it was for the truth, the last excuse for every cruelty. But now I think it might have been for much less than that. I think maybe I ruined him because I could not believe in something much smaller. Three simple words. An answer to my prayers.

II.

I FIRST MET him on a snowy morning in Concord, New Hampshire. I was standing on the statehouse square across from the beetle-browed statue of Daniel Webster, which glowers eternally at the ostentatiously golden-domed capitol, when his van came down the street and he got out looking for hands to shake. There was no one around. He stood on the sidewalk in a charcoal gray topcoat, the snow falling in flecks into his coal-black hair, his hands held awkwardly together in front of him like those of an altar boy. He was tall and slender, handsome in a midwestern sort of way, with a fine jaw and long clean forehead, heavy eyebrows perched on top of gentle brown eyes. His mouth was his mother's mouth, feminine, a bit too full.

But then, you know his face as well as I do.

"Well," Thomas Crane said. "Clearly the world waits for us."

He smiled and it was a wonderful smile, crooked and boyish and lit with a gentle self-mockery that I think of as quintessentially American.

"There's a group waiting inside," said John Starke, his press secretary, who had tumbled out of the van after him, along with a nervous, overweight woman I did not recognize and two reporters, both clearly wishing they were still in bed.

Crane squinted into the snow, pounding his gloves together, and you could feel his concentrated awareness of being out on this street on this morning in this town with the heart of a nation waiting to be won. There was a pink glow, a newly minted brightness to his cheeks that was more

5

than the cold and it filled me with a faint sense of warmth.

"We've got a few minutes," he said. "Let's stay out here for a while."

There is so much about him I have learned from others over the last year. There are scenes where I was not present that I now see as clearly as if I had been sitting in the back of the room. This is what comes from having too long to think about things, too many days free to wander backward into the past, too much regret. But this first meeting was before all of that, and what I remember is the odd contrast between the stray melancholy that floated in the back of his eyes and the rest of his manner. Waiting on the sidewalk, he seemed the very model of the confident young politician, and yet there was this disconnection, this brief trace of something else when he let his gaze wander. I thought then it might be a kind of boredom, a reflection of an arrogance to which politicians are particularly susceptible, a conviction that any part of the universe not revolving intimately around their particular star is a lifeless void.

Those eyes, however, slipped back into focus as he saw the first voter of the day approaching: a woman in a Scotch-plaid hat dragging a dog dressed in a matching sweater through the snow. He crossed the sidewalk to shake her hand.

"I'm Thomas Crane," he said. "And I'm running for president."

She smiled and held the rat-eared dog up for inspection.

"A handsome dog," he said, "but I'm not going to kiss him."

"Hold him," she said, offering the terrier into his hands.

With a wry smile he let her place the dog in his arms.

"Tickle him on the tummy," she said. "He loves that so."

He tried to oblige.

"No, a little to the left. There. Now behind the ears. Down at the base. Yes. Okay. Now back to his tummy again."

Other people were out on the street now and they stopped to see what Crane was doing. He scratched dutifully and the dog's head rolled back, his rear end squirmed. A small crowd gathered, dressed in the mufflers, stocking caps and goose-down parkas of New England. They peered over each other's shoulders to see what creature was cradled in Crane's arms. The moment froze itself into a strange nativity scene. The woman leaned in protectively, instructing with a sharply pointed finger.

6

"Now the top of the nose, with a couple fingers."

He rubbed the nose awkwardly; the dog stared cross-eyed at his fingers.

"You did hear I'm running for president?" Crane said.

"And then right under the chin. That's right."

Crane patted tangled hair. Someone giggled.

"There, Snoogems, you're being petted by a man who might be the next president. Isn't that nice? There, there, darling, he's doing his best. You're doing your best, aren't you? A little bit more to the right, I think."

A southern voice drawled in my ear, "Roll over, Senator."

"What do you think, Snoogems?" the woman asked. "Should I vote for the man? Maybe, you say?"

"Why maybe?" Crane asked the dog.

The woman smiled and took Snoogems out of his hands. "He likes that other one, the one on TV who promises to knock the hell out of the Japanese in the trade talks. But he thinks you're a nice man."

Straight-backed and happy, she strolled on down the sidewalk. Snoogems gave Crane a last, lovesick look, then trotted obediently at the end of his leash.

"Ohh, play dead, Senator," the voice whispered.

Crane stared at his hand, covered with terrier hair, as if searching for some explanation. Another giggle escaped from the back, but the crowd watched him in its quiet New England way, waiting for the clever thing he would surely say next.

"Folks, come on into the diner with us," Starke said quickly. "We're going to have a cup of coffee, talk about the issues. Join us. We'll even buy the coffee."

Inside, the smell of frying eggs, sausage, bacon and hash browns filled the air. A handful of men were bent over heavy porcelain mugs along the counter. Crane slipped into the washroom and emerged with a fresh smile on his face. That is the thing about politics—every encounter is a new chance to be loved.

He worked his way down the counter slowly, listening carefully, knowing when to touch a shoulder, when to laugh. He reached a pale, long-haired man wearing a baseball cap tipped back on his head and a green down vest over a denim workshirt. The man told Crane he was a welder who worked at the bus factory on the edge of town.

"But I lost my job last summer, after working my ass off for that company for seven years. What can you do for me?"

Crane sat down on the next stool. "I've got an eight-point economic plan—"

The welder cut him off.

"That's very nice, but that could take years. I mean, you wouldn't be elected until next year and then, who knows. What I want to know is what can you do for me *now*?"

Crane's smile seemed oddly stuck. "I would have to get elected first," he confessed.

The welder stared into his coffee cup in disappointment.

"Sure."

The drawl in my ear earlier had come from a tall, thin southern aristocrat employed by the *New York Times*. His graying hair was a bit unkempt in the morning and his skin a sallower yellow than normal, but his voice had not lost its icy, bitter tang.

"Ah, the can-do spirit of America."

It was my first day on the campaign trail, and I had arrived dreaming all the usual dreams. Now, here I was, in a sour little coffee shop on a cold morning, with the smell of dog hanging over the man who would be the leader of the free world, in a country where people want things now, right now. A presidential administration glimmered like the ocean down a desert highway and disappeared. Inaugural speeches and State of the Union addresses crumpled and blew away. Entire cabinets fell back into their graves.

Crane sat there on his stool and searched the welder's face as if there had to be something more, some glimmer of hope he had missed. The scene seemed to pain him in a way that I took again for a form of disbelieving arrogance.

A commotion turned his head. A shaved skull flew through the door like a bullet. The man beneath it landed on his knees and then scrambled back to his feet, shouting at the top of his lungs, shouting that Crane hated gays because he had not backed a certain bill. A half dozen ACT-UP members tumbled through the door behind him. They began a frenzied, hoarse chant that filled the diner. Their coats fell like cloaks; one of them was carrying two pieces of rough wood; one was wearing a robe; he stretched his arms out and they tied the lumber to his arms and down his back, a cross. A crown of thorns appeared from somewhere. The chant had changed. *Kill us, Kill us, Kill us*, it went. The words were so hoarse they were hard to understand. When the cross came out, I realized they thought television was going to be here. They had been misinformed.

For a moment Crane seemed paralyzed. He stood warily, his hands out, a sign of peace, asking for quiet. The chant continued, but changed again, *Act up! Act up! Act up!* Their shout had the mindless fury, the desperate assertion, of a dying scream. Crane tried again for silence. The chant only intensified. Finally, he turned to the rest of the room and shrugged his shoulders. He headed for the door. Scattered applause, intended to show support, arose from the diner's patrons.

The protesters followed him outside, but his car was waiting. It was time for his next engagement anyway. Before leaving, he paused by the open door and surveyed the protesters as if they were raw fish laid out in a supermarket stall. He lifted his fine chin and shook his head sadly.

We ended that night at a meeting with the strikers at a shoe factory outside of Portsmouth. A wet sleet was falling and a dozen men, worn and creased and drained of color, waited beneath a tarpaulin stretched between four poles. A trickle of water ran off the back and beneath their boots into a greasy puddle shivering with muddy light. They'd been on the line for thirty days, marching back and forth in front of a low brick factory blackened decades ago, the sole survivor in a dinosaur park of rusting iron skeletons and sagging brick carcasses sinking in a field of ash.

He joined them, shook hands and began to speak. He talked about the plans he had to provide tax credits for business modernization. He talked about his plans to retrain workers in dying industries. He spoke about the need to believe that things could be better. The need to believe we could change the course of our lives together. He was earnest and confident and they stared at him out of the death throes of American industry and after a time it was as if they had slid underwater and were watching him through drowned eyes.

We were walking back to the cars in the dark with the sleet falling down our backs when I ended up beside him. You could feel the whole bone-wearying slog of the day in his every step. He didn't say anything for a while. Then a smile curled up one side of his mouth, and he raised his head and fixed me with a sideways glance that had in it a stubborn refusal to go down, a strange and imperishable joy at where he had arrived in his life.

"I don't care what that woman says," he said. "I still think I got that dog's vote."

If this is a story about multiple seductions, about the delicate tide of faith on which we rise and fall, then it begins here. Because I confess I was a little bit gone on him from that moment on.

III.

FOUR MONTHS earlier he stood in the bay window of his townhouse on Capitol Hill, watching the light fade in the small park on the other side of the street and listening to advice. He had been the junior senator from Illinois for only seven years, with six before that in the House. There had been a brief flurry in the Washington press when he'd first been elected to Congress because he was a Democrat victorious in a Republican district, another smaller flutter of attention when he had been elected to the Senate because he was relatively young and less relatively handsome. Since then he'd been a good, if not great, elected official who did his job professionally and in good humor, which is to say he had been invisible.

Angela was sitting behind him on the couch, a small woman with dark hair, olive skin, and dark eyes a little too large for her tiny face. She is always described as delicate, but that is a trick of the cameras, which play up her finely carved cheekbones and her eyes. She was an attorney with the largest insurance litigation firm in Washington at the time, and in the way she handled the men who came to her with inevitable condescension in their courtliness, certain such a lovely piece of legal decoration could be no threat, there was nothing delicate at all.

She sipped from a glass of Brunello and considered her husband with a sympathetic, unclouded gaze.

"I'm not sure it's time," she said.

Across the room, Timothy Blendin, the political consultant, sat awkwardly in a Queen Anne chair, holding his legs out to keep the ragged cuffs of his jeans away from the furniture. He wore a University of Minnesota sweatshirt and had the unkempt look of someone whose family had been mad, iron-range socialists who once made their living salvaging shipwrecks on Lake Superior, all of which was rumored to be true. He glared at the antique rug as if it was threatening to crawl up his leg.

Steven Duprey, Blendin's junior partner, stood behind the chair, watching their client with pale blue eyes. It is from Steven that I know this story and many others, spilled out on the nights later when we had enough on each other to forge an uneasy alliance.

"It's going to take at least ten or eleven million," Duprey said finally in his soft Texas accent. "Lose and you could be paying it off for ten years."

The object of their attention stood in the window and they could see his eyes reflected as black pools in the glass but they could not read his expression. He had his jacket off and his sleeves turned up one crisp turn, and set against the night, his narrow shoulders appeared to be drawn in quick, sharp lines.

"It's only money," he said quietly. "Give me a real reason."

Blendin grunted and shifted his bulk in his seat. The floor creaked.

"How about the fucking president of the United States? The goddamn bastard's going to be unbeatable down south unless Jesus Christ and Mother Mary come back and register as Democrats."

Angela sipped her wine. "You think that would do it?"

"It would get you close," Duprey said. "But they'd hurt you with the NRA vote."

There was a faint but growing puttering sound outside. A police helicopter dropped a restless cone of light into a corner of the park, twitching along the steep shadows of a hedge.

"I talked to Senator Daschle earlier today," Crane said. "He told me to wait. He doesn't think I have a chance in hell."

He had the kind of voice in which the inflections were all modest and reasonable, the kind of voice that could announce "I am the greatest" and have it sound like an apology. But it was tinged now with a vague peevishness, as if this calculation imposed some unfair burden. Blendin & Duprey had handled his last Senate race, and Duprey remembered how much he hated to disappoint anyone.

"I gotta be straight with you, Senator," Blendin said. "The nomination is going to be tough enough. It's a real steep hill. Name recognition, money, it's a *real* fucking steep hill."

They contemplated his starched white shirt as he stared quietly into the darkness. Now is the time, Duprey thought, to recognize how far you have to go. Now is the time to tell us you'll wait four years.

"I've been getting a lot of calls from home, from people who think this *is* the time," Crane said. "I've spoken to Mayor Daley and he's with me. He says there's money waiting in Chicago."

"There better be a lot," Blendin said.

"There isn't," Angela said.

Crane smiled at his wife through his reflection in the window.

"Win and there's always money. A lawyer ought to know that."

Angela looked up at her husband with dark, twinkling eyes, and Duprey knew he was only watching familiar patterns of respect and affection play themselves out.

"I'm only providing due diligence, Tom. The husband of a lawyer ought to know that."

The helicopter rose like a hummingbird on the other side of the park and flitted over the house, the light flashing briefly against the glass in a nervous stutter. Crane set his wine on the windowsill and pushed his hair back with long pale fingers. When in private, he had a habit of playing with his face, pulling his ear, tugging at his chin, as though he was surprised to find them there.

"I think the experts are wrong about everything," he said. "I think the president's like a piñata. Whack him and all the votes are going to come tumbling out. I think it's going to be a really good year to be somebody new, somebody people've never heard of before. I think there's going to be a new president next November, and if we wait we might be waiting eight years."

Blendin sat up in his chair, his permanently wrinkled forehead corrugating like tin siding. "Hell, Senator, they're always ready for something different. The question is what?"

They waited for him to explain. But Thomas Crane only held his hand lightly against the window, as if he could feel the pulse of light in the glass.

"So why's he running?" my editor asked four months later. We were in the Cannon Newspapers bureau on the ninth floor of the National Press Building, and I was standing beside her desk. I didn't know yet about the evening in his townhouse, not that it would have explained anything.

"He says the economy, health care, children, etc., etc."

She nodded impatiently.

"So why's he running?"

"I don't know. I'll find out."

In her businesslike fashion, she had been typing while she spoke, but now she pushed a chestnut hair salted with silver out of her eyes and contemplated my hopeful face with sympathy.

"I don't suppose it matters. He'll last through Iowa and New Hampshire, probably South Dakota. You'll get a couple of months on the road. Do good work and next time we'll give you a contender."

My father had been a small-town newspaper editor for forty years and the closest he'd ever gotten to a presidential candidate was watching John Kennedy from the end of a runway when he flew through Montana in 1960. My career had started in the same state. I'd made my way east after more nights spent covering county commissions and state boards than I care to remember, arriving at Cannon Newspapers' Washington bureau with my western pedigree and my degree from the University of Minnesota only to discover I was working for a chain enamored of bored twenty-five-year-olds from the Ivy League. I was thirty-three years old, I'd been a reporter for twelve years, and this was my first presidential campaign. No one said so, but I understood Thomas Crane's candidacy was my shot at proving I could overcome the disadvantage of my origins.

I've always taken my work seriously. I am, by nature, too serious a person, too serious and too solitary. I was told the latter by the person I lived with before she left, and it was a fair criticism, even if none of the rest were, even if there might have been reasons. I told myself I would draw on my flaws when covering Crane. I would concentrate as I never had before and make more of this candidacy than others thought possible.

But life on the road was not what I had expected. There is an offhand feeling about the start of a campaign. Things are informal, without the Secret Service and all the clanking apparatus of a Prussian army that comes later. Crane traveled in his van with Starke and, usually, Duprey, though Blendin sometimes appeared, ranting, trying to generate heat by rubbing enough words together. The handful of us assigned to cover Crane trailed him in a haphazard caravan of rental cars. We listened to the same speech until we had it memorized. We watched him shake hands and lift babies into the air. We cringed when he did that stunt you may remember where he folded the dollar bill in sections as he explained where your tax dollars went. At night we ate together and drank together and told stories of indignities suffered from editors, hotel clerks and waiters, who were all considered of the same class.

Every morning I called my editor. Then I went where Crane went and watched what he did, and at the end of the day I called her back and we discussed what had happened and the various stories the bureau had under way. We'd worked together for three years and our conversations had the clipped, distant intimacy of an old married couple.

Days went by when I didn't have to write at all, and I drifted along feeling wonderfully anonymous and free of obligation. Secluded in strange hotels in strange cities, the world narrowed to the intimate circle of a bedside lamp, I read late into the night, mostly histories, the last of Catton's three-volume history of the Civil War, Morris's life of Theodore Roosevelt. I've always loved history for its sense of larger possibilities. If I couldn't sleep, I turned the lamp back on and read a while longer, sliding back into other lives, grander purposes. Like Crane, I imagine, I felt time slipping away with no sense of how to make it gain significance.

After two weeks I visited Crane's hometown of Berthold. When I returned, the campaign was in New York for a fund-raiser and a meeting with the city's senior congressman, a gaunt, acerbic Brooklynite fond of quoting the classics and himself. I had nothing to write but a brief summary of their meeting and an even briefer update on Crane's fund-raising, which was going poorly. I finished, clicked a phone line into the back of my laptop, waited with the slight apprehension I could never shake until it signaled the story had been sent, and called my editor. She told me to check back in an hour for questions. I knew there wouldn't be any. I glanced at my watch and felt a sudden, pervasive satisfaction that it was only six o'clock and I was in New York City and done for the day.

The bar was on the top floor of the hotel and Midtown glittered through the glass wall. The jumbled towers of commerce were a formal composition in the dark, the crown of the Chrysler Building visible in a space between buildings, a soaring pinnacle of automotive silver hung in its frame, an exaggerated notion of all the exuberance that once lit the American Century. I felt like raising a toast.

Myra Barnes waved from a table. She was seated with Stuart Abercrombie, the pale southern gentlemen from the *New York Times* I'd met my first day on the road, and Nathan Zimmer, who twisted in his seat to flag down a waiter.

"The representative of Cannon Newspapers. You in?"

"Of course."

"Pull up a seat. We'll get you a drink."

Myra sat in a pool of blue light, her feet on another chair. She wore a denim skirt with the outline of clowns on it and bright red cowboy boots, the stitching fluorescing in the light. Her hair was short and businesslike, flecked with gray. The crescent moon of one silver earring dangled near her collar like a dime-store charm. She smiled and kicked the chair under her feet my way.

"I've been saving it just for you."

"You're such a pal."

"Your den mother of the road."

"My den mother never wore boots like that."

"Can you be sure?"

Nathan twisted back in his chair to face Stuart, returning to their conversation. "Did you see how he looked when Crane's hand came down on his shoulder?"

Stuart laughed. "It looked like his scrotum was curling up. My friends, he is a pompous clown."

After meeting privately, Crane and the congressman from New York had strolled down a hallway together for the cameras, a rolling grip and grin. At the end, Crane leaned a bit too close, whispering as his hand settled intimately on the older lawmaker's shoulder. There was something proprietary and assertive about the gesture and the congressman stiffened, manufacturing a smile that would have seemed false at Madame Tussaud's.

"Now, now," Myra said to Stuart. "He's one of your congressmen."

Stuart pushed his lank hair back and, as he moved, the hollows of his gaunt face filled with shadow. He was a compulsive runner and had that look of strained tolerance for the slovenly world around him that runners sometimes have.

"He is that," he said. "I'm afraid I know the esteemed gentleman better than anyone. Did I tell you I once quoted him quoting Cicero in a story? He called me at two a.m. the *night* it came out—he'd had somebody read it to him when it hit the street—to say I'd gotten the quote wrong. I'd written, 'The good of the people is the first law.' The line is 'The good of the people is the *chief* law.' He demanded a correction."

"Well," Myra said. "I hope you ran a correction."

Stuart scowled. "It's the *New York Times*. We did run a correction."

Myra winked at me. "It's the *New York Times*."

Our waiter arrived. I ordered a scotch and soda and he nodded seriously without speaking. Stuart began describing an elaborate concoction of crème de menthe, vermouth and assorted other liquors, but seeing the waiter's eyes go blank, he stopped and in a childlike drawl asked for a bourbon and water.

Nathan sat with one leg folded beneath his body, rocking as if a small electric current was being pumped through his spine.

"The thing is," he said, "our guy got the photo he wanted. The two of them together. Pals."

"They can all get that shot," Stuart said.

"Yeah, but there's something he doesn't like about our guy."

"What is that?" Myra asked.

"Maybe it's all that damn good cheer," Stuart said.

"Maybe they agree on too much," I said.

"There you go," Nathan said. "The old liberal lion feels threatened by the cub."

"Please," Stuart said. "Centrists. Haven't you been listening?"

A blonde strolled by in a second skin of spandex that halted startlingly at midthigh. Nathan tugged one starched cuff the proper half-inch out of his jacket. He was always fastidiously dressed, today in a three-button camel's-hair sportcoat the buttery color of fine leather, a light blue shirt and a dark blue silk tie. He was forever tucking and adjusting things to hold the presentation together, and I had a brief vision of him ironing socks at three a.m.

Myra watched the blonde. "New York, New York," she said.

There was a moment of silence. The city winked at us through the glass wall. I realized the bar was slowly revolving.

"You know," Nathan said. "He looked good today."

Stuart looked down his nose. "And so what?"

"Well, it is still early."

"It's way too early for him," Stuart said.

"Maybe."

"Come on."

Nathan shifted in his seat. His standing as a cynic was at stake, but he couldn't help himself. "All right, all right. But let's just *say* he wins Iowa or finishes second, because he's a small-town boy from a neighboring state. I know the caucuses aren't that important this year, but just say it happens. Say he rides that into a second place in New Hampshire behind Wilson. Then he's back in farm country with South Dakota, and farmers seem to like him. Say he wins there—"

Stuart's laugh was like the dry snuffle of a horse. "Say say say."

"—he'd be in the race. That's all I'm saying."

"The *race*. When Wilson starts spending money, there isn't going to be a race."

Theodore Wilson, the dyspeptic governor of Pennsylvania, was the favorite among the press then, largely because they respected his bitter outlook on life. He had amassed a healthy war chest, largely donated out of fear, which he was hoarding like the skinflint Yankee traders of his ancestry.

"He doesn't have the money or the name recognition. And there's something else." Stuart stared across the room, a green light behind the bar emphasizing the sallowness of his skin. "I don't know that he has what it takes . . . I think he's the type that blushes at harsh language, do you know what I mean? I think you could make his knees shake with what they used to call a saucy story."

"Let's think of a saucy story to test him with," Myra suggested. She worked for the *Chicago Tribune* and had watched Crane longer than the rest of us.

"What if . . ." Nathan said, searching for a further argument.

Myra patted the edge of the table in a riff.

"Nathan, Nathan. What if? What if he turns out to be the king of Siam? What if he turns out to be a woman dressed as a man? What if he gets drunk and they throw him in the can?"

Nathan smiled slowly and surrendered. "What if an ex-wife shows up dead? What if he kisses someone on both cheeks and a horse's *head* winds up inside their *bed*?"

Myra clapped. "What if he comes out against school *prayer*? What if— listen to this—what if that's not really his *hair*?"

I sat back in my chair. The winter night on the other side of the glass felt archaically gentle. The chittering firefly of a helicopter sailed across the rooftops. A carnival flood of traffic drifted far below. I saw that this was how it came together, the consensus that someone should be taken seriously, that someone else is finished. Thomas Crane was sinking and he hadn't even set sail.

Through the glass wall I could see windows in other buildings. Dashes of yellow like the windows in the train that ran west through Havre, Montana, when I was a child: *The Empire Builder*, a chain of silver cars passing in the night, windows elongated as it picked up speed on the edge of town. When I was young I sometimes kept my father company while he pasted up his newspaper and it would be late when we left the shop and *The Empire Builder* would be rattling along the tracks in the distance, and he would stop and watch it disappear, the same look of wonder and mystery always in his eyes. The train was the train of his childhood, of an infinite world unfolding out of reach in the dark.

"Cliff, you know where that train's going?" he would say.

"Sure."

"Over the mountains and on to the sea. All the way to the sea."

I was very young and I imagined the train traveling right to the water's edge, silver cars on a moonlit beach, the round light in the nose of the squat engine searching the waves for passage.

The art-deco lighthouse of the Chrysler Building slipped into focus, brightly reassuring, a succession of gleaming arrows aimed heavenward. I took a sip of scotch, warm and tasting of oak. I felt suddenly how good it was to be out here, where all the questions would be answered. How good it was to be sitting at a bar in New York City, sipping a fine scotch someone else was paying for, contemplating the future of a man who hoped to rule the country, and knowing, as long as the odds were, that I would be there to see his chance unfold. How good it was to be talking to these people around this table about these things with the satisfying prospect of an evening in the city ahead of us.

It had been four hard years since my father's death, but I felt some cumbrous thing lifting and passing into the glow of the sky. A deep and foreign satisfaction settled inside me, a sense of having managed somehow to arrive at exactly the right place at the right time. I've got nothing to lose, I thought. Thomas Crane goes as far as he goes and every day is another one I gain.

I realized I was happy. Happier than I had been in a long time. The feeling would last all of three days, but I remember it so clearly, this brief sense of clarity and peace, this awareness of both ordination and duty.

We were all quiet in the bar, perhaps the others taking their own renewed measure of Crane. Myra shifted restlessly in her seat.

"What are you looking so smug about?" she asked.

"Nothing."

She pinged her empty glass with a frosted fingernail.

"Well, even if he goes under in a week," she said, "he got us to Manhattan on expense account on a Friday evening. Dinner anyone?"

IV.

THREE DAYS later a woman hiked across Daley Plaza in Chicago on an afternoon as bright as cut glass. She came steadily my way, ignoring the enigma of the gangly metal Picasso, crossing the stone with the measured steps of someone certain where she is going. An old man in rags and a pith helmet approached her and she reached into a pocket and handed him change without breaking stride. Her blond hair fell to her collar. Almond eyes stared out of a round face. The day was unseasonably warm and her jacket was open. She was wearing baggy jeans, as she often did, over her long legs. Her sweatshirt was several sizes too large, as it always was. I saw CRANE FOR PRESIDENT stenciled above the breast and my heart skipped.

She stopped a few feet from my bench, considered me dispassionately, then managed a smile. She still had a silly Cupid's bow of a mouth.

"Hello."

"Hello," I said. "This is a surprise. Finally leave Washington?"

"No. You?"

"I've joined the traveling circus. I have to sweep up, but they promise me I'll be performing death-defying stunts on the high trapeze any day now."

She sat down on the bench.

"That's too bad. From what I remember, you'll look silly in tights."

"Then maybe I can be shot out of a cannon."

She shrugged. "No need for a helmet."

And that seemed to exhaust that. We sat there for a moment.

"I'm afraid I've joined the circus too," she said. "I joined the campaign staff yesterday."

An old woman pushing a baby carriage full of broken dolls approached us. Robin reached in her pocket and handed the woman a quarter. I shook my head. Across the plaza Thomas Crane's car came around the corner from the Palmer House. He was making his last political calls after the fund-raiser and we would be moving soon.

"Congratulations."

"Thank you," she said carefully.

The woman with the carriage stopped to watch Crane's long black limousine. Slowly she lifted one of the dolls, blackened and burnt on one side of its face and missing an arm, and pointed to the car. She whispered secretively into the doll's charred ear.

"Not press," Robin said quickly. "I'll be traveling some, but it's a deputy policy post, rural issues."

"Rural issues?"

"Don't laugh."

"Hell, no. We'll call you Aunt Bee."

Robin stared across the plaza at the limousine and I could sense her resolve. I had greeted her kindly enough and this conversation was headed in the direction she wanted. She had only to finish it up and she could get on with the day's march. Her hand slid nervously along her thigh.

"This is important to me, Cliff," she said.

"Me too."

"I wanted to talk to you. I wanted to know if there's going to be a problem."

A harried commuter in an olive trench coat hurried across the square. I thought about the place I had reached, how hard I had worked to get here.

"No, I think it's been long enough," I said, "more than a year. I'll mention it to my editor, but there shouldn't be any trouble. A decent interval has passed."

She snorted softly, a half-laugh, half-smirk. "That's funny. That's what Kissinger said he wanted when the United States pulled out of Vietnam."

"What's that?"

"A decent interval before the collapse."

The afternoon light over the top of Chicago was the work of a turn-of-the-century urban impressionist, the buildings thick-shouldered against the sky. Our cities are best seen from the top down these days. On the plaza the rag man was trying to remember if he had hit us up yet and the doll lady was sitting on the stone, talking earnestly to two of her charges, one held in each hand. They were broken, of course, both of them.

"I'll try not to collapse," I said.

She kissed me on the top of the head.

"It'll be fine," she said. "We'll have dinner sometime."

I watched her walk away. She moved with a lilting precision, like a sliver of mercury drawn between two points. The way she'd always moved. I watched her cross the plaza and turn a corner. The sun was so bright it blurred my vision and the last I saw was a flash of her wrist, maybe a bracelet, shining in a pinpoint of radiance and she was gone. But not gone, not gone at all, of course.

I am a reporter and my life is measured in the ephemera of the news business. Yesterday's disasters, scandals and controversies are the markers I use to locate myself in time. So I seem to remember that she left me on a slow news day. A revolution in Africa, perhaps, or a typhoon in Asia, but nothing that mattered to American readers. I remember there were sirens in the street and the flag above the White House was still. I remember the sky was gray. I know I was standing by a window, waiting for the day to end. When the phone rang I was startled. I dropped the receiver once.

"I'm not coming home until Sunday," she said. "I've decided to stay here a couple of days."

That was all she said, but I knew what was happening. She spoke the way you speak to a condemned man, someone for whom the verdict is in, appeals exhausted. She spoke in the tone you use, all emotion carefully excised, when you are finished with a person. I asked her what was going on and she was evasive. She had to go. She'd talk to me when she got back.

She returned in a dark business suit and sat on our couch with her knees primly together, the lacquered shells of her shoes lined up side by side, her shoulders squared and her hands squeezed so tightly they turned bloodlessly pale in her lap. She told me she'd met another man, but I should never,

ever think that was the reason she was leaving. I should never be allowed to give myself that excuse for failure. I should never be allowed to feel wronged. She was very clear on that. I must understand that the responsibility, the error, the cruelty were all mine.

Is this how modern women say good-bye, I wondered? But that was unfair.

I tried to bargain. I promised all the things you always promise. I remember talking for hours while the sun went out beyond the window and there was only my voice in the darkness while she sat with the pale arch of her neck catching the light from cars on the freeway seven stories below and my voice, hollow and foreign-sounding and speaking too fast, and then finally exhaustion and silence.

"What's he like?" I asked.

"He's wonderful," she said.

Washington that night was afloat in light, the cavernous buildings ghostly in their artificial illumination. I walked past the White House. I watched flag shadows dance along the Washington Monument. I walked down the Mall, turning at the glass mausoleum of the Air and Space Museum. Across the black lake of the reflecting pool, I saw Grant slumped deep in his cloak atop his stone mount, while beneath him the grim shadows of his soldiers bent to their conquest.

Fourth Street was deserted and my footfalls echoed under the railway bridge with the sound of solitary applause. The Southwest Fire Station was quiet, lit yellow windows above closed yellow doors. I came to Mick's Office, where the jukebox sent the painted window shuddering. I stood in front of the bar for a long time before going in, feeling the dull thud of the music in the back of my neck, staring at the beat of light against crimson glass.

The floor shook with a strange assortment of dancing couples, men with little girls in ivory dresses, women with young boys wearing baggy sport coats or garishly colored athletic wear. I found a spot at the corner of the bar and ordered a scotch. I drank three quickly, the bartender watching me out of the corner of his eye as he deliberately poured the third. Understanding of the simplest things seemed to arrive from a great distance. I was watching parents dance with their children, as if I had stumbled into a wedding celebration, but I couldn't see a bride or groom anywhere. The bartender followed my eyes. "Thursday night, neighborhood night," he shouted. The boys strutted. The little girls wavered between strutting and twirling like ballerinas. Their parents swayed with concentrated frowns to "River Deep, Mountain High." There was an enduring bliss in the way they moved across the floor without touching.

I set my glass down so hard it shattered, slicing my hand across the palm. I left my barstool carefully, holding my hand closed by my side. On the way to the door someone tripped me accidentally, and I stumbled but righted myself and, looking straight ahead, made it to the street where the music was only a mocking heartbeat.

The offsale down the block sold me a bottle of scotch. The Waterfront Mall was closed, so I went a block east, through the projects. I didn't care. I settled on a wooden bench along the Potomac, watched reflected lights float like drowned moons, heard the creak of wooden boats along the pier, smelled diesel oil, rotting vegetation and brackish water. The wind came down the river and I curled up like a question mark. The cut in my hand was white, peeled open like cellophane. Everything hurt. Everything hurt more than I thought it could.

I drank until the lights smeared in the current and the Washington Monument lost its spine and did a mocking mambo across the sky. The world slid down into darkness, but I was all right until a round face with almond eyes and a silly Cupid's bow of a mouth swam up and whispered that I should never ever think there was an excuse. I should never think that I was not to blame. The fault was all mine. I crawled to the railing and vomited into the river.

Myra came walking across the plaza carrying a cup of coffee. She sat down beside me, idly picking an invisible mote of dust off the sleeve of her purple jacket, which was decorated with astrological signs.

"I saw your old girlfriend," she said.

"She's joining the campaign."

"Oh boy."

She pried the lid off the coffee and offered me a drink.

"You wanna talk to momma?"

Across the plaza the rag man was dancing with himself, arms up in a shambling arabesque.

"You got a day and a half?"

Myra took the coffee from me and sipped it.

"We've got fifteen minutes. That's why I came to find you."

I watched the rag man spinning on a broken heel, sure of his elegance despite it all.

"She comes from a long line of idealists," I said.

Myra sighed. "You poor boy."

"Never fall in love with an idealist. You're bound to disappoint them."

She laughed and waited for me to say more. When I didn't she threw the cup of coffee into a trash can.

"Come on. We're heading out."

"I'll be there in a minute."

She gave me a look and then walked away without glancing back. I watched her go and wondered if it would have felt better to talk about it. It was just an old story, anyway. You love a woman more than you thought you could love anyone. You bet everything on her and move to a place where you can start over together. She leaves and you don't think you can live but you have to find a way.

Here is what you do, Myra. You rebuild your life through detail. You get out of bed and you shower and you dress. You tie your shoes, you fasten your belt, you straighten your tie, and you think hard about all these things as you do them. If voices start to whisper, you go for a walk, counting each step, or you swim hard at your apartment's pool, moving up and down each lap with measured strokes until your arms and legs are made of clay. You keep a bottle of something that doesn't make you sick by the bed and you drink until you sleep and your dreams are a Dali landscape where all things, the hands of time and the pale hands of a woman, melt in the end. You get up the next morning and you shower, you dress, you tie your shoes, you fasten your belt, you straighten your tie. You face the simple complications of the outside world. You find it easy to work harder than you ever have. You focus on your job as if it rests at the end of a gun sight, standing in the Capitol's shabby hallways late at night to catch senators

26

leaving twilight budget deals, taking the body watch in the rain at Andrews when world leaders visit, volunteering for the night shift at the Pentagon during the international crisis of the month. You monitor arms talks, trade talks, labor talks, reform talks. You shave. You tie your shoes. You straighten your tie. You swim until your breath comes in ragged gasps and you drink from the bottle at night until the world sighs into blank darkness. You do these things. You do them every day until you wake up and you stare in the mirror and you know that you have won yourself back.

You have been stripped of a lot of things, but you go out into the world with what is left, and if you are a romantic sort, or endowed with a wry sense of humor, you pretend that you have found your truest self, this thin duke arisen from the grave.

You find that you have done your job so obsessively you are given the chance you've always dreamed of, to cover a presidential campaign. You take your leftover self out to face the new world and you find life is still out there.

Then one sunny day in Chicago she strolls across the plaza, kisses you on the head. "It'll be fine," she says. "We'll have dinner sometime."

V.

WATCH THE world go by outside a window for a while and it is odd how insubstantial it becomes, odd how easy it is to let go of the small familiarities that tether you to day-to-day existence: the walk to the train, the light across the rooftops, the smell of the elevator, the greeting in the hallway. It is strange how simple it is to become a passenger, how easy it is to surrender to someone else's plan. We traveled nonstop the next two weeks, flying back and forth in the tiny jet that was all Crane could afford, watching the country slide by in planes of darkness broken by the solemn clusters of lights that are small cities seen from above at night, and it was possible to drift and not think too much about what was waiting down the road, about the incomplete circle that suddenly seemed to be the past three years of my life.

There were only four of us traveling full-time with Crane then. Nathan, Myra, Stuart and I sat on facing benches in the back of the plane, drank wine, listened to R.E.M., and repeated the jokes forming between us while Starke glowered from his seat and Crane read beneath a lamp that filled the hollows of his angular face with darkness. I noticed he read almost every spare moment, heavy tomes that he cradled in his lap, the titles hidden from us. Sometimes Angela was onboard and she leaned in a tiny bundle against his shoulder, sleeping while he bent over his book, never coming back to visit us, ignoring the disdain inherent in the melancholy music we chose.

We followed him to union halls, senior citizens centers, high schools, cafes, sometimes no more than a street corner where two or three bundled-up, anonymous figures stood clutching signs fragile on their wooden stalks:

29

CRANE in blue on an angled field of red and white. He spoke to anyone who would listen; he ran ads he could not afford in both Iowa and New Hampshire, and his numbers moved not at all and his money trickled away in advertising and motels and signs that fluttered in disrepair across two states. He had closed his Washington office and his staff had gone without pay for a week when we arrived at the first debate.

Crane climbed out of the van, brushed crumbs off his slacks, ran a hand through his dark tangled hair, and stared at a ridiculous hotel, a cartoon of a Bavarian chateau set down in the middle of New England. He was less than five hours from an appearance that could determine his future and yet, as his brown eyes climbed up the Teutonic façade, they filled with delight.

Starke followed Crane out of the van. "You start with a meeting of the leaders of the nurses' association," he said. The debate was being held in front of a national health care conference.

"Good. My God, what a place."

"Susan Peldrona is the president. You've never met her. She's tall with dark hair. Beverly Kees is the vice president. She testified a year ago before your committee. She's blond, wears glasses."

"Fine."

"You'll get some pretty technical questions about Medicare reform."

"Great, John. The nurses are no problem."

Myra and I wandered up. She was wearing a quilted full-length coat with a Mandarin collar straight out of the Chinese imperial court.

"Senator, are you saying nurses are easy?" Myra asked.

His eyes drifted down reluctantly.

"Only easy to talk to."

"Okay." Myra smiled hopefully.

He fixed her with a blank look. A snowball whizzed over my shoulder and exploded at his feet. Two small boys disappeared laughing behind a car.

"I'm under attack," Crane said, "and I haven't even spoken yet. I guess I better retreat."

We followed him across the parking lot and toward the hotel. Halfway there he turned to me unexpectedly.

"I read the profile you wrote, Cliff. You did a nice job writing about my brother. A lot of people can't get past his accident."

A day earlier the Catton book had fallen out of my bag as I was passing his seat and Angela had picked it up and handed it to him with a smile. "Oh, God, there's another one of you on the plane."

He looked at the cover and then at me curiously, even shyly. "You're interested in Civil War history?" he asked finally.

I nodded, feeling awkward. We are supposed to know everything about them and they aren't supposed to know anything about us.

"Have you ever been to Galena?" Crane asked.

"I hope to do it during one of my trips back to your state," I said.

His enthusiasm was surprisingly boyish. "It's wonderful. They've kept the old house. Did you ever read *Captain Sam Grant*?"

"Yes. I liked it a lot."

"It's a great book. You have to go then."

I stood in the aisle and we looked at each other; it was one of those suddenly intimate moments, both of us smiling, aware of an unexpected connection, uncertain what to say next. He handed the Catton book back to me.

"We'll have to talk about it sometime, Cliff."

That was all, but things had been different since. The day before he had greeted me with a quietly wry aside about the history of Portsmouth. Now I walked along feeling self-conscious. There is nothing that fills a reporter with doubt as much as being complimented by someone he is covering.

"Bill's a good guy," I said.

Crane smiled. "My brother was meant to be a member of the Grateful Dead. Only he was born tone deaf."

"He never mentioned that."

"I'm sure it's the only thing he missed. Anyway, I thought you did a good job."

We reached the entrance to the hotel and he took a last breath of fresh air and composed himself. His forehead smoothed out and the skin around his eyes relaxed. His eyebrows slid up and curved into a position of polite curiosity. His mouth widened slightly into a modestly attentive smile. His lifted his chin and, with his coat collar turned up, he was all dark and sharp angles. He ran his fingers briefly through the hair along the back of his neck.

"Susan Peldrona, tall, dark hair. Beverly Kees, blond, wears glasses, met

31

her last year," Crane said with an amused glance at Starke. "Let's go meet the nurses."

Myra and I fell back as we crossed the lobby.

"I get snarled at. You get complimented," she said. "Obviously, he doesn't realize who we work for."

Two hours later Crane was in a hotel suite preparing for the debate and we were left to kill time in the lobby. The other candidates had arrived with their own entourages, and I saw reporters I knew from Washington, including those from my own bureau assigned to people with a realistic chance. We greeted each other with that combination of enthusiasm and hesitancy, a confusion of solidarity and independence, that comes over Americans when they bump into each other in a foreign locale. Night fell outside the plate-glass window as the lobby filled up, and I had a sense of Washington transported, as if half the city had been rolled in on wheels. David Broder strolled by, looking as cheerful and enthusiastic as ever. Sam Donaldson held court with stentorian authority by the men's room for half an hour. The significance of the event settled on me with a chill. The Media, in all its generalized, capitalized, reviled and secretly revered splendor, was about to clear its throat and pronounce.

Stuart shifted in his chair and, with a discontented rustle, set down the newspaper, with which he had been hiding from the world.

"What did you think about the story in the *Inquirer*?"

Nathan had been busy picking a loose thread from the sleeve of his silk jacket with a look of mild dismay. He glanced at the headline.

"That they're canceling the ad buy, saving everything for the last week?"

"Yes."

"Makes sense. I asked Duprey and he wouldn't say a word."

Stuart watched a bellboy dressed as a Hessian soldier tote a pair of bags past the giant cuckoo clock on the landing.

"I say New Hampshire and we go home."

Nathan shook his head.

"Through South Dakota at least."

"Ten bucks."

Nathan smiled. "Fifteen."

Suddenly I couldn't listen to them any longer. I surrendered my seat on the couch and wandered down the hallway toward the ballroom. I was standing by its closed doors, staring absently through the glass wall at the parking lot, when a young woman appeared beside me.

"They're going to be marching out there in an hour."

I couldn't see anyone in the gloom. "Who?"

"Some group supporting the homeless. They drove up from Boston."

"Why?"

She shrugged. "God knows. The new housing act, is that still around? Socialized medicine, maybe. All I know is that I've got orders to shoot them if they show up."

She squinted into the darkness, a prematurely world-weary expression on the face of a cheerleader. Television producers are usually young, sustained by frantic energy behind which perpetual exhaustion hangs like a cynical, leering ghost.

"So I'll end up doing my job as artfully as I can," she said, "and they'll look like a lot bigger deal than they were, and if nothing else happens, we'll run it, and they'll have gotten what they want."

A bleak sense of my own profession gathered around my heart.

"Well," I said, "it's that kind of business."

"There probably won't be more than a dozen of them," she said. "But I can work with that. We'll make it look like the Super Bowl."

She tossed back her blunt-cut bangs and excused herself to go to work. Five minutes later she stuck her head out the door.

"Hey, can you come in here for a second?"

Chandeliers hung like swollen mushrooms across the ballroom ceiling. Rows of red vinyl chairs marched backward from a temporary stage. A dozen technicians were working around the elevated, half-moon desk, unrolling cables, moving monitors into position.

"We need to do a color balance," she said. "Could you go sit up on the stage for a minute?"

"Let me guess. You chose me because I look like a born leader?"

"You have a blue jacket and a white shirt on. That's what they all wear."

So I climbed onto the stage and sat down. From the floor the desk was a gleaming crescent in red, white and blue, but up close you could see it had been cobbled together out of plywood and indoor-outdoor carpet. The television monitors were placed on both sides at angles so the candidates would be able to see themselves. I looked at the empty hall and tried to imagine what it would be like when it was full, when the lights were on. My face rolled up on the monitors and there I was, too pale, too somber, too young. What must it be like to make the basic transaction, to face a nation and reveal yourself in the fashion modern politics demands, to trade the intimate details of your life for anonymous affection, to engage in the calculated bargain of the talk show?

"I have suffered through an unhappy love affair," I said into the camera. "But I have survived."

"I HAVE SUFFERED THROUGH AN UNHAPPY LOVE AFFAIR BUT I HAVE SURVIVED," rasped from speakers in every corner.

Heads turned slowly my way.

"Mike check," I said. "Did someone want a mike check?"

There was a moment of silence.

"Not yet."

"Great."

An hour later the television lights came on with an audible pop and the crowd filing in picked up its step as if awash in a phosphorescent fountain of youth. On the tube political debates are sterile things, but in person they have the visceral feeling of a prize fight. Well-dressed men preened like Vegas sharpies as they took their seats, hailing each other with voices a little too loud. The Democratic Party's heavyweights gathered in front of the stage, chests thrown out, squeezing each other's shoulders and grinning until their faces glowed as if they'd all been nipping from a bottle around a campfire. A woman in a red dress, diamonds glittering across her bosom, blond hair launched in a reinforced cone toward the heavens, paraded by on her way to the czar's last ball.

Myra slid into the seat I was saving for her.

"Stick and move," she said. "Stick and move. That's what my daddy used to say."

The candidates were introduced one by one as they strolled across the stage and took their seats: Wilson, with his professor's rimless spectacles and the mincing way he pursed his lips; Brill, with the pasted-on slab of black hair and the almost audible grinding of gears when he moved; Harrington, with the hollow heartiness of the aging beach bum. Crane scratched his cheek absently as he settled in his chair.

The moderator, a former governor of New Jersey, a gentle, white-haired, ice-cream scoop of a man with pink cheeks and a thin, wavery voice stared intently at the camera in front of him until the red light came on.

"I'd like to open this evening's deba—"

From the center of the crowd came a shrill, giddy whoop. I turned and saw people rising, clenched fists leading their way into the air. Someone was shouting, but I couldn't make out what he was saying. The lights were down and a camera obstructed my view, so he came together in pieces, a raised arm, scarecrow shoulders, a brown suit, a goatee trimmed like the fluted point of a hunting arrow.

His voice was high and sharp. ". . . Governor, I say *again*, why is the Democratic Party shutting itself off to one of its *candidates?* I am on the ballot in seventeen states already, Governor. I have raised nearly a million dollars. Governor, how can this party call itself *Democratic* if it shuts out the voice of the *people?*"

The governor, the pink spreading from his cheeks, squinted into the audience. "I'm sorry. This is out of order. I'll begin again by introducing—"

There was a clamor around him as the man with the goatee slashed the air. "Out of *order?* Out of *order!* I've been out of your *order* my whole life—"

"Oh Christ," Myra said. "It's the Reverend."

And it was, the Reverend Lucas Wain, the storefront preacher turned presidential candidate whose message of black self-reliance and white injustice had found an audience across much of inner-city America. Somehow he and more than a dozen of his supporters were standing in the middle of an invitation-only crowd of well-heeled doctors and party faithful.

"I have more than a *hundred thousand* signatures on ballot petitions across this country!" The Reverend's chin stabbed the air with each word. "Why am I denied?"

Awareness of who was speaking rippled back through the ballroom and then bounced forward in a groan of discontent.

The governor's voice wavered like a badly played cello. "We had a selection process for candidates here agreed on by . . ."

"Why am I not to be considered?"

"The Democratic Party and the organizers of the conference agreed—"

"The Democratic Party? Aren't these people around me part of *the Democratic Party?*" The Reverend's finger stabbed in time to his chin. "Is there some reason my supporters are not part of *your* party?"

The people gathered around him roared. Someone in the back of the ballroom shouted *Sit down!* to a smattering of applause. Two policemen had made their way to the Reverend's row and now they slid between the chairs. There was a sudden tussle, the cameras swinging around and flooding the scene with confused crosscurrents of light. I saw a shoulder thrown into a chest, a fist swinging wildly, bodies turning in a whirl, the Reverend standing in the middle of it all like a lighthouse.

On stage the governor looked helplessly to the other men behind the desk. Wilson stared back, his eyes dead fish in the aquarium of his spectacles, his mouth as tight as a bottle cap, waiting disdainfully for the governor to regain control. Brill was as still as a wax dummy, his gaze fixed on a far corner of the room. Harrington shrugged.

"Why don't we invite the Reverend up?"

It took the crowd a while to realize someone had spoken from the stage. There was a camera slightly to my right and, through the monitor, I saw Crane in close-up. He stood framed by the blue backdrop, the strong lines and planes of his face softened by the hint of melancholy in his eyes. The lens transformed it into something more ambiguous, a kind of knowing compassion.

But that was only part of the alchemy. There is an indescribable something some people have when lights and television cameras are on them, something they have without saying a word. It comes together in a hundred details, the tilt of the head, the way the hand is placed in the pocket, the set of the mouth, the way the weight rests on one carefully placed foot. He always had it, I think, the ability to impress from the proper distance. We are in an age of false intimacy and he had the precious gift of looking at ease in the arenas of our illusion.

Now he smiled and his chin dipped toward the center of the audience.

"It's hard to see up here, but I believe that's the Reverend Wain, am I right?"

Crane seemed to be looking at the Reverend, but with the light in his face, it had to be an act of blind faith.

"He's got a point. He's got a right to be heard." He glanced at the New Jersey governor frozen behind the moderator's desk. "I know it bends the rules a little, but a single vote hasn't been cast yet."

He paused, as if he wanted everyone to have time to ponder this.

"Why don't we stop yelling and try listening for a change?" Thomas Crane said. "We've got nothing to be afraid of from each other."

There is a moment of which every politician must dream, when the public's sentiment is captured in a phrase, articulated in words they have been groping for themselves. Anger has always been an engine in American politics, but so has unexpected reconciliation. There were those who said it was the Reverend himself who started the applause, but I think it began in the back. First, no more than a hollow clip-clop, then sweeping forward, swelling until it was the sound of a thunderstorm on a tin roof, and the whole crowd stood with the dazed look of a family that has just learned an ancestral fortune has been reclaimed.

"Jesus!" Myra said, looking around us.

Crane was the first candidate into the press room afterward and they thronged around him. The debate had been his from the moment he stood; he had been quicker to the point, more forceful and at the same time more reasoned than the others. I caught a glimpse of his crooked, confident smile before he disappeared behind a forest of cameras, boom mikes and microcassette recorders, and I thought I saw a quick wink tossed my way, but I told myself it was only my imagination.

One of the last questions came from Myra.

"Senator, were you surprised by the Reverend's appearance tonight?"

He cocked his head and waited until they were all grinning in anticipation, but when he spoke his voice was quiet.

"I think we were all surprised, Myra. But needless to say, I'm glad he found a way in."

I found a seat in the back and got to work. Stuart and Nathan settled around me and we were all silently busy but for the plastic click of our laptops, Nathan bent like a praying mantis over the keys, Stuart sitting erect, occasionally staring at the ceiling like an Episcopalian bishop waiting for the word from on high. None of us spoke until Nathan rocked back from his computer.

"Well, what do you think now?"

Abercrombie pursed his mouth. "So his momma taught him how to act when poor relations come knocking. So what?"

"Come on," Nathan said. "You've just witnessed the birth of a campaign and you know it."

An hour later I was standing, stretching the kinks out of my back, when a hand touched me on the arm in an unmistakable way. She always placed two fingers just below the shoulder, gently but firmly turning you toward her.

"I didn't know you were going to be here," I said.

"We fly back to Iowa tomorrow."

"Rural issues."

"That's right. Rural issues."

Robin tucked a stray lock of tangled hair behind an ear. Out of the corner of my eye I could see Stuart trying not to stare. Nathan stared.

"It's been quite a night," she said. "I need some fresh air. You want to go for a walk?"

The snow was eggshell under our shoes. The hotel loomed out of the dark like some madly lit castle, gap-toothed battlements oversize in silhouette. We walked across the parking lot and found a path descending into a promenade of evergreens. Robin walked with her hands in her pockets, elbows out like a skinny kid, taking deep delighted breaths.

"I just needed to burn off some energy. I'm so wound up. This is all still really new to me."

"Yeah. Well, those who know tell me it only gets crazier."

A joyous smile bobbed to the surface. She stopped to look me in the eyes.

"He was great in there tonight, wasn't he?"

"He was pretty good."

Her head went back and she laughed.

"Good? Pretty good? You fucking reporter. He was great!"

"I believe the words I used were 'appeared to be in command.'"

"'Appeared to be in command.' Yeah, right. Like fucking Napoleon."

"Now there's an interesting analogy."

"Naah, too tall. No short-man complex."

"Probably wouldn't fire cannons into the mob, either."

"I don't think he could hurt a fly."

"He tagged Wilson pretty good a couple of times."

"You know what I mean. I don't think he'd do anything to hurt *people*."

She said the last words with a genuine fondness for the truth she felt within them.

"You know his life, right?" she said.

"I spent four days in downstate Illinois talking to everyone I could find."

"I think he was born to this. It's so natural to him. He's the kind who's always been chosen first, who's been class president in every class. I know his family was poor, but it all seems to come to him, and he sort of expects it. When the time comes, he never hesitates . . ."

Those last words were sad, or that she ever said them was sad, because they started the train of thought that would bring us all down. Would I have worked it out anyway? Would someone else? I don't know. But those words started it all.

Standing that night in the gentle curve between the trees, I only knew that her words bothered me in some indistinct way, struck a false note that I pushed aside. I looked at Robin and a thousand ghosts arose unbidden. A first kiss, snow slanting through a streetlight, eyes closed, her face upturned, her mouth a luminescent heart melting as it reached me. Walking in the wintry park in Billings, red mittens in the dark, her breath against my neck, sliding on the river ice, the sound of her laughter in the frozen air. All those moments I had buried climbing out of the grave and taking their first breath of life in so long.

Robin looked back at the hotel towering above the trees. Her hair hung over her collar, buttered the palest yellow by a brush of moonlight

"You know, I always wanted this . . . A chance to be part of something that mattered. When we first came to Washington together, it was never

39

there and you were struggling in your job and I was so scared of failure. I wanted to do well, really well. It didn't seem like we were going anywhere . . . And you were impossible then, you really were."

Staring at the stars, back arched like a swan, she spun slowly on her heel.

"But now it's turned out good for both of us. I mean, not together. But this, here we are."

She kissed me lightly on the cheek, a whisper of a kiss.

"Anyway, I'm glad for both of us."

I told myself it was nothing but the romance of the night, an absolution granted through the acts of others. But it was still a surprising breath of warmth amid the cold bosom of the snow gathered beneath the firs. How I wish now it had all stopped there. With forgiveness.

We followed the path deeper into the trees, descending in a curve, breathing the hushed air, the evergreens dark and sheltering, until we came out and stopped. A silver-plated river appeared beneath a footbridge and hurried toward a distant railroad trestle. Sheltered from light by the crossed beams beneath the trestle, the morning star watched us with the knowing eye of a great, sad beauty.

We were silent, left breathless by this casual assertion of the material world.

A skater slid out from under the trestle, a slanted shadow suspended above skates winking in the dark. He floated past and toward the bridge, his blades scissoring the ice with a chill sound in the dark.

"I would like to do this again," I said.

The skater's back was a suspended patch of gray. The sound of his skates came down the river like a series of faint, painful incisions. And I knew I had gone too far.

Robin shivered and gathered herself, lifting her chin, straightening her back. A hand came up and tucked her hair behind her ear.

"We have to get back," she said. "They might be waiting for me."

"All right."

"It was a nice walk. Thank you."

She turned and walked quickly back up the path, the castle leering at us over the top of the evergreens.

I dreamt that night of Robin skating on the rink beside the Natural History Museum. It was the place she went to remember home the first winter we spent in Washington, the winter we knew no one and she could not find a job. In my dream I sat on a bench beside the green, wrought-iron pavilion and watched as she glided around the ice and slowly disappeared, her legs fading first, then her waist, then her shoulders, growing fainter with each circuit until all that was left was her bobbing hair and the flash of her skates.

I woke up and it was a long moment before I remembered I was in a hotel in Boston and the muffled throb I heard was early morning traffic. I knew I wouldn't be able to fall back asleep, and I stood at the window, watching the city take shape in the quartered light of dawn, and thought about how Thomas Crane never hesitated, never hesitated, and I remembered my visit to Berthold and knew why Robin's words bothered me.

VI.

I HAD VISITED Crane's hometown for the first time on a Saturday afternoon in January. I drove down from Springfield through rolling farm country, came over a hill no different than the last hill and saw Berthold on the left side of the highway a half mile ahead.

The town hung low in the gray winter light like a raft barely afloat. The road behind me was deserted. I stopped and stood by my car, leaning against the door. I could see the backs of two brick buildings, a red house between skeletal trees, a ramshackle grain elevator clinging to the sky, a cemetery on a hill. The town was no larger than it had to be to survive; any smaller and it would disappear in the first heavy snow.

I thought of the prairie towns that had flared up suddenly in the darkness when I rode the train across North Dakota on my way home from college, the way they filled me with a feeling that God sat crouched over the world, contemplating each pale yellow farm light.

I had spoken to Crane's sister, who lived in California, by phone before my trip, and I hoped to visit with his brother, who still lived in the old family house. But I'd been told to start with his cousin, Eddie, who would show me the town. I was here to find out about his life, but I had already begun my investigation and the beginnings glimmered in my mind.

I knew he had been born without a name at three in the morning on a sultry night in August. His sister remembered sweating at her mother's bedside while they waited for the doctor to come from Springfield, forty miles away. He just made it before the baby, the youngest in a family of three children, came squalling into the world with a full shock of black hair and a healthy set of lungs. His sister remembered Tom Crane and his mother dozing on an old iron bed that night, while through the open window the cornfield swished with the sound of a woman softly brushing her hair.

I knew he was born in a small house on the edge of Berthold, a simple square white cottage with a front porch sagging like a pair of old shoulders and a tile roof the color of moss. He was born with a dying father who would take years to die. His father's hacking cough, the rattle of lungs burned by coal dust, carried easily through the walls at night, and his sister remembered that you heard the cough, then his mother toss in bed, then a strange creak that sounded as if someone was coming up the cellar steps. In the winter the house smelled of the menthol rub his father kneaded into his chest.

He was not given a name his first four months. No one remembered why. He came six years after the last child, and his sister thought her parents may simply have been out of ideas; his brother told me later they couldn't agree. Without a name, the parish priest would not baptize him, and his sister remembered being deeply ashamed to have a child crawling about who would be confined forever to Purgatory if something terrible should happen, where he would never, ever see the face of God. She watched him as if he were made of glass, never letting him get near anything that might scratch his cheeks or bruise his hands. He was coddled and anonymous, a perfect every-baby, which is how they thought of him: the embodiment of precious infancy without further identity. She thought her mother might have liked it that way.

When they finally gave him a name it was a serious one. Thomas Hart Crane.

Eddie was standing beside his pickup outside the town bar, a short, broad man with thick wrists and heavy hands that hung open at his side. He wore a ski jacket, blue jeans, square-heeled boots.

"So you're the reporter." His speech was clipped, the consonants hard and unfriendly on the teeth, unlike any Illinois accent I had heard.

"I am that man." I shook his hand.

"Cannon Newspapers," he said slowly. "Don't believe I've heard of it."

"It's a chain. About forty newspapers around the country. The biggest is in San Diego."

"So that's where you're from then?"

"No. I work in Washington. The company has a bureau there."

He spat and rubbed his neck thoughtfully. His face was heavily seamed and the only hint I could see of his famous cousin was in the squareness of the jaw and the amiable way the skin crinkled around his eyes.

"That where you were born?"

"Nobody was born in Washington. I grew up in Montana. A little city called Havre, up near Canada, about halfway across the state."

His eyes softened a little. He stuck his hands in his jacket pockets and shrugged.

"I'll take you around this burg if you want. Not that there's that much to see."

He drove me up and down Berthold that afternoon, stopping every few feet to tell me another story. I heard first about the coal mine, the shuttered remains of which crouched in a cluster of trees a half mile away. The mine had provided work for most of the men in the town for the first half of the century. I heard how they worked on their hands and knees in the narrowest tunnels, earning seventy-five cents for every ton mined, burning the mine out of their heads at the same time they burned up their paycheck in the half-dozen bars that once lined Main Street.

They were all gone but one. There was a post office and a single bar on the block that qualified as Main Street. The town was no more than a couple dozen houses scattered among vacant lots and the tumbled-down remains of old sheds and cars with weeds sprouting through glassless windows. The gravel streets ran in a simple square, the one stray branch climbing the hill to the cemetery.

Eddie and I retired to the bar and I heard how Thomas Crane's family had been one of the poorest in a town where almost everyone was poor once the mine started to wind down. Still, the town knew he was something special before he was twelve—when he was already playing baseball with the high school boys, racing around the bases in a skinny-legged, pell-mell blur that left you feeling he would surely come apart. For the next three days I listened to Eddie and others, and I soaked up the entire Thomas Crane iconography, the story that would become so familiar to all of us, even if it turned out to be no more true than any legend. I heard how he had gotten into the private Catholic school in Springfield because some of the wealthiest farmers in the area had gotten together and agreed to pay his tuition, how he headed out every morning that first year before dawn, standing on the highway and waiting to hitch a ride into Springfield. I heard how he succeeded at St. Thomas Aquinas High School beyond the town's hopes, becoming class president and the school's best athlete. I heard about the scholarship to Princeton and the two years in the army in Europe. I heard how he came back home when his mother died unexpectedly, flying all night from a post-army trip through Italy to make the funeral and then staying to arrange his father's medical care, proving he hadn't gotten too big for his hometown or his family, no matter how far he'd come.

For three days I drove back to Berthold every morning, circled its gravel streets, talked to anyone who remembered Crane, and absorbed the story I would later help to sell to the public as a small model of our national aspirations, our best sense of what is possible for someone who has a particularly American combination of athletic grace, faith, and keenness of desire that we persist in idealizing, despite all jaded protestations otherwise.

I admired it too, but there was something else that I never got into print, because I was writing for Cannon Newspapers and we publish our stories in black-and-white. As I put the man I had seen on the road together with his past, Thomas Crane came to seem the embodiment of a certain midwestern kind of ambition, no less determined for being cloaked in the self-effacing manners of the region. I heard stories of charm, but I saw striving, striving, striving. Private school. Princeton. The army. Graduate school. And then, so quickly, his first congressional race.

On my last night in Berthold, I drove into the country with Eddie to visit one of Crane's early patrons. Roger Amb was finishing his chores and we sat in his pickup truck when he was done, listening to the bump and swish of cattle milling in the twilight by the barn. Amb pulled off a glove and ran a dry and cracked hand through the high widow's peak of his gray hair. His face was narrow and sharp like a bird's.

"I guess I've been one of his biggest supporters since he first ran," he said. "That's true."

"You've given to every campaign?"

"Yes, I have."

"How much?"

"Well, the maximum, I guess. What is that now?"

"Five thousand dollars."

"Right."

"And you've known him since the beginning. I heard you helped him go to high school at St. Thomas Aquinas."

He stared absently out the window at the darkness swallowing up his barn.

"A few of us helped him out. That wasn't anything, really. He was a smart kid and his family was poor. I hope you won't put that in your story."

I stopped writing. I could write it down later.

"What I really wanted to talk to you about is why you've supported him the way you have."

Amb pulled a crumpled pack of Marlboros out of his pocket and held it in his lap.

"Oh, I don't know. He's a good man. I've been a Democrat for years, and I just thought, from the first time I heard him speak, Tom Crane is going places. I agree with almost all his positions and those I don't, well, I tell him."

"You helped organize the rally on the Capitol steps that kicked off his presidential campaign?"

"Yeah, he called and wondered if I could help set things up. No big deal. I was glad to help."

"Why do all that for him? Because he's a hometown boy?"

He shrugged. "Maybe that's part of it—we got a little pride here, you know. But he's a good man like I said, a smart man. He came from a poor family and look at him now, not only is he a senator, he's made a lot of money, handled his investments well. I don't think he needs any money. He's smart and he believes in the things he says. We could do worse in the White House, I'll tell you that."

"It seems like he's had a pretty charmed life here politically," I said, "almost foreordained."

47

Amb lit a cigarette, rolling the window down an inch and watching the smoke curl into the darkness.

"You'd think so, but you know, we had a hell of a time getting him to run the first time. The House seat was just sitting there, waiting for him, and so a group of us went and talked to him. He'd been active in the party since he came back and people were already buzzing, but it took him a week to make up his mind. He and his new wife were living in Springfield then. He didn't tell us, but he came back here for a couple days before he told us he'd give it a shot. Same thing when the time came to make the Senate run. He took his time and wouldn't say yes right away. He was in Washington then, and he came back here before he made up his mind. It took him another week."

I jotted down words absently. "Came back here?"

"I saw him on the highway south of town. He disappeared and we had to keep after him for a week," Amb said. "So I guess maybe he's not quite as driven as you people all think."

The Illinois countryside felt close inside the pickup, the stolid shuffle of the cattle, the sweet and sour smells of hay and manure, the trees creaking in the cold.

"He's running for president," I said. "You don't usually do that by accident."

I thought nothing more about it at the time. There are unaccountable moments, odd hesitations in everyone's life. But standing by the window in Boston, watching dawn move in a hammered copper sheet across the Prudential Building, I wondered. Thomas Crane pausing irresolute on the ladder of his destiny, disappearing while he vacillated—it was a little thing, but it failed to fit with the man I knew, and as the day spread to the streets below, I found myself coming back to it again and again, like a sensitive tooth you can't keep from touching.

VII.

THE DEER jumped out of the morning fog, an arc of brown and white crashing onto the damp highway in front of us, and our driver hit the brakes and the van slid and came to a teetering halt sideways on the road.

Crane was sitting in the front passenger seat and I had been leaning forward between the seats to do my interview. I had asked him about his mother's death and he had hesitated and said something about how hard it was and then the deer slid on its rear hooves into the middle of the highway. I don't think there was any real danger; we never left the road and we never felt close to tipping over, but we were slammed forward and knocked off balance before the van stopped. I ended up sprawled over the transmission hump.

"Jesus Christ!" said the driver, a pale, crew-cut college student. "Christ, I'm sorry. He came out of nowhere . . . Man!"

He turned and looked at Crane for understanding, and Crane was staring out his window. The deer was staring back, inches away on the other side of the glass, frozen with fear, the long brown petals of its ears stiff, nostrils distended, brown eyes damp and wide and very alive. Crane looked at those eyes and a shadowy recognition filled his face.

The deer reared back suddenly with a strange little hop, white chest flashing high, before it turned and sprang into the trees along the road, rear hooves disappearing in midair as they punched a hole in the fog.

We sat silently askew in the middle of the highway as Crane stared through an empty window until his eyes changed focus and he saw himself in the glass.

"Is everyone okay?" he asked.

"God, I'm sorry," the driver said again, voice half an octave too high. "I never saw him, Senator. Honest."

Crane's hand rose absently and squeezed the driver's shoulder. "It's all right. There wasn't anything you could do. Let's get back on the road."

He looked out the window again, as if he could see some faint trail hanging in the air. Then he remembered where he was and I watched him fashion a rueful, abashed grin to be presented to me in the rearview mirror.

"Six more inches and there went the animal rights vote."

I'd gathered myself back into my seat and was trying to ignore the runaway train pounding inside my chest. "Not to mention everyone who saw *Bambi*."

The driver straightened out the van and headed down the road, creeping along at fifty-five miles an hour, his wrists corded with tension. I glanced behind us and saw the staff car on our tail and the first car full of reporters behind it. They'd all be wondering what the hell had happened.

"All right," Crane said briskly. "What was I saying?"

"We were talking about your mother. When she died."

"Yes." The smile was swallowed up in a word. He looked out the window. We were coming into the outskirts of Manchester and he watched a Texaco sign slide by. It was the morning after the debate, a morning for exhilaration. They had been waiting for him outside the hotel, waving signs as if his campaign had started the night before. We had three camera crews with us and the advance staff said a giddy crowd was waiting at the high school.

"My mother. She was a complicated woman, had a lot of expectations for us. But she held our family together. She was really the glue, as they say. Have you ever lost anyone close to you like that, Cliff? A parent?"

"My father."

"Well. Then you know."

We had brushed up against another intimacy. I glanced down at my notebook.

"You came back home then," I said.

"I came back home."

"But you didn't stay."

50

"That's right." He pursed his lips as if I was inferring something unfair. "You have to make choices."

Our driver came to a stop sign and inched us around the corner.

"You have to make choices," Crane said more firmly. "You have to decide what you're going to do. I had to decide if I was going to stay in Berthold and take care of my father. I had to decide what my life was going to be about. It was that kind of moment . . ."

He stopped and looked down the street at the approaching high school. The day was so clear a bead of winter light sparkled along the edge of everything. You could see signs waving in the parking lot, red, white and blue.

"Oh man," the driver said. "Look at them out there."

"History," Crane said. "We always end up talking about history."

I knew something had slipped away, something I should pursue, but I didn't know what to do about it. I had only a few seconds left and there was one more question I had to ask.

"There's one other piece of history. A friend of yours, Roger Amb, mentioned that you were a little hesitant to run for both the House and the Senate. That you took a few days to think about it and came back to Berthold each time."

He stared out the window and I thought he hadn't heard me.

"I don't remember that."

"He said he bumped into you outside of town the second time. I've never read anything about those decisions and I just wondered if you could remember what was going through your mind. Why you came home."

"It was a long time ago. I went to see my brother. I wanted to talk to him about the decision. You know better than anyone we've always been close."

We turned into the parking lot and a man in a red down jacket, bundled up like the Michelin man, stepped in front of the van waving his sign back and forth like a flag. You could hear them cheering. Crane straightened his coat and reached for the door. He stopped and turned in his seat so that we were looking at each other. I expected him to unshutter that crooked smile I had seen blind so many, but what I got was something softer, less certain.

"You know I always enjoy talking to you, Cliff. Maybe next time we can forget Crane and talk about Catton."

He stepped out and entered the crowd, shaking hands, moving toward the doors of the high school. The driver turned to me, his young face still full of horror.

"I didn't see that deer," he said. "He just came out of nowhere."

"Hey," I said. "You got us here in one piece. Somebody who was half a second slower than you and it would have been a mess."

He leaned back in his seat, placed both hands on the wheel and, slowly, he grinned. "That's right, man. Mario fucking Andretti."

Starke was waiting for me outside, his waxen cheeks pulled tight in the cold. He frowned.

"We should have put this off, you know. He needed to be thinking about this stop on the drive."

"John, I appreciate it. I really do."

"What happened up there? We all saw the deer."

"Nothing. It just jumped out of the trees. The kid did a good job."

He shook his head, offended that nature refused to follow the morning's preprinted schedule.

"You going in?" he said.

"In a minute. I've got to organize my stuff."

I walked to the rental car I was sharing with Myra, who was already inside the auditorium, and settled in the backseat. I checked my tape to make sure it had recorded. The recording was hollow, full of wind noise, but I could make out his voice. I marked the tape and tucked it in my briefcase. Then there was no escape. I leaned against the seat, closed my eyes and remembered, as well as I could, my visit with Thomas Crane's brother during my trip to Berthold.

I didn't see a doorbell so I knocked and waited on the sagging porch of the old cottage. I'd been told to wait patiently for several minutes, then if he didn't come, jump up and down on the porch. Sometimes he doesn't hear a knock, they said, but he always feels the floorboards vibrate in his wheels. I waited instead.

He opened the door slowly, rolling his chair back with one hand. He was wearing a red plaid shirt and faded blue jeans. He had tightly cropped gray hair and a gray mustache shaved neatly at the edges of his mouth. His neck and his shoulders were as thick as a bull's. His legs ended a few inches below his knees.

He stared up at me silently. I introduced myself and told him why I was there.

"Well, I knew you'd start coming by sooner or later," Bill Crane said, the deep creases in his face bending into a smile. "Follow the rambling wreck."

He took me into the living room. There was a picture on the wall in which he sat astride an old Harley. He saw me looking at his two good legs in the photograph and nodded.

"Used to have long hair, a beard, and two feet. I was a regular wild man back in the sixties. Had a hog, drove the damn thing everywhere. Never had a thing happen. And then I'm driving a four-door Ford and a damn grain truck sideswipes me down an embankment and this is what happens. I wrote Harley-Davidson I'd do an ad for them, swear that the bike ended up being the safest thing I ever drove, but they weren't interested. Can't figure out why."

He winked. When I smiled he reached up and punched me lightly in the arm. He had the face of a Prussian officer, but when he smiled everything bent into a confidential grin, as if he was sharing a naughty but harmless joke.

"But I bet you'd like to see the old pictures of Tom."

"Sure."

Opening a cabinet, he bent double in his chair to rummage in the bottom shelf. He pulled out an album covered in brown vinyl and sat up with a sigh. I knelt beside him.

"Don't have a whole lot. But here they are."

The photographs were black-and-white, the ancient kind with serrated edges. They started with other members of the family. I saw the gaunt profile of their father, his awkwardly cut hair protruding like a thundercloud over his forehead, his shirt hanging loose around his consumptive chest. Crane's sister, wearing a loose dress in a print of oversize roses, was almost pretty. Bill was barrel-chested with short, stocky legs. Their mother was tall, big-boned. She wore her hair up and she might once have been beautiful, but central Illinois had burnt and creased her skin, stolen her waist, and swelled her ankles. Still, she stood with chin high, eyes fierce, mouth set provocatively.

Thomas Crane first appeared as a small boy, balanced on his father's bony lap, toddling down the sidewalk in patched pants, peering from beneath the hood of an oversize parka, sitting on the edge of the porch, a flop-eared dog at his feet. He was skinny and his smile had the nervous brightness of someone who wants too badly to believe in his own happiness.

"He looks a little tired," I said.

"He had a hard time sleeping when he was a kid."

Bill handed me another album. Thomas Crane was older in these photographs, staring into the lens with budding confidence. He was still slim but had a lanky grace. He bent over the open hood of an ancient Model A with a friend; he posed in his baseball uniform, leaning on a bat like a cane; he wore a blue sport coat while holding the arm of a girl in a pink dress, a corsage pinned modestly above her right breast. She was pretty with a Donna Reed hairdo and plucked, quizzical eyebrows.

"An old girlfriend?"

Bill considered the picture and shrugged. "Believe it or not, he was kind of shy with girls, but I think he had a crush on that one . . . Maureen something. Took her to a couple big dances."

"Really? She still live around here?"

"Somewhere south, I think."

He flipped to the last page in the book.

"This one was always my favorite."

The picture was of the two of them, the Crane boys, on a hillside. The photograph had been taken from slightly above, looking down. Ragged clouds and the town floated indistinctly in the background. Their arms were around each other and they were wearing suits. I lifted the page so the glare fell from the plastic. The face I had seen so often stared at me in a clarified version of itself, as if everything since had been no more than the inessential embroidery of time, as if everything that mattered was already there.

"We don't have many of us together," Bill said. "That was when our mother died. He was about twenty-five, I think."

It's funny how you don't see things when you're not looking for them.

There were pallid stones tilting in the grass. They were holding on to each other in a graveyard.

"You two still spend a lot of time together?"

Bill rolled his chair back from the cabinet into a square of yellow light falling from the window. His profile looked like the marble bust of an old soldier.

"He doesn't get back here much. But he calls. He called me when he was thinking about running for the Senate and when he was thinking about this whole show. We talk about things." A faint blush creeped up his thick neck. "He's just checking up on me, really. He's a good brother."

I opened my eyes in a high school parking lot in Manchester, New Hampshire. He *called* me. He didn't visit. He *called* when he was thinking about running for the Senate. I thought of something else and rummaged in my bag for the manila folder that held the clips and notes I used for reference. It was a story in the *Miami Herald* by Mary Voboril, one of their best writers. I found the paragraph: "The strange succession of tragedies that befell the Crane family continued that March when Bill Crane was injured in an automobile accident. Both legs of the former high school football player were amputated slightly below the knee and he spent two months in a Springfield hospital recovering."

March. Fourteen years ago. The same month Thomas Crane was considering whether to make his first run for the House. He couldn't have gone back to Berthold to visit his brother then. His brother wasn't there; no one was living in the Crane home in Berthold at that time. He had lied to me.

The parking lot was full, chrome glittering in the sun. The snow was freshly fallen from the night before, the sky a flawless blue. He had lied to me and I couldn't imagine why. I ran through it again in my head and got nowhere. I didn't even know enough to guess. It could be anything, nothing, a mistake, a conspiracy, a forgivable vanity, the key to his existence. I closed my eyes again and tried to remember exactly how he had looked as he told me he had visited his brother, but I couldn't bring the moment into focus. All I could see was the odd twinning in the window of his eyes and those of a terrified animal, both damp, brown and filled with a profound sense of dislocation.

I sat in the car and fought a sense of betrayal that made me angry because of its naiveté. I had been a reporter for ten years and I knew the first mistake you can make is to think you are friends. You are never friends. *Then you know*, he said and I had wanted to believe it was true. I wanted to believe we shared the feeling of losing the person you have always measured yourself against. But did that have to be false because something else was? Or because something else *might* be false? I didn't want to think so.

I put the folder in my bag and left it on the floor when I locked the car. The auditorium doors were open to let the heat escape and, as I climbed the steps, I heard a raucous high school cheer. He was crossing the stage as I slid inside, a sheepish look on his face as he listened to the noise. He stood at the podium and I noticed he had loosened his tie and his hair was slightly mussed. He tugged his ear, head cocked; his gaze swept across the tiered seats sweeping up into the shadow of a roped-off balcony. A look of displeasure crossed his face and then a swift, elusive calculation, before he smiled, as if truly engaged for the first time, and raised a hand for silence.

"I'm going to talk to you about a bunch of things," he said in his flat heartland accent, which I realized was the voice of a thousand television actors. "But before I do, there's something I've noticed waiting up here. I noticed you've segregated yourself. We've got the African American students sitting over here"—He pointed to the seats in the top left corner of the auditorium—"and we've got the kids with long hair there against the door, and then we've got everybody else here."

He pushed a hand through his hair and eyes turned mischievous. "In the words of Robert Kennedy, this is crap. I'd been told this school had the most diverse student body in Manchester. In New Hampshire. But it doesn't matter much if you keep yourself separate, does it? Let's mix things up a little bit."

His chin pointed into a dim corner. "Some of you guys, come on down here where there's some seats. You laid-back types by the door. Over there. The rest of you spread out. Take some of the open seats."

They shuffled their feet and looked uncertainly at each other. Crane strolled around the lectern. He pointed at the camera crews set up in the aisles.

"Come on. This is the first real attention I've gotten this campaign. You gonna make me look bad on television? They'll never come back." He waited, one hand stroking his chin, a conspiracy born in the light-hearted glint of his smile.

"You've got nothing to be afraid of from each other," he said.

We learn our cues so quickly these days. A kid in a red flannel shirt stood and then a girl and soon they were all sliding back and forth with the sheepish reluctance of teenagers since time immemorial. Crane watched from the front of the stage.

"Careful, now, no talking to each other. We don't want to go crazy."

A bright, summery wash of laughter rose from teenagers too pleased with themselves to feign indifference. They were part of a brand-new show and they knew it was a hit. They moved in a jostle of baggy pants, flannel shirts, backward caps, hockey jerseys and unlaced baseball shoes, punching each other in the arm, exchanging low-fives and embarrassed grins, all the while stealing glances at the figure watching from the stage, sipping from the age-old communion between audience and star.

Stuart was going to lose his bet. We were going to be around after Iowa and New Hampshire.

Myra was standing beside a camera crew.

"Can you believe this?" she said. "Television. It's the hand of God."

VIII.

HE WON the Iowa caucuses on a night when the moon hung over Des Moines like a new silver dollar encased in velvet. He won the New Hampshire primary a week later with snow falling across Manchester and a lightning storm of camera flashes in the hotel ballroom when he stepped on stage. The last two weeks had been a haze of shopping malls, five-hundred-watt radio stations, Holiday Inns, weekly newspapers. And then, of course, there had been the endless variety of the American midway: the girl who brought him a model of the White House made completely out of twist ties; the man pushing a wooden cross in a wheelbarrow across America who paused to offer his blessing; the ice fisherman who asked Crane to hold the line while he ducked behind the cabin to take a leak; the mechanic who wanted to arm wrestle for his vote.

He traveled trailing a phosphorescent glow, for television was falling in love with Thomas Crane. It is a wondrous thing to see a man reborn through the lens, to watch his life refocused and broken into primary colors. He emerged in brilliant fragments: his angular frame, crooked smile, the perfect miniature of his wife, his midwestern gift for clarity, the gentle irony with which he often seemed to observe his circumstances (fulfilling television's theological precept that the principal virtues are simplicity and an irreverent sense of self). There was the uncomplicated melodrama of his youth: Berthold made the perfect backdrop for poor-boy-made-good stories, and I glimpsed the town so many times on the screen, floating forlorn between ruined hills and metallic sky, that TV's distant perspective began to superimpose itself on my memory.

The *Times*, the *Post*, the *Atlantic* and other publications cleared their throats and wrote the usual articles raising the usual questions about his experience, proposals, political substance. The Washington press corps resents anyone it has not had the chance to dismiss. But the cynicism that passes for wisdom was momentarily swept aside by features on everything from his addiction to Diet Coke to his passion for history, and by the image of a boy on a blue road at dawn, taking slow but steady steps toward his future.

So in Manchester balloons bounced through the strobe-lit air and Crane hugged Angela and waited for the crowd to cheer itself out. When it was making no more noise than a fraternity on a Saturday night, he leaned into the microphone.

"They said we didn't have enough experience. They said we didn't have enough name recognition. They said we didn't have enough money"—he paused—"we still don't have enough money." Laughter, whoops of delight. "They said we didn't have a chance. But we had two things they didn't understand . . . We had a message and we had the people!"

He stepped back and let them go at it for a while. He was wearing a dark suit that in the stuttering light seemed like a tailored scrap of night; his smile was modest, and the melancholy in his eyes was buried in a glittering attentiveness, as if he would not let the farthest corners of the celebration escape his memory. I was standing near the back and I felt my own heart pound and my own breath quicken. He pushed a hand through the hair above his ear and stepped back to the microphone.

"Before I go any further, there are some people I want to thank. And I want to start with the most important. Always the most important. My wife, Angela."

He turned to her and she leaned forward, one leg kicking back like a sixteen-year-old, kissed him and whispered something in his ear, and he laughed and lifted her off her feet before swinging her back into place. She pretended to be dizzy and the crowd loved it. His hand came up in a half salute stolen from some old war movie; he let the photographers have his profile for a last battering of flashes. Those of us flying out with him threw our stuff together and scrambled after him as the cheers swept us down a hall, out a side entrance and onto a street where snow crunched startlingly beneath our feet.

Steven Duprey stopped on the sidewalk.

"Where's the car?"

"Where's the car?" Starke said to a campaign volunteer. "We need the car."

The volunteer turned to an eighteen-year-old holding open the door. "Where's the car?"

Nathan spread calfskin-gloved hands in dismay. "They don't even have a car waiting for him. How can we be expected to take this campaign seriously?"

Myra buried her nose in her collar. "It's just a car, Nathan. It's not like they're recounting the ballots."

"Just a car? You want to turn the nation over to people who can't even find the service entrance to a hotel?"

"I don't want to turn the country over to anybody. But it's just a damn car."

Stuart stood behind them, hugging his birdlike shoulders through a tweed coat. "Would you two quit bickering?"

"It's what we do to keep from freezing to death," Nathan said.

"Or going crazy," Myra said. "Besides, he's wrong all the time."

"What? I'm wrong?" Nathan's voice had a high New York twang. "You think this is a smoothly running show you're seeing here? You think this is a Carnival cruise?"

"Oh God," Myra said. "Yes, Nathan, I think this is *The Love Boat*."

She looked up into the tumbling snow, laughing, and I remember everything so clearly: the mob of us in the dark; Crane down the sidewalk, head tilted to keep a cell phone dry, speaking into the distant sunshine of Hollywood as he desperately tried to turn the evening's elation into more durable currency; Angela holding his free hand and listening to every word, calculating behind her smile; the Secret Service glancing nervously up and down the block; Duprey standing in the middle of the white street, light shining off his balding forehead, waiting for the uncertain caravan of our future to come clattering out of the dark.

Crane spent four frantic days making sure South Dakota didn't slip away. He shook the hands of buzz-cut ranchers at the Sioux Falls stockyards, managed the Corn Palace with only the faintest smile, raced down highways drawn with a ruler to towns rising like islands in a winter sea. Behind the scenes all was chaos: the campaign was running on money borrowed on the flush of rising polls—only the ghost of a structure had been set up outside New Hampshire and Iowa—and suddenly offices were needed everywhere. We were late all the time and sometimes the rally was in a different restaurant and often the hotel clerk looked at us blankly when we stumbled in at two in the morning. When he was on the road with us, Blendin could be seen pacing like a bull in the lobby at the end of the day, compulsively picking more holes in his tattered sweatshirt as he shouted commands at newly recruited volunteers with the frenzy of a pyromaniac in charge of a fireworks display.

Crane flew out of Rapid City cursed with the title of front-runner. Wilson still had more money and the better organization, and both were expected to show themselves when we reached the great slew of southern primaries held on Super Tuesday. But first came primaries in Maryland, Colorado and Georgia. We traveled through a blur of hotels and airports and rallies. The peaks of Colorado slid past the plane windows and the hills of New Hampshire seemed a distant memory. The pine trees in Georgia rocked in a sullen breeze and the arctic stillness of South Dakota seemed to belong to another life. Then the wind blew ice into our eyelashes in Maryland and we'd circuited the seasons in a week. Myra stood in the sleet in a light jacket with quilted swans parading across the back, imploring the heavens: "I give up. I'm out of clothes. You've beaten me. Where next, Alaska?"

The campaign was swollen by success, requiring a full-size jet, a bus, limousines, vans. We traveled in motorcades and took over entire floors of hotels. At rallies a host of starry-eyed volunteers appeared to push and prod us in the right direction. So in late winter the world in which I would live for so long took final form: a world of hotels and airplanes and buses, crowds and deserted tarmacs late at night and unknown cities on the horizon distant and obscure, an artificial but strangely intimate community of reporters and staff and Secret Service agents, all pressed together, watching America pass through smudged glass, hearing it in a thousand interrupted conversations, wondering always what was in its heart.

We were in Baltimore and I had finished a long night working on a setup piece when I ran into Steven Duprey at a bar down the street from the hotel.

"Hiding out?"

He gestured to a spot beside him. "Not any longer, I guess."

We had known each other since Blendin & Duprey handled a Montana senate race four years earlier. We'd gotten along well from the beginning. We both came from small western cities, the same kind of place, even if separated by two thousand miles, and we liked each other in the quiet, unstated fashion that exists between Westerners.

"I'll buy you a drink," I said.

"Only if you don't expect me to say anything newsworthy in return. It's been a long, hard day."

I signaled the bartender. "How's Susan?" His wife was five months' pregnant.

"Still throwing up every morning."

"So being on the road isn't all bad?"

His gentle smile escaped through his beard. He raised his glass. "To my lovely and very patient wife."

We drank quietly for a while. The bar was almost deserted.

"There's a stupid little thing I've been meaning to ask you about," I said.

Duprey sipped his beer. "Stupid little things are my life. Shoot."

"You ever know your man to go through periods of self-doubt? I mean, about his political career?"

He set down the bottle. "Self-doubt? Come on, Cliff. What's the next question, the real question?"

I raised my hand in a gesture of peace. "When he was first asked to run for the House and the Senate, he went back home and spent a week making up his mind. It just struck me as interesting. I wondered if you knew why."

Duprey was dressed in the cowboy boots and jeans jacket he always wore on the road—the perfect disguise, a genuine part of himself that had nothing at all to do with what he had become. He was working now, sipping his beer while he tried to decide if he needed to be worried about this conversation.

"You doing another profile?"

"Updating an old one for the future. I was just going through old notes when it struck me as curious."

He shrugged. "We didn't do his House races. You and I were probably in high school during the first one. I came on board for his second Senate race. I don't remember him saying a thing. Why don't you ask him?"

I gestured to the bartender for another round.

"I'll have to do that. It's probably nothing."

The bartender handed us our beers and Steven paid.

"So you and Robin getting along all right?" he asked.

"We've only seen each other a couple of times. But sure. Very professional relationship."

"Cold?"

"I didn't mean it that way. We're getting along fine. Friends."

"Good. You know she's doing a great job. They promoted her a couple of days ago. Assistant policy director. She flew in last night. You'll see her on the plane a lot more often. She's working her buns off, learning about everything, and we need someone like that on the road."

"Great," I said. "That'll make her happy."

"She deserves it."

Through the window you could see the shadow of Camden Yards squatting along the horizon. The streets were empty.

"When did you first introduce me to her?" he asked. "In Washington someplace?"

"A reception . . . in the Interior Committee room, I think. I can't remember why we were there."

Duprey smiled. "Probably something of tremendous importance at the time. Probably all over the front pages."

"Probably."

"Well, always a pretty woman, and smart."

"True enough."

He hesitated. Decided he knew me well enough, I guess.

"She ever marry that photographer?"

"I don't think so."

He rocked his empty bottle gently on the bar, the sound like the amplified roll of a coin settling in place.

"You'll probably be seeing a lot of each other."

I tipped my beer back and swallowed.

"We promise not to pull each other's hair in public."

He looked at his hands.

"Did it ever occur to you that politics is just junior high in suits and ties?"

"Finally, Steven, a quote I can use."

He smiled. "Which means I better call it a night. You know how it is, tomorrow is *always* another day."

I watched him leave. The question about Crane had been handled badly, probably a stupid idea from the beginning. But for two weeks I had pondered, turned things over in my head, and done nothing. It wasn't like me. I knew my own weaknesses as a reporter and hesitation had never been one of them. Uncertainty, yes, but never hesitation.

Duprey wouldn't bother Crane about it anyway. Consultants were like lawyers. They never pressed their clients about anything that might bring complicated news.

The bartender swabbed around my beer. "We're closing up soon, sir. Last call if you want one for the road."

I looked at the beer in the bottom of my bottle and stopped pretending I was thinking about my job. Robin would be traveling with us. I'd known all along it was just a matter of time.

The next morning I woke early and stood in the hotel window staring at Baltimore's inner harbor fifteen stories below. The USS *Constellation*, the old clipper ship, bobbed along the boardwalk, masts swinging like tired metronomes. Farther down the dock, the National Aquarium melted into the fog, cubist and cold.

Another morning, another hotel room, the depressing familiarity of the unfamiliar. I stumbled through my rituals. I took the battery that had charged overnight out of my computer and replaced it with the backup, to charge until the last minute. I sat on the edge of the bed and discarded old campaign schedules, briefing papers, press releases and torn newspaper clippings from my Lands' End bag. I checked the cell phone in the bathroom, plugged in beside my shaving kit as it always was, to make sure it had charged.

All this done, I sat on the edge of the bed in my underwear. I had another hour I could sleep, precious time on the road, but I knew her habits too well.

I shaved and showered and packed my garment bag, leaving it outside the door of my room with the campaign tags on it. Someone would be along to pick it up at seven and transport it to the plane, or so they always promised.

The hallway was quiet, the restaurant downstairs empty. I ordered coffee and a sweet roll and sat at a table in the lobby reading the *Sun* and the *Post*. The papers were already looking ahead to Super Tuesday. Crane was behind almost everywhere in the South, but closing in fast in Missouri and Kentucky. I read and, after a while, as I knew she would, Robin came in from running, wearing smudged gray sweats from the University of Montana and breathing hard. A thin trickle of sweat slid from her pulled-back hair down her temple and past one pink, translucent ear.

"You're still running," I said.

She stopped and glanced around the empty lobby. "And what are you doing?"

"Still not sleeping."

Robin hesitated, then took a deep breath and sat down at my table.

"Well, it's good to know that wasn't my fault."

"Not for a while anyway."

"Very funny. Can I have a sip?" She slid my Styrofoam coffee cup her way.

"Of course."

She sipped the coffee, wiped her forehead with a sleeve, and shuffled her feet across the carpet. Her eyes wandered to the newspaper and around the room, taking everything in.

"Congratulations on the promotion," I said. "Welcome aboard."

She tried, but could not stifle her satisfaction. "Thanks."

Robin leaned back in the seat. Her breathing slowed, raising and lowering the delicate bones of her shoulders and the swell of her breasts.

"What else you doing? Still reading a lot of history?"

"Some."

"Still the Civil War?"

"Sure, but don't worry. I'm not going to turn into one of those guys who dresses up and marches around in a field on weekends, shooting a musket at strangers."

She looked into the coffee cup, a wry and then slightly sad light in her eyes.

"No," she said. "You never were a joiner."

The first bedraggled volunteers were arriving in the lobby, bleary-eyed, clothes twisted, unbuttoned and wrinkled. Robin watched them gather around Aaron Siegel, the road manager.

"It's been wild in Springfield," she said. "We started out with almost nobody and now we've got people bumping into each other. We're setting up a computer system so we can respond to any claim by our opponents within the same news cycle. All Crane's votes and everything he's ever said that we can get our hands on is being entered into the system. We've got kids working all night long."

She smiled at me, wanting to share the joy she felt.

"How about you? Has it been fun?"

"The 'Cornheads for Crane' buttons in Iowa were fun," I said. "And there was this supporter of yours in Bedford, New Hampshire, who put up a hot air balloon the night before the election. He had an electric sign hanging beneath it, but one of the letters blinked out. 'WE WANT RANE!' it said. That was fun."

She smiled again, offered me the coffee cup. I shook my head and she drained it.

"Think how proud your father would be if he knew you were doing all this."

I thought of my father in his shoe-box office with sunbleached books and newspapers piled up to the ceiling. He worked until his heart gave out, toppling forward in the print shop when, despite the doctor's warnings, he insisted on lifting bundles of his newspaper onto the truck for delivery just as he'd done for thirty-five years. He'd never cared for smart-ass features, the ironic tone, and the concluding editorial judgment that have become the staples of his trade.

"He was pretty old-fashioned," I said lightly. "I don't know what he'd think of the stories we write today, laying the candidates out on a psychiatrist's couch, doing features about their pets."

"Crane's dog is named Rex. Got a feature coming?"

"I know its name, and it's probably only a matter of time."

Robin watched the lobby slowly filling up with people.

"Do you think he can do it?" she said.

"I don't know. Nobody thought he'd get this far. He's going to get hammered down south. But maybe. Who knows?"

"You're always so careful, Cliff."

The old differences glimmered up out of the past like a snakeskin in the sunlit grass. We watched to see if it moved.

"I always thought *thoughtful* might be a fairer word," I said.

A curled strand had fallen from behind Robin's ear and wrapped itself underneath her chin. She wove it back into place, gold on gold.

"I don't think so, but maybe."

"Maybe thoughtful?"

"Maybe thoughtful or careful wasn't what I needed then."

She squeezed my hand across the table, cool fingers sliding up the back of my hand.

"Oh, I don't know, Cliff. Maybe. Maybe not. Maybe I was crazy. Maybe we both were. Maybe it wasn't ever meant to be. Maybe we screwed up. Maybe it doesn't matter anymore. Maybe maybe maybe. But ahh me, this is no longer necessary."

She laughed, embarrassed, and stood up. She bent and touched her toes quickly, then stretched as if just getting out of bed, arms wide, small fists curled.

"Anyway, he's *got* to do it. And I've got to shower. You know what they say. Miss the bus and you miss the day."

"I'll see you later," I said.

She smiled. "That's right. You will."

When she had gone, I bought myself another coffee and settled at the same table. Other reporters drifted down, hair still damp, eyes puffy, skin pale. We had a long way to go and I wondered what we would look like at the end. The coffee burnt my tongue and I set it down. *Ahh me, this is no longer necessary.* That was something her mother used to say, usually when discussing Robin's haunted, ruined father. *Maybe it doesn't matter anymore.* I wanted to believe that more than I could say. But I knew it wasn't true. If there was one lesson in our history, it was that the past always, inescapably, and forever matters.

IX.

EARLY ON a December morning Robin is riding a horse along the Yellow-stone River. The hills she has known all her life are white and brown. She crests a ridge and the river glimmers below like a bent tongue of silver. She sees the ghost of the moon and the last stain of night in the folds between the mountains. Standing in the stirrups, she takes a deep breath, and as she exhales and fog rises in her vision in a curtain, she lets her eyes fall to the huge white house on the river.

She stays for less than a minute, and when she tells me about it that evening, her voice is so flattened out I am not sure how much it means until I see her small hands, balled up into fists that rest in her lap like stones.

I have been a journalist long enough to know that you can tell any story countless ways. This could be a story of two people who misperceived strength, it could be a story of the misplaced faith humans have in the redemptive possibility of change, it could be a story of the seductive power of an aggrieved sense of injustice, how the crusade leeches simpler plea-sures out of the crusader. All these things are true, and the lessons can be taken in such abstract terms if you wish. The world seems to need morals these days and so I give you these.

But we were a skinny son of Irishmen and a skinnier daughter of old Scots, and we lived beneath any larger point the way we lived beneath the sweaters and parkas that swaddled us through the Montana winter. I am telling you about the only person I have ever loved, and to me we are a tangle of arms and legs, the brush of a wordless tongue against a roaring ear, and to me this story is in those hands.

It begins not with the pampered child who once rode a pony out from that house, but with her father. He was the son of a rancher who hated horses and spent thirty years working for the U.S. Forest Service. Robin's family moved twice as he slid up the bureaucracy, living in Washington for a year when she was an infant, and in Arkansas when she was in junior high, but always returning to Montana. Her father had been a blandly successful careerist, his political beliefs safely stapled shut for decades, by the time he ascended to the regional director's post. The position made him one of the most prominent federal officials in Montana. He was an old-fashioned forest man who accepted the need for logging, who enjoyed hunting and fishing, and who had no time for city folk who believed the American wilderness was a fragile garden to be preserved untouched. I can't imagine the men in charge thought they were going to have any trouble with him.

I don't know when he first noticed that the Forest Service was being robbed. But something compelled him to a laborious private examination of the wide swath of forest being cut down by the multinational companies that held the principal logging leases in his region. He spent months putting his case together, traveling alone to isolated valleys where he calculated harvest rates and the size of the cuts that ran like brown scars up and down the mountains. When he knew for certain, he went to Washington with evidence the companies were illegally deforesting many square miles of land.

His end came swiftly after that. He made his report in the sixth year of a Republican administration, a time in which the men who ran industry and the men who oversaw the regulation of industry had become interchangeable. He clutched his picnic basket full of truth to his chest and marched into a haunted forest of corporate lawyers and government officials on sabbatical from the companies he was accusing. His charges were buried in official denials and bottomless studies conducted by consulting firms that were part of the industry. That might have been enough, but he had spoken out publicly and so he had to be discredited; his earlier work was attacked in anonymously leaked stories; doubts were whispered about his mental stability. He found himself accused of the misuse of government property. (Exhibit 1 was the times his wife was spotted in his Forest Service pickup at the hardware store.) His management of the day-to-day operations of headquarters was portrayed as chaotic. His expense accounts were examined and, inevitably, a few receipts were missing. When they fired him, it was for every reason but the real one. He would never hold a steady job again.

The family had long been prominent in Billings. Robin's great-grandfather, one of Montana's lesser land barons, had built the big, white Victorian house with its wraparound porch, where on slow summer evenings you could watch the sun set red on red along the Yellowstone rims. But the family inheritance had been frittered away over the years and Robin's childhood home was sold within a year. After her father lost his job the family's fortunes arced downward with the helpless grace of a diver. Still, there was no sense or justice in what happened next, only a strange intimation that some unseen law of momentum propels disaster. Six months before I met Robin, her younger brother slid the bright red convertible bought for him in better circumstances off a mountain road and tumbled end over end to land upside down in a stream. He was wearing his seatbelt and in a very dry state he drowned.

I didn't hear that story until some time after I met Robin at the *Billings Gazette*. In Montana they don't believe much in speed limits or government safety programs. They post whitewashed wooden crosses on the side of the road where accident victims fall, a simple reminder from a state that believes you take your own chances. Robin and I were returning from a story assignment, one of the few times we worked together, when a cross on the corner ahead was suddenly and starkly there in the bloodless glare of our headlights.

"See that cross," she said. "That's where my brother died."

I had not known she had a brother. But that night she told me the story of her family while the road fell toward Billings and the mountains tore at the stars.

I think I was half in love with her by then. I remember the first time I saw her in the newsroom. She was arguing with an assistant editor about something, arguing fiercely; then they were both laughing and the change in her mood was as abrupt and hypnotizing as the edge of a summer squall.

I was introduced to her that afternoon. She nodded in recognition.

"Cliff O'Connell. You came from the *Great Falls Herald*, right? Political reporter?"

"I'm afraid so."

She smiled. "And your father owns the paper up in Havre?"

"Owned. He died half a year ago."

It's something you get used to saying, like you get used to the dutiful moment of compassion in response. But the pain in Robin's eyes was genuine. The connection she must have felt is obvious now, but then I only knew I was touched.

"I'm sorry," she said, then, fumbling on, "How come you're not running the—what is it—the *Tribune*?"

"The family's selling it. It never made much money."

Which was at least half true. My mother was selling the paper because I had refused to come home and take over. As far as I could determine the decision had been the signal act of cowardice in my life. Havre sat there, forty miles below Canada, hard along the Bear Paw Mountains, and it was my childhood and the ghost of my grandfather raising a sledgehammer and slamming spikes into railroad tracks marching west, and my father's fingers arching in a similar manner and slamming the keys of his old Underwood, nailing down the truth as he saw it. The town was theirs, and when the time came to step into my father's job, I knew I could never take the place of either of them.

Across the newsroom Peter Jensen, the state editor, stuck his head out of his glass office and called Robin's name. She glanced at his door in irritation.

"Christ . . ."

"What?"

She hesitated. "Oh, I'm trying to get them to do a story on environmental problems on the Yellowstone, but they're not interested."

"Why not?"

"I don't know. We've been going around and around about this for a week, and they think I'm being a jerk . . ."

She stood in front of my desk and we considered each other uneasily. Her anger was much sharper than it should have been. She stared across the room.

"I can't get along with him. He doesn't seem to understand. It's important . . ."

"How about Prescott?" I asked. He was the managing editor.

She managed a jaundiced smile.

"Oh, we've had our disagreements, too."

I noticed that the balding, pink-cheeked cops reporter sitting next to me had gotten busy, his nose buried in a file. I was too new to the paper to wade into newsroom politics, but I wanted to say something. She was young and beautiful and her anger floated awkwardly across her face and I was already on her side.

A copy aide approached holding a sheaf of photographs toward Robin like an offering. I glimpsed a strangely mutated, white-faced creature seemingly mounted on a pedestal.

"Now this is something else entirely . . ." she said. "Have you heard of our feature, 'Critter of the Week'?"

She flipped through the photographs and placed them gently back in his hand. She smiled finally, a real smile, and I had an excuse to look at that silly, sublime Botticelli mouth.

"You know," she said gravely, "any way you look at it, a two-headed calf is still pretty much a two-headed calf. You can tell Julie they all look good to me."

Then she shook her head and laughed and I felt she had captured some crazy, elusive essence of this business in which we worked.

I've pondered since how quickly we fell in love. Something about the romance was liberating for us both. We snuck off at odd hours to make love, crawling between cold sheets in the middle of the afternoon while through my window an old man tossed a spray of sunflower seeds to sparrows in the winter sunshine. Robin had been living in a room above a laundromat while sending her mother half her check, and almost overnight she moved into the bungalow I rented by the park, more of her clothes magically appearing in my closet or scattered about the bedroom floor every day, tossed from her old life into mine in a frenzy until one day she was there all the time. We were a couple. People invited us to things together and we had to sort socks. We lay in bed and sometimes I could not sleep, so I listened to the bungalow's old bones creak in the cold and the floors groan about having to hold themselves up one more long night, and the bed swam as it can when you are very tired, sliding down a steep canyon, and it felt good to let it take me where it would.

I had come to Billings to escape the vague failures and inadequacies of my recent past and I had met this woman who was smart and beautiful and trying so very hard. More than anything I think I was captivated by her defiance. For her part, I think she thought I was someone with destinations in mind. All my life, I have had my reticence mistaken for resolve.

Robin skated on the rink at the old park almost every night in winter, racing around the oblong moonlit eye with long, hurried strides. She borrowed a friend's horse and rode across the arroyos and barren ridges in the foothills, turning him hard and galloping back and forth in a restless, invisible box. She was tiny on the broad white back, holding the reins high, bent forward slightly at her waist, riding until the horse was lathered and worn. She rode hard but rubbed him down carefully afterward, whispering to him what a good horse he had been.

At the *Gazette* she argued and shouted and worked harder than anyone and it got her nowhere. The editors of the paper never let her near her father's story, of course, but she fought back with every word she wrote, trying to tilt the scales of justice toward whatever victims she found or imagined. She clenched her fists so tightly in her sleep that they sometimes cramped and she awoke in the middle of the night with a start.

We lived together for seven months in Billings. In May we stood on a bridge above the Yellowstone as a flatboat appeared out of the darkness and raced below us with the current, a blur of Christmas tree lights hung in loops along the railings. The air was warm and full of spring. We leaned forward to watch the boat disappear beneath the bridge, then turned to watch it reappear and hurry down the river. The voices of the passengers drifted up glittering, diaphanous, along with a splash of ragtime piano.

"I think you have to do it," Robin said. "Let's go. It'll be exciting."

"I don't think that boat's ever coming back. The current's still too strong. Look at it fly."

"You're lucky they asked you. It's really a compliment, Cliff."

The Christmas lights receded like a swarm of fireflies. They rounded a bend and disappeared.

"I know that," I said.

The sloshing sound of the flatboat and the revelry of the passengers gone, the river seemed strangely quiet. You could smell spring grass on the hills and the sweetly sour mud churned up below. Robin's chin rested on her arms folded across the top of the railing, but she fidgeted, one tennis-shoed toe restlessly rasping concrete.

"Jesus," she said, "what are we going to do? Spend the rest of our lives making out in the darkroom and pasting Jensen's misspelled memos on the bulletin board to be naughty?"

"You have to admit, both those things were fun."

She smiled. She was never really mad at me then.

"Sure. It was great. But—"

"We're happy here," I said. Some unexpected self-doubt was rising out of the dark.

"But we're not doing anything," Robin said. "There's no future here for us. It's such an opportunity."

My reporting had gone well at the *Gazette*. I'd stumbled upon a small scandal in the governor's office and, of course, I came with the pedigree of my father's reputation in a business that, like all others, doesn't want to admit how much it relies on mindless credentialism to make its choices. Cannon Newspapers, which owned the *Gazette*, had offered me a job covering Congress in Washington. It was the lowliest of beats there, watching the elected officials from the Dakotas, Montana and Wyoming, but it was Washington. So at a moment when our romance was a seamlessly woven magic of time and place, we were about to change it all.

Of course we thought we were unhappy.

"I know I'll find work," Robin said. "Jensen says he'll help me."

"Sure. You'll do great. You'll probably do better than I will."

"I don't know about that. But it's an opportunity." She stared at the ghostly slip of a sandbar down the river.

"I'm tired of trying so hard here," she said. "I'm tired of trying so hard not to give a damn. I could use a change."

Maybe we have used this place up, I thought. I knew the urge to move on. I'd been discarding pieces of my life since the day my father died. Standing on the bridge with Robin, I was twenty-nine years old and I felt that the sum of my material and spiritual worth could be packed in a small box and shipped on ahead without loss.

"Where was the first drink we had?" Robin asked.

"At the Western. We thought everything was funny."

"What was our first date?"

"We went to see *Dune*. A really bad movie."

"Where?"

"The theater in the mall. A really really bad movie."

"Our first kiss?"

"In the storm."

"Our first . . ."

"My place," I said. "A Friday night, I think."

"Very good. A Friday night and the wind blew that damn branch against the window. I was awake all night. You slept like a log."

"Men do that when we've been carnally satisfied. We have innocent hearts—troubled by nothing but lust."

"Yeah, right."

I decided to play. "The first meal you made?"

"Beef stew. Romantic, huh?"

"But very good. The first flowers I sent you."

"A dozen red roses. Predictable."

"I like to think of it as time-honored."

"I love you so much," she said.

A quarter-moon sat high over the mountains. Tomorrow's clouds waited along the saw-toothed horizon. A hawk materialized out of the black, gliding low along black water. A splash. We listened. A faint rustle along the bank, nothing more.

Robin slid along the railing toward me, leaned into the circle of my arm.

"I need the chance to do more than I have," she said. "In newspapers or whatever. I just think . . . I just think I've worn this place out, or it's worn me out, or something. There has to be something better ahead."

You can smile at us, two innocents for whom Washington, possibly one of the most institutionally corrupt cities in the world, shimmered like some Edenic island on the edge of the sea. You can wonder how we could not see things that now seem so obvious . . . the fragility of our joined shadows quivering in the water.

But most wrong turns are taken in optimism. Robin's head fell against my shoulder and on a bridge outside of Billings I took a deep breath and let myself believe I was undaunted by the prospect of reinvention. We were still young enough then to feel that life, by definition, is promise. We believed we had talent; we thought we put fine faces forward to the world; we knew we were in love; we felt our lives had an inevitable charm that must carry us forward.

Did I ever truly believe all this? I don't know. Maybe Robin did and I chose to believe her.

She turned in my arms and I could feel her hips slide close to mine, her breasts softly pointed against my chest, the lovely mop of her hair under my chin.

"Okay. We'll go," I said. "It'll be fun. If we bomb, we can always come back."

She smiled, closed her eyes; in the small of my back her hands squeezed me tightly within her dream.

"We won't bomb," she said. "It's the start of our lives."

On a morning in March, in a hotel lobby in Baltimore, at a table of green enameled wrought iron, Myra sat down beside me. Her hair was plastered back and she had a drawn, stretched look around her eyes.

"Good morning," she said. "My damn shower didn't work this morning. Nothing but cold water. I feel like I've fallen off the goddamn *Titanic*."

She took my second cup of coffee, swallowed a big gulp and shivered.

"Is the air conditioning on in here?"

"People have been going in and out of the door."

She pulled the cup toward herself and warmed her hands on the outside.

"I need to go home," she said. "I need new clothes, I need to see if my cat's still alive, I need a warm shower, I need to watch a dozen reruns of *Mary Tyler Moore*, I need to not hear Thomas Hart Crane say, 'I want a nation true to its best instincts . . .' one more goddamn time."

The past picked up its skirts and fled, casting a last ambiguous glance over its shoulder.

"That must have been some shower," I said.

"Very cold."

"When do you get a break?"

"After Super Tuesday. You?"

"I love this. I might stay out here forever."

She scowled, sipped more of my coffee.

"Saw your old girlfriend going up the elevator."

"Yeah, she was down here."

"Want me to have her killed?"

"No, maybe a year ago."

Myra slid my coffee cup back my way. There was a single swallow left in the bottom. She tapped the side of the table in a drum roll.

"So you're recovered?"

"Absolutely."

"Twelve-step program?"

"More like a hundred little steps."

"Good. Safer that way."

"Sure."

She ran a hand through her damp hair and sourly eyed the campaign staff milling about the lobby in hastening disarray.

"Because if you wanted to get even, you'd have a hell of an opportunity right now, cowboy. A hell of a chance to work out a grudge."

I watched a dirty yellow bus pull up on the other side of the plate glass. Laugh at me now, but in a hotel lobby in Baltimore, in the stained light of March, I felt pure of heart.

"It's okay," I said. "It doesn't matter anymore."

Myra glanced at my coffee cup and grimaced as if something distasteful had settled on her tongue.

"That's the heartbreaking thing about romance," she said. "By the time you figure out how to get even, it's always too late."

X.

COLORADO. Maryland. Crane won them both despite last-minute advertising blitzes by Wilson, but he lost Georgia to the dour governor of Pennsylvania and we were back in the air before the final tallies were in. The great slew of southern primaries came next and we flew over swamps and mountains and hills with farms sagging like piles of scrapwood in the middle of lovely hollows. We rode through somnolent small towns and Sunbelt cities popping out of themselves like stevedores splitting their shirts.

The press is reductionist by nature, sooner or later simplifying everything to a matter of stark contrasts. If one candidate is salt, the other must be pepper. So it came to be the conventional wisdom that Wilson was the more conservative of the two and would do better in the South, which was now without its own candidate. Political momentum rides on gossamer wings and there were more than enough delegates at stake to crush the faint brush of the new that had carried Crane this far.

From my seat in the front of the plane's press section, two rows from the galley, I could see the first-class seats where Crane and his staff were sequestered. At night when the galley emptied, I could see the back of Crane's head as he sat in his seat by the window. Sometimes I would think he was sleeping and then he would turn. I could just make out the tilt of that dark shock of hair and long forehead as he stared out the window and I used to wonder what he was thinking.

I now know there were certain things that occupied him. One was the continuing bargain to be struck with his profession and the tenor of our times. Thus, it was one of those nights, after even I was asleep, that Blendin perched on the arm of the seat next to Crane.

"Three days in five markets," Blendin growled. "Five fucking markets and we can stop this." He waved a crumpled piece of paper filled with dimly printed numbers, the edges bent and crumpled with sweat.

The campaign's first attack ad was ready to go: a thirty-second spot in which an actress with a voice one could associate with the Virgin Mary told the story of the Christmas crèche that Wilson ordered out of the Capitol Building in Harrisburg after the American Civil Liberties Union objected.

"We've begged, stolen and borrowed and we've got the fucking money for three days," Blendin said. "Have you looked at this, Senator? You're down ten percent with people who strongly identify themselves as Christians. You started out as a nice guy who didn't owe anybody anything, and now you're a godless northern *liberal* and Wilson is Saint Fucking Francis of Assisi."

Crane rubbed his eyes. "Plus I want to kill millions of unborn babies."

"Plus you want to kill babies."

The protesters were showing up in the back of the rallies by then, kept a safe distance away by the crowds, by his popularity, but at quiet moments you could hear the muzzy rhythm of their chant, and if you looked, you could see their signs, each with a bright red splotch in the middle like a curled-up comma.

"Tim. We've gotten this far saying we don't play by the old rules," Crane said.

Blendin held up the sheet of polling data. "That's exactly right. We've gotten this far."

Blendin could say things to Crane no one else could. I think he recognized Blendin provided something he lacked. Crane almost lost his first campaign for re-election to the House when his opponent attacked him savagely in the final days and he was left groping for ways to respond. Since then, he had hired consultants who liked to get dirt under their fingernails. No one survives long in politics in innocence, and he may have kept his hands clean, but he was not innocent.

Crane tugged at his ear and looked out the window at the stray lights passing below.

"When I was a kid I used to watch jets like this flying by at night. You'd see them way up there, like another star. I used to wonder if there was somebody looking down right then, out the window like this, and if he was wondering if anyone was down there looking up at him."

"Everybody's done that," Blendin said impatiently.

Crane smiled as if his consultant had missed the point.

"No, Tim, I thought it was an epiphany. The thing is, it seemed like an unbelievable life to me, to be up there in that plane. I used to think about flying, how I would have to take trips like this someday. You know what? I worried that I'd be airsick. That I wouldn't like it."

He ran his fingers along the side of his jaw.

"Let me ask you something. Why do we do this? Why do get off and on this plane eight times a day? Why do we eat bad pizza at eleven o'clock at night? Why do we stay away from our families for days on end? Why do we do all this?"

Blendin shook his head in irritation. "I can only speak personally, Senator. But I'm hoping this leads to a career on MSNBC spouting whatever bull-shit I want for three hundred thousand dollars a year."

"We do this because it's what people expect. It's what they expect of a candidate. You know the other thing they expect of a candidate? They expect he'll finally descend to their worst expectations."

"And there's a reason it happens. Because it works."

"Until it's not what they expect."

"You should look at these numbers."

"I look at the numbers all the time, Tim. I see the numbers in my sleep."

"Three days, Senator. In four markets."

"I don't think so."

"Ahh fuck." Blendin crumpled the poll and tossed it toward a sleeping Starke two rows ahead.

The plane thrummed along, the rest of Crane's traveling staff sprawled asleep across seats, the cabin dark, the press on the other side of the galley quiet, the night passing, Blendin sitting on the armrest gloomily wondering how much of the fishing season in Minnesota he would catch when this campaign was over and Thomas Crane was back in Washington with his sanctimonious notions about the American electorate safely tucked away where they could do no more harm. Then he glanced down to see his candidate watching him with a merciless eye.

"Don't worry, Tim," Crane said. "I will do what's necessary. But this is the wrong move."

"What then, Senator?"

Crane looked out the window, and I wonder what he saw, how much he imagined, how much he really understood.

"You remember the spot we ran in Colorado on the environment? Take the money and get that on in the university towns. Run the radio spots on the campus stations. We'll be okay."

I don't know what I would have thought if I had known about that conversation then. I had ambivalent feelings enough when, two days before the vote, I caught a cab from the Omni Hotel in Atlanta to the Buckhead neighborhood. Latrelle Gregory was waiting for me at a table when I came into Bones. He sat with the stolid concentration of a middle-aged burgher considering the huge menu propped before him on the table, a glass of scotch perched inches from his left hand.

"You are buying, am I correct?" he said in his fussy Georgia accent when I sat down.

"That drink and everything after."

Gregory smiled. He had thinning hair and a round, pink face with a thin mustache that lent him an air of pleasant dissolution. He had been slim when I knew him two years earlier in Washington, but now there was a comfortable thickness about the middle.

"You look as if you're settling in nicely down here," I said.

"I am home, Clifford. That is a comfort."

"And how is the governor?"

"The governor is a man of vision and perspicacity. A gentle, yet firm and clear-eyed soul. The governor is one of the great leaders of the New South and quite possibly our nation. The governor is, I tell you confidentially, quite possibly a genius. The governor is, above all, the man who signs my checks."

I pointed to Gregory's scotch and held up two fingers. A waiter nodded and slid gracefully into the shadows.

82

"Washington misses you, Latrelle," I said. "No one has used the word *perspicacity* since you left."

He folded the menu and placed it carefully on the tablecloth, as if it were delicate and to be cherished.

"But I do not miss Washington. At least not more than a little." He smiled, reminding me briefly of a Teutonic Buddha. "And how about you, Clifford? When I left you were covering those eternal hearings we held on the Farm Credit Act, and now look at you."

My scotch arrived and settled as if by levitation in my hand. "To quote one of your region's fine senators," I said, "Howell Heflin, I believe it was, 'Even a blind pig can find an acorn now and then.'"

"Thomas Crane is no acorn."

I raised my glass in a toast.

"Well, it didn't make any sense when Heflin said it either. To the old days."

He sipped and smiled into the glass.

"And what is it you want to know, Clifford?"

I hefted the menu and pretended to study it for a moment.

"You were with Crane in the beginning, right? When he first came to Washington?"

"Yes. Somebody in the Speaker's office suggested me to him. He needed a few veteran hands sprinkled throughout the happy, corn-fed children, just to keep the office running." His smile slid up both cheeks. "Ask me what I think of him and I'll tell you what I've told everyone. I think he was a good legislator and I think he'll make a darn fine president."

"I'm sure that's true. You stayed with him through his first year in the Senate?"

He nodded and waited, enjoying himself.

"But you left after that. Why?"

"A difference in styles, Clifford. Nothing more. You know how you people from the North are: you shave in the shower because it saves time and you count your change every time the waiter sets it on the table. I wished for a certain latitude."

I set the menu down with the vague impression the plains of Texas were being depopulated to provision this one restaurant.

"Actually, I have nothing to ask you on the record," I said. "I don't even

83

have anything to ask you for use without attribution. I just have something that's been bothering me, and I was hoping you could help clear it up." And I told him about the two unaccounted-for trips by Crane.

Gregory sipped his scotch.

"You ask me something unexpected."

He was wearing an old tweed jacket with a vest the color of dying pumpkin beneath it. He reached down and slid a thumb absently along the buttons on the jacket.

"How much do you know about his past?"

"Quite a lot."

He nodded. "Everybody does these days. You can't open a newspaper without a story about the poor boy from Berthold who made good. My favorite are the ones that start with young Thomas Crane standing on that highway, hitching rides into Springfield in the dead of winter so he can go to that Catholic school."

"Aquinas."

"Yes. Saint Thomas Crane going to Saint Thomas Aquinas. I love those." He lifted his drink and looked meditatively into the glass. "What is that line from Hemingway? 'I distrust all frank and simple men, particularly when their stories hold together.' You all love that story too much, my friend."

"I always thought you'd be a Faulkner man."

"You like it because it fits into sixty seconds or four paragraphs. Because it has a recognizable form. Because it's part of an accepted myth that doesn't require you to think. Its utility blinds you. No road, Clifford, is that magical."

He was working up to something, so I waited.

"Here is a story no one has ever heard," Gregory said. "When I was first with him in the House there was a simple protocol—if his door was closed, you left him alone. If the door was ajar, you knocked and entered. I don't remember what it was I had in my hands, but it was something I was reading, and when I came to his door, I pushed and, since it was ajar, entered without remembering to knock. He was on the phone. We had those absolutely dreadful offices on top of Rayburn then and he had his chair swiveled so he could see the little patch of the city you could glimpse through a corner of the window . . ."

84

Gregory took a slow drink. His Adam's apple bobbed and he went on, avoiding my eyes.

"Anyway, he was on the phone and I heard him say, 'I want to send you a check.' The person on the other side said something. Then Crane said, 'I know I don't have to, but it lets me sleep better at night, do you understand?'" Gregory's eyes grew clouded. "Something like that. I think those were the words. Anyway. I am sometimes foolish, but I try never to be stupid. I knew I had made an unfortunate error walking through that door without knocking. I took half a step backward and dragged my feet as if I'd just come in.

"The congressman looked up and this is why I have remembered this all these years, Clifford. He looked so young those days, you remember?" He waved a hand. "I forget you were still feeding at your dear mother's breast. He always looked young then, but that day it was like there was someone else, a separate child, staring at me. Like some scared child peering out from inside a costume who knows he's on stage and can't remember his lines."

"What happened?"

"It only lasted a second, and then it was Thomas Crane again, and he asked me if I could come back in ten minutes. I believe I made sure the door clicked when I left."

Gregory settled back in his chair and his full cheeks glowed in the candlelight.

"It's a more complicated story, isn't it? How poor boys get rich and who they owe when they're finished. He had debts back home, Clifford. They all do."

"Do you know who was on the other end of the phone?"

He shook his head. "We could talk about that all night, but it would be idle speculation. This is what I can tell you: There were people who helped him, helped him get into school, helped him when he left for Princeton, helped him later. Debts come with obligations. You let me know when you find out more and we can talk again."

He was finished, at least for a while. We were both quiet.

"But you like him," I said.

He smiled like a child with a bug on a pin. "Of course I like him,

85

Clifford. The man fired me, but I have nothing but admiration for him to this day." He hefted the menu again and stared into its silken depths. "We must order. I'm sure you have a long day ahead of you tomorrow. What are you going to have?"

"I'm not sure. You?"

"The largest tenderloin they have, I believe. Rare."

"Rare?"

Gregory's gaze rolled up the menu. "I am a southern boy, Clifford. We like our meat the way we like our politics. Raw."

We flew from Atlanta to the Carolinas, stopping at Duke and the University of North Carolina and the Charleston harbor, where the Old Fort floated like a desert citadel in a glimmering sea-sky. We flew to Florida and touched down in Orlando and then Sarasota, where the Chicago White Sox were in spring training. We tumbled out of the hot and diesel-smelling bus and squinted through the sunlight at a world of primal green and blue.

Crane stepped out of his limousine wearing a White Sox cap. He stood blinking in the sunlight and then turned to the gate held open by a wizened security guard who seemed about to doff his cap.

The woman stepping down in front of me was a twenty-three-year-old television reporter from a local station, blond with a powdered face, a bright pink mouth and a canary yellow suit ready to take wing. When you travel around the country, you find that an amazing number of local television reporters are former Miss something or others, and the woman stepping off the bus had the determined good cheer of a beauty contestant. She waited for her cameraman to join her.

"This is an odd stop," she said.

Myra was beside me, wearing a pair of baggy khaki shorts, a Stub's Bar and Grill T-shirt and a checkered blue bandanna.

"Come on, it's baseball," Myra said. "America. Apple pie. All the eternal verities. Who doesn't want to be tied to baseball?"

Crane stood by the batting cage, his tie gone, the sleeves of his dress shirt rolled up his slender forearms. A small circle of players and coaches gathered around him, and outside them, a wider circle of madly clicking photographers.

"Where are we exactly?" I asked.

"Sarasota," the television reporter said as if I had hurt her feelings.

"Don't worry about it," Myra said. "Tonight we'll be back in Charlotte. You remember Charlotte? You like Charlotte."

The grass felt luxuriant beneath my feet. Laughter rose and fell in a loping rhythm from the outfield. Crane gripped a bat and waggled. He was talking to the cameras, but seemed to be addressing a tall wide-shouldered player with a round, boyish face: Frank Thomas, the all-star first baseman.

"I played in high school and a year in college before I got too busy with other things," Crane said. "But I don't think I was ever much of a threat to your career."

The players laughed politely.

"How's it look this year?" Crane asked.

An old man scratched the salt-and-pepper bramble of his hair. "If some of our young pitchers come around we'll be in good shape."

Crane smiled at the cliché, straight out of baseball eternal.

"I followed every game the Sox played when I was a kid," he said. "I used to stay over at my cousin's whenever I could because he had a radio and we'd pretend to go to bed and then lie in the dark and listen to the games. Nellie Fox was my hero."

The players listened dutifully. He was talking about a time before they had been born.

A photographer yelled from the back. "Take a few swings, Senator!"

Crane looked at the bat in his hands.

"I can toss you a few," said a small squarely built player.

"Who's that?" Myra asked.

A photographer glanced up. "Martino Benitez. Their ace."

"Come on, Senator, just a couple!"

Crane waggled the bat and then glanced at the photographer who had issued the challenge. The wounded look surfaced in his eyes, and his expression steeled into a resolve I took to be a reflection of the quiet arrogance beneath it all, an arrogance that touched off admiration despite myself. He stepped into the batting cage, pulled his White Sox cap low on his brow, and took an upright stance. Benitez trotted behind the wire screen that protects pitchers during batting practice. The rest of us formed a V that bottomed around the batting cage and fanned out along the foul lines.

The bat was cocked behind Crane's ear, the barrel moving in a small nervous circle. His hands couldn't keep still on the handle.

"All right," he said.

Benitez hitched his glove, kicked his leg, turned and lobbed a pitch like a spill of milk over the middle of the plate. Crane swung early off his front foot and fouled the pitch weakly to the left. He smiled, but when he saw the cameras recording everything, his expression went dead.

"Go ahead, give me a pitch," he said. "You don't have to make it soft-ball."

The cameras whirred. Myra crossed her fingers.

"I can see the lead already," she whispered. "Thomas Crane struck out in Florida Saturday. Please please please."

Benitez hitched his glove, kicked, spun and came over the top with a gentle, batting practice fastball. He threw just hard enough that the pitch looked like a real pitch, but wasn't.

The ball sailed across the plate and Crane swung in rhythm this time, the barrel of the bat coming out to meet the ball with the weight of his hips behind it. He was a bit stiff-legged but his head was tucked nicely and his shoulder was closed and moving forward when the bat came around in its arc and sent the ball rocketing in a starched rope toward left field. It hung on a line for what seemed like a long time, then dipped, hit the soft grass once and thumped off the wall beside a Marlboro ad.

On the mound Benitez grabbed his heart and pretended to faint. Beside the cage Frank Thomas tipped his hat up as if to get a better look. "Nice rap," he said.

"There's your TV clip," I said.

"Christ," Myra said. "The Natural. I can't stand it."

It could be nothing, I thought. Trips home to see an old friend, a check that got lost in the mail, an old staff member who can't forgive someone for seeing clearly what he was. It could all be nothing.

XI.

R ED, WHITE and blue bunting was already sagging in the heat when I arrived at the party on the night of Super Tuesday. Crane posters were spaced along the walls, and he stared at me from a dozen different angles with glassy-eyed optimism. Myra leaned against the wall, dodging elbows, clutching her notebook to her chest.

"This is worse than New Hampshire," she said. "Why is the room never big enough? I know, I know, so the crowd always looks big. But, come on, give us some air."

"Crane might be saying the same thing by the end of the night."

She jotted some stray thought in her notebook, tucked up in front of her nose.

"He's running for president," she said. "It's not supposed to be easy."

We had arrived in Lexington a few hours earlier, stopping first at the university. Raindrops pelted from tumescent clouds and Crane hurried indoors with his hands deep in his pockets. We had been campaigning nonstop for two days and you could see exhaustion in the way he fell forward into each stride, turning fatigue into an illusion of momentum. There hadn't been quite enough money, organization or time and now they were voting across the South.

In the hotel ballroom a young woman with wide blue eyes and a brown ponytail sipped from a paper cup and tried to keep her eyes on the earnest young man next to her with a similar ponytail, but her eyes strayed to the television cameras going up next to the stage and then to the willowy actress who wandered in our midst, untouchable in the soap bubble of celebrity. The crowd pressed and jostled her and her eyes danced with delight and her ponytail switched happily across her neck.

The actress slid by and Myra, sensing her presence by the awed hush, glanced up and watched her pass.

"She once bought a whole southern town, didn't she? I wonder if she owns any of these people."

"I think that was in Georgia."

"I don't know. Watch for ankle chains."

The big-screen televisions, squatting like Easter Island totems in the corners of the room, squawked to life. Myra teetered on her toes and peered over a shoulder. I read the early, inconsequential vote tallies scrolling down the screens to her, and she settled back on her heels with a sigh and halfheartedly jotted down numbers. The room came back to life with heightened, electric chatter.

"This is going to turn into one hell of a wake if he goes down," Myra said.

Four men wearing the black satin jackets of the coal miners union shouldered past, their cologne settling on us like marsh gas. Their eyes rolled sideways, considered the brightly colored planets and stars decorating Myra's jacket, rested briefly on her smiling man-in-the-moon earrings, then flew forward.

"But there's always the fun we can have in the meantime," she said.

An hour later I was finishing the first draft of my story when CNN called Missouri for Crane and the crowd roared as if watching the opening kickoff of a football game. In the press room, demarcated from the party only by a half-open folding wall, Nathan's eyes twinkled with intimations of disaster.

"If all Crane wins is Missouri and here, it's trouble."

Everything came down to a measurement against expectations. It didn't matter that two months ago Crane was at 7 percent, that he didn't have real organizations in half the states voting tonight. Win only where he was expected to win and he'd done nothing. Governor Harris Wilson stepped inside the magic lantern and his shadow was tossed larger than life against our cave walls.

"He's still got a chance in Tennessee," Nathan said. "But I don't know if that'll do it."

No, I thought, Tennessee wouldn't quite do it. The feeling of heaviness that settled over me was like waking from a dream of flight.

"He's running for president," I said. "It's not supposed to be easy."

When CNN called Kentucky for Crane, I was in the ballroom interviewing an old woman with campaign buttons blanketing the front of her moss-green vest. She was telling me how collecting them had been her hobby since the Kennedy administration, when she froze in midsentence. Behind her the young woman with the ponytail stared at one of the televisions. A hand flew up to her mouth and she gasped, bending from the waist as if breathless. I could see her mouth the words behind the fluttering hand. *Oh my God. Oh my God. Oh my God.* I wondered how many hours she had worked for this moment, how many doors she had knocked on, how many phone calls she had made.

It was time for Crane to appear and claim the victories he had in hand. The crowd shifted expectantly toward the stage. Half an hour later they were still waiting. In the press room we tinkered with our stories and watched the minutes tick away. We needed a quote. We needed Crane.

Stuart Abercrombie stroked the pale parchment of his chin. "Something's up," he said. "The North Carolina gap's down to a point. And too many precincts are still out."

"Where?"

"Chapel Hill and Durham. My desk says they temporarily ran out of ballots."

The table we were working at was an eddy of silence.

"Jesus Christ," Nathan said. "College kids."

"Are they allowed to vote?" Myra said. "No wonder this country's such a mess."

"Shit," Nathan said. "He could win North Carolina."

"No."

"Hell, yes. You know how he did with college kids in Colorado and Maryland."

"That's why he hasn't shown up," Abercrombie said. "They're waiting up there." He pointed toward Crane's suite somewhere above us in the hotel. "They know something's happening."

Nathan hopped on his chair like an admiral taking the bridge in a high sea and dialed his office. "The polling data is being revised . . . They're rolling the new numbers now . . . Jesus Christ. No, really? Hell, here we go. All right, let me get this down."

He cradled the phone in his neck and scribbled. "Yeah . . . yeah . . . got it. All right. Twenty minutes, I know." He glanced at us. "He's got Tennessee, and the new numbers show him winning North Carolina by one and a half. The next raw vote total will move him ahead. It's coming out of the college precincts. I've got the numbers."

A roar built next door, a long hoarse exultation. I looked up to see faces turned toward televisions like flowers facing the sun, filling with light as the world spun on a pointed toe and swooned at Crane's feet.

Then he was making his way forward through the crowd. The roar climbed a notch. His hand rose in a triumphant fist. They pulled at his arms, they reached for him so the room swayed at his every step. He slid through the chaos, Angela by his side, disappearing and reappearing until he reached the stage, hugging local party leaders as he worked his way to the microphone. We tumbled out of the press room and pushed ourselves into the back of the crowd, standing on chairs, sliding around tables, holding tape recorders and cameras above our heads.

Crane raised his hands for quiet.

"I'd like to—"

A crack split the air behind us. Crane was looking at the podium and he seemed to take a very long time to lift his head. His eyes filled with a strangely serene curiosity, as if he heard someone knocking on a door. His wife grabbed his arm. There was a flash of light and then a lingering echo.

He straightened himself and smiled. Heads spun around, locating the noise. An ice sculpture at the buffet had shattered in the heat, an air bubble perhaps. We faced nothing more severe than the death of an ice swan.

"Jesus," Nathan said. When the statue cracked he had jumped and knocked over a bottle. Seltzer water was fizzing all over the crotch of his pants.

"I know you're excited about this man," Abercrombie said, "but please."

92

Crane leaned into the microphone.

"As I have been saying . . . We've got nothing to be afraid of—"

He was drowned out. They tossed confetti, paper cups, napkins, anything they had into the air. Rolls of crepe paper bounced above the crowd, tossed back and forth until the room seemed to float beneath a slowly collapsing sky of red, white and blue. Crane stood at the microphone with both hands up, his sleeves sliding back on his jacket, his dark hair tangled in a nimbus of confetti. He tried to wave them to silence but the noise rolled on and on, and we all knew we were on our way to the convention in New York and the race against the president. Thomas Crane had gone south and won four states, twice as many as the polls had predicted. The media had set a standard and he had performed the best possible trick, exceeding it right on deadline.

I stood unsteadily on a chair, trying to see into the knot of staff gathered to the right of the stage. Robin was wearing a gold sweater and her hair was damp across her forehead. She held her hands above her head, clapping with the crowd, and you could see her laughing, her eyes sweeping the room, swallowing it all in, letting it get inside her, fill her up, radiate back out in unalloyed joy.

As Crane finished speaking my editor and I were shouting at each other over the phone.

"What?"

"Fifteen minutes. Just a new top."

"I know. I'm recasting it. I'm going to use the—"

"What?"

A man with a handlebar mustache staggered into the press room, swinging a beer bottle like a baton. He climbed on a chair, raised his arms and toppled backward, boot heels flipping into the air like a pair of startled cartoon eyes.

"I'm recasting it. I'm going to use the 'common fears, common hopes' quote—"

"Good. Fifteen minutes. We'll fill in here."

"All right. You've got the Brill stuff out of Virgin—"

"What? I'm having a hard time—"

"The Brill stuff—"

"The Bill stuff? Who's Bill?"

"Brill. Congressman Brill!"

"We're fine. That's fine. Everything but the top."

"All right."

I worked with the controlled panic and attention to detail of someone launching a lifeboat with water lapping over his shoes. In fifteen minutes I was watching my computer, thinking *send send send*. I called and made sure the story was there, stood and stretched my back, fought my way past reporters hunched in mental carapaces over their laptops, sweat in sagging crescent moons beneath their arms, eyes glazed, lips murmuring odd scraps of story. I tiptoed through the tangle of phone and power cords, trying not to hit anyone's elbow, until I found a warm can of Coke by an empty cooler. I carried it to my computer and went back to work.

In the ballroom the television crews were doing interviews and their portable spots swung back and forth, illuminating bodies in elongated cones of light. Voices rose and fell in fervent swoops, one shrill laugh floating above them all in a mad, fluted solo. A country-western band led off with a raucous electric fiddle, and the actress-who-did-or-did-not-own-a-town danced a jig with a coal miner, the girl with the ponytail waltzed across the floor with a torn poster of Crane clutched to her chest; a senator from Alabama slapped John Starke on the shoulders. Someone passed out party hats and soon they all looked as if they'd escaped from some eternal New Year's Eve roaring on in hell.

I worked hard for another hour and a half, sending three more updates of the story, the last for our West Coast papers. On other primary nights my job had been relatively simple. The main stories had been written by one of the bureau's veteran political analysts, reporters who did not follow any one candidate but roamed the countryside, thinking deep thoughts and going wherever their wisdom took them. My role had been to feed them information and fashion a small sidebar about the Crane campaign. The phenomenon is known as getting "big-footed," stepped on by a reporter with more clout. I may have lucked into the candidate rising like a bottle rocket, but I was still on my first campaign and wasn't to be trusted with the final word. It hadn't mattered that much to me; I had been too happy to be on the road.

But tonight the big feet had guessed wrong and were sitting in Wilson's campaign headquarters in Florida. I was writing the main story and they were feeding me. I wasn't leaving my computer until every possible update had winged its electronic way to the farthest corners of the tidy little empire that was Cannon Newspapers, Incorporated.

By the time I was done, the party had drained out of the ballroom. A couple sat holding hands and whispering in one corner; a drunk slumped over another table, humming to himself. The room smelled of stale beer. Half-empty glasses left damp half-moons on the tablecloths, and sodden crepe paper hung everywhere like shed snakeskin.

The phone was ringing when I entered my room. Latrelle Gregory's lugubrious voice greeted mine.

"Clifford, I was beginning to think you'd joined the all-night bacchanal."

It was after midnight and I had been working for hours. My thoughts felt like they were plodding through mud.

"How'd you get this number?" I asked.

"Your office, of course."

"Of course."

"There is something else, Clifford. Something I remembered after we spoke. There was another sudden trip to Berthold—or at least back to Illinois. I checked my old office datebook today to be sure. I keep them all, you know. During his first year in the Senate. June fifteenth to be exact . . . Yes . . . He was scheduled to attend a hearing of the labor and human services appropriations subcommittee. It was important because of Medicare reforms. We had a long list of questions prepared. Then at five o'clock the evening before he tells us he won't be attending. He asked Julia to get him a ticket to Springfield for early the next morning. Listen. I have jotted down here: 'Congressman clearly upset.' He came back late the next night. . ."

His voice trailed off and I heard him breathing a little too hard. I thought Gregory had celebrated Crane's southern triumph with a toast or two.

"And he never offered an explanation?"

"No. I don't have this in my notes, but I remember that he wasn't much good for a couple of weeks after. Spent a lot of time away from the office. With Angela, I believe. Whatever else one says about the man, he always put his shoulder to the grindstone. So that lodged in my mind."

"Well . . ."

"There's one other little bit. I can't be sure. But I remember checking his desk for something else when he was gone. He's a tidy guy, you know, but I remember he had scrawled a name down on his blotter. Joe, I believe."

"Joe?"

"I seem to remember so."

"No last name?"

"No."

"And you don't know who it might be?"

"No, I'm afraid I really couldn't say."

"Okay . . ."

"Yes, well. I thought you would find it interesting. So how is the celebration?"

"I don't know. I just finished working."

"Clifford, Clifford. I am many hundred miles away and yet I can tell you that in some crowded room at this moment are young women flush with the passion of the moment. It bubbles inside them like champagne, Clifford. They have never felt so good and they want to share it. You have sympathetic eyes, my boy. Tonight is the night to put them to good use."

"Thank you, Gregory. I'll act on that immediately."

I put the phone down and looked in the mirror. Sympathetic eyes. Eyes begging for sympathy, maybe. There *was* a party in the room next door. The wall thumped and I heard shrill notes of laughter above the din. I wondered where Robin was. Any one of a hundred places. The phone rang again.

My editor's voice was dry, exhausted. "I tried to call earlier, but your line was busy. Who the hell were you talking to at this time of night?"

"No one. An old friend."

"I'm on my way out the door. I just wanted to tell you, you did a great job tonight. They're jealous as hell right now down in Florida."

"Great."

Something in my voice stopped her.

"Is there anything else?"

96

"I don't think so," I said. "Not now."

When she was done I pulled off my tie and walked to the window. I didn't have anything yet, not enough to let the bureau know. Tell them now and they'd be all over me for a story, and I didn't know it was a story, not yet. I had been lied to, though. I had to remember that. I had been lied to. Or was it a mistake, one anyone could make? So many years ago. Two different visits confused.

The hotel was old enough that the window opened. I yanked it up and the damp night air flooded in, brushing the curtains back. The noise from the party came in louder. Another sound came from the street, faint and struggling to be heard. I leaned forward and followed it down to the sidewalk. Five figures passed from circle of light to circle of light, carrying signs on their shoulders. A curled red splotch on the signs. Their voices floated in a singsong: "Crane the Killer. Crane the Killer. Crane the Killer."

I watched them for a while and then I pulled the window closed and sat down on the edge of the bed. I had to plug in my equipment. I had to pull out tomorrow's clothes. We were leaving at nine, but I was too tired to move.

Crane the Killer. Crane the Liar. We were all out for him now.

XII.

WE FLEW north and the primaries melted into one another. Michigan, Illinois, Connecticut, New York. Crane did not win everywhere, but he won often enough that the result was never in doubt, although we spun endless fantasies in print and on videotape pretending otherwise. The protesters I heard that night in Kentucky were with us from then on, not always, but every few days, floating at the edge of our consciousness like a troubling, half-formed thought that recedes as you pursue it, but refuses to disappear.

So March passed and April bloomed on Lexington Avenue with Crane standing on a flatbed truck while faces appeared in window after window, a crowd terraced above us, leaning forward to catch snatches of his words rising on a spring breeze. When he spoke, laughter, applause, smiles rippled from the street up into mirrored reflections of the city, and in their warmth, the long winter was somehow banished.

We slid into May and I saw Robin often when we were both on the road. I took days off and she went back to Springfield for as long as a week at a time, but when we were traveling we talked and sometimes we had breakfast together. We talked about Billings, but never about those awkward, final months in Washington. Our conversations were full of the ever-exploding present. There were strained moments, of course, when we got too close to the past, and then she was too busy to see me for a few days, but they were rare. I look back and it seems we talked mostly about nothing at all, and I realize how essential that was, how much we needed a gentle changing of the seasons.

I got up in the morning and left my bags outside my door and got on a bus and went where they took me and wrote what other people asked me to and I never did a thing about what Latrelle Gregory had told me until one day John Starke leaned over and said, "The senator would like to talk to you."

We were on the plane. Starke's fine hair was cropped close and brushed back above his pink forehead. Light from the window caught his ear and I noticed the waxy stubble of just-clipped ear hair.

"The senator wants to see me?"

He nodded and smiled, as always, with less joy than anyone I've ever seen. "If you've got a moment."

I found my tape recorder and notebook and stood up. Our assigned seats were two to a row, the middle seat left empty. Nathan sat next to me. He stood up to let me out, his eyes bright with curiosity.

"Tell him I'll be in next," he said.

"Sure you will," Starke said.

I stood in the aisle trying to get my bearings—fifteen seconds earlier I had been slumped against the bulkhead with my eyes closed. The press section of the plane slid slowly into focus with the reassuring familiarity of home: the torn-out pictures and headlines pasted on the walls, the odors of sweat, half a dozen meals, spilled soft drinks, dirty bathrooms and greasy luggage. Taped to the bulkhead by my seat was a picture of the vice president of the United States visiting one of our proxy guerrilla armies in Central America. He was posing ferociously with a grenade launcher, holding it backward so it pointed at his shoulder. I stared at it until my head cleared while Starke waited impatiently.

"Just preparing a brutal chain of questions," I said.

He led me through the galley and into the front of the plane. One of the flight attendants winked at me as I passed, as if to say, aren't you a lucky boy. My eyes strayed to Robin's seat when I entered, but she was in California preparing for our arrival.

Crane had his jacket off and his sleeves rolled up one crisp turn. He sat in one of a set of seats facing each other. He had the table down between them and in his right hand he held a small book with covers of worn and cracked black leather. He smiled when he saw me.

"Cliff, sit down." He gestured to the seat across from him. "I wanted you to see this. A man who read your article about my reading habits gave it to me."

He handed the book to me. The covers gave beneath my fingers, as soft as old cotton.

"It's an edition of Grant's memoirs," he said. "Published in eighteen ninety-four."

I turned the translucent pages carefully and read: *My family is American, and has been for generations, in all its branches, direct and collateral.* The words were full of an unexpected resonance, and I hovered over them uncertainly.

Crane watched me carefully. "So, have you gotten to Galena yet?"

I shook my head.

He seemed mildly, but genuinely disappointed. "You should try if you get a chance. Did I tell you they've got the family home restored and a great exhibit at the museum? A nice piece of history. They're very proud of the whole thing."

"I've read this," I said. "It's a great book."

He nodded with boyish enthusiasm. "He was a beautiful writer."

"Of course, there are those who say Mark Twain wrote most of it."

He considered me with those eyes and I watched a reappearance of the quietly haughty candidate I had glimpsed before.

"Yes. Every time a politician opens his mouth, there's someone who looks behind the curtain to see who's pulling the strings. Yet somehow we remain creatures of free will."

The conversation seemed to be teetering on a fence, capable of falling in either direction. Crane looked over my shoulder.

"I've been thinking about something you asked me a while back. You asked me about my mother's death and I said something like, 'It was hard. You have to make choices.' I regretted that after I said it. I thought it sounded hard . . . harsh."

I had set the book on the table. He picked it up and stared at the cover.

"I don't know if you remember that conversation, but I wanted to correct it. I don't know that there were that many choices. I had plans, and I knew she wanted me to accomplish them as much as anyone. They were her dreams, too. She deserves more credit than I gave her, than she's ever gotten."

He paused. I could feel Starke hovering behind my shoulder, hating the direction of this conversation.

"I know you were close," I said.

Crane shifted uncomfortably in his seat.

"There is all this stuff written about me these days," he said, "and I have yet to see a story that gets this right, that gives her the credit she deserves. She had a sense of larger things. That wasn't that common. At least in Berthold."

His tone was strangely aggrieved, defensive. His fingers slid absently along his temple.

"It wasn't always easy, but without those goals, who knows where I'd be? That's what I wanted to say."

I nodded. Starke shifted behind me, and I thought I was about to be dismissed.

"I remember you told me once you grew up in a small town," Crane said.

"Havre. It's a small city in Montana."

"I thought maybe it wasn't so different."

"Maybe not."

"Are your parents still alive?"

"My mother. My father died a few years ago."

"I remember you told me that the same morning. What did he do?"

"He was a newspaper editor."

He smiled at me, as if clearly apprehending something he had only sensed obscurely before.

"I bet you made him proud."

"He died before I got to Washington," I said.

"So did she."

My ears popped. We were descending. I heard Starke clear his throat. I knew this was the time to ask Crane about the thing that had been bothering me, to point out gently that he could not have visited his brother when he said, to ask him about the sudden trip to Berthold, to ask him what kept bringing him back. I knew this was my chance.

"Thanks for letting me see the book," I said.

Crane slid the book across the table.

"Take it with you for a while, Cliff. You can give it to John when you're done."

"I wouldn't dare." I nodded toward the back of the plane. "It's like bringing china into a zoo."

Starke snorted with satisfaction. Crane grinned. "Remember you said that, not me. I hope we can talk more about Grant later."

Myra's seat was directly in front of mine. When I got back she propped her arms on top of the row, resting her chin in her hands, examining me with a mocking look of astonishment. I felt Nathan twisting in his seat.

"So?" she said.

There is a protocol among reporters on the campaign trail. Words said in public by the candidate are shared by everyone. Words said in a private interview are your own. She was asking if I had anything I wanted to share.

"So nothing," I said. "He had an old book he wanted to show me. We had a discussion once about history."

She cocked an eyebrow as if I had just admitted I was building a time machine in my basement.

"And?"

"Nothing."

"Nothing?"

"Nothing," I said. "Nothing at all."

I looked out the window at a patchwork of gold-and-brown hills rising to meet us. I heard Myra settle back in her seat. The day was full of the saffron light of the West Coast, still the light of eternal promise. I thought about my father. When I was young he never explained the point of his work to me that I can remember, but once. We were standing near the railroad tracks that divide Havre into rich and poor, white and Indian. He had written a story that traced the last hours of a carful of high school students who killed themselves in an accident coming down the road from the Rocky Boy Reservation. It was an annual spring rite in Havre, the graduation party at the reservation, where the police had no jurisdiction, followed too often by the death of a carful of teenagers on the way home.

My father had written about the three girls in the car and the two days of drinking that preceded the accident. They were all popular, all from well-to-do families, and the community was furious. We were walking near the tracks and the mother of one of the girls saw us. "Lying bastard!" she shouted and crossed the street to avoid him. I was twelve years old and

I was mortified and then full of self-righteous rage.

"Those girls were just what you said," I told my father. "Just what you said."

He was a gentle, easily distracted man by then, who wore old corduroy pants that rustled when he walked, so he always seemed to be having a murmured conversation with himself. He looked at me through his glasses with watery eyes, and I saw that I had hurt him. "I never said they were anything," he said.

He walked another few feet and stopped again. "Most people never look at the world the way it is, just the way they want it to be. That's a nice way to live, Cliff. You want to live that way you go work in a university." He looked across the street at the disappearing back of the mother. "I never said those girls were anything. I reported the evidence. I just reported what they did."

It was an old-fashioned creed even then, many would say based on a simplistic notion of the truth, as if the truth can be assembled from the physical detritus of our lives, as if we are the muddy footprint on the carpet, the smiling face bent toward the makeup mirror, the offhand remark in the hallway. Who is to say any of this is truth?

Nonetheless, I don't know of any other creed for a journalist that starts in humility and proceeds without bitterness. I know of no other way we can operate without committing greater sins of arrogance and presumption. Maybe it is a frail and incomplete faith, but what else do we have? I had raised this tattered pennant through all my defeats, all my thirty-three years of small failure and paltry evasion: I had never been afraid to gather the evidence. I had never been afraid to ask the question.

We banked through reefs of sunlight and landed at John Wayne International Airport. While we were waiting for the bus, I walked far enough away from the plane to escape the noise. I stood on the shimmering tarmac, thinking about Thomas Crane and his mother and my father and small places where dreams are all about the things you will do when you leave. I thought about how I liked him and how I knew he liked me and then I tugged my phone out of my bag. My editor answered on the first ring.

"When I get back to town, remind me," I said, "there's something I've got to talk to you about. It's probably nothing, but I need help checking it out."

XIII.

IN CALIFORNIA, where the sun sets on the primary season, we filed early to meet East Coast deadlines, and the night stretched before us like a sudden holiday. I don't know San Francisco well, but we were near the Embarcadero Center in a beautiful hotel with rooms of Japanese simplicity, silk prints on eggshell walls, lacquered woodwork shining like obsidian. Chinatown and North Beach were somewhere above us. We climbed a hill and chose a restaurant where the drawn red carcasses of ducks hung by their necks in the window and the smells of ginger and garlic drifted out of the open door.

We sat at a huge table with a dolly in the center, sharing heaping platters of Kung Pao chicken, sweet and sour pork, Szechuan vegetables, shredded beef in garlic. We'd been living for months on sandwiches tossed into the plane and Mexican food served from press-room buffets, and a bottomless hunger had seized us all.

"More of these," Nathan yelled, holding up a plate of prawns. "And another round of beer."

Myra stared through a beer bottle, sloshing it back and forth, the muscles in her face slowly relaxing.

"You wouldn't think he could put that much down, would you? I guess it feeds his twitches."

"Little guys always eat a lot," said Randall Craig, CNN's correspondent. "Haven't you noticed?"

Craig was smooth and suntanned, with heavily lidded eyes, delicate wrists and long fingers. He had a precise, European way of speaking picked up in a bureau overseas, only rarely betrayed by the vestiges of a Brooklyn accent. His hair was a remarkable ornament, silver and black, sweeping back into a widow's peak like the beak of a hawk. He was eternally bored and always seemed to be having a splendid time.

"I'm a high-energy guy," Nathan said. "Never gain a pound. Never run, never lift weights, never do anything. Type real fast."

"Verbal calisthenics, you may be an Olympian," Stuart said, sipping a glass of wine and pursing his lips as if there were ashes at the bottom. The happiness of others worked on him that way.

Steven Duprey's face disappeared and reappeared between decanters of soy sauce and bowls of peppers. A paternal smile parted his beard. Those of us in the press had been articles to be managed, handled, massaged for months, and now, at least temporarily, we could do no more damage. He watched us with the pride of a parent whose children have learned enough to be taken to a nice restaurant.

A round-faced aide sitting next to him waved a bottle of beer above his head.

"The spoils of victory! Enjoy! Enjoy! Enjoy!"

Randall Craig raised his glass and nodded at Duprey. "To victory. Who would have thought it possible?"

"I believe I predicted it from the beginning," Nathan said with his mouth full.

"You predicted *everything* from the beginning," Myra said. "You were bound to be right sooner or later."

"An amazing campaign," Craig said. "Brilliant and, of course, luckier than God."

Duprey raised his beer. "To being luckier than God. The key to political genius."

"No false modesty, Duprey," Myra said. "It doesn't suit you."

Steven's half-moon of forehead seemed to be grinning with reflected light.

"Didn't I just call myself a genius?"

Nathan lifted a dripping forkful of broccoli to his mouth.

"You want to know genius? Those public forums are genius. That speech in Colorado where he promised to clean up Rocky Flats if it takes a thousand years—*that* was genius."

"If you want genius in this campaign, there's one place you find it," Craig said. "The first debate. When the Reverend stood up and Crane welcomed him to the stage."

"He does rise to the occasion, doesn't he?" Duprey said.

Stuart sourly swallowed the last of his wine. "You'd hardly think it possible."

Duprey smiled mildly. "There are worse things in politics or life than being underestimated."

"Let us give credit where credit is due," Craig said. "It isn't often that a politician comes along who remakes the rules, but Crane may be one of those men."

The round-faced aide waved his bottle. "Hear! Hear!"

Craig had a smile that appeared like the suddenly white underside of a fish. "And that doesn't mean we won't do our best to drag him back to earth with the rest of us."

Duprey raised his beer. "Hear, hear."

A cigarette wraith of a woman, with jet-black hair cut in a severe bob and lipstick the color of dried blood, slid up to the table. She was Randall Craig's producer, but she ignored his gesture toward an open seat and stood until we all stopped and looked at her.

"ABC's running another overnight on Crane versus the president," she said. "I called a friend to get the prelims."

We waited while she enjoyed her moment on stage.

"Crane, thirty-nine," she said. "The current president of the United States, thirty-eight, a virtual tie—"

"*Ohh yeaahh!*"

The aide's hands shot into the air and beer poured down his arm. A waiter came hurrying from the corner of the room.

"It's nothing," Myra said. "Our friend is celebrating his future seat in the cabinet."

Duprey scratched his beard and covered his smile with his hand, staring above our heads at something on the wall.

"Congratulations," Craig said. "Of course, it doesn't mean a thing."

"Not unless they've moved the election up five months," Stuart said.

"Nothing at all," Duprey said. "Waiter, could you bring me another beer?"

We finished in the restaurant and tumbled out onto the street, laughing and talking too fast. The night was warm and the city was wide awake and full of light. We came to the barber pole lights of North Beach and Stuart stopped, casting a pipe-cleaner shadow across the damp street.

"I'll see you all tomorrow." He waved a limp hand. "Behave as the distinguished members of the establishment I know you are."

We watched him disappear, sunk in his private gloom. Craig led us down an alley and through a neon arch into a cavern filled with college kids wearing clothes made up of holes, men in elegantly formless jackets, and women in black stockings that made their legs disappear so they floated on upside-down buttercups of colored silk. A shock of white hair hung in the barmaid's night-of-the-living-dead eyes. We found a corner where we could stand together and yell in each other's ears over music thudding from another room.

Euphoria leaked out of us somewhere in the middle of the first drink. Nathan and Myra argued listlessly. Steven drank quietly behind his beard. The young aide boogied with his eyes closed. The producer raised the painted circle of her mouth to Craig's ear and he nodded his sculpted chin and his mouth settled into a lazy smirk. All of it struck me, suddenly, as a tired road show, a brittle comedy of manners that had been treading a succession of flimsy stages for too long.

I patted Nathan on the shoulder and mouthed good-byes to everyone else. Myra grabbed my arm.

"Come on," she shouted in my ear. "We've just about determined exactly what states Crane's going to win this fall. We need your insight into all those flat rectangular ones. You know, West Dakota, East Montana."

"He wins everywhere," I said. "He conquers the world."

"That's too easy. There has to be uncertainty. There has to be drama. We're wondering about the moose vote. Is that solid?"

"The moose vote is solid. He wins East Montana. I guarantee it. Good night."

Duprey finished his beer. "I'll walk out with you."

We waved and left the last, shipwrecked remnants of our party watching as we waded toward the door.

The sidewalk was damp, and we sent rising and falling shadows before us as we descended. We let the ringing in our ears recede. We breathed the ocean air.

"Well," I said. "He did it."

Steven shook his head as if in astonishment.

"He did do it."

We walked a while.

"It's strange," I said, "how such little things, a word here, a gesture there . . ."

"It is, isn't it? That's the thing that's amazed me since the day I began in this business. You run for months and you can win or lose in fifteen seconds . . . Not always, but sometimes."

We passed an alley and the sweet odor of rotting fruit. Something moved in the shadows. A cat.

"We have nothing to be afraid of from each other," I said. "Such simple words. Kind of hackneyed. Who would have thought the country was waiting for that?"

I could see Duprey's smile in the dark.

"The mysteries of public affection," he said.

"It all flowed from that," I said. "Everything. Nobody would have given a damn if it hadn't been for that night."

"You like it?"

"I'm saying it's the only line we'll remember from this campaign."

Duprey laughed. The fog curled like cigarette smoke around the lights marching down the hill. We were both a little drunk.

"Off the record, my friend."

"No."

"Come on."

I knew I shouldn't do this.

"All right."

"Never to go any farther than this conversation?"

"All right!"

"I know that line was good. I wrote it."

"What?"

"We heard the Reverend was going to try to crash the thing. How do you think they got tickets? I know someone who knew someone with the Reverend . . ." He waved a hand dismissively. "Anyway, we had a good idea what they'd try and we were ready. Chaos creates opportunity for the underdog. A political maxim. Came up with it myself. Just now. Anyway, I wrote the line about an hour before the debate. Suited Crane well, don't you think? It always helps if they believe the stuff."

I felt like a child who opens a cellar door to find an entire world full of shining, unknown things growing in the dark.

"You bastard," I said. "I should write that tomorrow and screw you."

We came down a steep block, the sidewalk uneven under our feet. Steven stared at the hotel lights below and his gait never faltered.

"But you won't. I've known you long enough to know your rules."

"I should."

"But you won't."

The lamps in the lobby spread honey on the glass. We stopped at the door.

"I'm going to walk for a while," I said.

Steven stroked his beard.

"You won't," he said.

"No, I suppose not."

"I should have kept my mouth shut. Look, I'll give you something before the end. Something no one else has. Maybe I'll give you this after the election. Who knows? We're going to go on a vacation to Greece after it's over and I may not give a shit by then."

"Go to bed. Don't worry about it."

"But something, all right?"

"Sure. See you tomorrow."

"Tomorrow and tomorrow and tomorrow."

He waved and went through the door. I watched him disappear into the elevator. He never looked back. I stood on the sidewalk, feeling the ocean out there somewhere, faint and damp, heavy with fog. Maybe I would get up early tomorrow and see the Golden Gate Bridge. I never had.

I thought of my father. The train had reached the sea and its light was searching the waves. Where did we go from here?

The campaign turned around and followed Thomas Crane back across the country. The real race, the race against the president, was just beginning. I was going back to Washington for the break between the primaries and the convention. The bureau had a reporter covering campaign spending, but I had decided to go through all of Crane's financial records: Federal Election Commission reports, congressional financial disclosure forms, even state filings. It's a complicated story, Latrelle Gregory had said, how poor boys get rich and who they owe when they're finished. Well, I would start with the paper trail.

But not tonight. I didn't want to think about it tonight. I followed the coils of fog toward the ocean, passing shuttered coffeehouses and boutiques with dazed arrays of summer pastels prostrate in the windows. I walked until I came to a bar, Whistling in the Dark, and laughed and went in.

The interior was dark enough, clarinets and saxophones collecting dust on the walls, jazz scratching across a tape. I ordered a beer from another pale bartender, sipped Anchor Steam and thought about what Steven had said. Crane's signature moment of genius and it had been worked out in advance. I wished he hadn't told me.

A familiar voice, high and fast, drifted out of a booth. Robin was telling a story. I turned and I could see her hands move, slender fingers held straight for emphasis. Her hair swung like a curtain back and forth across her face. The young man seated across the table leaned forward listening, stiff as a bird dog on point.

Well, of course.

I turned back to the bar and downed a fourth of my beer. When I was seventeen I once sat on the shore of the reservoir outside of Havre, listening to a party gathered on the other side of the water around a bonfire. Couples danced on the beach while the fire rose in a whirl of cinders. Their shadows reached halfway across the lake, cavorting across a thousand shivering slips of the moon. I wanted to join them, but I knew the uninhibited dance wasn't in me, no matter how much I wished it was. The urge to join the circle around the fire, yes, always, but not the dance. You find out about yourself at odd moments. I was seventeen and I knew I would always be one of those watching from outside the circle.

I turned to leave and Robin stood behind me, a pleased, silly smile on her face.

"I didn't see you come in. You looked so morose standing here alone, I wanted to come ask you to join us."

I looked at the table where the young man and another woman were waiting.

"I don't think so. Not tonight. Thanks."

"That's too bad. I'd buy you a drink."

I managed a smile. "*A* drink? You owe me more than one."

"So come on."

"I can't. I have an analysis to write tomorrow. I should have gone to bed hours ago."

A line creased her forehead.

"Are you all right?"

"I'm just tired. Tell your boss to stop making news on deadline."

She laughed. "We'll try to wrap it up around noon in November. Come on and have a drink. You'll like Randy and Beth, they're great."

I shook my head. "Thanks."

"You're sure?"

"Yeah."

"All right."

"Well . . ."

I dropped a five-dollar bill on the bar and turned to go. Robin touched my arm.

"There's something I should have told you a while ago."

She looked past my shoulder, her eyes too bright.

"Danny and I split up. I didn't know if you knew that."

"No. I didn't know that."

"Before the campaign."

"I'm sorry."

"No, it's all right. It was bad for a long time."

I didn't say anything.

"Photographers," she said. "It's like being a kid with five thousand dollars worth of toys and people who will fly you anywhere to play with them. Growing up is a liability."

112

I reached for my beer and it had disappeared. I very much wanted something to hold in my hands. I held on to the edge of the bar.

"Anyway. We split up a few months ago. It's a relief, really."

Neither of us knew what to say. We looked at each other, and it was as it is sometimes between two people who have known each other a long and difficult time, when suddenly everything, everything you feel and have ever felt, is right there in front of the two of you.

"I should go," I said.

"You're sure?"

"I can't make small talk tonight, Robin. I don't know why."

She glanced at the booth.

"I'll walk out with you. Just give me a moment to say good-bye."

We walked up the sidewalk, our heels echoing in the fog.

"Now that we've won, I've got to go back to Springfield for a while," she said. "I probably won't see you until the convention."

Streetlights appeared like Chinese lanterns hung in midair. Buildings slipped in and out of the fog. Robin slid her arm into mine and I shivered.

"Cold?"

"It's the ocean. You can feel it in the air."

Robin took a deep breath, arching her back to fill her lungs.

"We've run out of country," she said, "and now we turn around and go back."

"Tired of it yet?"

"Cliff, I don't want it to end. I don't ever want it to end."

We walked across a square and the hotel took shape on the far side, an island of hazy yellow light. She leaned against my shoulder and I felt the sway of her long swinging gait.

"I don't want it to stop," Robin said. "I don't want to look back. I don't believe in history, not the way you do. I believe in *this*, this chance we have, all of us, right now. I believe in second chances, Cliff. I believe in rebirth. I always have."

She turned to face me, her round face pale and moonlike, the scent of champagne sweet on her breath.

"You know what I remember about you?" she said. "I remember the time that ferret got into the house. And you were going to protect me and you stuck out the broom, and it crawled over it, and you jumped back and ended up behind me. And then we could hear the woman calling out on the street, *Timothy, Timothy.* And I realized it was just somebody's pet, and I picked it up."

She laughed. "I liked that you never pretended you weren't scared. You always told the truth. You never pretended to be more than you were."

"I thought you thought I knew what I was doing."

"No, Cliff. I thought you were sweet and I thought you were honest. I wanted you to be strong."

We were so close I felt each word beat softly against my skin.

"It doesn't matter," she said. "Now everything is new."

"I want to see you again," I said.

"Oh, God."

She looked past my shoulder into the dark.

"I want that, too," she said.

There was a noise in the fog, a drunken hurrah, and when we turned a half dozen campaign aides were spilling out of the hotel. They recognized Robin and shouted her name and staggered toward us, some of their bodies strangely square, boxes with arms and legs. When they were a few feet away I saw the square ones were wearing campaign posters tied front to back like sandwich boards. They were all young and their clothes had the rumpled look of people who have been hugging and grabbing each other all night. They circled us.

"A party. Come on, Robin! It's on a yacht! *Everybody's* there."

Robin shook her head but her eyes danced with delight.

"Robin! Robin! Robin!"

"Go," I said.

"No . . . it's okay."

"Go ahead. You've earned this."

She looked at me gratefully.

"I'll see you when—"

"Right."

Robin squeezed my hand and slid into line. They whooped with satisfaction. She winked and her hair fell in her eyes. They grabbed each other around the hips and congaed down the square. "*Crane! Crane! Crane!*"

they chanted and his dark, sad eyes bounced past larger than life. I watched them disappear into the fog, dreamlike laughter echoing long after they were gone. I stood there, hands deep in my pockets, the bemused expression of a professional observer securely fastened on my face, but the thrill of their pounding feet arched up my spine and the rhythm of their chant caught my heart, and I surrendered to the sudden surpassing joy of it all.

★ ★ ★ ★

BOOK TWO

I.

THERE WERE fireworks over the Hudson on the first night of the convention and a party in Bryant Park where thousands moved restlessly across the grass in search of an elusive sense of privilege crushed by the weight of collective desire. Myra and I stood the crowd and the dinosaur rock stars entertaining on stage as long as we could, and then escaped through the police line and walked to the end of the block to gaze at the lions on the steps of the New York Public Library. They gazed back through proud stone eyes, and we stood in contemplative awe as the celebration vaulted the library and settled around us in a faint cacophony of feverish voices and electric guitars.

The second night I was sent to a club on the East Side for a reunion of the 1972 campaign. The club was a warren of rooms done up in red and black, too small for the crowd of middle-aged men and women who gathered around their candidate, an unassuming man who once carried a tattered flag for peace in a time of war. He was the center of attention until the World's Number One Box Office Attraction, famous for movies of ritualistic weapon use and mass homicide, appeared behind a phalanx of bodyguards. The crowd slid his way like water in a tilted glass. The party rolled along, but I had a brief, dislocating sense that the more esoteric physicists were right, and the universe must be collapsing in on itself, and it was only a matter of time until we were all scuttling backward into the sea.

On the third night I stood in back on the floor of Madison Square Garden, bodies pressed against me. The lights were down. The stage rose at the end of the hall like the prow of a ship pushing its way through a human ocean. The giant screen at the back came to life, and it took me a few seconds to realize what I was seeing. The Crane family stood in front of their Berthold home, a sepia tint added to an old photograph. The cottage seemed warm and quaint. The family smiled with a cheerful and alien resilience.

A hallucinatory version of Thomas Crane's life unreeled on the screen, all uplift and achievement, determination and tragedy bravely overcome. The hushed narrator moved back and forth in time, and we saw Crane as a crusading college student, a young army lieutenant, a bright-eyed groom, a youthful congressman, a child holding a flag on the Fourth of July.

Now a young man wearing a baseball uniform stepped on to a porch, grinned shyly and loped off down a street gentle in the hazy light of dawn. A quick cut to the young man swinging a bat and sending a ball rocketing toward an unseen outfield, then a slow dissolve, the grainy film replaced by videotape, and the young man became Thomas Crane in Florida, at bat again. The swing was much the same and the ball rocketed onto a corner of the outfield and you felt a swelling satisfaction at promise fulfilled, dreams realized, an entire mythology falling into place and settling in your stomach like a solid meal.

A voice came down from on high, the voice of God, or at least James Earl Jones: "The Democratic nominee for president, the next president of the United States of America . . ."

He appeared wearing a suit so black his face and a single hand floated disembodied above us. The noise rolled down from the highest seats, filled the air with the sound of a hundred locomotives charging down a mountain. The lights on stage came up and Crane filled out in our presence, standing before us with a boyish smile and eyes that briefly closed, as if to hold the thunderous ovation within himself.

I had pulled one morning of pool duty during the convention, and we'd gone to a day-care center in the Bronx, where Crane was briefly surrounded by toddlers. They tugged at his pants and held their arms out to be picked up, and I saw something complicated and defenseless happening in his face, an expression that brought back a vague memory I could not place. Then he remembered the cameras and glanced at me with a look of comic helplessness.

"Do you have any children, Cliff? Maybe you can help me out here?"

"I'm afraid not, Senator."

He held his arms out as though he were overwhelmed, and knelt suddenly, his long legs folding up, looking a surprised black child directly in the eyes. They gazed at each other in mutual astonishment and then the child smiled, and Crane swept him up in one arm and a little girl in his other arm, and I thought how easily came this expectation that he could win the hearts of innocents and the jaded alike. It was something you wanted to resist and, yet, there was a child in his arms, and here were thousands screaming until their throats were raw, and here you were, very professionally keeping your voice quiet, yet with your shirt sticking to your back, your eyes seeing blue dots, your heart racing like a runaway roller coaster. Here you were, with all the rest, carried aloft.

I didn't want to leave, but I had work to do. I slid through the crowd, ducked under a curtain and hurried down the halls and tunnel that led to our temporary bureau on the stage of the Paramount Theater. I turned over the quotes I had collected about the party's chances in the fall to the reporter doing the story and joined my editor, who had swiveled her chair to watch Crane on one of the televisions set up across the bureau.

"He's not going to mess this up?"

"I don't think so."

She searched for the remote control in the miniature landfill on her desk, found it, and turned the volume down. I noticed silver was weaving itself further through her hair and there were new lines around her eyes. I wondered how many hours she was working each week. During my years in the bureau I had watched her change. She came from San Diego as a tanned, squarely built athletic woman, the kind you might see playing soccer in a park on Sunday morning. Her principal gift had been a willingness to work hard. It had won her a chance to edit the campaign coverage, and over the last year everything else had been stripped away as she transformed herself into a vessel of pure efficiency. Once there had been a woman named Ellen Herrin who played racquetball on Saturdays, loved to cook Italian, and kept too many cats, but the campaign had swallowed her like so many others.

"They think you're doing a great job in San Diego," she said, her eyes

121

on the television. "They want to keep you out on the road from here on in."

San Diego was the home of Cannon Newspapers' corporate headquarters. Praise from offices above the bay arrived through acolytes like blessings from Mount Olympus.

"That's okay. You know I don't mind."

"How are you getting along with Robin?"

"Fine. We don't see each other all that much."

"No problem, then?"

"No. It's just business. The world's full of politicos and journalists who've slept together and then screwed each other all over again in the light of day."

She looked at me. "Is that right?"

I knew I'd made a mistake. "I don't know. Anyway, it's not a problem."

The bureau had been set up in hasty disarray amid a nest of cables and cardboard boxes. A dozen reporters and editors sat at metal tables, clattering away at keyboards while Crane's voice drifted through the clamor: *Charity. Responsibility. Community. Independence. These things are not contradictions.* Applause rose from the unseen audience and reporters looked up briefly across the bureau and focused absently on a close-up of a face radiant with reassurance. I wanted to be in there. I wanted to be in there to hear him and for another reason. I had been trying to reach Robin for three days. She'd be here tonight, but if I waited too long I might not find her.

Ellen lowered her voice.

"About the other thing. What you and Kelly found. You're sure you can follow up on the road?"

"Yes."

"I haven't said anything to anyone else. It's still your lead."

"Yes. I'll be fine."

"Kelly will help whenever you need it."

"I know."

Her blue-green eyes arrived on mine without apology.

"You're not too tired?"

"I'm tired. So are you. I'm not too tired."

"You haven't fallen in love with Thomas Crane or anyone working for him?"

"I have a crush on John Starke, but I'm fighting it."

She smiled and glanced back at the television.

"You're in a hurry to get back in there?"

"I'd like to see the end of the speech."

Her hand slid absently over the papers beside her terminal.

"Why don't you round up a few react quotes and call it a night. I know you head out early tomorrow morning."

"Thanks."

"It should be a hell of a ride, Cliff. Don't fuck up."

Crane's voice echoed indistinctly down the hallway. I stopped in a small bathroom hidden behind floor polishing equipment in an alcove and found Steven Duprey throwing up into a toilet. The door to his stall had slipped open and he was on his knees, clutching the toilet paper dispenser for balance.

"Oh Christ, not you."

"Are you all right?"

"Sure. I dropped something."

"What?"

He was seized by dry heaves and bent over the toilet.

"I don't know. *Something.* Can't you please walk out the door now?"

He caught his breath and stood unsteadily, wiping his mouth with a wad of toilet paper, his skin pale, sweat popping in beads of pearl across his forehead.

"It's going awful, isn't it?" he said.

"The speech?"

"The speech." He said the word as if it was a mountain he had tried and failed to scale.

"It's fine. It's good." I'd heard only a few sentences.

"I knew it was too long. I should have cut the middle. It was self-indulgent not to cut it."

Then I understood. "You wrote it."

He nodded and then quickly shook his head. "Mostly him. He went over it in longhand."

"It's okay. Listen—" You could hear the tidal roar of the audience through the walls.

Steven nodded weakly. I dampened a paper towel in the sink and handed it to him. He wiped his forehead, dabbed at his mouth, took another deep breath.

"This is going to look great in print," he said.

"You'll come across as human."

"That means pathetic."

He bent over a sink and splashed water on his face. He did it several times. When he looked into the mirror, his self-control had returned.

"Maybe we could make a deal," he said.

I thought about the night in San Francisco—he was building up quite an account. But I had no desire to write about Steven Duprey bent over a toilet; it meant nothing in the larger scheme of things, and the fact that it would be repeated everywhere represented all the things I hated about journalism. Besides, I considered him a friend—and I knew the value of the debt.

I handed him a dry towel. "Everybody gets the stomach flu. I don't think it's news. At least not today."

He dried his face and looked at me sideways in the mirror. "Thank you, Cliff."

I had to go. Once people started leaving I would never find her. Steven tossed the towel in the trash. We walked out the door together, and I could not help but smile.

A sour look crossed his still pale face. "What?"

"Nothing, Steven. I just never knew you cared."

I reached the floor as circles of foil came tumbling out of the rafters, red on one side, silver on the other, winking as they fell, delegates laughing and reaching for them like children, then balloons, drifting out of the netting in a lazy red, white and blue waterfall sent bouncing back into the air while the orchestra launched into Copland's *Theme for the Common Man* with a flourish of trumpets. I saw Duprey hovering at the back of the stage, recovered, as inscrutable as ever. I saw Myra on the edge of the Illinois delegation, her hair wrapped in a bright red bandanna that made her impossible to miss. She grabbed a balloon the size of a small man and, pinning it against her chair, stabbed a pen into its side. It exploded and a chorus line of delegates in Uncle Sam hats staggered and fell like dominoes.

I saw everyone but Robin. She had been hidden away for days, working with the platform committee, but she wouldn't miss tonight. I knew she was here, but it was like trying to see through a hurricane. A circle darted and landed in my mouth, tasting warm and metallic. I brushed another out of my eyes.

I saw her nearer the stage. I wedged myself past a heavy woman in a straw hat, between a pair of weeping young men, beneath a swinging flag. Bodies were massed solid, and I leaned against a broad back until I felt the crowd surge and my feet were lifted up and I was carried forward. I saw Crane descending a stairway on the front of the stage, bending toward a forest of hands. Balloons bounced off my head. I struggled to breathe in the heat and the damp exhalation of sweat, and then I found my feet and pushed, and when I looked up Robin was only two feet away.

I reached across a stranger and touched her on the shoulder. She smiled, scraps of silver foil tangled in her hair, and I saw her mouth my name. I leaned hard against someone's side, and the crowd slid clockwise in some oblique shift of Crane's gravity, and we were facing each other, pushed together and laughing.

"God, where have you been?" she said.

"I've been here! Where have you been?"

"I've been stuck in a closet for three days with the most anal—Oh God, it doesn't matter." She tossed her head back. "Isn't this wild?"

We were turned by the crowd, pressed so close I could feel her against my stomach, smell lemons in her hair.

"Dinner tonight," I said. "Whenever you get through. I'll buy."

"Oh God, Cliff. I have to get ready for tomorrow. I'm going to be up all night. I'm sorry."

"On the road then."

Her eyes were a glittering patchwork of reflected silver. "Soon. I'm sorry."

Crane came down the stairs and stepped into the delegates. I felt an elbow in my back and an arm slid across my sight. When I could see again,

Robin had been carried forward. She lifted one hand and let the crowd sweep her away, mouthing good-bye. I leaned backward and fought to stay in place. It was like fighting a tide when it releases and you stumble backward onto the beach—suddenly I was free and backpedaling down the aisle. I settled beside the California delegation and watched people sway to the music and the signs swinging back and forth and the silly hats and costumes and felt the noise pound against my heart. I found enough stray delegates in the hallway to get all the quotes anyone could need, stopped by the bureau, checked with my editor one more time, grabbed my bag and left.

A torrent of bodies spilled out onto Eighth Avenue. Policeman sat regal on their mounts, whistling and pointing like heroic statues while bright yellow cabs turned into traffic with an existential disregard for the laws governing moving bodies. I walked toward the theater district. The crowd moved around me, but almost no one spoke. Halfway to the hotel I passed a wig shop, blank-faced heads in the window, echoing in their immobile apprehension and hope the blurred mass of faces I had seen turn toward Crane.

My room was on the twenty-first floor of the Omni Hotel. I left the lights off, pulled a Heineken from the mini-bar, opened the drapes, and let the neon of Times Square flood the walls with light. A message scrawled across the electronic ticker tape far below, but I could only make out two foreshortened words. *Thomas Crane.*

For two weeks in Washington, Kelly Williams, the bureau's financial reporter, and I had waded through the vague financial records required of American political figures. We'd found nothing. Then late one night I looked up. "We're starting from the wrong point."

Kelly brushed her straight black hair out of her eyes and waited. A quiet woman, slim and teacup pale, with an unfussy prettiness in her pursed mouth and curious eyebrows, she was most at home with numbers and the obscure but irrefutable language of official documents.

"Everything we have here commences with the start of his public life," I said. "But Berthold isn't part of his public life. It's all from before. What started this were three unexplained trips back home. When I asked Latrelle Gregory about it, he indicated that Crane owed a debt to someone back there."

126

I held up a sheaf of disclosure forms. "We're looking for some slipup here that other people have missed, although these things have been gone over a hundred times. But it has to be earlier; if it brought him home it has to be earlier. What Latrelle Gregory said was, 'It's always fascinating what poor boys have to do to become rich.'"

Kelly's pale blue eyes fell to the papers in her hands.

"He's not really rich," she said. "He might be worth a few hundred thousand dollars, but *rich*, by today's standards—"

"But compared to where he came from. That's the point. He came from a family so poor they used to scrounge coal from alongside the railroad tracks. Look at this from his first House race." I held up the form. "He already had twenty-nine thousand dollars worth of stock. Where did that come from?"

"They asked him about that at the time," Kelly said. "He made a ten-thousand-dollar investment in Teltronics and the stock nearly quadrupled in the space of a year."

"But where did the ten thousand dollars come from? I know it's not a lot of money. But the thing is, it was to him. He'd been a graduate student two years earlier. He'd just gotten married. Where did the money come from?"

Her eyes went blank and then filled with the pride of a document hound.

"There was a small biz page story in the old *Chicago Daily News*"—she ruffled through a thick folder on the table—"that talked about investors who hit the gold mine with Teltronics. It mentioned Crane briefly. . . Here it is." She produced a faded computer printout and read: "The money came from Roger Bushmill. A loan. Crane paid it off at the end of the year out of profits. This is before he ever met your friend Latrelle."

"And who is Roger Bushmill?"

She blinked. "Bushmill Industries. They own two different plants that make high-grade opticals, mostly for the military."

"But that's not who he is to Crane," I said. "To Crane he's one of the guys who used to pick him up when he was hitchhiking into Springfield."

Kelly looked at me blankly. Five-thousand-dollar donations and soft money contributions were her obsession, not Crane's life.

"When Crane was fifteen he got into a private Catholic school in Springfield. It was the start of everything. But his family was so poor he had to hitchhike into town. After a while, he had a handful of people who picked him up regularly, made sure he got there. Roger Bushmill was one of those."

Kelly set the papers in her hand down as if they had disappointed her.

"So what are you saying? This is all worthless?"

We were in an office in the bureau, deserted after midnight. Across the street the garretted roof of the Willard Hotel reflected scraps of moonlight. A lamp was on in a round window and I saw an eggshell blue wall and then a hand, as perfect as if painted by Michelangelo, reach for a book on a table. Then it was gone, the room transformed by its unseen presence.

"You don't just lend someone ten thousand dollars," I said. "There's a preexisting relationship there. A pattern of trust or reciprocity or *something* has already been established."

"Are they still friends?"

"Not that I've heard of."

Kelly ran her hands through her hair and stared at the ceiling.

"So, Cliff, what do we *do*?"

I looked at the papers spread across the table. Crane's life wasn't her beat, it was mine, but she was a good reporter, and I had to give her something to do.

"We need to find out everything we can about Bushmill. Check him out against all this"—I swung my arm to encompass the mess on the table—"and anything else you can think of. When I get back I'll look through everything I have on his past again. We'll figure it out from there."

I left Washington for a three-day trip through the Carolinas, Georgia and Florida to assess the chances of the democratic ticket across the South. When I came back there was a message waiting for me. Kelly's voice was rushed and faintly euphoric.

"Cliff, I did what you suggested and it's amazing! You run a search and Bushmill's name shows up everywhere. Regular contributions right up to the allowable limit. And listen to this! They were briefly partners in a group that invested in gulf drilling. Oil drilling. Five people. They put in two hundred thousand total." She took a breath. "I did a little research on him. Bushmill. He still lives in southern Illinois, near Phillips. That's only about thirty miles from Berthold." Her giggle was one-part exhaustion. "I think we're on to something here. I don't know what exactly. It just feels right. I'm going to start looking farther back now. I've got some ideas."

A police car raced across Times Square, lights spinning like tops, strangely peaceful without the wail of sirens. I watched it roll past the ticket kiosk and disappear down Broadway. The restlessness I had felt since leaving the convention welled up. There were parties everywhere tonight. I should go to one, get out, escape into the collective amnesia of the celebration.

I sipped from my beer, warm now. It was too late. The night was populated with ghosts sliding backward into the past.

I remembered standing in a similar window staring at a different city. Robin and I had gone to Baltimore, hoping a weekend away would help. I wanted desperately to recapture some lost buoyancy, some stray lover's magic that once floated us above it all. I wanted us to be light, but we were as heavy as a pair of tombstones. She was silent through dinner and I knew it was something I had said or done, some minor offense for which I was not to be forgiven. I knew it was my fault and I knew it was unfair. I started a fight and we argued as we walked along the harbor, shoulders hunched and heads bent together like two old men leaning on each other for support. By the time we got to the hotel room we weren't speaking.

She stood in the window, staring at the city, arms across her chest, shivering in her T-shirt. "My brother's anniversary," she said. "My brother's anniversary. Why should you remember?"

When she was finally asleep I slipped out of the covers and went to the window. The Bromo-Seltzer tower stood bathed in light like some misplaced fairy-tale battlement. In the distance I could make out the turrets and false buttresses of the First Maryland Bank. Her brother's anniversary. She meant the anniversary of her brother's death. Lights began going out in a nondescript building down the street, lopping off each floor, the building shrinking before my eyes until all the lights were out and the silhouette came back, haunting and larger than ever. I stared out the window for a long time, and I knew it was useless. I would never see the world through her eyes.

Across Times Square the Fuji sign flickered as if worn out by a long night of dazzling tourists. I leaned against the window and the glass was cool against my forehead and I felt myself pulled against my own reflection, the cold shadow of inescapable desire.

I was half undressed when I heard the knock on the door. I opened it and she was standing in the doorway with a half-empty bottle of wine hanging in her left hand. She stood with the yellow light from the hallway tangled in her hair and her eyes wide and tired and very sober.

"I got done early."

Without thinking I reached up and put my hand on her shoulder.

"Tell me this isn't the stupidest thing I've ever done in my life," she said.

She started to say more, gave up and slipped from the light into the darkness of my room just before she kissed me. I felt her hips settling against my thigh as they always had, her arms around my neck, her mouth against mine and everything coming back and I knew it had always been there, always waiting.

We slid backward to the bed. The lights from the window flashed along her cheek and when she opened her eyes they were a neon blue-green and stared at me with the surprise of a creature sprung from television. I felt her breath along my neck and then buried in the front of my shirt, damp against my chest. Her hand slid down my stomach and then all the old patterns reestablished themselves, memory taking over and leading us. We had always had this. This had always been fine. I rolled her toward me and her breast settled in my hand, and I must have smiled or laughed because it was there as it always had been, and I felt her smile as she kissed her way down my stomach and her fingers climbed my ribs like a musical scale. Then it was all the same but new, and every shadow we threw against the wall, every breath cut short, every shudder of the bed, every arch and descent carried us deeper into the past. In the end, when she burrowed her nose into the hollow of my shoulder and fell asleep, I stared at the ceiling, watching the reflected lights and, one by one, they went out. I wanted to see Times Square in the dark, but I couldn't move without waking her, so I lay in bed and tried to imagine cornices and pediments and gargoyles perched on crumbling ledges reasserting themselves in the insubstantial moonlight.

II.

WE LEFT Manhattan in seven buses festooned with signs, pennants, and red, white and blue bunting, rolling down stained brick canyons in a symphony of rattles and gnashing gears, the morning throngs waving and holding their thumbs in the air, until we came to a bridge and floated out over the gunmetal river. Then more city and industrial park and the flat scrubland of New Jersey. Cars on the other side of the freeway slowed as we passed, gaping at the spectacle: police cruisers with blue lights whirling, motorcycle cops, a Secret Service van, two black limos, all smoked glass and menace, then the happy circus of our buses, and a final, abashed police car.

I sat in the third bus and watched the country pass. Robin had been gone when I woke from a dead, dreamless sleep. The note on her pillow crumpled beneath my hand: *Early staff meeting. See you on the road.* I held it above the bed and a mote of reflected sunlight caught a corner, and I was holding a peel of orange flame that spread slowly through the translucent flesh of my hand.

Myra slumped in the seat beside me, a hand draped across her eyes. When she groaned I could no longer ignore her.

"You all right?"

"Never try to drink with a Chicago alderman," she said.

"Where'd you go?"

"Oh, God, you know, Amalgamated Polluters, or maybe it was United Weapons Technologies. Some hospitality suite. There were free drinks and food and there was this evil man who rules part of the Southside, and I had to swill scotch with him for half the night . . . We have hard jobs." She squinted at me through a flat, gray eye. "How about you?"

"In bed like a good boy."

"I thought you might be out with your ex-squeeze."

"She had to work."

Myra batted a puffy eyelid like an aging chanteuse.

"Too bad. Manhattan. Moonlight. The sweet smell of corruption everywhere. There's nothing like politics for causing you to toss your scruples out the door."

I stared out the window.

"Is that right? The alderman teach you that?"

"The alderman. The alderman could corrupt Mother Teresa. But I remain pure."

"In a relative sense, of course."

"Now, now, Cliff O'Connell. We've known each other too long for you to get petty."

"We haven't known each other that long at all."

"It's not the years, it's the mileage."

"That's very good."

"I stole it from a movie."

"Of course."

Nathan leaned forward from his seat, holding the *New York Times*. "Did you see this Johnny Apple piece? He breaks the party's prospects down region by region, goes over the strategy."

Stuart, sitting in front of Myra, looked as if he'd swallowed a piece of chewing tobacco. Apple was the senior political correspondent at the *Times*, and a small, relentless wheel in the infinite rack that was Stuart's existence.

"Lord, the strategy's been the same forever," he said. "The Democrats always come out of their convention looking good, saying they're going to challenge the Republicans down south and out west—make them defend their base—then take the two coasts and enough of the Rust Belt to win. You always get these Lil Abners in Georgia and Alabama talking about how they might stick with the Dems this time. It always sounds great. And then it falls apart."

"Apple says Crane's running slightly ahead across most of the South," Nathan said, "and he's way up out west."

"It's been a holiday so far," Stuart said. "Wait till the other side gets going."

A CNN cameraman, portly with a pair of glittering button eyes in a soft pillow of a face, listened from across the aisle. The buses were packed with members of the press who'd taken advantage of the relatively cheap cost of ground travel to climb on board for a few days, jittery with their first hit of campaign adrenaline. But the cameraman had been with us from the beginning, always dressed in red suspenders, green T-shirts and white tennis shoes. We called him Santa.

"It's like the Three Stooges," he said. "The Democrats are Curly and the Republicans are Moe. You know how it is. Curly's walking along feeling good."

He fixed his face in an expression of blissful ignorance and waddled down the aisle.

"He bumps into Moe."

He popped his eyes.

"And it's whap, smack! Whoob-whoob-whoob-whoob!"

He poked his own eyes and punched himself in the stomach.

"It's taxes! Bam!"

A wild roundhouse on the top of the head.

"Or the death penalty! Pow!"

He boxed his ears.

"Or burning the flag! Nyuk! Nyuk! Come here you little . . ."

He pulled himself across the aisle by his nose.

"Owowowow! And Curly never knows what hit him, but there he is, sitting on his ass in a vat of molasses with a crowbar wrapped around his head."

He rocked back and forth, rolled his eyes and slumped to his seat. The bus broke into applause. He stood and bowed somberly.

Myra had opened both eyes. "The Three Stooges as a metaphor for American political debate. Wait until the French get ahold of this."

"Maybe this time *he's* Moe," Nathan said, meaning Crane. "And the president's Curly."

A general shaking of heads. No one thought he was Moe.

"The only real question," Myra said, settling back in her seat, "is whether he's Curly or not."

Our bus growled up an exit ramp. Local police cars, spread along the road in a blue daisy chain, fell in behind us as we rolled toward a steel-sided building in an industrial park.

"But what can they use?" Nathan said. "He looks clean as a whistle."

"They'll find something," Stuart said.

We stopped outside a chain-link fence and the driver swung the door open. Reporters were pouring out of the buses ahead of us. We grabbed bags, cameras and tape recorders, scrambling for the aisle. Myra watched through a cocked eye.

"If he's not Curly," she said, "we sure are."

I saw Robin only briefly that day and the next. We rode through West Virginia, Pennsylvania, and back into upstate New York, living off sandwiches and granola bars tossed into the bus as if we were animals at the zoo. We stopped in cities and small towns and flat spots on the side of the road where small crowds huddled. We piled out of the buses in a paratrooper drill at every stop, throwing ourselves out the door to catch up with Crane, who always seemed to be ahead of us.

Cannon Newspapers believes in interviewing the public obsessively, so I wandered along rope lines and talked to people doing well, people without work, people with sick children, people who had come to see a celebrity, people who had come to scoff, people who believed, people who wanted to believe. They reminded me of the men and women who trooped into my father's newspaper office every week, the ranchers, teachers, ministers, small businessmen. In another way, they reminded me of my grandfather, who came over from Ireland when he was fifteen and, despite a lifetime of hard labor on the Great Northern Railroad, held with quiet fidelity to his love for his adopted country.

Hearing them, I thought some dam of public skepticism had cracked. The polls might show that people didn't believe in much of anything politicians said anymore, but on the road you felt that was, at least in part, a bluff. If it is possible for an entire nation to become mediawise, then it had happened to the United States. The public knew cynicism had been established as the only knowing stance, and when the pollsters asked, they gave the answer expected.

But they came and they listened, and, although it is a truism that you can't tell anything by the people who come to cheer, the veteran correspondents said these were the largest crowds they had seen this early in a campaign. And late at night, even with all the cynicism journalists horde as a defense against inevitable disillusionment, there was no denying the figures on the side of the road, waving flags, holding up handmade signs, or simply waiting for a chance to applaud an indistinct figure in a passing bus.

We ended up in Chautauqua, New York, on a beautiful afternoon, the sky a taut blue, women holding their summer dresses against a warm breeze, heels clicking across sidewalks baking in the sunlight.

The Victorian cottages were painted in the elaborate patterns of the period, bright blues and forest greens outlining windows and doors in descending frames of color that stepped backward through time. The stage had been set up on the steps of a brick hall at one end of the commons. The press room was in a cottage with a wide porch generously provided with rocking chairs. I sat in one and read a history of Simon Bolivar my aunt had sent me. Bolivar's fortunes were at low ebb; he was hiding from the Spanish in a swamp, up to his chest in dank water, when he began declaiming loudly how he was going to retake all of Spanish South America. The officers hiding with him quivered—Spanish soldiers were nearby—but nobody dared suggest he lower his voice. He went on at the top of his lungs, a declaration before God and his enemies, and within three years he made it all come true, a man so certain of his destiny he could summon the future into existence while half-submerged in a swamp.

The book was too dark for the gentle nature of the day. I put it down and stared through whispering trees at the sky. When Robin leaned over the railing all I saw at first was the top of her head.

"Come with me," she said. "You've got to see this."

She led me down the street to a house where the Secret Service stood on the porch and a limousine waited out front.

"He's in there meeting the local Dems," Robin said. "He'll be out in a second to ride down to the stage."

She edged us around the small crowd along the sidewalk.

"Do you see her?" Robin asked.

"Who?"

She whispered the name of a writer famous for eviscerating the powerful in heavily psychoanalytic prose squeezed between the perfume ads in *Vanity Fair*. I didn't recognize her at first; then I saw a short woman with brown-and-gray hair piled in a matronly bun. She was older than I expected, her face wrinkled and weighted down with a second chin they covered up on television. She spoke to a bald photographer with skin the color of Silly Putty.

The Secret Service agents came to attention. Crane stepped onto the porch and stopped, as if the brilliance of the day surprised him, then strolled down the sidewalk. The people along the line called his name.

"Watch what she does when he gets to the door of the car," Robin said softly. "This is so great!"

Crane entered the funnel of people around his car. He shook a few hands and, as he stopped beside the limousine to sign something, the magazine writer pirouetted around the fender, bent backward, precariously balanced on one leg, turned so she was looking at her photographer as her face slid close to Crane's. It was an illusion—she was three feet in front of him—but they appeared to be cheek to cheek.

Her photographer snapped the shot, capturing a surprisingly girlish smile.

"Yess!" Robin squeezed my elbow. "I've been watching her. She's done this twice before. She almost tripped him to rub up against his shoulder in Erie."

"Really?"

"She's a groupie."

"She's a killer on the page."

"That's different. That's business."

Robin spoke as if the distinction was a fraud. She put her hand on my

136

shoulder and her dress swished against my hip. She'd been on camera a lot since the convention and she'd taken to wearing skirts and dresses, often with a gold necklace I had given her many years earlier.

Crane's car pulled away and we walked back down the street.

"One thing I have learned on the trail so far," Robin said.

"What's that?"

"The famous will disappoint you."

There was a brief rustle of applause, reaching us like a breeze moving through the trees. A local congressman was on stage.

"What famous have led you to this conclusion?"

Robin's smile was full of secrets.

"They're sent to us for private briefings. Rock stars, movie stars."

"So like who?"

"Bono. Tom Cruise. Barbra Streisand. Ringo Starr even stopped by. He's a vegetarian now, did you know that?"

"He always was the lovable one."

"He wanted to talk about animal rights." Robin tossed her hair back and it flashed as if sloughed off by the sun. "You can't write any of this, you know. You have to get it somewhere else."

"Okay."

She waited a moment, teasing me, her cheeks a high pink. We strolled under the trees, staying along the edge of the crowd. People looked at us and smiled.

"You know how it is. They come back after the rallies and they all want to meet him. They all have their causes now. So, after he gives them a few minutes, they get sent my way and I run them through the campaign policy on whatever it is they care about, and then I listen to their spiel. That's really what it's all about—listening to them."

"Does he really give them only a few minutes?"

"Well, he gave Robert Redford half an hour. The environment, you know. *I* got to spend half an hour with the heavy metal band the Stiffs."

"Yeah?"

"They're all for condoms."

"Thank God."

"The lead singer thinks they should be provided free in little bowls in

137

public restrooms, like mints in a restaurant. He was really concerned that they aren't available in airports. I think a lot has happened to him in airports."

Crane stepped to the microphone and I looked at the faces turned toward the stage. I know you all, I thought, I have seen you before. The way you lift your chin and the light of hopeful surrender comes into your eyes. I know you, I have you: this secret about yourselves even you do not admit. I will have you always.

"I'm sorry I've been busy every night," Robin said. "I didn't mean to disappear like this. For two days. Maybe a little, maybe that morning, when I woke up and there you were . . . just like before. But I wanted to see you before today. It's just been crazy."

Crane said something and the crowd around us let out its breath, a gentle exhalation like the sigh of a wave sliding down the sand.

"We still have our jobs," I said.

She faced me. "Steven told me you bumped into him at the convention when he was . . . plagued with a moment of self-doubt. He said you decided not to write anything. That was nice of you, Cliff."

"We made a deal."

"Sure you did."

"Let's get together tonight in Buffalo," I said. "I'll rent a car and drive you to Niagara Falls."

"Cliff! It'll be two in the morning by the time we get in."

"I don't care. Let's go. It'll be wild in the dark. Don't you want to see it?"

Robin laughed. "We could stay for a couple of hours in one of those motels? The kind with a heart-shaped bed?"

"Sure. Why not?"

"We'd be back before anyone woke up in the morning?"

"I promise."

She looked into the sun. Crane's voice rose like a sail catching the wind. ". . . and they say we can't do anything about the failure of our schools, the closing of our factories, the crime. They say the government can't do anything about any of this. They lecture us about working harder, playing by the rules, behaving properly . . ." The words were as familiar to both of us as the rosary to a nun.

"Oh God, tell me this is wise," Robin said.

"They have heart-shaped beds. What else could it be?"

John Starke stood down the street with a bespectacled young man at his side who clutched a notebook and pen. Starke saw Robin and waved for her to join them. She nodded and then turned back to me, her eyes rising slowly and then filling with light.

"I don't know," she said. "I don't think I can make it. But I'll try to think of something else. I promise."

The rocking chairs were full so I sat on the porch railing, turning my tape recorder on for the last part of the speech. They were almost always the same, but you could never be sure. I leaned against the wall of the cottage and tried to see him through a swaying maple branch.

The stage was dwarfed by a huge banner strung across the pediment overhead, *Crane* fluttering in majestic rhythm across the sky. Below it he seemed small. He stood behind the microphone stand, his weight on the heel of one ebony loafer, his index finger touching the air as though the point he was making was a physical thing, right there to be pinned down. "You've heard what I want to do," he said. "Job training, healthcare reform, child welfare. But everything I have said today, everything I believe this nation can accomplish, none of it will get done if we continue to suspect each other's motives and divide ourselves by race, by class, by sex, by religious beliefs . . ."

He was reaching the end. I closed my eyes on the porch and the sun colored my eyelids a drowsy yellow, spectral trees rising in red and blue. Crane floated among them, an afterimage breaking into phosphorescent fish that swam away in a sea of words.

"I have been accused of excessive optimism. I plead guilty. I have been accused of a naive belief that our differences are not as great as what unites us. I plead guilty."

I felt the crowd stir. A thousand lips began to form the words.

"We have nothing to be afraid of from each other," Crane said as they joined in ecstatic chorus. On the porch reporters mimicked the line halfheartedly, more out of habit than malice.

I opened my eyes in time to see Crane toss off his patented wave and disappear off the back of the stage. Around me reporters stirred lazily into action. I pulled my cell phone out of my briefcase and called my editor.

"I've got nothing to file."

"Kelly wants to talk to you," Ellen said. There was a click and Kelly came on the line.

"Listen, Cliff, I've gone through every database I could find looking for stuff about Bushmill and Crane. There's a little bit about Bushmill in the business pages, but nothing much. I think he keeps away from the press. There's nothing else . . ." I heard her take a quick breath. "*So.* I decided to call the local library down there in Phillips, where he lives. I asked them to send me their clips from the local paper—it's a weekly—and Cliff, I've got a story. Listen to this. Crane attended a ribbon-cutting at an addition to Bushmill's plant outside of Phillips. It's when he was a freshman congressman . . . and . . . Here it is. Bushmill was asked about Crane and he tells the reporter. 'I've been impressed by this young man since I first saw him hitchhiking to school. I've been glad to help him since the days he came back to Berthold after his mother died.' At first I read right by that, and then I thought, why would he say something that specific? 'The days he came back to Berthold after his mother died.' Why did he mention that time? What did he do for him then? I went back and read your profile, but I couldn't find anything . . . Do you know?"

I stared at the crowd shuffling down the street. When Crane's mother died he was hiking across Tuscany. He'd just finished his service in the army and it was a trip he'd promised himself for more than a year. He was staying outside of Florence in a farmhouse with a view of a three-hundred-year-old monastery on a hill. He checked with American Express and found the message waiting for him, and he was on the next morning's flight out of Rome. A day later he stood beside her grave while they buried her on a cold October afternoon. The other children fled, but he stayed on, always the responsible one, sorting through his parents' papers, trying to get his father into the veterans' hospital in Springfield. For two months he stayed in the old house with the same ghost walking up the cellar steps at night, the same drafts sneaking through the windows, and then one day he was gone, fleeing back East to graduate school in Princeton. His cousin remembered it as one of the loneliest times in his life. I didn't know how he had been helped by Bushmill. I thought about it and a young man hovered gray and indistinct, disappearing into the darkness on an autumn evening more than twenty years ago.

"I don't know," I said.

"Do you want me to try to talk to Bushmill?"

On the street people were standing on tiptoes, looking into the distance and breaking into smiles.

"Not yet," I said.

Silence on the other end of the line.

"I'll see Gregory soon," I said. "Let me talk to him first."

"You're sure? Ellen thinks we've got to get going on this."

"I'm sure. We'll move fast enough."

The limousine appeared as I hung up. The door opened and Angela Crane stepped out. The people along the street pressed toward her. She waited by the car while members of the staff unrolled an orange rope and then she walked alongside, briefly touching hands, stopping to listen, to take small gifts handed to her and pass them to an aide. She was wearing a sleeveless red dress with white polka dots and she seemed so small and delicate it was hard to remember she was an insurance lawyer. How do women do this, I wondered? How do they balance the disparate roles expected of them?

Myra drifted out of the cottage and stood beside me, watching Angela work the edge of the crowd. A small child, a girl with a tangle of brown curls held back with a red ribbon, slid under the rope. Angela knelt and lifted her to her side, smiling down at her until their noses almost touched.

"I always wonder why they never had children," Myra said.

Angela whispered conspiratorially into a tiny pink ear and handed the girl to her mother. She moved a little farther down the line to a place where the crowd had an oddly pleased look about itself. From my distance, the waiting faces had a hypnotizing similarity. An old man, a boy, a young woman, a llama.

Angela drew her hand back as if stung. The llama eyed her apathetically from behind the rope, gray-brown, donkey-eared head peering out between a proud couple.

"Bring it out," the photographers said, and soon the llama was stand-

141

ing in all its shaggy glory in the middle of the street, while they clicked away madly and a chant began. "Kiss the llama! Kiss the llama!"

The sun was high and the trees, cottages, and shops shimmered in its unencumbered light. Ten thousand people watched while the wife of the next president of the United States and a llama eyed each other.

"Kiss the llama!" they shouted. "Kiss the llama!"

Angela Crane leaned over and kissed the llama on the top of the nose.

The cheer rippled back through the crowd until those raising their voices could have no idea what it was they were celebrating beyond the sky, the light, the lake, the day.

Robin appeared by my shoulder. "Come on inside for a moment."

We slipped inside and up the stairs without anyone paying attention. Robin led me to the second floor and a room at the front of the house, where the sound from below rose through an open window and mottled green light drifted along the floor.

"No one is using this room," Robin said, "and I have the key in my pocket."

She locked the door and placed her hand on my chest, unbuttoning the first button with a twist. Laughter rose outside in a muffled wash and she placed her mouth against my ear and whispered, "And we're not going anywhere for an hour. And there is no news today." Her hand slid lightly down and pulled the second button loose and we slid backward toward a couch beneath the window.

My back slid along the matted hair of the old couch and I felt the warm air along my chest and down my stomach to my hips where it disappeared in a different warmth. Robin rose above me in the aquarium twilight. I saw her chin and the tangled corona of her hair and her shoulders, delicately concave under the bone, before the white swelling of her breasts and then her ribs and the shadow of her stomach, hollow and tight, and her hips rocking warmly against mine. She smiled and slid hard against me. She moved and the old couch groaned. In the corner of my eye I saw the leaves of an oak tree sliding back and forth against the screen and I turned my head, and the room was at sea and hot and crossed with thunder and she was pale and tall above me.

And it is so strange that I remembered a winter night in Montana. We had been fighting earlier. She was always enraged then about some injustice or another and there was something inside me that always resisted judgment. We argued and later we went to bed. In the winter the wind blew from the North, and the skeleton hand of an oak tree scratched the window, and our bedroom was always cold. Robin's clothes lay in a collapsed ghost in the corner. She rose above me in bed that night too, settling herself on me suddenly. Then she rocked forward, her eyes wide, her hair falling around us like a parachute, and she whispered hotly in my ear, "I'm right."

Splayed fingers pressed themselves into my shoulders and I opened my eyes to the sea-green light and her arched and lovely form and then there was only this joined part of myself rising and falling and the twin engines of our breath racing toward the familiar tunnel of darkness.

While somewhere in the distance . . .voices floating up from the porch, a radio reporter piecing together his report, snippets of Crane's speech running back and forth, cut into delicate slivered ribbons.

"We have nothing to be afraid of . . . nothing to be afraid of . . . to be afraid of . . . from each other."

III.

WE RETURNED to the air and the days passed in collage. Leaning against a brick wall to dodge the blistering sun in a Polish neighborhood outside of Cleveland where we ate sauerkraut pierogies on paper plates and watched dancers in heavily embroidered skirts melt while they performed. Tripping over ducks waddling through a Memphis hotel on their way to a fountain in the center of the antiquarian lobby. Shooting pool with Steven Duprey in a press room set up in a pool hall off the tumbleweed-dry square of a Texas town while the locals peered from the shadows beneath their hats. An Elvis impersonator dispensing wisdom from a pickup bed at a truck stop in West Virginia. A woman dressed as the Statue of Liberty following us for two days through Pennsylvania.

Crane faced swelling crowds everywhere. Thirty thousand filled downtown St. Louis at noon on a Thursday. Twenty thousand waited in Detroit. Seven thousand lined the banks of the San Antonio River when he came around the bend, standing in the prow of a barge and wearing sunglasses like MacArthur. The most fervent crowds were in the small towns left behind in the age of airport-to-airport campaigning. They were rediscovered this summer, and when his staff realized how good they looked on television, we made a lot of one-day bus trips to visit these places where the old vision of America survives.

On a clear night in Waco, Crane led a candlelight procession across a bridge in honor of a high school teacher slain the week before. We waited in a park on the riverbank while a field of fireflies moved in solemn procession through the air. Somewhere in the distance the methodical chant of protesters floated in and out of the hum of traffic. Something about Jesus. Something about God.

The night was unseasonably cold and the crowd waited hushed and huddled as the march curved down the bridge and appeared before us. Crane's gray trenchcoat was a cloak in the darkness; his candle cast his elongated face into a mask. The teachers and students behind him held melted candles aloft in ghostly, translucent fingers. There was a pinpricking moment of silence and then the pent-up roar of the crowd swallowed us. And I thought that there was something in the sound we didn't understand, some deep-throated pitch of intensity, some desire that escaped those of us in the press.

Our journey was refracted and distilled every night in the shadow universe of television. Those of us traveling with Crane glimpsed this more perfect reality in airports and hotel lounges or late at night in our rooms. It brought a realization that we traveled at the center of a web of electronic perception, what we saw and heard broken down into glittering facets and reassembled into a jeweled miniature. There was Thomas Crane on the news in front of another flag-draped background. There were his ads: Crane, sleeves rolled up, at a chalkboard in front of a rapt class of high school students, explaining what it would take to see that they had decent jobs waiting for them in the next decade; Crane discussing job retraining with unemployed workers standing in line to collect benefits in Youngstown; Crane blasting two clay pigeons out of the air before talking about how his position on gun control was being misrepresented. The news and the ads were all part of the miniature, reflected and gleaming without distinction. All of it, despite the dithering of the talk shows and the ponderous mulling of the *Times* and the *Post*, trading on a swelling implicit faith: that he could be trusted, that he was different than the others.

The last night of the Republican convention, when the president accepted his party's nomination for the second time, Crane and Angela and his senior staff watched in a hotel room in Houston. They listened as a small, white-haired man with the eyes of a falcon called on old allegiances, evoked primeval fears of the unknown. When the speech was over they watched the commentary and then Crane turned off the tube, and this is how Steven Duprey, fulfilling one part of his debt, remembered the evening:

There was a reflective silence as the light on the screen shrunk to the null point, and a nervous shuffling until John Starke cleared his throat.

"Well. That was the same old same old. You know what the voters are going to say to that? Fool me once, but not twice."

A chorus of assent trickled out as they waited for Crane. He stared at the dead screen, rubbing his jaw absently with his fingers. He turned to Angela, who leaned against his side, feet curled up on the couch.

"What do you think?"

"It's close, but I still like the other guy better."

The aides laughed. Crane waited. She shook her chopped black hair uncertainly.

"I don't know. There's something missing. Don't ask me what. He said all the things he should say and he slammed his fist at the right times and he looked like the president but . . ."

"Resentful," Crane said. "He looked resentful that the public's making him go through this again. He looked angry that he's tied in the polls with some senator from nowhere, after all he's done for the country. And it makes him look old. Proud but old."

Duprey leaned against the wall beside the television.

"Old means tired," he said. "No matter how many times you pound on the podium."

Blendin stumbled out of the bathroom, zipping up his fly, his dirty T-shirt caught in the zipper. He yanked until his khakis slid past his belly-button and he looked like a hundred-year-old man.

"*Goddamn this* . . . I don't know if old means tired, but I'll fucking tell you this. Resentful means nasty. Like a cornered fucking animal . . . *This fucking* . . . And nasty means a campaign just like every other presidential campaign for the past twenty years. You define or you get defined. You bite or you get bit . . . *God-fucking-damn this thing!*"

He held the torn piece of T-shirt in his right hand and finished zipping up his pants.

"Now can we get back to work?" he said calmly.

Two hours later, when much of the staff had dispersed and all the polls had been reviewed, the money allocated, a half-dozen complaints, pleas and petitions from state campaign managers dispensed with or dismissed, Blendin handed a sheaf of papers across the table to Crane, who read silently, passed them on to Angela, and slid back in his chair and closed his eyes, as if suddenly tired.

"Rough," Angela said. "Can we back this up? The one about the administration's relationship with Mekron Chemical?"

Duprey ran his finger down a sheet of paper. "Fifty-seven thousand dollars in campaign contributions from various corporate executives and three visits with senior administration staff on the deregulation bill."

Angela blinked. "And they're the company being sued in the Wyoming pesticide case?"

Blendin sipped from a Budweiser that had been sitting at his elbow for an hour.

"That's right. In the water and fucking tumors the size of grapefruit."

Crane spoke with his eyes closed. "The administration held two business roundtables on the pesticide deregulation bill, and they met with half a dozen companies each time. Is that where they met with Mekron?"

"Research gave me the dates," Duprey said. "I don't know who else was there."

"Does it really matter, Senator?" Blendin asked.

Crane looked across the table at Blendin until the consultant averted his eyes, glancing at Starke asleep on the couch.

"I know how this has worked so far," Blendin said quietly. "I hear them in the back of the plane. *Saint Thomas*. They might not like it, but I know how valuable it's been. But this is a different game. No more intramurals. You're facing the Oakland Raiders now. They bite, they spit, they've got bad breath, they tell stories about your momma."

Crane stood and walked to the hotel room's glass wall, contemplating the banal geometry of the streets below.

"Tim Tim. Yes yes. They play *hardball*. It's *total war* . . . Please."

"All we want to do is film two spots," Blendin said. "So they can go on the air quickly if they're needed."

Crane had been troubled by a problem stomach since he was a child. He couldn't handle junk food or meals at midnight, and he had been losing weight during the eight months he'd been on the road. When he stood against the window Duprey could see his shirt hanging on his shoulders. It was a beautiful shirt, carefully tailored to leave those shoulders looking fuller than they were. Duprey thought about how careful Crane was about his appearance. He remembered seeing Crane backstage, holding in his right hand what appeared to be a dove. He held it at his waist, considering a pair of fallen white wings while the applause mounted, and only when he stuffed it hurriedly into his pants pocket before stepping out did Duprey realize this indecision had been about whether to wear a pocket handkerchief.

"What do you think, Angie?"

His wife looked up from the pages in front of her.

"You don't have to use everything you bring into the courtroom. But it's nice to have it all there if things go haywire."

Blendin slammed his beer on the table. "Exactly right."

Crane stared out the window and I wonder what he thought. So many cities. So many anonymous landscapes. "Texas," he said. "An amazing state. At the Battle of San Jacinto, Sam Houston and his troops defeated thirteen hundred Mexicans. Caught them by surprise. You know how many prisoners they took?"

Duprey stroked his beard. "That first night? None."

Crane smiled. "We have a son of the Lone Star State in our midst. That is correct. None. At the time, a few newspapers denounced them for having descended to savagery. It turns out they were just ahead of their time."

He placed a hand on the glass briefly and returned to the table, stopping behind his wife, putting a hand gently on her shoulder. The familiar melancholy slipped from his face in a stiffening of the jaw, a thinning of his mouth, until he considered them with a strangely blank composure.

"It has been my experience that no ad filmed for a campaign ever goes unused," Crane said. "But go ahead."

We moved across the South. I followed along and wrote what I had to write and waited for the nights when Robin had dispensed with the day's final crisis, and she slipped through my unlocked door, and we entangled ourselves in a succession of motel rooms that linger in my mind today in the smells of industrial laundry soap and cheap disinfectant, in phantom coughs through threadbare walls, the slamming of doors in my dreams, the murmur of televisions at dawn. It was too dangerous for me to come to her room—staffers could be interrupted at any moment—so I waited on a string of beds like life rafts, sometimes falling asleep, and then surprised by her hands sliding up my back, long fingers pushing themselves through my hair before I turned around and felt her shivering warmth as she slipped in beside me, then her mouth, arriving in a rush, without more than a word. The nights were separate from the days and from the formal pretense that we had managed to become friends, nothing more. The days passed and only rarely did I let myself dream of a time when we could settle into someplace for more than a night and our future would unfold like a brightly colored map. I saw all the things you see on that map, a house and kids and a riding lawn mower and beat-up loafers and the Sunday paper and fruit in a bowl on the kitchen table, the whole damn thing. All of it. But I knew it was a mistake to let myself see such things in the sunlight.

The days were when we did our jobs. Robin had hers and I had a course I had set myself on much earlier. And so, when our southern swing took us to Atlanta, I went to Fulton County Stadium, where my ticket was waiting at the Will Call window.

Latrelle Gregory was already in his seat. Ponderous clouds were piling up in the evening sky and the air was humid and still. We were seated halfway up the second deck, the stadium hanging around us in artificial midday like a giant dog-food bowl, a soulless, utilitarian artifact. The field glimmered green and geometric below; the players looked like children's action figures lost in the expanse.

"Clifford, I feared you might not make it."

His beer rested comfortably in a childlike hand on his knee. He wore a lavender knit shirt and pressed khakis, the shirt a little too tight and the pants a bit too short. His face gleamed as if we were sitting in the sun and I could see his scalp through dancing wisps of calcified hair. He smiled at me.

"Los Bravos, as we call them here, are ahead three nothing. The Mets have already committed one grievous error, thus lending a particular joy to the evening for the home folks, who do dearly love to see all Yankees, and New York Yankees in particular, embarrassed whenever possible."

The beer vendor's harsh call echoed up the seats and I waved at him.

"How sad for you then," I said, "that you have to settle for the Mets."

Gregory nodded and sipped his beer.

"How true."

"Have you eaten?"

"I have eaten some, Clifford. I have not eaten all I intend."

"I'll buy you whatever you recommend as a specialty of the house."

"I believe I'm drinking the specialty of the house."

The beer vendor arrived at the end of our row. "Two," I said, and after money and beer had been exchanged, I settled into my seat in time to see a Met ground out to second. The fans around us applauded without fervor.

"Thanks for the ticket," I said.

"Comps, actually. But you're certainly welcome. I'm afraid we might get rain."

"You a serious fan, Latrelle?"

"I love the Braves, Clifford. They have more money than anyone else, a mad tycoon of an owner, they buy the best players, and they win all the time. They are the embodiment of my nation's spiritual essence and I embrace them."

"You want to watch the game for a while?"

"Don't be silly."

I told him what Kelly and I had discovered about Crane and Roger Bushmill. When I finished he was smiling. He sipped his beer.

"That is a name I thought might show up."

"You know him?"

The batter snapped a line drive to left center and the runner on second wheeled around third. The crowd stood as he launched himself toward the plate, the ball arriving on a line that terminated in a cirrus of dust and flailing limbs. Gregory waited until the cheers had died and we were seated again.

151

"Mr. Roger Bushmill. Mr. Roger Bushmill visited our offices a few times. I would say Mr. Bushmill was greeted very cordially. Mr. Bushmill had a problem with the disposal of certain chemical byproducts used in his manufacture. I can't for the life of me tell you what they were, but disposing of them was a touchy business and Mr. Bushmill needed a waiver of EPA regulations concerning storage of those byproducts at his plant site. I believe you will find that a young congressman, Thomas Crane, helped Mr. Bushmill with this problem, arranging a meeting in his office between EPA officials and Mr. Bushmill's people. After which, the EPA did see fit to grant a waiver. I believe you will also find that young Congressman Crane had spoken out forcefully during his campaign on the need for greater vigilance when it comes to the environment, but saw the error of his ways after meeting with the providential Mr. Bushmill."

Gregory tilted his paper cup back, swallowing until a rivulet of beer ran down his chin. He let the cup fall to the cement, where he crushed it underfoot.

"Of course this was very long ago, and the problem is long gone."

When we had been talking about other things Gregory had spoken boisterously, but when we turned to Crane he spoke in a subdued and reasonable tone, the kind of voice that does not demand attention, and I noticed his accent grew less distinct.

"I could provide you with dates and times, all off the record, of course, should you wish."

Thunderheads towered at the far rim of the stadium, a reef of flickering darkness. We were between innings and the crowd milled down the stairs with their eyes on the sky.

"Was there any further problem?" I asked finally.

"What do you mean?"

"Was there any further problem with the stuff they stored? Did anything happen?"

"Not that I know of."

"Was there a discernible quid pro quo? Was there something said that indicated an obligation on Crane's part that went beyond what he would have had to help any well-heeled employer in his district?"

Gregory rubbed a soft bead of sweat above his upper lip.

"Clifford, you give me a name and I tell you what I know. He didn't treat everyone like Mr. Bushmill. You forget he was a congressman of integrity, Saint Thomas, the *pure*."

I watched the first batter for the Mets settle lethargically into the batter's box, stalling for time, hoping for the rain. Gregory sat beside me quietly.

"What is this, Clifford, a change of heart?"

"You know, Latrelle, I don't think I ever mentioned it, but my name isn't actually Clifford."

The first batter flied out with an underwater thunk. Half the seats around us were empty, their occupants inside, waiting for the storm.

"I'm sorry, Latrelle," I said. "There is nothing at the core of this. It started because I couldn't understand two trips back to Berthold and then it became something else and now it's this and there's still nothing at the center of it all. No proof of anything. Nothing. No *thing*, where you know suddenly what's going on, where you see what it's all about, even if you can't prove it . . . I've seen reporters do this. We hypnotize ourselves. We stare into the bushes long enough and we convince ourselves there has to be a snake in there. And pretty soon we're seeing a snake every time a shadow moves. And it's just bullshit."

Gregory turned to face me.

"Clifford. Cliff. I was not aware it was your responsibility to answer every question you raise. I thought it was enough that the questions themselves be legitimate. There are reporters who would write based just on what I've told you about Bushmill."

I stared at the field, colored now with a strange Mediterranean light.

"Have you gone back to Berthold?" Gregory asked quietly.

The batter had stepped out of the batter's box and the players were all looking at the far end of the stadium.

"No."

"Then maybe the answer is at the starting point."

The rain began falling in big fat drops. The few people still around us fled toward the tunnels. Gregory held a hand over his eyes as if squinting into the sun.

"You fear you will destroy a good man," he said. "But he is what he truly is, not what he appears to be in a nineteen-inch box, not what he becomes when the fools in your trade trip all over themselves because he's some-thing *new*. Politics is only bearable when the frauds come with a wink, or end up with a prison sentence, Cliff."

My anger was gone. It felt like some distant storm I had watched along the horizon, something that had nothing to do with me.

"Everyone's a fraud, Latrelle," I said. "Look at you. You're pretending to like baseball."

They were pulling the tarp across the infield. Gregory watched them with a pensive, doubtful expression, biting his lower lip in a fashion that made him look like a school boy about to be punished. He reached into the pocket of his baggy shorts and pulled out a small envelope, holding it beneath his cupped hand and his wrist to keep it dry.

"I was uncertain about this," he said. "I still am."

He slid the envelope into my lap, still shielding it with his hand.

"Don't open it in the rain," Gregory said. "Don't ask me to say another word about it. You can't use it directly. You can't make it public. I don't know how you got it. I don't know where it came from. It never comes up again. If you have any hesitation on these ground rules then I am afraid it goes back in my pocket."

"You know I can't promise any of that without knowing what it is."

"It'll be quite obvious. You'll see it's all right. And I give you my word it's genuine."

"What is it, Latrelle?"

"You remember when I said there was a third trip to Berthold? This is from then."

He lifted his hand slowly from the envelope and I covered it with my own when the first drops spread gray stains across the paper. He stood up, hunching against rain falling now with a heavy slap.

"Come on! Even Yankees know enough to get in out of the rain."

"In a minute. I'll meet you inside the tunnel."

He stood there for a moment, his hand above his eyes, his shirt stick-ing to his belly like the skin of an overripe melon. He watched me push the envelope deep inside my pocket and shrugged.

"Cliff. Clifford. You folks up north have always taken yourselves too seriously."

The real rain arrived after he left, blowing up the stadium in a billowing curtain that hit like a waterfall, washing the world away in a roar that drowned all without judgment or clemency. I sat alone among fifty thousand empty seats, my head back, my eyes open, and let it pummel me until I was blind.

IV.

THE ENVELOPE held a blurred copy of a phone bill, dozens of pages listing calls from Crane's Senate office in Washington. There were too many numbers to track down, and I sat on the edge of my bed and flipped through the pages with a growing sense of futility until I came to the credit card calls. *This is from the third trip to Berthold.*

The bill listed both the numbers from which Crane had called and the numbers he had dialed. I could trace his trip from the airport in Springfield to Berthold. He called the office back in Washington once when he arrived; then he tried a number in southern Illinois. I recognized Berthold's area code. Half an hour later he tried the number again from a different location. I picked up the phone by the bed and dialed. The phone rang half a dozen times.

"You have reached the Clark County Clinic. Our hours are from nine to five. In an emergency please call . . ."

I listened to the message twice and hung up. He had called about seven years ago. The number could have changed. It was a clinic—why would the number change? Had his brother been in for treatment? It could have been Bill Crane or a cousin or an old friend or he could be part of an organ-running ring stealing kidneys from baby children. There was no way to know.

I put the bill in my bag and unpacked tomorrow's clothes. I plugged in my cell phone and computer, making sure the battery had discharged completely first. I called and got my wakeup call, and it was only when I was lying in bed, watching the red numbers click down on the bedside clock that I felt the dead weight of not knowing. What could a clinic in Berthold have to do with a chemical manufacturer? What could it have to do with Crane? A politician rushes home three times. The first two are just before he runs for office. The third time he stops on the way and calls a clinic twice. He was very poor once. He made money. He has a wealthy friend. The friend helped him long ago. Did he help the friend? If so, so what? Did he break the law? Why did he go home? Why did he lie about it? Did he lie about it? Each thought slid and turned like a fleck of light in a kaleidoscope, but nothing coalesced. Watch long enough and you will almost always find a pattern, but I could see no design, only the reassuring sprawl of chance as the clock clicked down and Robin did not knock on my door and I waited and waited and fell asleep dreaming of an endless line of telephones, each ringing and then falling silent just as I reached it.

When I pulled back my drapes the next morning the parking lot was bathed in light, and I had that illusory early morning feeling of acute clarity of perception. The world seemed as bright and uncomplicated as a child's watercolor. We checked out, rode our buses to the airport and waited on the tarmac for Crane. The time before the first flight was always one of the best, a chance to sip coffee and enjoy the day, knowing that responsibility still lay hours distant. Robin was nowhere to be seen. Staff and reporters chatted in small circles, but I stood by myself near the wing, enjoying the sunlight and the rain-washed air. The less sleep you have the brighter the morning's brief illumination of the mind, and I felt brilliantly clearheaded.

At the foot of the stairs leading into the tail of the plane, a Secret Service dog was digging in Myra's bag. Its wet nose slid across her notebooks, its wet tongue dug past her sweater. It snuffled, growled and pulled a curl of sausage out of the bottom of the bag.

Myra stared at the sausage in astonishment, then glanced wildly around the plane. I heard Nathan laughing underneath the other wing.

Standing in a ragged line at the edge of the tarmac, reporters and staff held cellular phones to their ears, sharing gossip with distant friends. I knew I should call my editor, but I sipped my coffee and watched a biplane steer across the edge of the sky, trailing a banner advertising Ford trucks.

I strolled to the back of the plane, where Myra paged through a pocket notebook, making a face as she separated pages sticky with German Shepherd saliva.

"Did you see what happened?"

I nodded.

"I'm a cat person myself," she said. "No self-respecting, professionally trained, federally employed cat would debase itself sniffing around for a dried-up hunk of pork."

"Have you and Nathan considered a truce?"

Myra closed the notebook in disgust and bent it in two to mark it for the trash can.

"Not now, for God's sake. Besides, what else is there to keep us interested?"

Randall Craig strolled up, immaculate in a blue suit, gray shirt and striped tie.

"She's right," he said. "What else is there? Did you see this morning's *New York Times*?"

"The dog ate my *Times*," Myra said.

Craig shrugged as if nothing he failed to understand could be too interesting. "Crane's up nine. He's even up down here in Dixie."

Myra looked at me and smiled. "It's amazing, isn't it? Remember following Crane around in the snow in New Hampshire?"

"Who would have thought it?"

"He's not there yet," Craig said. "The president's started hammering him out west. I guess the ads are *hard*."

The biplane banked overhead and sunlight glittered on the edge of a wing. The sound was like a lazy mosquito on a hot summer afternoon. Randall's cameraman walked by chewing on a roll the size of a brick, the smell of cinnamon floating above the odors of asphalt and aviation fuel.

"He's not there yet," Myra said. "But sometimes it feels like it."

A thin crowd pressed up against the wire fence at the edge of the tarmac. A single sign waved in back: CRANE in red letters on a field of white.

"See someone you know?" Myra asked.

The faces were visible through the interlaced diamonds of the fence. I know you all, I thought. I know who you are and what you want.

"No . . ."

"Come on, who's your buddy?"

"I was just remembering something Duprey said to me once, something about the mysteries of public affection."

She blinked. "He said that?"

"I believe he did."

"There's no mystery," Craig said. "There's greed, there's self-interest and there's revenge, fucking the other guy. That's always big. And at the bottom of it all, there's fear. People do everything they do because they're afraid, or because they want to stop being afraid."

"Christ, Randall," Myra said. "It's eight-thirty in the morning."

"I think there's more than that," I said. "I think this campaign's about something more."

He snorted. "This campaign. This campaign has had a sweet run, but it'll turn out like all the others. You saw Dan Balz's story in the *Post*."

Balz had written the day before about a split within Crane's campaign. There were those, led by his chief pollster, Susan Douglas, who thought it was essential that he narrow his message. Robin's name had come up as one of those opposed to the idea.

"They'll be polling on the color of his ties by the end," Craig said, "or what kind of shoes he should wear."

Craig's producer waved at him frantically from the edge of the runway, a cell phone held a foot from her ear. He strolled over to join her. Myra watched him leave.

"Never vote for a wingtip man," she said.

"Oxfords?"

"Okay. Dependable."

"Slip-ons?"

"Depends. Tassels?"

"Sure."

"Give the country away."

"To who?"

"Tassels? Anyone! Commies. Welfare mothers." She hunched her shoulders and whispered, "The French!"

The crowd behind the fence stirred, unfurling a homemade banner:

"Georgians for Crane!" They held it across their chests, pressing against the fence, the words chopped into pixels of color, broken fragments of their smiles trapped in silver above the cloth.

"I woke up a couple of days ago on the bus," Myra said, "and I didn't know where I was. We were heading into some city and I thought for a moment I was back in Chicago, riding the bus home. Then I saw this woman standing on her lawn with this dog, a terrier, that she'd dressed up in red, white and blue with an Uncle Sam top hat stuck between the poor dog's ears. And I thought, no, I'm on the road with Thomas Crane." She swept her eyes across the crowd, the tarmac, everything. "You see my point?"

"Not at all."

"Randall doesn't know what he's talking about. None of us do. This country: go figure."

Myra peered into the bottom of her bag with disgust.

"I better clean this out or I'll be chased by every dog from here to Canada."

She crossed the tarmac with a jaunty, elfin stride, wearing stockings with miniature cartoon tongues running in a neat line down the back of her legs. This country, I thought. This country, indeed.

I heard the people by the fence stirring and looked up to see Crane's limousine rolling through the gate. I stepped out of range of the jet engines and dialed the bureau on my phone.

"The prodigal reporter checks in," my editor said dryly.

"It's been crazy."

"Kelly wants to talk to you."

"We're boarding here. I'll call her later."

"Don't let it wait."

"Right."

"Do you have anything daily?"

"I don't know. I'll call you when I see what the schedule looks like."

The limousine door opened. Crane and then Robin stepped blinking into the sunlight. I watched her pull her hair out of her eyes and lean forward to speak into his ear.

"Talk to Kelly, Cliff."

"Right. I've got to go."

Crane was at the fence, reaching through the wire to touch fingers stretched toward his. Robin stood by the limousine watching him, the morning sun diaphanous in her dress, one hand still frozen in her hair. Her bare arm was the color of wheat when it catches fire in the high summer light. When Crane smiled, she smiled, when he frowned, you saw it reflected like a faint cloud shadow in her wide blue eyes.

We flew to four rallies that day, floating from small sunbaked airport to small sunbaked airport. We made four stops, and I didn't make a call from any of them. Starke fought his way through the crowded aisle of the plane as we rumbled into the air one final time to tell me there had been a message for me in the press room at the last rally. "Kelly someone. She says to call as soon as possible." I thanked him and when the giddy, exhausted chatter had fallen off and reporters had returned to their seats, most of them sleeping to the reassuring roar of the engines, I saw Robin standing in the galley, a glass of wine in her hand. She waited until she was sure I saw her, and then she slid back into the front cabin.

Hours later, when I got to my hotel room, the red message light was blinking on the phone. I listened to Kelly's whispered, nervous voice imploring me to call, hung up and watched the light go out. I sat in the chair beside the bed and thought about the things I should be doing and watched a sliver of light along my door, which I had left carefully ajar, and heard footsteps down the hall and saw Robin's thin, unwavering shadow fall across the doorway. And only when I heard the hiss of my door sliding across the green hotel carpet did I feel a sudden, scalding sense of shame.

V.

WE FLEW into Washington early the next afternoon. The day was bright and hot. Tourists swept across Independence Avenue at every intersection like dazed tropical fish suddenly pulled blinking and gasping into the air. The federal buildings were a washed-out imperial white against a lifeless sky, and the city shimmered distant and remote on the last day of August.

We rode up Capitol Hill into the shade of the historic, officially labeled trees, and the police waved us into the east parking lot where John Starke waited in the middle of the pavement like a pale Brooks Brothers mannequin. "You'll be pleased to know the first debate has finally been scheduled," he said. "Senator Crane and the president will meet at the Ford Auditorium in Detroit next Wednesday."

The debates had been floating on the horizon since the Republican convention, the last known obstacle on the trail, the one we knew could still wreck the journey, and there was a moment of silence while we collected our thoughts.

"The format?" someone asked.

Starke looked at the piece of paper clenched in his hand. "The format will be an hour and a half, the first hour a question-and-answer period with three members of the press. In the last half-hour, there will be a direct exchange, with each candidate addressing the other twice on a topic of his choice and then the other candidate being given the same amount of time to respond ... two and a half minutes each. Then five-minute closing statements."

"The panel?"

"It will be jointly announced later."

"Why not now?"

"It will be jointly announced later."

"Why?"

"We're notifying the members."

The press scrum had gathered around Starke, those trapped in the back jumping up and down, holding their recorders above their heads. The boom mikes swung down from above and it looked as if he were trapped under a nervous spider. There was the usual babble of questions until Randall Craig's voice cut through the others.

"The president's staffers have said that they were demanding the direct exchange. They thought it was their best chance to illustrate the president's greater experience in both world and domestic affairs. Is it true you fought the direct exchange?"

"Not at all. The senator looks forward to the chance to meet the president on an equal footing."

"Are you worried about your candidate's relative lack of experience?"

Starke's mouth pursed and his eyes grew waxen. "Senator Crane has fourteen years of experience in national politics . . ." he began in a monotone that droned on until I drifted loose. Anything else that came up would be in the pool report, and there was something in the eager circle that filled me with dread.

Nathan Zimmer was bouncing on his toes a few feet away, swinging his arms so the back of his blazer billowed out like a lady's bustle. He saw me and his face broke into a wide grin. "We'll find out," he said. "We will find out."

After that, the press conference with the Democratic leadership was anticlimactic. We waited outside the caucus room until Crane and a group of middle-aged men in dark suits appeared. They solemnly announced that they had all pledged to pass Crane's economic revival package immediately once he was elected. I heard Stuart snort and someone laugh and there were a few shouted questions about the debate, which Crane ignored, and then we were free for the rest of the day.

I caught a cab and, as it plowed up Constitution toward the National Press Building, I thought about my apartment, old magazines on the coffee table, a single dried plate by the kitchen sink, the dust of eight months everywhere. I would be staying there tonight and I pictured myself inspecting my own belongings like an amnesiac searching for clues to his past.

The cabby saw me staring at the colonnade of the Canadian Embassy. "You visiting Washington?"

"No. I've just been away for a while."

"Vacation? You go someplace cool?"

"No. . . I'm a reporter. I travel with Thomas Crane."

In the mirror I saw him purse his lips and shrug.

"I had George Will in here last night. He had dinner at the White House."

I was home. I looked out the window and wondered what Robin was doing.

Once, the old-timers said, the Cannon Newspapers Bureau on the ninth floor of the National Press Building had the atmosphere of a genuine city room, clattering wire machines, battered metal desks, black telephones heavy enough to use as murder weapons. But that had been before newspaper companies had metastasized into media conglomerates, corporate soulmates to insurance companies in their unceasing devotion to avoiding risk. The bureau I knew, with its burgundy carpet, indirect lighting, broad expanses of laminated mahogany and dashboard gray plastic, could have been an underwriters' office.

"The conquering hero." The receptionist handed me a sheaf of pink message slips without looking up from *People*. "I've been telling people you're dead for the last week."

Ellen sat in her usual spot at the far corner of the copy desk. She was wearing a sweatshirt and jeans, a vestige of her beach-jock past, and yet her skin had the pale, dried-out hue of someone who has not seen enough natural light. I told her the press conference was worth maybe six inches and asked if she had gotten my message about the debate. She pushed her chair back and rubbed her eyes.

"They made the same announcement at the White House. Thomma's going to handle it. I need to talk to you."

165

She stood and walked into one of the glassed-in offices along the wall. After I followed her through the door, she closed it. Long ago, we had come to know each other in that intimate, professional way that moves past courtesy to candor. When she faced me, her expression had room, if warranted, for sympathy, but none for sentiment.

"What the hell is going on?" she said.

I sat down.

"It's been busy. It's been hard to keep in touch."

"You have a cell phone, Cliff. They work anywhere. You've blown Kelly off for two days."

I watched the receptionist stroll past in slow motion, eyes rolling sideways to steal a glance through the wall.

"I'm sorry. I just got . . . distracted. Where is she?"

"I sent her out."

The way she said it made me look at her. "Where?"

"I sent her to interview Roger Bushmill."

"He doesn't speak to the press."

"He's going to be in Iowa appearing before the state legislature. He's trying to build some sort of plant there and he wants a tax break. She's going to catch him afterward."

"I know people in Iowa," I said.

"I know you do."

"Can I still reach her?"

"Maybe at the hotel tonight."

I know there are worse things than failing to do your job, but it has always been my private vanity. I couldn't think of anything to say.

"How's the campaign going?" Ellen asked.

"What?"

"How's the campaign going? How's it look from here on in?"

". . . Good. I mean, anything can happen, particularly with the debate coming up, but it looks good. You've seen the numbers."

"Crane looks good?"

"Yeah. He's getting great crowds . . . You are reading my stories?"

"I read every word you write," she said gently. "They've been fine stories."

"I am reassured."

166

"How do you feel about him? Crane. Do you think he'll make a good president?"

I looked at the desk behind her, a pile of newspaper clippings, a Webster's collegiate dictionary, a stained coffee cup. I knew I was to blame for this question. I was to blame and that made it much worse.

"I haven't gone native, Ellen," I said.

She sat down and I saw she was trying to be kind. I wasn't the only one with something at stake here. In her own way she had bet on me from the beginning.

"Cliff, maybe you need a week or two back here. Just a shift in focus."

"Don't take me off the road. Not right before the debate."

She looked over my shoulder uncertainly.

"Have you called the people in Berthold to find out what was going on between Crane and Bushmill back then?"

"I'm calling this evening."

"It might be better if you went out there."

"I'm not sure it's worth it."

"Explain that to me."

"I've thought about this a lot. Listen. What crime do we have here? What evidence that Crane has broken a law, betrayed the public trust, done something unethical? We have a little piece of his life that doesn't make sense. We have a few half-assed allegations from a former aide. We have early help from a friend. Okay, that friend is wealthy, an important constituent. But if a close connection to a wealthy constituent is a crime, then we better lock up Congress."

She stared through the wall at the office.

"How long have we worked together?"

"Three. No, almost four years."

"There are forty reporters in this bureau. There are reporters who write better than you do. There are reporters who are better at going through records—like Kelly. There are reporters who have more talent at finding an angle. There are reporters with a lot more swagger." She smiled wearily. "But you're on the road with the man who's probably going to be the next president. You know why? Because there was nobody who worked harder than you did. I fought for you to get this chance, Cliff. I said we had nobody who was more honest in their basic approach to our business, nobody else who always made the extra phone call, always checked the last possible source."

Ellen slid her chair closer.

"Maybe it all adds up to nothing. Maybe we'll wake up tomorrow and it'll be on the front page of the *Times*. But we still have questions. You know that as well as I do. I don't understand what's going on here."

I could see the watercooler through the wall. Two reporters lingered, pretending not to watch us. My back was to the newsroom, but I could feel its weight, figures slumped over keyboards in airless cubicles, fingers moving like nervous crabs as they struggled to tap-dance life into the latest GAO study, the latest hearing of the subcommittee on interior appropriations, the congressman's latest fatuous statement on whatever. Picking through the shit for seeds, I once heard an old editor call it. This was where I had been for three years. I didn't want to go back.

"I'm just trying to be fair."

She opened the door.

"We'll be fair when we know what we're being fair about."

I went back to my desk and wrote six inches on the press conference. I finished in twenty minutes and tried to reach Kelly at her hotel. She was gone and I left a message telling her I'd be home tonight. The call made me feel like a fool. I thumbed through message slips while other reporters stopped by to offer the greetings attendant upon the returned warrior. If I was in trouble, it was between Ellen and Kelly and myself, and for that I knew I should be grateful.

By seven-thirty the bureau was almost deserted. I dialed Bill Crane's number in Berthold.

"This is Bill Crane," his recorded voice said. "He's a great brother, I think he's going to win, and I think he's going to be a great president. Good-bye and God Bless the Democratic Party."

I hung up and listened to the horns on Fourteenth Street for a while. I felt stale and dull, like an old man who has stared out his window at the same landscape for so many years it has ceased to have any meaning.

The night editor, a friendly woman with a shock of red hair, glanced up when I passed her on my way out the door.

"Calling it a night?"

"Just need some fresh air. I'll be back."

I walked down the long sloping street past the gray buildings until I came to the Mall, where I sat down on a park bench. The sun hung low over the Lincoln Memorial and the Washington Monument cast a shadow halfway to the Capitol. That peculiarly marbled light of early evening in Washington fell across the thick grass and the gravel paths crowded with tourists, runners, and the last remnants of the bureaucratic army that occupied the city every dawn, only to flee before dark. The bells in the Old Post Office tower began to chime and startled pigeons rose in a swirl.

A woman with long, beautifully tanned legs jogged by, black hair in a ponytail, eyes raised above the glances of the men she passed. Her stride kicked up a small stone that settled next to my shoe.

I thought about how I had come to love this city. The disdainful part that couldn't be bothered to look you in the eye. The hustling part that filled the streets east of Fifteenth. The tourist part with its dinosaur bones and famous flying machines. I loved the way the figures in Statuary Hall grew more severe late at night, the hollows of their eyes deepening in unforgiving judgment. I loved the giant shadows of the flags flapping across the Washington Monument, Jefferson's somber silhouette when the lights went down on his stone cage.

It had always been night when the city felt most mine, when I felt I had earned some small claim on its secrets. You finished covering Congress late and crossed the marble paths on the Hill with your footsteps echoing in the silence, the Capitol dome floating behind you like a Roman helmet, the ancient trees on the East Lawn, so manicured in the light, reclaiming their rightful mystery in darkness. The policemen in their black uniforms stood in pools of light on the corners, guarding the congressional office buildings as if each were some sacred ruin left here by catastrophe only dimly understood. There was a tremendous comfort and sense of belonging in the familiarity of it all.

From my bench I could see the green, wrought-iron light poles for the skating rink next to the Natural History Museum. Robin skated all the time the first winter we were here, a frantic circular chase to reclaim one piece of a world she understood. I wondered what she thought when she saw the rink now. All she had really wanted was to earn that feeling I had when I left the Capitol late at night, the feeling of having won the right to take your role seriously. She wanted it more than I ever had.

I remembered coming home to find her staring at the Capitol through the glass wall in our apartment.

"I got word today from *Congressional Quarterly*," she said. "They're still not hiring."

We had been in Washington four months and she had learned that her experience as a reporter in Montana might as well have been in Montenegro for all it counted here. The first set of resumés had been sent out in a flush of excitement, as if she could feel a new beginning waiting for her behind a half-open door. The second set had gone out with steely determination. The third had been sent with a kind of grim fatalism. The fourth in a daze. I spoke to the bosses at Cannon and they made calls and a few interviews came through, but nothing more. I thought that if someone could just sense how much she wanted to belong to something, how completely she would throw herself into the cause, they would have jumped across the room to hire her. But desperation is the muffled bomb tick to employers, the warning of past and future explosion.

The first few weeks I came home she was waiting for me on the balcony, watching so she could wave as I appeared on the sidewalk. She sat on the couch with her knees tucked under her chin "Tell me what it's like," she said. "Tell me what happened. Where did you go? Tell me who you spoke to," and I tried at first and then I found I could not really share the experience. I was struggling in my own fashion, trying to master a new job in a city where no one helps you learn the ropes, and I sensed, in some inarticulate way, how important this was to the rest of my life. And I have wished a thousand times since that I had told her this, told her how I felt I needed to hoard what strength I had to deal with each day, but then I only knew that the thought of talking about it filled me with a sense of weightlessness, as if I was one of those cartoon characters pedaling madly across thin air, knowing the one mistake I could make was to look down.

And maybe this is bullshit, maybe I am blaming temporary causes for a permanent condition, maybe we all find excuses for who we are.

The squeal of tires floated up to our apartment from the Anacostia Freeway seven stories below.

"I'm sorry," I said. "I don't know what to say."

"That's okay," Robin said quietly. "Why should you?"

She ran a hand through her tangled hair and it fell lank and untidy across her forehead. A line of red splotches ran down one temple, as if her knuckles had been pressed hard against the side of her head.

"I've got an interview at PBS Thursday. They need a research assistant. They told me over the phone it's unlikely I'm what they're looking for, but they'd give me an interview . . ." Her voice trailed off.

"That's great."

"I need to put my stuff together tomorrow," she said. "I want to practice what I'm going to say. Can you help me?"

We had been through this before, and I knew how the night would end: her loathing and then anger as she faced the inadequacy of her qualifications, tears and defeat and a desperate reaching out for assurance I could not give.

"Sure," I said.

I walked into the claustrophobic kitchen, turned on the light and scared a single cockroach, who scurried behind the toaster. I found some frozen chicken and put it in the microwave. I was making a salad, chopping an onion, when I heard a tearing sound in the next room.

"Robin?"

She sat in the dark on the edge of the couch, elbows on her knees. Scraps of paper fluttered to the carpet from her hands.

"Don't say a thing," she said.

She picked up another page from a stack beside her on the couch and slowly tore it in two. The sound was agonizing, like skin tearing. She tore the halves in two again and then tossed the pieces into the air. I picked one up. It was a page from her resumé.

The next day at work was hard, and when another reporter in the bureau invited me to join a group going up to the press club for a beer, I jumped at the chance. I told myself I would only stay for one, but I stayed for several and soon it was later than I had realized, and it was too late to call.

I saw her skating when I was walking home. I stood in the darkness on the edge of the rink and watched her. She wore black tights and a red ski jacket. Her hair was pulled around and pushed out sideways beneath a stocking cap and she skated slender and fierce, leaning out over the ice, blades flashing. I watched her and saw, as if for the first time, how beautiful she was, and felt, with a hollow pain, how much I loved her, and knew I had failed her in some immeasurable sense, not just tonight, but every day since we had arrived, and she was going to leave me.

The rink was quiet now, unlit, disappearing as the sky turned the color of wine. I closed my eyes and tried to remember her turning a pirouette, the ice flying in slivers around her ankles. Instead I saw her on the road, standing by a nameless stage in a parade of nameless stages, smiling at me through the crowd. She had what she'd always wanted.

What did I have? These nights amputated from the rest of my life, hanging over the days with a dull ache like a phantom limb? What happened when the road came to an end? I knew the things I wanted and they weren't special things. They were ordinary things, but I knew them, and I knew who I wanted them to be with. But we had tried. We had tried before. What else did I have? I had my job.

I walked back to the bureau and dialed my editor at home.

"I don't want to miss the days before the debate. I want to cover the buildup. I'm the best reporter to cover the buildup. I have the best connections. But I'll fly to Berthold the morning after it's over. You can get someone to cover for me. I'll stay down there until I know it doesn't make any more sense."

I heard her take a deep breath. "Good."

"Ellen," I said, "Kelly hasn't called me back. If I don't get a chance, tell her I'm sorry."

I set the telephone down and then despite myself there was a moment when I almost dialed Robin. I held the phone and it seemed as if it would be so easy, as if I could step through a door into a world where the rules would change. I wanted so badly to believe it could happen. But I had just rededicated myself to the truth.

VI.

THE CRANE for President campaign ran its first attack ad the following week, a thirty-second spot that opened with a black-and-white shot of a school in Wyoming where chemicals seeping into the water had left twenty-seven children seriously ill. The ad went on to tie the administration to one of the worst groundwater pollution cases in the nation's history. The spot ran in the West and was paid for by an independent political organization, maintaining the tissue-thin fiction that the campaign was not responsible. It could have provoked a backlash, but the press, which can rarely think of more than one thing at a time, was already caught up in the countdown to the debate.

Those who managed Crane's campaign used their success with the ad to press for more changes, and so there came a night when he sat in a hotel room watching a chart of the public's affection for his every word displayed on a television screen. We are all undone by the vagaries of love, and maybe it was too much to expect him to be different.

They played him a dial poll, in which a selected sample of voters watches a speech or ad on television and registers approval or disapproval by turning hand-held dials. The results are superimposed along the bottom of the videotape, so moment-by-moment emotional reaction can be measured. The possibility that the voters might go home, spend a night thinking about things, and change their minds is a quaint notion to modern political handlers.

Steven Duprey told me this on the condition he could not be identified and the story could not be used until at least a week after the debate, but he told it well. Crane with his tie undone and his feet up, sitting in an easy chair, following the graph climbing and dipping at the bottom of the tape. They played and replayed slightly different wordings he had used while talking about the economy and, as the strange pulse ticked along at the bottom of the screen, Duprey said you could feel Crane's heart reluctantly, inevitably, start to keep time.

"Play it again," he said.

And they did, repeatedly, until they winnowed all the words he had said on character and community down to a handful of sentences, all the words on the economy down to a simple phrase: "Jobs with a future, not a dead end." The tape rolled to an end and Duprey thought Crane might ask to see it again, might have it played over and over like a song that reminds you of the first girl you ever loved.

"Millions and millions of words," Crane said. "And you never know. Amazing."

They waited and he glanced away from the television absently.

"'Jobs with a future.' That's what they want to hear?"

"Yes."

Watching him closely, Steven Duprey thought Crane measured the phrase as if it had to satisfy him in some abstract sense unattached to its message, as if he weighed its worth in some hidden currency. Why is he running? my editor had asked at the very beginning. If I had been there to ponder that question at this moment, the answer would have seemed farther away then ever.

"I'll work it in more often," he said.

Blendin jumped up from the couch. "All right. We don't eat, sleep, shit, smoke or breathe anything but 'Jobs with a future' when it comes to the economy."

"There's one more thing," said Susan Douglas, his chief pollster.

They slid another tape into the VCR and Angela appeared on the screen. She looked like a china doll behind the podium, but her voice carried as clearly as a wind chime and her olive skin seemed to glow. The graph at the bottom of the screen soared giddily to the top and stayed there. Crane smiled.

"We know Angela prefers to stay out of the limelight," Susan said. "But the public loves her. They love everything about her. How tiny she is. How she looks. The way her voice sounds. I don't know that she has to do much more than read the phone book, but it would be nice to get her out front more. It's less than ten weeks now."

"She's not comfortable with it," Crane said. "She's had a hard career and she would just as soon not become a center of attention."

"It could help," Blendin said. "You wanna see the tape again?"

Crane stared at the blank television.

"I'll talk to her, but we're not going to push. We'll do what she wants."

He stood up to leave and the room came to informal attention. He pushed back the veil of exhaustion long enough to smile slyly.

"Jobs without a future. Like the vice presidency."

So he went out drawn in bolder and simpler lines, but I am not sure any of us noticed, so eagerly did we look ahead. The days before the debate were spent looping across the Midwest, our pace slowed to give Crane time to prep. We rolled through Ohio State University, the University of Wisconsin, and other places that melt together into a long sunny afternoon with the waving pennants, glinting coronets and martial foot-stomping of a college football rally. We were the home team everywhere, and there was only one dark moment I can remember.

In Paducah, Kentucky, the buses had stopped in a light rain when something hit the window next to Stuart's seat. He jumped at the same time I became aware of the chant. A red stain ran down his window, bleeding pink in the rain. Stuart settled back in his seat, running his fingers down his long nose as more blood hit other windows, plastic bags exploding with a sodden thump. On the side of the street, the signs with the fetuses bobbed up and down like an angry mob while the protesters beneath them stood oddly motionless behind the police line, only their mouths and their arms moving.

"This is a bit much," Stuart said, returning with theatrical aplomb to the *Atlantic Monthly*.

The reporter from the local radio station was unsettled. "I don't get it. Why does he make them so mad?"

Nathan leaned forward from the seat behind them. "Hey, he's a Catholic boy. Even went to a Catholic school. That makes him a traitor to the faith.

175

Plus, he conned them when he was a congressman. You go back and look at his speeches, and he's talking about how uncomfortable he is *personally* with abortion. You know who Daniel Smith is? The head of Shepherds of the Unborn? That's the group you see out there, mostly. He thought he had Crane's assurance he was with them." Nathan smiled. "He was everything to everybody then. It wasn't until he got to the Senate and he had to vote that they smoked him out. They thought they'd been betrayed. Smith thought *he'd* been betrayed."

The radio reporter stared at the diluted blood pooled in his window frame. "They've been blocking a clinic here off and on for six months. Don't you ever wonder how long this can go on?"

Stuart turned a page. "The crusades, young man, lasted three hundred years."

We rode through rural Indiana and then we were back in one of the places we started, but now it was late summer and Iowa was a different country, a quilt of green and gold and black. The buses were parked in a yellow dotted line along a country road, a single cloud floating across their windows as if on a roll of film. Beneath them Robin descended the hill surrounded by a tail of reporters. They came straight toward me and I could hear the conversation clearly.

"So you say you're holding foreign aid to the same level?"

The words rattled out of the mouth of a reporter I had never seen before. He was short with a balding crown, and he jogged alongside Robin to keep up with her long strides, his houndstooth-check sportcoat billowing behind him.

"The same or a couple hundred million dollars lower," Robin said. "But basically the same. That's right."

"Then I think you've got a bit of a problem," the reporter announced.

They stopped, the other reporters circling around Robin and her interrogator. He held a crumpled copy of the Crane budget outline in his hands. His pen scrolled down a page until it came to a line where it hovered.

"Because you say on *this* page that you plan to raise spending on food aid to the Third World by one billion dollars."

The pen came up and pointed at Robin's chest. The other reporters waited. Robin's eyes fell to the pen and then climbed to the balding reporter's face. Her smile was small, contained, but I saw clearly how much she was enjoying herself.

"That's because the Food for Peace program, which handles food aid, doesn't come out of the foreign aid budget. It comes out of agriculture. And we make corresponding cuts in an export subsidy program to pay for it."

She gently bent the pen earthward.

"That's all right, though," she said. "It was a good question. Keep us on our toes."

When they were gone, the reporter in the houndstooth-check coat shuffling along defeatedly, Robin sidled over and stood looking at the stage beside me. We watched a blond girl in white cowboy boots toss a silver baton into the air.

"You've been avoiding me?" she asked.

"No."

"I thought you might call in Washington."

"I almost did."

She looked out at the countryside and nodded.

"What a beautiful day," she said.

The baton twirler was replaced by a quartet of teenage girls dressed as bobby-soxers. Three of the girls began singing doo-wop, moving in synchronized dance steps.

"Tonight," Robin said.

"Maybe."

She looked at me out of the corner of her eye. "I have to fly back to Illinois for a week right after the debate. I won't be around for a while."

The fourth member of the quartet, a thin slip of a girl, wide-eyed with a touching wisp of a nose, stepped to the front of the stage. She reached for the microphone with long gawky arms. In a crystalline voice she sang, "I found my thrihhill . . . on Blueberry Hihhill . . ."

"What happens when all this is over?" I asked.

Robin's eyes lost their focus and she lifted a hand up to block the sun, as if the future was floating out there somewhere in the back of a wheat field in Iowa.

"What do you think you'll do after the campaign? Are they going to ask you to cover the White House?"

"They might."

"The big job, Cliff. A thousand years ago I thought you were headed somewhere and now it turns out you were."

The girl on stage was singing each note in a voice without hesitation or doubt. The crowd stood transfixed, as if watching someone on a high wire.

"I hate the White House press corps," Robin said. "I hate the whole fucking attitude. The shallow cynicism. The way they whine. When one of them turns up on the plane, it's like having somebody from the court of Louis the Fourteenth on board."

"I promise not to whine."

"I'll be there too. On the other side."

"Just like now."

"No. It'll be different. You know that. *This*"—she waved a hand to take in the stage, the crowd, the press tent.—"this is summer camp. The White House will be different. Different sides day after day. Different choices."

"I'm not on any side. I'm on your side."

Robin smiled sadly. "Cliff, you are the infinite and eternal bystander. You're God's man on the sidelines."

"That is such bullshit. Give me a chance."

She stood there pale in the sunlight, and I wanted to grab her and shake her until she understood.

"They're calling for you," she said. "Listen."

My name drifted up from the press tent, repeated over and over again.

"Wait," I said. "I'll be right back."

I hurried down the hill and grabbed the phone handed to me by a volunteer who stepped back with a queer, uncertain grin.

"I spoke to Bushmill," Kelly said. "It just happened."

I tried to concentrate. "Good."

"He's this crusty old guy, with a face like splintered wood. He looks like a cowboy who's been out in the sun for fifty years. He comes into this committee hearing and he tells them in this gravelly voice, 'We need twenty-three million dollars worth of roads, seven million dollars worth of sewer system and two years of deferred property taxes or we're on our way to

South Dakota. That's my testimony, gentlemen. I'll answer any questions.' It was great. You should have seen the committee."

"So you spoke to him."

"I caught him in the hall afterward. I knew I probably wouldn't get more than a couple of questions. I don't think he's wasted two words in his entire life. So I decided to go for broke. I said, 'Mr. Bushmill, I wanted to talk to you about the money you lent Thomas Crane shortly after his mother died.' And *he* said, 'That's a private matter.'"

She paused to let the remark sink in.

"So he turns and I grab his elbow. 'Just one question,' I said. 'Did he pay you back?' And he said, 'That money was never intended to be paid back. But as a matter of fact, he did.' Then his attorney stepped between us and he disappeared down the hall."

She waited for me to say something.

"Cliff? Do you *understand?* I got him to confirm. He gave him money back then! There's an early and private financial relationship nobody knows about."

"That's great. Good job."

"Thanks." Her voice was full of gratitude. "Well? What next? Do you think maybe you should ask Crane about it directly?"

"Let me go to Berthold after the debate. Let's do that first."

"All right." I could feel her impatience. She was out in the field and she had the scent. "I've been thinking about this a lot," she said. "I've been thinking about what you told me about his childhood. How poor they were. I've gone back to the earliest things I can find about his finances. I don't think it adds up, Cliff. You're right. He had too much money too soon."

"All right," I said. "We'll talk more when I get to Berthold. You did good, Kelly. You did great."

I was looking up the hill but Robin was gone. I stood there and people stared as they passed until I realized I was still holding the phone by my ear, the single unbroken note of the dead line ringing like a car alarm into the summer air.

That night we came to what had to be the last county fair held that summer. We came around a bend and you could see the grandstand and the midway with a Ferris wheel turning in a bright circle of colored lights. We parked in a field of dried mud and when we got out of the buses there were cheerleaders waiting at the edge of the crowd. "Hey hey press this way," they chanted, and we followed them. There was another group waiting at each corner, high school girls, faces flushed in the unexpected heat, cheering us on, pointing us toward the bright globe of yellow light that was the grandstand.

I was filling in for Nathan on pool duty, so I found my way to the stage and identified myself to the Secret Service. The head agent was balding and his forehead struggled up the great dome of his skull in increasingly red folds as if he were a thermometer on the verge of exploding. He was about fifty and loved to quote from U2's *Achtung Baby*. He lifted an eyebrow and considered me with a mild skepticism I did not understand.

"There's a member of the staff looking for you," he said. "That blonde with the legs and the walk."

"Where should I stand when he's on stage?" I asked.

"Offstage to the right," he said, still considering me oddly. "I'll be nearby."

So I stood behind the stage waiting for Crane to appear and watched the Ferris wheel turn lazily below the moon and listened to the hoarse shouts of barkers, the hollow pop of balloons and air rifles. I could smell sausages frying and caught the sweet scent of cotton candy. When Crane mounted the stairs at the back of the platform and passed through the door in the backdrop, I took my place to the right of the stage. I was looking up at him from an oblique angle and not thinking of anything when Robin peered over my shoulder.

"There's something I want you to see," she said.

"I've got pool duty."

She smiled mysteriously. "It's okay. You'll be fine."

We walked to the back of the stage, and she led me up the stairs, past two Secret Service agents. It was dark and the sound of Crane's voice was muffled. The head of the Secret Service detail loomed in the darkness as large as a planet. He saw Robin, considered me speculatively again, as if trying to decide if I could possibly be worth it, and then nodded curtly to her. There was a narrow passage between an outer wall and the backdrop facing the audience. She took my hand and led me between the two, into darkness broken by the narrowest slivers of light. I could feel my muffled heart pounding. Robin's mouth came up to my ear and whispered. "Right where my hand is. *Look.*" I saw her finger pass like a shade over one of the slivers and I felt her leaning against me, steering me toward this star.

I pressed my cheek against unfinished wood, seeing only an opalescent blur. Then my eye adjusted, and I was staring over someone's shoulder. Beyond us a lip of a stage, a bank of stage lights, and between them, floating in a blue haze, faces, row upon row of faces hanging in flattened perspective, watching with a blurred, identical expectation. The bleachers behind them were lost in the darkness, but the shadows moved with palpable significance and you could feel the larger crowd out there, feel them perched above you, pressing on you, all watching, all waiting.

I was so close to Crane that when he turned his head, I had the odd sensation of having slipped inside his skin. When he spoke his voice made my spine crawl, the way you could see it ripple across the faces floating out there.

"This is how it is," Robin whispered in my ear. "Every day . . ."

Crane said something, I missed exactly what, and it was like watching flowers unfold: smiles widened, eyes danced, heads snapped up, chins bobbed as if on a spring, hands rocked back and forth in repressed fervor. They were tied to your heart, hanging on every hesitation in your breath.

Then Crane said something funny, and the tether snapped and they were all laughing, loving him more for knowing when to let go. His head turned and I saw his strong chin and long forehead edged against the lights. A thin sheen of sweat glistened along the side of his jaw. His expression was detached, but with a distant melancholy, the melancholy of mysteries removed, the melancholy of the final connection.

I could feel Robin's lips brush my ear. "This is how it feels."

I snapped back from the hole, blind. She moved me gently aside and her breath caught as she lowered her eye to the vision. When she was done, we slid back out of the passage. The Secret Service agent eyed us with clinical pity as we passed. When we were back on the ground at my assigned station, the carnival spinning on in mad neon circles behind us, Robin took a nervous breath and ran her hand through her tousled hair.

"I just wanted you to see. I wanted you to see what he means."

I felt my heart pounding. There had been something too intimate about what we had done, like peering into a keyhole and catching someone you have always respected undressing before a mirror.

"I never told you this," Robin said, "but after my brother died, I had the same dream over and over again. It was night and I was walking up the steps to my parents' house. The big one down by the river. But it wasn't my family. I was a visitor, going to see my brother. I'd be walking up the steps and across the porch and I'd be happy, because I'd be thinking, I'm going to see Tim. And I'd walk through the door and my parents would be in the middle of the room crying and then I'd remember he's dead. And it would be this terrible sense of loss, all over again. Every time. Like it had just happened."

She ran her hand through her hair and there was part of her that looked ready to run and part of her ready to stand and fight.

"You want so much to believe in something at times like that," she said. "And what do you have but other people. And they're bound to let you down."

"Listen—"

She grabbed my arms.

"Listen to that."

The crowd was cheering, the sound sweeping up and filling the grandstand like some vast migration of souls taking wing.

"I hear them," I said.

"But *listen* to them."

"I am—"

"No. You're not. Don't you see how much this is? Don't you see how special? Don't you see how lucky we are to be here, right now, together?"

"This ends," I said.

"Yes! It does."

I heard Crane coming down the stairs. The crowd swung around the stage to get close to him and the line of cops behind Robin swayed like a wind-blown daisy chain.

"I asked too much from the future before," Robin said. "I don't want to make that mistake again."

"We don't have to," I said. "We have nothing to be afraid of—"

Robin smiled at the sky. "Oh Christ, Cliff."

Crane swept around the corner, the crowd calling to him, moving, trying to get ahead of him for a chance to touch his hand, meet his eyes, tell their story.

"You've got to go to work," Robin said.

I slipped into his wake and it pulled me toward the crowd. I turned once to look for Robin but she had disappeared. I stood behind Crane while he worked his way down the rope line. A dozen hands reached for each of his as he bent into the crowd. They struggled and shifted to be near him and you could hear their voices like a ragged chorus of children calling for his attention. He shook hands, slapped palms, held children, bent deep into the tangled mass of bodies to touch the fingers of a particularly devout woman while the Secret Service agents in front and behind him watched apprehensively, eyes flitting back and forth. Heat rose from the bodies and his shirt turned a stained gray as he moved down the line. All the time he kept up a steady monologue *how are you . . . need your support . . . thanks . . . we will, we will . . . how are you . . . thanks . . . how are you . . .* until a man stopped him with a story and he listened while the crowd knotted around them, and he spoke quietly to the person who had poured out his heart before moving on.

We worked our way to the end of the rope line and then we reached the parking lot and he turned and waved at the crowd streaming toward their cars. His face was red and sweat made him blink. The cheerleaders were climbing into a bus and he watched them file past, glancing at him with shyly excited eyes as they climbed through the door.

He took it all in as if it had belonged to him since birth, his eyes registering that faint disappointment, as if the world could never quite measure up, and I found myself angry at his presumption, the false sense of ordination, as if the world came with promises for anyone.

"How many of these people, Cliff, do you think can tell you more than ten words of what I just said?"

The words left my perception in ruin. I could cause him trouble by repeating that line. It was so exposed, an expression of such essential trust, that I stood ashamed of myself.

"I have this sense sometimes," Crane said, "of someone leaving from the back of Lincoln's Second Inaugural saying, 'Well, he's tall and he wears a good hat, but what's all that stuff about the bondsmen and the lash?'"

"And you don't even have the hat," I managed.

He was watching the crowd, but he smiled.

"I don't want the hat."

"What do you want, Senator?"

He hesitated and I thought for a moment he might answer, and I would have the whole thing explained to me.

"Malice toward none," he intoned. "Charity toward all. Firmness in the right as God gives us the strength to see the right."

"Charity toward all."

My voice sounded like the voice of the dead. Crane placed a hand on my shoulder, and I could tell he wanted to say something that would help, but he didn't know where to start, which only made the gesture all the more intimate.

"Or a few words half as good as those, anyway," he said. "But maybe you'll write the phrase people remember this time."

"I don't think what I do is that grand, Senator."

John Starke was leading an elderly couple our way, the woman in a formal blue dress with a string of pearls, the man in an undertaker's suit, both of them moving with great dignity, as if they were concluding the essential pilgrimage of their lives.

Crane smiled at them, welcoming them forward, and then, in the brief moment of their passage, he faced me and said, "Don't ever sell yourself short, Cliff. It's the first mistake people from places like ours make."

I watched him until he was safely in the limousine and then I couldn't find the pool van, so I climbed into the regular press bus. Nathan was sitting in a front seat, frantically going through his notebooks, nothing but empty pages riffling by under the dome light. I heard Myra's stifled laughter as I took a seat in back.

I watched the flat, black country pass and found myself thinking about the day I realized I held the power to shape the story of someone's life. It was my first job, with a weekly newspaper in Rothko, Montana. I had put the paper out the night before and had taken the morning off to golf in a light rain. I had just teed off on the first hole when the police car came rolling out of the mist. I walked to the fence and talked to the chief through his rolled-down window.

"There's been some kind of accident on the railroad tracks," he said. "Thought you'd want to know."

I loaded the Nikon in the car, ratcheting the film into the camera carefully, afraid it would thread improperly. I drove to the center of town where the railroad tracks ran past the grain elevator and a long warehouse the color of ash. The ambulance sat between the two buildings. Men from the city rescue crew, wearing elbow-length green rubber gloves, walked along the track, bending now and then to pick something up. The rain was falling just hard enough to sting my eyes. I watched the grain and coal dust that covered the siding turning to paste. I saw two members of the rescue crew coming up the track. They carried a heavily sagging green bag, one at each end, moving as if something fragile was inside. They came partway and one of them raised a hand and they set the bag down. The one in front bent over and picked up something that was a deep bruised red, heavy as a stone, a tattered green strip of cloth with part of a foot attached. He set it into the bag and zipped it closed. He stood and they both stood without lifting the bag for a moment, the man who had done the work holding his arms out so the rain hit his gloves and the rubber fingers began to drip water the color of weak tea.

"Franklin Nies," he shouted. "Sat down in front of a coal train. We talked to the engineer on the radio. Didn't even know he'd hit anything."

I was new in town but I knew Franklin Nies. He had owned the hardware store for thirty years before turning it over to his son. He had a boxful of souvenirs from his time in World War II that he loved to show strangers: a strange Italian sash picked up at Anzio, an old German helmet, an officer's sword.

I took pictures of the ambulance and the men working in the rain. I drove to the home of Franklin Nies's son. He had been called by the police and he was there with his wife, waiting quietly. He didn't have any idea why his father would sit down on the tracks. He said his father had been going down to watch the trains for weeks, but they never thought anything about it. "I didn't think he was sad," he said. "He seemed the same."

The rain was falling harder by then. I went back to the office, and I was shaking out my jacket when one of the older women who wrote our local social notes asked me what had happened. I told her and she shook her head.

"Poor Franklin. What are you going to do?"

I was twenty-one and full of my father's ideals. The truth was the truth was the truth. "I'm going to write a story," I said.

She looked at me through her owl-rim glasses. "It's a shame you have to tell people," she said. "Franklin did so much. He was too many things to be remembered as a suicide."

Too many things. The bus jounced up the gravel road. We were on a curve and I could see the whole unlikely caravan strung out ahead, police lights, headlights, tail lights. We were the entire illuminated world. The windows in Crane's bus had a faint opaque pumpkin light, a reading lamp on inside, perhaps.

I listened to laughter in the front of our bus, a soft voice telling a story I could not make out, a story that seemed, as I listened, to be the story of a life, a midnight confessional rolling on and on in somber, then hushed, then buoyant tones, punctuated now and again by a companion's gentle laughter. Too many things. We are all too many things and most of us are lucky enough to die without an epitaph. We are all too many things and who was I to decide what mattered and what didn't? We are all too many things and I couldn't put the world inside my own heart in order.

The bus turned onto pavement with a rocking motion like a boat, and then we picked up speed and the voice in front was lost in the sound of the pavement thrumming beneath us.

VII.

SPECULATION about the debate grew all week until it reached the kind of frenzy that only the American press, careening downhill like an out-of-control circus train, can manage. The two candidates traveled toward Detroit in a narrowing circle of opinion that flickered across channels, through newsprint and back into the airwaves until it swallowed its own tail of argument and prophecy. So the conventional wisdom was established: Thomas Crane was young and what was there, really, in his record to justify his popularity? Surely, the president would take apart that record and then proceed, with all the gravity of his office and his years in public service, to shred the magic carpet upon which Crane sailed. After all, the president had the *history* with the public, and if there was a strangely unsettled sense in the land of things gone wrong, the plain facts were that it was not that bad. He deserved more credit than he was getting. The president, the conventional wisdom proclaimed, simply had to remind the public of his record.

Thomas Crane had to prove he belonged on the stage.

I arrived at the Ford Auditorium to find Myra eying a half-dozen members of the White House press corps, who had settled around Duprey with the lazy disdain of ladies-in-waiting commandeering a scullery maid.

"Just kill me if I ever get like that," she said.

"With pleasure."

She was wearing at least seven metal bracelets on her left arm, charms dangling in a hysterical tinkle: toy spaceships, Christmas ornaments, silver poodles, Mickey Mouse ears, a peppermint-striped Eiffel Tower, crucifixes, stars, Elvis, a half-dozen Thomas Crane buttons. I was transfixed.

"What did you do? Hold up a five-and-dime store?"

She held her arm out in front of her

"You know how Nathan is always locking his briefcase when he leaves the press room? You know how incredibly anal that is?"

"I hadn't noticed actually."

"Well, he does, cowboy, and it is. Except . . ."

She fingered two small keys on the third bracelet.

"Not anymore," she said.

"What if it's already locked shut?"

"Oh, don't tease me."

The president's press secretary stepped into the room. The floor tilted and all kinds of things slid his way, reporters, cameras, microphones. Myra and I held onto the edge of a table as they tumbled past. The flood trickled to a close with those who had been enjoying the free buffet in another room. They struggled by holding half-eaten sandwiches, chewing frantically as they fumbled for tape recorders and notebooks. At that moment, the televisions lined up across the front of the room came to life with a clap, and an empty stage with a flag hanging above two glass podiums was repeated in shimmering perfection on screen after screen.

"God," Myra said.

"Yes."

Two men face each other on a stage. A nation is watching. They stand fifteen feet apart but it looks like more on television. One of the men is tall and slender and, although he has aged in the last six months, could be said to look youthful. The other is shorter but carries himself with a solemnity that lends substance to his appearance. His hair is a fine silvery white and his long face has attractive lines like a well-broken-in bookbinding. He has a reedy voice, but very narrow, very blue eyes that have held him in good stead through the years with the voters.

There is a sign and an American flag behind the two of them. There is a panel of three reporters at the far left of the stage. The floor has been polished and shines with a moonlike gleam. The curtain is blue. The audience is out there behind the lights, never seen, but heard often and felt at every moment. But really there is only these two men all alone, two men and the light and the silence that is the held breath of a nation, two men and their words.

The president speaks with the confidence of one who has done enough to know what more awaits him. He speaks with the dignified anger of one who does not feel he should have to remind the nation of what he has tried to do. He turns to his opponent with the look of the circling hawk who is waiting for movement in the snowy field below.

Thomas Crane seems oddly off balance, his smile a bit too bright, the measured clarity of that midwestern voice suddenly too thin, without deeper chords of authority and experience. He answers the first questions about the economy and foreign affairs with words he has used a dozen times and, for the first time, they seem too pat. He stands with his hands folded slightly below his waist and it strikes one how thin he has become, how the campaign is paring him down. His blue suit hangs square from his shoulders. He reaches up now and places a hand on the glass podium, the fingers long and thin.

"I'm glad you asked that," he says and it sounds too eager. "I disagree with the president," he says and it sounds self-conscious. "The problem is not as complicated as you make it sound," he says and, for the first time, one wonders.

The press is in the balcony, scribbling on their knees. Myra is seated two seats down from me. She leans across two annoyed reporters and whispers, "Pretty boy needs to land a punch."

Crane is being asked about welfare reform. He listens with one elbow resting in the palm of his other hand, with his finger absently running across his lip. Standing as he is, he seems all angles, a good-looking suit hung on a wire hanger. He smiles and, despite the gray seeping into his temples, despite the melancholy in the back of his eyes, he looks a little too much like an honor student who knows he has the answer.

"As you know, Peter," he says to the television anchorman on the panel, "I have a detailed proposal that will turn America's welfare program into a job training program . . ." And he is off for five minutes into a monologue sprinkled with facts and numbers.

When Crane finishes the president is staring at the glass of his podium. He waits several seconds, letting precious time elapse; when he looks up a thin smile gleams like a razor and his eyes are narrow and filled with the light of the hunt.

"It's nice to hear that Senator Crane has another *plan*," he says. "As near as I can tell Senator Crane has a *plan* for everything, including the common cold." He turns his head then, considering Crane the way a wise old sailor might consider somebody fumbling with the canvas in a stiff breeze. "I listen to you, Tom, and I keep remembering that story about the train trying to go up the hill, *I think I can, I think I can*." After the crowd stops tittering, he continues: "It's nice to have *plans*, but it's better to have accomplishments. Let me tell you what this administration has already *done* and what we're going to *do* over the next four years . . ."

Crane blinks and for a moment I remember the deer staring at us through the window. Myra leans across the seats, ignoring the protests. "He looks like Bambi after they shot his mother," she says as if she can read my mind.

The debate moves on to the direct exchange. You can feel the crowd's anticipation. On stage the president waits with the impatience of a boxer who knows the last round ended with his opponent's knees buckling. The lines around his eyes are gathered. He leans forward slightly at the podium, impatient to be done with this intrusion upon greater matters. He brushes aside Crane's first thrust on foreign affairs with a plainspoken lecture on the situation in Eastern Europe that leaves his challenger's platitudes about human rights sounding like the musings of an eighth-grade class president. They move on to economics and the president's narrowly aristocratic lips cannot help themselves, they curl into a grimly satisfied smile as he recounts his personal negotiations at the last economic summit and how they led to an agreement lowering trade barriers throughout much of the industrialized world. The lights on stage are so bright it is a world without shadows, a world with no room for hesitation.

Crane stares at his podium, as if he has lost something there, his dark eyebrows arched in mildly bewildered surprise. He seems young, unfocused, uncertain.

"I'd like to turn to the child healthcare bill that died last year in the

Senate," he says. "As you know, the bill would have guaranteed that no American child would be without healthcare, regardless of how poor, or how rich—"

The president nods. One finger taps impatiently at the edge of the glass. "We had hoped that bill could be passed," he says. "It wasn't perfect—there were concerns about cost—but it was unfortunate that the committee voted it down."

"You had hoped the bill could be passed . . ." Crane's voice trails off.

"That's right." The president's voice has an edge to it. "There were those who said the bill was a budget buster, and we were worried about that. But nothing is more important than our nation's children. It wasn't perfect. But we knew something needed to be done. We were working on a version that could be passed in committee and make it through Congress."

The president turns, so he is no longer looking at Crane but into the crowd; his lean face softens, his cropped gray hair transformed by the light into a grandfatherly haze. I imagine families across America leaning forward on their couches.

"I have seven grandchildren myself," he says. "And although they've been lucky enough to grow up in families where they're well taken care of, I know some of their friends haven't been as fortunate." He smiles. "You know, children don't care if their friends are rich or poor. They just know who they really like. In that way, they treat everybody equally. Those of us who are older could learn something from them. As adults, those of us who have been lucky in life shouldn't forget those children who haven't."

He steps back from the podium with the auditorium, and maybe the country, in the palm of his hand. Crane is motionless, his head hanging on his chest so he appears to be lost in thought. A world spun of silver words and threads of faith until it took shape complete with continents, oceans and mountain ranges is tumbling like a broken web in his silence. The camera is on him, and I wonder what it looks like in close-up, this collapse of a beautiful, hypnotizing shell.

"There are eleven million children in the country without any kind of healthcare," Crane says absently, as if unable to veer from a prepared text. "The legislation would have guaranteed coverage to all of them in the case of serious illness. Catastrophic care, they call it, I guess."

191

The president is considering him with pity. You can feel the crowd shifting nervously and out there in a million living rooms you can imagine the fallen chin and downturned eyes trapped tightly in the merciless box. When he looks up it is a surprise.

"Angela and I haven't been lucky enough to have any children," Crane says, "but I guess children do know a lot of things. One of the things we expect them to know is the difference between right and wrong, the difference between the truth and a lie—"

"Hold it—" the president says.

"—You know David Yates, a reporter for the *Washington Post*, Mr. President? You once called him one of the best, most reliable reporters in Washington. Yates is writing a book about the battle over children's healthcare and in that book, which is due to be finished in a month or two, he got Senator D'Amato to speak about what happened."

The auditorium is silent. The president leans toward Crane, bent at the waist as if preparing to take a blow to the stomach, his mouth half-open. In the infinite space of this moment, Crane glances at the papers in front of him.

"Let me just read to you what Senator D'Amato told Mr. Yates: 'It came down to my vote, and I thought the bill was flawed, but I might support it. The White House let me know they needed it killed quietly. It was a tough vote and I decided I wasn't going to give it away. We needed their support for a half a billion dollars worth of work on the thrustate freeway and I thought, If I'm going to do this, I'm going to get their support for the damn highway. So that's what it came down to. They wanted the bill held up in committee, and I wanted the highway, and we worked out a deal—'"

"Now wait a minute—"

"—Let me read you just a little more: 'They'—he means you, Mr. President—'thought the bill would wreck their budget plan, but the White House wanted it both ways, kids and bankers.'"

He says the last word without disdain but with a wistful sadness at the absurdity of the comparison. I have seen him so many times under so many circumstances that when he looks up finally to consider the president, I can picture how he must appear on the screen, this tall man with something lonely in the too-perfect planes of his face, facing an older, less honest man, without anger, but also without sympathy.

"Maybe we *can* learn something from children," Crane says. "And it starts with the truth."

The word breaks a dam. I hear Myra whoop beside me. The auditorium rustles and hums. The president coughs once, violently.

"Bullshii—nonsense! How dare you question my integrity? We supported the bill and we will support it when it comes back next session. I haven't seen the book you're discussing and I don't believe a—"

"I have the pages right here," Crane says. "I'm happy to share them."

He leaves his podium, walks slowly across the stage, calmly breaking all convention, and places a piece of paper on the president's podium. He holds it between his thumb and forefinger and it flaps gently in his hand as he crosses the space between them. When he lets it go, the paper settles with a swanlike swoop on the glass. Speechless, the president watches it fall.

After the handlers had lined up to spin us all in the front of the press room, after all our deadlines had passed, we piled into the buses and headed out across Detroit, a mad babble of voices bouncing off the walls as we tried to unwind. "I thought he was sunk, man, who knew . . ." "*President* Thomas Crane, never in a hundred years . . ." "The difference between right and wrong, the difference between a truth and a lie, Christ . . ." "I tell you, the president is going to see that paper falling in his dreams." "Dreams? Hell, we're all going to see that paper falling on the tube every day until the election."

Nathan rocked back and forth on his knees as he addressed me and Stuart in the seat behind him. "I think . . . he may . . . have done it."

A crowd was waiting in the parking lot when we reached the hotel. It spilled out into the street and down the block. Crane had already stepped up onto the hood of his limousine to address them. His coat was off, his shirt a ghostly white below the mystery of his face. He raised his voice to cut through the clamor, pulling the words up out of his stomach. "As you know, we've just come from the debate. The press has yet to render their verdict, but I think I did all right." Laughter. "I think we found out something about the president tonight."

The sound that swept through the crowd was a cross between a growl and a mutter of sad recognition. I leaned against the bus and looked at all their faces, sweating, dazed, expectant, a sea of faith reaching back into the darkness. Robin stepped in front of me.

"I leave for Illinois in five minutes," she said. "The car's waiting."

I nodded. Her cheeks were flushed and she radiated the triumphant heat all Crane's staff had in the press room.

"But I'll be back in five days."

She stepped closer and I could feel her rapid breath against my neck.

"I can see you then."

"Then," I said.

She stepped back and pushed her hair nervously out of her eyes.

"Yes. Then. I want to. *Then*. Doesn't that matter?"

The crowd around us was laughing, faces antic with joy. The sound echoed, rolled back inside my head, settled into a sibilant hiss of derision.

"Of course."

She searched my face hopefully and I saw her push through confusion and frustration to settle on a careful suspension of judgment. "All right," she said and turned to leave.

"I may have to write a tough story soon," I said.

I watched her thin back and the way her weight stopped on her forward heel and the graceful way she swung my way.

"You've written tough stories before."

"I mean a harmful story."

Suddenly I was a distant figure moving across a foreign landscape.

"Your car's waiting," I said.

Her hand ran up into her hair and tangled itself.

"I'm sorry," I said.

She started to speak and then stopped and backed up along the buses, watching me as if I was about to disappear before her eyes. A horn honked and she turned and ran another bus length before spinning around.

"Call me! Cliff! Call me first!"

When she was gone I looked up and Crane was still speaking, shouting to be heard without a microphone, his exhausted voice rasping harshly near the end, sealing the covenant with every word. "I may make mistakes. I may not always succeed. But I can promise you one thing. I will never lie to you. I will always let you know where I stand. I will always let you know who I *am!*"

God, they made noise then. I felt it pulling at my chest, lifting me up and out of myself in a rush toward this pale ghost of a man standing above us. I stood with my back against the bus and wished Robin was still here. I wanted so badly to share this moment, this consummation. I wanted her to know that I was present, that I heard, that I felt. That I could believe.

VIII.

I CAUGHT a plane to Springfield the next morning and before noon I was heading down a familiar highway. The day was bright and clear, but as I approached Berthold the hills and fields became freighted with the chill of winter. Even with the corn swaying top-heavy in the breeze, the wind had a sharp edge, and despite the sun and swaths of green and gold, the knocked-about houses looked forlorn. Summer had no power here. There was too much borrowed memory clinging like December frost to my vision of the town.

I stomped on the porch of Bill Crane's house when he didn't answer my knock, but there was no one home. I walked around back and tried the door to the kitchen, then stood for a moment listening to the wind in the cornfield. On the far side of the field, the stand of trees around the abandoned mine gathered darkness despite the day.

The bar was empty. I sat in one of the booths and sipped a Coke. The television was on above the bar and I watched Crane tour part of Cincinnati with the governor of Ohio at his side. Myra floated briefly in the background, a square-brimmed black hat lending her the air of a vaudeville gangster. The sound was down and I felt as if I had snuck outside my own life and was peering back in through the keyhole. Crane stood in front of a storefront; you saw black faces behind a rope, and then a woman was rowing a canoe across a kitchen sink. The bartender turned her head and smiled.

More than twenty years ago Crane needed money. A few years later he came home twice without telling anyone. Six months ago he lied about it. Latrelle Gregory raised the possibility he had been bought, but there was no proof. But he had gone home unexpectedly a third time. I had a phone record that proved it. He had gone and he had also visited a clinic in the town of Phillips, which was near Roger Bushmill's estate. Where did this leave me? On a barstool in Berthold about to sift through the ashes of his past one more time. Comb through any life long enough and you will find enough to build a mystery, enough to imagine anything you want about your subject. We are all saints and all demons when viewed from the proper angle. We are all beyond hope and worthy of redemption.

The ultimate and eternal bystander, she said. Was that fair, Robin? Would that be the lingering, last word when all this ends? Because this ends. You said so yourself. Yes, it does.

CNN returned from a commercial and I saw footage of a burning car, shattered windows, a man on his knees, blood pouring from his forehead while strangers taunted him in a semicircle, grotesque shadows dancing across the pavement. Here was another question: What did the crimes of the past matter in the face of the overwhelming need of the present?

"So you missed our little burg?"

Eddie Crane stood above me, heavy blunt-nailed hands hanging awkwardly at his side, shoulders moving with his thick neck as he turned his head to slip my gaze while his square face bent into a shy smile of recognition. He settled onto the stool beside me.

"So what's my famous cousin up to these days?"

"About fifty-seven percent in the polls."

He nodded and glanced at the bartender, who slid a glass under the beer tap.

"Thanks for seeing me again," I said. "I'm sure you've had enough of this."

He reached across the bar and took the glass as it slid toward him, raising and half-emptying it in a swallow.

"You know it's a funny thing, but you people were all over the place at first. Christ, I thought we were going to have to start charging admission. But you know, hardly anybody comes by anymore. It's like this part of the story's been told."

"Did you get the copy of the story I sent you?"

"Yeah. You did a nice job on that. Didn't make fun of us half as much as some of the others."

We sipped our drinks, Eddie waiting patiently as I tried to figure out where to start.

"I'm doing another story like that one," I said, "and I'm just trying to get some new stuff. I've heard from a couple of people that Tom came home to visit when he had to run for the House and the Senate, and yet his brother says he didn't stop by the house, and so I'm just sort of wondering where he went, who he talked to. I thought maybe he stopped to talk to you."

Eddie rubbed his neck, thought for a moment, and shook his head. "We see him at family reunions and things, but he hasn't come to visit us in a long time. I don't remember anything like that. Maybe he went to see some of his big supporters like Roger Amb." He smiled. "The boys with all the money."

"I don't think so. But Amb said he bumped into him. Out on . . ." I pulled my notebook out of my back pocket and flipped it open. "County 123."

Eddie shrugged. "We don't live out on that side of town."

"Do you know who does?"

"Sure. But besides Amb I don't know who he'd be visiting."

"Does that road take you to Phillips?"

"Yeah. That would be the way you'd go. Why?"

"You know anyone he might go to see there? I heard he stopped by the clinic."

He sipped his beer and stared at the bar. Finally, he shrugged his shoulders. "Lots of people up near Phillips. You're paying a lot of attention to a couple of trips a long time ago, aren't you?"

"Just curious. Thought it might be interesting who he talked to for advice back then. It's hard to find something new after a while."

Indirect light came softly through the narrow windows. The two deer heads mounted behind the bar floated in a somnolent haze. On the television children were fleeing across a narrow stone street somewhere far away, a bomb exploding in a silent shower of dust that seemed to push them through the air.

"I remember talking about the time when Tom's mother died and he came home for the funeral," I said. "I've been thinking a lot about how hard that must have been."

Eddie nodded.

"Tom stayed around for a while, right?"

"Yeah, he had all kinds of stuff to take care of. I mean, Bill, he's all right now, but back then you couldn't count on him for a dime."

"What kind of stuff?"

Eddie shrugged shoulders that moved like a pair of frozen hams. He drained the last of his beer and the bartender, leaning forward on her stool, slid another glass under the tap.

"I don't know. He had to get old Johnny—that was his dad—into a vets' hospital. He had to see that somebody took care of the house."

"It must have been hard. I remember you said the family didn't have much money."

"Hell, no."

"How'd they manage, do you know?"

"You mean after she died?"

"Yeah."

"I don't know. Tommy finally got the old man into the hospital up in Springfield and I suppose that took care of it."

"But money for the funeral and everything. How'd they manage all that?"

Eddie sat his beer down and swiveled his head and shoulders to look at me, his eyes strangely small and damp in the center of his broad sunburned face.

"Wasn't much of a funeral," he said.

I drained my Coke and glanced absently at the drowsing bartender, as if my question hardly mattered.

"That's too bad. It sounds like she was quite a woman."

He swiveled back on his stool and pawed his beer glass. I knew I needed to back off for a while.

"You said he spent time with you when he came back?"

"Yeah."

"And your other cousin and a woman, Maureen. An old classmate, right?"

"Mo, yeah, that's right."

I recalled the photograph Bill Crane had shown me, a girl with a sweet smile and a hairdo that bent in two curls under her face. She'd been holding Thomas Crane's arm as they prepared to go to a dance. What where they then, seventeen?

"They dated in high school?"

"A little. They were friends. We were all friends."

We both stared unhappily at dust-encrusted bottles of forgotten liqueurs on a shelf behind the bar.

"I'm just trying to understand a time in his life that seems important," I said. "You read my other story. I've been fair."

Eddie glanced at the drowsing bartender. We were the only customers this early in the afternoon. Perched over his stool, both hands awkwardly in front of him on the counter, he reminded me of a circus bear who has been asked to ride a unicycle. There was some trick expected of him he did not want to perform.

"Yeah," he said finally. "That was the hardest time he had. Just between you and me, that's the only time I ever saw Tom get drunk. We'd go driving and we might get plastered, sit out on the old bridge down by the river and watch the stars. I think he was lonely—he'd left everybody he knew back east—Mo and me were the only friends he really had here anymore. He was never close to that many people, really. I think maybe he cried on her shoulder a bit. Don't use that, 'cried on her shoulder,' okay? I mean, hell, I don't know."

"Maureen Barstow."

"Yeah. She was always sweet. Didn't stay in town much longer than Tom did."

"I don't remember much about her in any stories."

Eddie smiled the kind of sly smile he would never have dared the first time we met, but he knew me a little now, and he was prone to those sudden confidences that erupt awkwardly out of Midwesterners.

"You reporters," he said. "You read each other's stuff and you all come here and ask the same questions. If it ain't in the last story somebody wrote, you don't bother with it."

I felt a weary disappointment in my craft.

"You know where she is now?"

Eddie shifted on his seat. "Haven't talked to Mo in years."

"But you don't know where she lives?"

For a moment I thought he wasn't going to answer. He looked up at me for a long moment and then he shrugged. "In Phillips. Works at the clinic, I believe."

His glass was empty and he was looking at the door.

"Eddie, there's one other thing," I said. "Roger Bushmill lent Tom some money back then, maybe several thousand dollars. You wouldn't know why he needed that, would you?"

He turned his whole body to face me and I had plenty of time to watch the small stones of his eyes slide underwater.

"I don't know a thing about money," he said. "But Tommy wouldn't take a dime if it wasn't right."

Information had no listing for a Maureen Barstow in or near Phillips, but the woman who answered the phone at the community library came up with an address. The town was forty miles down the highway, and it was the middle of the afternoon by the time I found the small bungalow on its postage-stamp lawn burnt crisp in the sun. Phillips was a farming community barely hanging on to life, and Barstow lived on the edge of town in a development of tract homes set down as nakedly as the toy houses on a Monopoly board.

I stood on the concrete step in the glare, considering the solitary crab-apple tree withering on the lawn and the Ford station wagon listing on its bald left tire in the driveway, when the door opened. A teenage girl wearing mirrored sunglasses and a baseball cap popped her gum and then dropped her chin to peer at me over the glasses.

"I'm looking for Maureen Barstow."

Turning her head as if she could hardly be bothered, she shouted, "Mom!" and slid down the steps and toward the car—tall, slim and sullen, I thought, until she glanced up from behind the wheel and smiled briefly and brightly before pulling out of the driveway.

"You should see her when she's in a *bad* mood."

Maureen Barstow stood in the doorway, wiping her hands on a green-and-white striped apron. She was shorter than I would have guessed from photographs taken more than twenty years ago. The girlish prettiness, round cheeks and gentle eyes, had been sculpted by the years into something harder and more handsome, skin tight around a sharp jaw, lined and drawn around slate gray eyes. Her hair was businesslike and short; she wasn't wearing makeup and she smelled like onions.

I told her who I was and she hesitated in the doorway.

"I really won't take long," I said. "I'd be happy to wait around town and do it after dinner if you'd prefer."

The prospect of losing her evening seemed to make up her mind. She stepped back from the door, and I followed her into a kitchen with black-and-white tile and white pine cupboards. A large kettle simmered on the stove and a pile of chopped onions sat on a cutting board. She pulled another onion from a wicker basket. I leaned against the counter.

"Smells good," I said.

"You're from Washington?" She had a surprisingly husky voice. "Have you ever eaten at Bistro Bistro in Shirlington?"

"I don't think so."

She tilted her head toward the kettle. "This is their white chili."

I must have looked surprised, because her broad mouth broke into a smile that seemed equally amused and defensive.

"You didn't expect to find someone out here making chili from Bistro Bistro? The recipe was in *Gourmet*. If you want me to fulfill a midwestern stereotype, I could whip up something with cream of mushroom soup and hamburger."

She chopped the onion with a short precise rocking of the knife back and forth, not bothering to look at what she was doing.

"How old's your daughter?"

"Seventeen. But you're not here to ask me questions about my daughter."

"No."

"What is it you want to know about Tom? Did we date? Yes, briefly in high school. Do I have anything to say about it? No, not really. He was a nice boy. He'll make the country a great president. We're all proud of him in this part of the country, you know."

203

"You knew him later," I said. "When he came back for his mother's funeral."

The knife made the blunt sound of an ax as it moved across the plastic board.

"We were still friends then."

"I guess that was a hard time for him."

She lifted the cutting board to the kettle and pushed the onions with the blade of the knife. They tumbled into the chili in a clump and broth splattered on the stove.

"Damn. His mother had died, his father was sick, his brother was off gallivanting around on his motorcycle. His sister came back for about a day and a half. Yes, you could say it was a hard time for Tom."

She leaned against the counter, arms folded across the apron, eyes red but not crying.

"Is that what you came out here for? To see if his mother's death was a bad time?"

"I'm just trying to understand a period I think is important."

"Really? Two and a half months before the election? Isn't it time to worry about the issues?"

"We have wiser men than I working on the issues."

"Really."

She pulled a paper towel off the roll under the sink and swabbed up the spill on the stove. Her hands were square with pale, businesslike fingers, one wrapped in a bandage. When she had finished, she leaned sideways against the counter. There was something in the way she raised her chin, the way her weight settled on one foot and she cocked the other leg, that reminded me of Robin.

There must have been a look of recognition in my eyes. It had the strangest effect on Maureen Barstow. She seemed terrified, and then slowly she smiled at me, as if maybe I held out the prospect of more understanding than she had expected.

"We were friends once a long time ago," she said. "There's really not much more to say."

"Did he say anything to you about his finances at the time?"

Maureen jumped as if pinched and spun toward the pot.

"Oh damn, I forgot the cumin. You're throwing off my cooking. I don't remember a thing about his finances. Why don't you just tell me what you're after?"

"He was loaned or given some money by a man named Roger Bushmill back then," I said. "And I just wonder why."

She fumbled inside the cabinet above the counter for her cumin, pushing spices and sauces aside. A bottle was in the way and she slammed it upright on the counter. She stopped then, staring into the cupboard, her face red.

"I don't know where it is. It'll be tasteless without cumin."

"Do you know anything about the money?"

"Tom never talked to me about his finances."

"Do you remember him mentioning Bushmill?"

Her hand clenched the cupboard door and she seemed unable to take her eyes off the inside of the cabinet.

"He owns a couple of factories not that far from here," I said. "Crane met him when he was hitchhiking into school as a kid."

She shut the door with a surprising bang.

"It was a long time ago. I don't remember who picked him up from school, for God's sake. I don't remember who he talked about. He was an honest man, that's what I remember."

She stood facing the closed cupboard, her forehead pink right up to her hair, her jaw set.

"I've got to go to the store," she said. "I'm sorry. You'll have to go."

"There's just one other thing," I said. "He came back here before he ran for the House and the Senate and one other time without telling anyone. I know he called you at the clinic the last time. I was just wondering why."

She sagged and her hand fell to the countertop, knocking the soy sauce over. It rolled off the edge of the counter and was falling toward the floor when I caught it. Maureen stared at the bottle in my hand as if waiting for it to explode.

"I don't have anything more to say about Tom," she said. "Good-bye."

Driving back down the highway I watched the sun set, a snarled ball of red that hung squat and heavy on the edge of the earth and then unraveled across the fields. The news came on the radio and I listened to the latest polls. Crane had gained five points off of the debate and, for the first time, analysts were talking about the possibility of a landslide. The president was down south trying to shore up his base, but that's where Crane was headed. The world had been rearranged and he was welcome everywhere. They ran a brief clip of his speech in Ohio and I thought I could hear a note of triumph escaping from deep within that carefully measured and reassuring voice: *In two months we can begin the work of rebuilding the American community* and the rest of the sentence drowned in cheers.

What was it? Was it the mention of money? Was it Bushmill? When had Maureen Barstow started to come unhinged? She had been on edge from the beginning, but that simply could have been the uneasiness of dealing with a reporter. What had started her toppling bottles and slamming doors? I tried to remember what I had said, but I couldn't be sure. The question that undid her, however, was clear. But why? Why shouldn't Thomas Crane call if he was in town? They had been high school friends. That was all she'd had to say. Old friends. A trip through town.

The last of the sun slipped beneath the horizon and the fields and hills went out like a blown match, but the sky flared even brighter, streaks of autumnal orange and vivid blue flung up casually in astonishing beauty. *Don't you see how lucky we are to be here? Don't you see how special all this is?* Of course I do. How could you think I wouldn't understand? How could you believe I can't see? But there are still questions, and maybe there are even answers. I saw a nervous hand falling again and a bottle tumbling toward the floor. I knew I should have let it break—to see what came spilling out.

But I'd wanted to catch it. I'd wanted her to hold herself together. I'd been glad when she told me to leave.

Bill Crane didn't recognize me at first when he opened his door; then an unaffected grin split his square face.

"Minnesota, right?" he said.

"Almost. Montana."

"Montana, Minnesota," he shrugged, rolling his wheelchair backward so I could enter. "I thought all you reporters were through sightseeing in beautiful downtown Berthold."

"Not me. I love the night life."

He laughed as we made the short trip into the living room.

"You know what the big entertainment used to be here twenty years ago?"

"No."

"Train wrecks. The bend used to be too tight on the Illinois Central just south of the cemetery. They'd come around and about once every few months some engineer would get to feeling cocky and take it a little too fast. They'd derail, stuff would spill all over hell and, that night, folks would go help themselves. When my father was a kid there was a time when a car full of Canadian liquor tipped over." Bill laughed, tipping that great big square of a head back. "The whole town was drunk for a week."

"Let's head out there. Maybe we'll get lucky."

He shook his head. "The train doesn't come through here anymore."

He settled in by the Formica table in the corner. Everything was exactly as I remembered, the sagging floors, the faded wallpaper, the crucifixes and motorcycle posters on the walls.

"Not much comes through Berthold at all anymore, except reporters," he said. "And I thought you were about done too."

"Not me," I said. "I've always got more questions."

"I've got one first," Bill Crane said. "How's he holding up out there?"

He had settled his bulk in the chair, looking as stolid as a bust of a British prime minister. But there were bags under his steel blue eyes and a pulsing vein along his temple not present on my earlier visit.

"You worry about him," I said.

He waved a hand and stared with a wounded expression out the window into the dark. "Naah, he's a big boy. I just wondered if they were treating him all right."

"He's holding up good."

I noticed something new on the fridge, visible through the kitchen doorway: dozens of newspaper headlines cut out and taped up—CRANE WINS NEW HAMPSHIRE. ILLINOIS SENATOR EMERGES FROM PACK. DEEP SOUTH UPSET. CRANE ROLLS THROUGH MIDWEST.

GOLDEN STATE SEALS CRANE NOMINATION. DEBATE KNOCK-OUT!—and on and on, crisscrossed and piled on top of each other across half the fridge.

Bill followed my glance. "One for each day of the campaign. Seventy days to go." He winked at me. "Now what was it you wanted?"

"He called you when he was going to run for the House and the Senate, right?"

"That's right."

"Didn't visit, did he?"

He shook his head. "No, I would have remembered that."

"You don't know what else could have brought him back here around then, do you?"

Bill looked at me, trying to decide if a trap was being set. He was a generous man, but there was no confusion about his loyalty. I waved a hand dismissively to take any edge off the question.

"I just heard he was back in the area then, and I was curious why."

"I can't imagine. People get confused about times."

The wooden legs on my chair were uneven. I placed both elbows on the table to steady myself and decided to leave Phillips and Maureen alone for a moment.

"I've been thinking more about when he came back to town after your mother's funeral. Money must have been pretty tight for this family then."

"Hell, money was more than tight. You got to have some money before it can get tight."

Bill's big ragged smile split his face and I knew I wasn't going to lead him on anymore.

"I heard that Roger Bushmill gave or lent him some money back then. Do you know what it was for?"

Bill rocked his chair back and forth, the old boards beneath him creaking in protest. He stared out the darkened window and his proud soldier's profile slowly turned grayer than marble. All of a sudden he was an old man in a wheelchair.

"I don't think it's anybody's goddamn business what happened when he was twenty-five," he said. "My brother's never taken a bent nickel. You better go."

I drove back to Springfield in the dark. Now I knew something had happened almost eighteen years ago, even if I was no closer to finding out what. His brother knew and Maureen knew. Eddie didn't know, at least not for sure, but he was worried. Maybe he suspected, or maybe I had just set him on edge.

Eighteen years ago, and fourteen years ago when he running for the House, and eight years ago when he was running for the Senate. Something that could still knock the wind out of Maureen with the mention of a telephone call.

It's always interesting how poor boys get to be rich boys, Latrelle Gregory had said. It was a clever line, designed to send me marching down a twisted path, but it didn't ring true for Crane. The thieves I knew on Capitol Hill didn't steal just once, they stole compulsively, like children let loose in a mint, stole until they got sloppy and got caught, or became committee chairmen and moved on to grander larceny on behalf of their entire state. Crane had powerful friends and I knew they'd helped him. But there was no sense that money mattered greatly to him, no sense of the political sensualist who revels in the material rewards of power, no sense of grosser appetites. He had always been an inner politician, the kind who lives on the warm breath of applause, who feeds on a purer sense of self reflected back at him. His vanity was spiritual. If it was vanity at all.

In my motel room I ordered room service, turned on the television and lay on the bed. CNN's *Week in Politics* was doing a montage of the Crane campaign, old clips from the beginning. I saw myself briefly, standing on the steps of a high school in New Hampshire, frozen crusts of dirty snow lapping at the stone. Then Crane was shaking hands in a snowstorm, startled pedestrians peeking out of their parkas. I thought about those days and how they had all changed the night of the first debate, and the next morning when we had driven to that high school in—where was it?—Manchester? Then the deer and the look in Crane's eyes as they stared at each other through the glass. A sense of inescapable recognition and loss. What had we been talking about? His mother. We had been talking about when his mother had died and he had said something about choices. Then the deer. No, *after* the deer staring through the window at us. That was when he lied.

We had been talking about the days after his mother had died, the thing that had brought me back here. The days after his mother had died.

Then the deer startled him, caused something he was hiding to surface. More than sadness or loss. Something else. Regret.

On the television screen Thomas Crane stood at the podium during the convention and behind him his life played on other television screens. He was a wide-eyed boy walking down a gravel street. He was a young lieutenant in front of a cathedral. He was a freshman congressman on the steps of the Capitol. He was a husband with his wife dreaming on his shoulder in an airplane. He was a dozen things, he was everything you, or he, or anyone could wish, but one thing.

You think it will be a piece of paper or something you can hold in your hand. You think it will be something you can hold in your hand and raise toward the light. But sometimes it is much less.

He was everything b ut one thing, and I understood what I had seen in his eyes when he stared at that deer on the other side of the glass. I knew the answer.

IX.

IN THE MORNING I made one stop before leaving for Phillips, but that stop took longer than I expected and the sun was high overhead by the time I was back on the highway. The day had the gentle clarity of late August, the red barns and white farmhouses glittering in the sunlight with the precision of a landscape in a dream. I thought the country had never looked so beautiful, and as sad and hopeless as this sounds, I found myself wishing Robin was sitting beside me so she could see it, and then I remembered her in bed the last morning we had been together, the rose light stealing up her pale cheek until her eyelids fluttered and she turned away from the window and buried her head in my shoulder.

I could smell her hair, and I wanted her so badly then I would have betrayed a nation for a chance to wake her gently, then insistently, one more time. I would have promised anything. I could see her in bed so clearly and I reached for her and we had time, time outside of history, time to explain, to come to understand, and I knew it was all an illusion, a concoction of light and perpetual motion. But for a moment it was all I could see, more real than the road ahead.

The same spindly tree stood on the Barstows' lawn, withered green apples the size of golf balls rotting in the brown grass. Maureen Barstow came to the door in an oversize shirt, untucked and rolled up at the sleeves, hanging down to her knees. She stood behind the unopened screen, wiping her hands on the shirttail, the articulated shadow of the wire mesh wrapped around her like a net of silk thread.

"You shouldn't have bothered," she said. "I don't have anything more to say."

"Are you sure? I have just a couple more questions."

"I'm sure."

She was about to shut the door in my face.

"If you'd give me a drink of water," I said, "I'll be on my way."

Reflexive courtesy is the Midwest's grace and its undoing. She pushed the screen open and led me into a narrow, neatly ordered family room with a pale blue couch and a corded gold rug. She went into the kitchen and I heard water running. Pictures of her daughter covered the wall above the television. Gentle brown eyes, a soft mouth. I took one off the wall and was holding it when Maureen returned. She stopped when she saw what I had in my hand.

"She's his daughter, isn't she?" I said.

She stood with a glass held toward me in a suspended and suddenly sad act of courtesy.

"Born seventeen years ago," I said. "Born nine months after you saw each other in Berthold. Born a little more than six months after you suddenly left town."

She pulled the glass back as if it carried the weight of an ocean.

"He fled east back then," I said. "He was disturbed. And when he had to decide to run for the House and the Senate, he came back here each time. To talk to you. What sense does that make? You had a secret you shared. He needed to know if it was safe."

"No."

"An old supporter of his saw him driving up County Highway 123. I drove up that same highway yesterday. It leads here. I know he phoned you. One of his staff members remembered a name jotted down another time when he left unexpectedly. The staffer wasn't sure, but he thought it was Joe. It wasn't Joe. It was *Mo*. That's what they called you."

"No."

"The money from Bushmill. I asked both you and Bill if you knew what he might need the money for. You answered by saying he would never take a dime for himself and would never do anything dishonest. That's because the money wasn't for him. It was for you."

"You can't prove any of this."

"I checked her birth certificate in Springfield today. No father's name, but you shouldn't have given her the middle name of Gretchen. His mother's name."

Maureen set the glass carefully on a table. She sat in a brown chair and her head fell into the chapel of a cupped hand. I raised the photograph of her daughter.

"His eyes," I said. "His mouth. I've spent months staring at his face, seeing it in my sleep. This is his daughter."

"No."

"Yes, it is."

Light fell in gold bars across the couch. Something ticked inside the wall. Her face moved behind her hand and I saw that her eyelashes lay still as powdered ash. You forget in Washington how hard it is for most people to lie when confronted with the truth.

"It's hard to see, really," she said. "Just the eyes. You'd never know unless you looked for it. She looks more like me."

She held out a hand and I gave her the picture. She stared at her daughter. Their daughter.

"Gretchen was a stupid choice," she said.

"It was kind."

When she had been in the kitchen, I'd set my tape recorder on the television, and its baleful red eye glared at us, but she hadn't noticed, and now she looked at me hopefully.

"Does she know?" I asked.

Her head shook fiercely.

"Were you ever going to tell her?"

"No. Never."

"Why not?"

"She's *my* daughter. I'm the only parent she's ever had. I wanted her all for myself. I was selfish. I didn't want to share her."

"I don't believe it was that simple."

She glanced at her hands. "It was that simple."

"Did he want her to know?"

"It was my choice. That was a long time ago."

"I don't believe you were selfish."

She stared past me at the wall, perhaps recognizing the meaninglessness of noble gestures at this point.

"I didn't want to ruin his life. Why should I? What bad thing had he ever done to me? Give me a daughter I love? Is that bad?"

"Of course not."

In the kitchen the coffeepot dripped. The little house was bright and neat, full of merry sunlight streaming through the blinds like an electrocution. Maureen sat in the brown chair with her red, chapped nurse's hands clasped in her lap, holding herself erect.

"And now you found out," she said, "and it's going to ruin him."

"I don't know. I haven't written anything yet."

"You'll write your story. You know you will, and that'll be the end of him."

"I don't know."

"Of course you do. You know it won't matter how he tries to explain. It won't matter what I say. It won't matter if I tell the world he's been a wonderful man. They have this view of him, all those people out there who want to believe in something, and this wasn't part of it. I saw the debate. 'I'll never lie to you,' he said, and now he has. It doesn't matter why. It doesn't matter what I wanted twenty years ago, or how scared we were, or how young. It'll ruin him as sure as if you tell the world he shot someone."

She lifted her square, honest face toward me.

"You know what I hope? I hope he doesn't say a word. I hope he tells you all to go to hell. Let you write whatever nonsense you want. Let people think whatever they want. The hell with all of you."

We were finished. I picked up the tape recorder. Maureen glanced at it blankly and then led me out of her house and into the sunlight.

"I knew," I said. "I knew, but I really didn't have anything. I didn't have a single piece of evidence that would hold up. You could have lied."

She stood in the doorway, not understanding at first.

"You really are from Washington, aren't you?" she said, and shut the door.

I drove halfway back to Springfield before I turned onto a gravel road and stopped the car. There was nothing in sight except a stunted pine tree in the ditch. I opened the door and stepped out. The sun hung low, as hard and red as a hammered railroad spike. Late afternoon, plenty of time before deadline.

I walked along the road, hearing small sounds in the grass, smelling the baked cornfields radiating heat. A spray of starlings shot out of the pine tree like darts. What could I do? What choice did I have? I was a reporter and I knew something that would change the nation's understanding of a man running for president. There was nothing complicated about my decision. It was simple.

I stood on the road and then I turned slowly on my heel and, as I did, I remembered Robin on the night of the first debate, pirouetting under the stars as she breathed deeply of the magic of the campaign. Cornfields rolled off in every direction, rising and falling in broad, golden swells that tumbled finally into the sky. I could hear the whole country out there, raising its voice, begging to be heard, clamoring for someone to listen. I had heard them for six months and I had seen him face them day after day and I thought he was trying, I thought he cared, I thought he was the best chance they had.

I turned on my heel and I knew I wasn't going to write the story. He was too many things to be this one thing forever. We want the character of our leaders to be etched in marble at birth, every man a tombstone. It's not fair. The answer isn't what we were, but what we are, what we're trying to become.

If my editors found out it would be the end of my career. But maybe that was all right. I'd been there with him from the beginning. I'd seen more than I'd hoped. I knew something about the country I hadn't. I knew its secret: despite all its knowing cynicism, in the face of a culture of compulsive mockery and disaffection, it wanted to *believe.*

Robin was standing outside my hotel when I pulled up. She yanked open the passenger door and sat down.

"Don't write the story," she said.

215

"What?"

"Don't write it, Cliff."

"How did you find out?"

She wore a silk blouse and it stuck to her under her arms and down her sides. She leaned toward me, the tendons in her neck defined as if carved out of wood.

"She called Crane to tell him. Duprey called me because I was in Springfield. I got here about fifteen minutes ago. Have you called your bureau?"

"No."

She rocked back in the seat, looked at the roof. A long breath slid out of her chest. "God, I was afraid I'd miss you."

Her door was still open, but she filled up the car, slumped against the seat in a boneless curve, breasts falling against damp silk, one leg bent, knee against the dash, slender fingers hanging over the seat, inches from my leg.

"You shouldn't be here," I said.

That brought her back. She turned, red-faced, eyes holding mine desperately.

"What happened between them eighteen years ago is a private matter that has nothing to do with anything. Nothing to do with politics or what kind of president he would make."

I heard echoes of Duprey in those words, maybe Starke, perhaps even Crane. I was watching an understudy read frantically from a cobbled-together script.

"You'll wreck the life of an innocent girl, Cliff, destroy the privacy of a family and you'll hurt Crane. And what will it accomplish? It has nothing to do with what he believes, how he has conducted his public life. How will the country be helped?"

"It would be the truth."

"A hundred things are the truth." The words rattled against each other. "It's the truth that the country needs him. It's the truth he can make a difference. It's the truth he's going to win. It's the truth it was a long time ago. It's the truth it doesn't matter. It's the truth—" She rocked backward, her breath hissing between her teeth.

"You know he's the best man for the job," she said.

"That's not my decision to make."

"Jesus, you sound like a lawyer. Are you a fucking lawyer? You know he's the best."

"The voters—"

"Christ, Cliff! Cut it out! You know he's the best."

"Sure."

"Then don't do this."

"Robin."

"Please don't do this."

"Robin."

"Jesus, Cliff, please don't do this!"

Her hand settled on my shoulder.

"Cliff, he's going to *win*. Think about that. Think about what it means. He's going to win. He's going to be president. But he won't if you write this."

"I don't know."

"Yes, you do, damnit. You know."

Her fingers moved frantically along my collarbone.

"Cliff, please, please please."

I almost told her what I had decided. I have thought back a thousand times and I will never know why I hesitated.

"Listen to me, Cliff," she said. "I love you."

Then I knew I had been fooling myself. You cannot escape what you know. I closed my eyes and felt her fingers against my skin one last time.

"I love you too," I said. "I always have. Get out of the car."

"I don't understand. I love you."

"Get out of the car."

I made my first call to Duprey. I had his beeper number and he called back in three minutes.

"Where are you at?" I asked.

"We're in the car on the way to the hotel," he said. "In Atlanta."

"Is Crane there?"

"Let's talk a little, Cliff."

"Put him on, Steven."

"Cliff, listen, we've been friends for a long time—"

"You can put him on the line or you can read this in the paper tomorrow."

Silence. His breathing. "For Christ's sake, Cliff."

The phone moved and Crane came on.

"Cliff. You don't want to talk about Ulysses S. Grant this time."

I could picture him in the back of the limousine, the manner in which he sat with his legs crossed at the ankles, the polished captoe oxfords, the blue suit, the way he watched the passing landscape of motels and fast-food restaurants and discount outlets, as if they must contain within their banal façades some greater explanation of the journey. I could see all this—I knew it, had been there, awed, hypnotized, converted—and it filled me with rage at the arrogance that created a universe of such false promise, a universe with a lie floating like a black hole at its center, bending and distorting everything in its presence until the world turned inside out and all you were left with were lies.

"She says the daughter is yours, Senator. Is she telling the truth?"

"Well, I don't—"

"Maureen Barstow of Phillips, Illinois. She said you are the father of her child, a seventeen-year-old named Kara. Is she telling the truth? Is she lying?"

"Could we get together to talk?"

"I'm in Illinois, Senator. You're in Atlanta. We can't get together. We're talking now. I'll ask you again: is this woman lying? She claims this is your daughter. Kara."

"Kara," he said, and the way he said the name was an answer, but not enough.

"Kara. If you won't comment I'll put that down. Is she lying?"

I have read that he closed his eyes, that he did not speak for ten seconds. I only know it seemed like a very long time.

"Maureen's never been a liar," he said.

"Not now?"

"Not now."

218

I heard a shout in the background. The phone changed hands abruptly.

"Cliff!" Duprey shouted. "That is not an admission of anything! Do you understand? Not a goddamn thing!"

"I know you will want to talk to my boss about this story," I said. "Do you have the number?"

When I called Washington I asked the bureau chief and my editor to get on the line together. When I finished talking, there was a long pause.

"You have it on tape," my editor said finally. "You have it all on tape? You have him on tape?"

"Yes."

"On tape? Everything they said?"

"Yes."

"Jesus," she murmured, "'*I'll never lie to you*' . . . Jesus H. Fucking Christ . . ."

Then there was the great debate, of course, about the rights and the wrongs of putting what we knew into print, the slow creak up the hill toward moral justification. I was on the phone for an hour, but the tinny ringing of jubilant bells never left their voices through all the hand washing, through all the tortured granting of self-absolution, and I knew from the beginning we were going to run the story.

★   ★   ★   ★

BOOK THREE

I.

WHEN THE worst of it was over, after the press conference and television appearances, I was given some time off and drove down to Ocracoke Island in North Carolina, as close as you can get in this country to the end of the world. I stayed for a couple of nights at a motel in the village on the southern tip of the island. I couldn't sleep and I went for walks early in the morning and watched the light gather over the ocean and the beach take on the color of human skin while sand crabs tried to bury themselves alive. I watched the fishermen and the birds and the tourists who came on the ferry to drip ice cream on the wooden sidewalks. I stood at the edge of the ocean and tried to imagine the green horn of another continent glimmering in the distance, and after a while I couldn't stand it any longer, and I took the ferry north to Hatteras and drove up the Outer Banks and turned inland and headed toward Washington.

I drove until I reached Norfolk, where I pulled into the Quickstop for gas. *Newsweek* was on the stand in front of the cash register. On the cover Crane was coming down the steps of his plane late at night, his shoulders slumped, his eyes on his weary feet. In the background the flash illuminated a hard circle of faces along a wire fence and they were ghastly in the light, mouths open, eyes like slivers of coal. There was no forgiveness in them, no pity, no understanding, nothing but anger. There were two tabloids farther down the magazine rack. Three other women were now claiming to have had Crane's children, one who said she had married him at age fifteen in a ceremony in Elkton, Utah. There was a computer-generated photograph of the two of them standing in front of a log-cabin church.

The man behind the counter recognized me, a pleased and baffled look creeping past his watery eyes and up the wrinkled dome of his forehead.

"I've seen you on television."

I nodded and signed my credit card bill.

"You're the one that caught Crane with his girlfriend."

A woman behind the counter came over to stare.

"She was his girlfriend a long time ago," I said.

"I never trusted him," the man said. "There was always something in the way he looked at you, like he was hiding something behind that pretty-boy smile."

The woman laughed from the back of her throat. "Hell, you were going to vote for him last week, Johnny. You said you wouldn't trust the president to piss on a campfire."

"I never *trusted* him," the man insisted, his eyes focused on me, seeing television. "Any man that cheats on his wife like he done ain't worth shit."

"It was before he was married," I said.

"When are you gonna be back on television? Are you gonna be on them Sunday morning shows again?"

"I don't think so."

He shook his head sympathetically. "You'll do better next time, son. Won't look so nervous."

Pine flats rolled away on both sides of the road, a gray Confederate sky following me up from the South. Rain swept around the car, steam rose off the highway, and the world blurred outside the windows. I clenched the wheel and hurried toward Washington, flying blind through sheets of water tossed up by trucks. I drove faster, feeling the car rise up on the road like a penny skipping across a river. My windshield began to fog and I let it climb halfway up the glass before I turned on the fan. I needed to get back home, back to the campaign.

I stopped in the bureau when I reached Washington. My editor caught me walking to my desk.

"You're back early."

"Tanned, rested and ready."

She pushed her dark hair out of her eyes and squinted at me dubiously. "Nelson wanted to see you when you came through."

Nelson Ambrose, the bureau chief, was watching television when we knocked on his glass wall. He stood when I entered and clasped my shoulder with the restrained affection with which a Victorian Englishman might have welcomed a son back from the war. He was short and trim and had the thoughtful, neatly cropped, salt-and-pepper beard that Cannon Newspapers liked on its editors. As he settled back in his chair, he absently straightened a shabby green tie across his blue oxford shirt, the two-tone flag of prep schools everywhere. He'd been born the son of a milkman in Nebraska, and the uniform was only one in a series of compensations.

"I thought you were due back in a couple of days." He had a mellifluous, quietly commanding voice.

"I found out I'm not a beach person. I'm ready to go back to work."

He tilted his chair back. The television murmured away behind his shoulder.

"Great. Can't say enough about what you've done, Cliff. I know it hasn't been easy."

"I guess you watched me on *Nightline*," I said.

He smiled blankly, a line of perfectly regular teeth appearing through the beard. "Of course I did. You acquitted yourself well."

Ellen bit her lip. "I'd like to buy you a new tie."

"So you're ready to get back to work?" Ambrose said, swinging gently back and forth in his chair.

"I thought I'd fly out tomorrow morning."

"You're sure you want to go back on the road with Crane?"

Behind him shells were falling on a village street. A woman in a scarf fled from one pockmarked building to another.

"What do you mean?"

"You're an important employee, Cliff. Just want to be sure this is what you want, returning to the trail."

"Yes. It is. It's what I want."

"That's great. Whatever you want, you have earned. You've done extraordinary work and I know it hasn't been easy. Just wondering if it might not be time to think *change*. We could make you a senior correspondent, writing think pieces on what's happening in the minds of the voters, talking to *real* people. Might be bracing. You could travel where you wanted. Do the stories you wanted. Maybe spend some time traveling with the president. God knows, you've earned it."

"I'd like to stay on with Crane."

Ambrose nodded as if agreeing completely. "What sort of access do you suppose you'll have?"

A woman was dancing across a kitchen on the screen. She opened an oven and a chorus line of dinner rolls danced out.

"I'll be there with other reporters," I said, trying to sound dispassionate. "They can't throw me out of the day's events. One on one, I know it's going to be hard, but I'll work around it. I didn't start out knowing anyone. I'll manage. Just like I've always managed."

He nodded again. "I wonder about the flash point of having you back out there. There are people in San Diego who are afraid it could be seen as a provocation."

I knew the company had been getting calls and letters since the story appeared. The last count I'd heard was in the thousands. Somewhere in San Diego, right now, they were watching the sun glimmer on the bay, thinking, we made 20 percent last year, Wall Street is happy, the stockholders are happy, the view from this office is beautiful, soon I'll go home to my lovely family in my nice house in La Jolla, I don't need this wild-eyed anger simmering up from that odd and unsettling country out there.

"I can see how they might worry about that." I pretended to ponder the awful possibility I could be making life difficult for people in big offices. "But there's another side to the coin that I'm sure has occurred to *you*, Nelson. If I get pulled off the beat, it's going to look like we're retreating. It's going to look like we're scared. Like we're backing off."

Nelson tugged at a cuff. "We wouldn't want that," he said uncertainly.

I shook my head sympathetically. "You know what it's like. If the other members of the press sense we're unsure about what we've done, we'll never have a moment's rest. We'll be answering questions from Howie Kurtz at the *Post* every other day."

Nelson's hatred of Kurtz, the media reporter at the *Post*, had been a small, carefully tended fire since Kurtz had ridiculed the bureau for an internal memo signed by one Nelson W. Ambrose announcing that Cannon

Newspapers was switching to "high altitude" journalism. The metaphor was meant to convey some abstract notion of reporting that took in the entire landscape. Practically, it meant nothing, as the previous year's switch to "high impact" journalism meant nothing. Dying industries, like condemned men, seek endless redefinition. But Kurtz's column caused a small tick that throbbed for a day and a half in a white patch of Ambrose's beard. Now he tilted his chair forward and sat up as if something distasteful had settled in the bottom of his stomach. After a moment he smiled at me.

"Just wanted to make sure this was what you wanted, Cliff. You know this campaign better than anyone. If you're up to it, you're the man we want out there."

Ellen was silent until we were seated at her desk, our backs to Nelson's glass wall.

"Nicely done," she said. "But why?"

"Like I told Nelson."

She brushed her hair out of her eyes. "Bullshit. You know it's going to be hell."

I saw a tarmac, infinite in the night, and on the edge, a haze of lights. I could hear the murmur of the crowd, a keening of anticipation floating like a fervent whisper across the asphalt.

"I've just come too far to get off now."

She closed her tired eyes and I knew she was weighing her job, our friendship. For the first time I realized we were friends in a final and absolute sense: we could no longer survive without each other.

"We'll try to help you back here," she said. "Fill in the holes wherever we can. There's probably somebody in the campaign still talking to Mary." Mary Finley was the reporter who filled in for me on the road.

"Thanks," I said.

"Have you eaten supper?"

It took me a second to remember. "No."

"You want to get a bite?"

"I really need to go back to my apartment and throw some clothes in the washer."

She waved me away from her desk. "Go home. Watch a movie, get drunk. I'll tell Mary you're coming out tomorrow."

My apartment smelled like stale bread. I opened the curtains and was surprised to discover the National Cathedral floating against a pink sky like some misplaced piece of Europe. An avalanche of mail sat beneath the slot. I sorted it into bills and everything else, until I found a letter from my mother: *Dear Son, It has been so long since I've heard from you. I hope you are doing well. I saw you on television and was so proud. I know your father would have felt the same. You have stayed true to the things he believed in, though I am sure it has been hard. The weather here has been hot and dry . . .*

I folded the pages and put them aside. There was nothing else worth opening. I sat on the couch and looked around. Four rooms. Wooden floors. High ceilings. Had I really felt at home here once, or had it always been a place of physical and spiritual storage? I couldn't remember, but I missed the anonymous comfort of a hotel room. I walked through the tiny dining room to the tinier kitchen and found a Rolling Rock in the fridge. Returning, I saw myself in the dining room mirror, a dark-haired fugitive with surprising circles under his eyes. The telephone rang.

"You need to turn on CNN," Ellen said flatly.

By the time the screen came to life, Maureen and Kara were fleeing their home, hurrying out the door into the desert sun of the television lights. An elderly woman helping them tried to block the descending circle of reporters, but the camera lunged closer in that jagged rush that has become the American perspective on shame. Kara stared directly into the lens. She had long dark hair and wide eyes in a round face. Then she was gone and the pathetic apple tree on the front lawn stood incongruously front and center, abashed and lonely in the light.

"I guess they've had enough of us," Ellen said.

"Where are they going?"

"Undisclosed location."

I used the remote control to mute the volume. The picture cut to videotape of Crane's press conference. I recognized the room at the Washington Hilton instantly. It was all smaller on the screen, smaller and more pathetic and destined to be played over and over again from now until the end of time.

"Cliff? Are you still there?"

"Yes."

"Turn it off, Cliff, and go to sleep."

"Sure."

"I mean it."

"I know. Thanks."

But of course I did not turn it off. I watched it happen all over again, and soon I was there, back against the wall, trying not to be seen, watching Thomas Crane's death march, the way the room took in its breath when he stepped out of the door and crossed the stage to the microphones, his gaze fixed on the far side of the stage, a scrap of paper clutched in his left hand so it bent in two, the staccato of the cameras rising in a wave that lent his movement the slow-motion grace of someone drowning in light.

On television it was all smaller, more tawdry and less tragic. He moved like a marionette and squinted when he turned to face the cameras. But in the room that night he appeared and reappeared between the silhouetted heads and shoulders of the crowd as if struggling through an impossible landscape. I felt Myra leaning against me as she stood on her tiptoes, the dampness of her shoulder in the overheated room. Someone else brushed up against my other shoulder, the person behind me pressed forward. It was so hot the air seemed to shimmer and bend.

The press conference had been called with only an hour's notice and there were rumors of a screaming match between his advisors in a suite above us, but no one knew what side Crane had been on, whether he wanted to be here or not. I wanted to believe he had made the final choice to appear, but watching him I couldn't tell. He stood in front of us and he placed one hand in a jacket pocket and on his face was a small, screwed-up ironical smile, a faint ghost of the old charm, the old distance he once seemed effortlessly capable of maintaining from the surreal carnival.

He was wearing a blue suit. His tie was silver. He had allowed them to put on television makeup and they had gotten too much rouge on his cheeks, a strangely cheery shine that made him seem both boyish and false.

"I'd like to begin by . . ." He stared at the shimmering rectangle of white in his hand. "I'd like to . . ."

He glanced helplessly toward the side of the stage where Angela was standing. She stared through him with a shell-shocked grin.

"Eighteen years ago when I was twenty five . . ." He blinked at the cameras as if they were something he did not recognize. "Eighteen years ago when I was twenty five, long before I entered public life, I became the father of a baby girl . . ."

The tension broke in a shuffle and a gasp and the feeling of the crowd moving, despite itself, toward the stage. "Jeesuss," Myra whispered, scribbling so her arm dug into my side.

The television cameramen were swearing and sweating. They'd been set up too far back. The campaign press corps and the media stars from Washington were jammed up front. The bodies around me were flushed with the heat and the feverish anticipation of catastrophe that sets reporters glowing like banked fires.

". . . Neither her mother nor I was ready for marriage. Nor did we believe we were particularly well suited to each other. It was the wishes of my daughter's mother, reached after many hard painful hours of conversation between the two of us, that she raise our daughter privately. I have honored that wish since then. It has not always been easy. But I have always felt I had to respect the wishes of her mother. I have provided regular financial support for my daughter since her birth, and I have been in regular contact with her mother since then, making sure her needs were seen to. Within the very limited role agreed on, I have tried to be responsible and faithful to my obligations as Kara's father . . ."

His voice had fallen into a strained singsong. It wasn't the voice we had known, but it seemed to gain strength. I thought he was going to make it to the end.

"The matter is, finally, a private one between Kara's mother and myself. No one else can understand or judge the choices we have made. No one else can know what either of us has felt over the years. No one else can say if we have done the right thing. You all know how I feel about this story. A child has had her privacy destroyed, her life changed and perhaps ruined for nothing she has done. This is your responsibility. You in the press. One you will have to live with . . ."

They were standing on the edge of the stage, Duprey, Blendin, Angela, as if watching someone teetering on a ledge, afraid an indiscreet breath would send him tumbling. You could see by the way they strained motion-lessly toward him they thought he might make it, that there would come a moment when they could reach out and take him in.

"... I know that I have dealt as well as I could with a very difficult decision and very personal decision made when I was very young. I believe the American public will understand that, and I hope we will soon be able to return to what really matters, the issues of this campaign."

He released his grip on the paper and placed it on the podium beneath the microphones and lifted his eyes as if waking from a dream. A separate child, Latrelle once said, peering up at me. There was an awkward silence, and for a moment I thought Crane was going to turn on his heel and leave us while he could. The first question came from Randall Craig.

"Senator, you told the American public you would never lie to them. On the same night, during the debate, you said, 'I haven't been lucky enough to have any children.' Was that the truth?"

Crane leaned toward the cameras. He had been prepared for this question, and in his answer, you saw a glimmer of the old confidence.

"I said *Angela* and I haven't been lucky enough to have children. That is the truth. I have never denied Kara was my daughter because I've never been asked. As I said, this was a private matter, as was my concern for my daughter's welfare. A privacy I believe should have been respected."

His chin came up as he finished and even this modest sign of triumph seemed to confuse us. The room rustled with reporters shifting their weight, scribbling in their notebooks to cover uncertainty. Stuart Abercrombie's voice broke the silence.

"Senator, have you ever met her—your daughter?"

"No, I've spoken to her mother ..."

"Then how do you know what she wanted?"

Walk away, I thought. Now.

Crane wavered behind the microphones.

"Pardon?"

"How do you know she wants this privacy you talk about if you've never spoken to her? How do you know she wouldn't like to meet her father?"

"Her mother wanted her to have a normal life ..."

"But, sir, how do you know what *she* wanted?"

His hair was damp on his forehead. He reached toward it absently. The room was so hot the air seemed ready to ignite.

"I think I've explained . . ."

Nathan spoke quickly. "Senator, have you ever sent your daughter a Christmas gift?"

Crane's angular face went soft, as if the bones had dissolved. His left hand fumbled out of his pocket and he grabbed hold of the podium with both hands.

"No."

"Have you ever sent her a birthday gift?"

"No."

"A birthday card."

"No."

"Do you think those things are part of fatherhood?"

"Yes."

"You've talked a lot about character in this campaign, Senator. What kind of father have you been?"

Crane's mouth opened and closed. The room was so quiet you could hear the klieg lights hum. He tried to smile and his mouth opened and closed again and he stumbled back a step from the microphones. Blendin crossed the stage in three wide strides and ended the press conference and then came the deluge, the questions shouted about birth control and abortion, and the woman in back who began screaming, *I know him, I know him,* and the fight that broke out between the two photographers who had been jockeying for position from the beginning. At the edge of the stage Crane reached blindly for Angela, who stood as still as a winter morning.

A knee clipped me in the shin as the press rushed toward the door to file, Myra squeezing my arm once before she disappeared. I waited in the back of the room until they were all gone, and then waited until they were down the hall, and then waited until the lights had all been taken down and then waited.

But none of that was on the television. On television Crane was frozen in close-up at the end, sweat rolling out of his hair, smile struggling and forever failing to be born. On television the press conference ended with his expression at the moment he heard the last question, the moment before he fled, the expression of a child walking into a new school and realizing that all the friends he has known his whole life are gone.

I sat in the dark and watched it all unspool again on the screen and I thought, *This. This you have done.*

II.

THE FIRST person I saw when I returned to the campaign was a radio reporter who had crippled legs and moved along on metal crutches. He was standing underneath the plane's wing in the rain while a mechanic hammered at something inside one of the landing-gear bays. A half-dozen other reporters huddled beneath the other wing, smoking, faces lost in the drizzle. The radio reporter noticed me and came swinging my way. Everyone liked him because he had to work harder than the rest of us to keep up, and he did it with unfailing good cheer, but we had never been close, and I stopped in surprise, touched and a little uncertain.

"Cliff," he said, panting. "Do you have time for an interview?"

Then I understood the way he had been staring at me. It was the way a surgeon might contemplate a discolored pancreas. I was now a news object, a part of the story.

"Let me get settled in first. Maybe we can talk at the first stop."

He nodded in disappointment and swung his legs back toward the plane. I showed the Secret Service agent my tags and carried my bags up the stairs, assaulted by the smells I knew so well, the sweat, the old food, the odor of dirty bags full of dirty laundry. I stared down the narrow cylinder at the defaced luggage bins, the crowded seats, the aisle milling with staff and reporters, and the world swung on a gimbal. The sense of return was vertiginous. This was home.

I threw my garment bag into the netted storage space in the back. One of the CBS cameramen was flicking Styrofoam peanuts across the aisle. He

235

aimed at my head and then stopped when he recognized me, the peanut poised on his thumb.

I was in my seat before other reporters gathered around. They crowded into the aisle and the rows in front and back of mine, people I had lived with for months, suddenly tentative and awkward.

"They let you come back," Nathan said.

"They did."

There were a few half-hearted welcomes. Stuart stood with his thin arms folded, peering down his nose at me.

"It might have been more merciful just to leave our boy alone from here on in."

The plane shuddered. You could hear the dull thump of a hammer beneath our feet. A campaign drains everyone; they all had looked tired when I left, but then the exhaustion had been tinged with euphoria. Now they looked battered.

The Associated Press reporter leaned across Myra to shake my hand.

"Good story. You lucky bastard," he said.

Randall Craig smiled at me from across the aisle. "Ruthless. And I always thought you were a softie."

"No, he's the quiet assassin," someone said.

A CBS producer, a small Asian woman, leaned against Craig's seat. "He's a killer. I'm just wondering, do you know how that poor little girl felt when she found out who her father was?"

Starke appeared from the galley. He hesitated on the edge of the group and then slid by, never looking at me, never saying a word, a trembling flush on his full cheeks.

The heart went out of the party after that. When everyone had drifted back to their seats, Myra lifted her Bugs Bunny sunglasses and considered me in a parody of wide-eyed amazement.

"It's Mr. Popularity. Back from television."

"Just get me up to speed."

She laughed. "Speed? There is no speed. You're the angel of death and this is a slow-motion train wreck. You done killed him, boss. What more do you want to know?"

"What's happening with the party?"

"Oh that." She shrugged. "The central committee met and it looks like he's going to survive. There's just not time to find another candidate. Besides, how do you do it? Recall the convention? He hasn't committed a crime. He didn't commit treason. He just had a kid and somehow forgot to tell the whole world. It's going to be close, but what're they gonna do?"

I didn't say anything.

"One thing, Cliff?"

"Yeah."

"A lot of fools on this plane, and I don't mean up in front, believed in this campaign. I recommend extreme caution, cowboy, from here on out."

The hammering stopped. The engines roared. I felt my heart straining to take wing, to return to the solace of flight, the false significance of travel. I felt my blood pulse in the rhythm of constant motion it knew so well.

In the front cabin Crane came out of the pilot's door. As he moved toward his seat he looked up and saw me. There were hollows around his eyes and a stain on his shirt sleeve. His skin had an exhausted, moonlit pallor. He raised his chin, almost as though he was about to nod, the way he used to when he recognized me at the edge of a crowd, and a surprisingly abstract curiosity seemed to linger in his expression, and for a moment I thought it might be all right somehow, that there was an explanation I could make if given the chance. But the question, if it was ever there, faded from his interest. His eyes, which seemed to have grown in prominence, went flat and he looked away.

Starke appeared at the entrance to the cabin and ripped the curtain shut.

"Welcome home," Myra said.

He spoke that night in an arena with a bad sound system, his voice muffled and flat as it bounced off the walls and girders. The crowds had become sullen while I was gone. The first reaction to scandal is often sympathy. The second is not. It had taken a few days for a sense of betrayal to settle in across the country, and it had taken a while for his opponents to organize their fury. But both sentiments flowered that night. I remember how motionless he was behind the podium, his jacket off, a thin man in a white shirt in a circle of light, while out in the darkness, the crowd moved restlessly and then broke into the chant we would come to know so well. *Crane Crane what's her name?* Then the schoolyard taunt of *Liar Liar Liar* starting in back and filling the audience briefly with sour glee before it broke up into catcalls. He turned pages with a lifeless hand and spoke in dull reverberating sounds and walked slowly at the end to the back of the stage, where he disappeared in three steps, legs, shoulders, head, without a backward glance.

He reappeared the next morning in reverse, climbing onto the stage at the last possible moment and reading his speech while a sleepy, sullen crowd gathered its bile. He escaped before they had time to jeer and then we didn't see him again until the afternoon. The curtain in the plane was pulled shut all the time now and it was only secondhand, in the vacant murmurings of stunned staff, that we heard he was sitting alone at his table between stops, reading a worn black book with orders that he not be disturbed. It was only through rumors that we heard he was sitting up at night, that he had stopped sleeping, and that he had given orders that no one ride with him in the back of the limousine or speak to him for ten minutes before he climbed up on each stage. There was talk he was drinking and I didn't believe it. There was talk Angela had started staying in another room and I didn't want to believe it. There was endless speculation about the book and I thought I knew the answer. I had handed it back to him one night on the primary trail when he had been trying to explain a time in his past, a remembrance that had been based on lies.

I wondered what he thought he could find in Grant's *Memoirs*, written by a far different politician trying to recover from disgrace. I sat in my seat and stared at the curtain pulled tightly closed and it was hard to shake the vision of Thomas Crane bent over that book in the middle of the night, turning worn pages in a search for explanation, consolation, redemption. It was hard to shake but it wasn't my fault. I hadn't told the lie that sent him scuttling toward a greater man's life for solace. I hadn't built a ruined kingdom around a false promise. I hadn't made the cardinal mistake. The only mistake I had made was taking so long to see the truth.

A long trip through the Bible Belt had been planned back when all things seemed possible. It should have been changed, but the schedule seemed to have gained a life of its own. At our first stop in Memphis, Crane spoke for only fifteen minutes before skipping to the last paragraph and finishing in a rush, his good-bye buried in a taunting chant. That night Timothy Blendin screamed at the travel staff, "I don't care. Don't put him out in another field like that where half the fucking lunatics in this fucking lunatic country can get at him. Change the venue! Get the party to hold a party event where we can control the crowd! Do you understand? Don't leave him out there like that in the open!" They stared at him with the bewildered, terrified expression of sheep caught in a thunderstorm, but it was too late to make the changes and the next morning's rally was at a landing strip where, for the first time, the audience waved dime-store baby dolls with frozen pouts and wide wanting eyes, held aloft like a children's crusade marshaled to expose his hypocrisy.

It was hard to be certain what was worse, the dolls or the signs with the aborted fetuses a bright red splash in their centers. They sprouted everywhere. In Memphis the signs slapped against the windows of his limousine, halting the motorcade before the police linked arms around the car. They pounded against the side of the bus as we passed, the dull chants of *Murderer Murderer* like a ghostly echo of the rain.

"I don't get this," Myra said. "He's going splat because she *didn't* have an abortion."

Randall Craig smiled through his window at the protesters, as if they were cheering us. "They were right about him all along. They said he was a liar and he is. They have the righteous rage of the prophets. And that, my friends, is one powerful, fucking rage."

"It's about hypocrisy," Stuart said. "The South knows hypocrisy in its bones."

I raised my eyes and beyond the signs I saw hundreds of other faces, blurred and indistinct, watching with a sullen silence. They were the ones that mattered, the ones who had taken a chance and allowed themselves to believe he was different from a ruling class they held in contempt. They were the ones you saw him searching for when he briefly, inevitably, raised his eyes during every speech and stared past the dolls and the posters for a sign of recognition.

When Starke had walked silently past my seat on my first day back, he had declared my status with unusual precision. I was a nonperson to the staff from the moment I reappeared. They could have kept me off the road—Cannon Newspapers would have folded if they'd insisted—but they'd been too dispirited at the time. Now I was as close to invisible as they could manage. If I made a request in front of others, they answered as briefly as possible. If I spoke to them privately they walked away without a word. Still, there was no other retaliation, and after a while I understood: The contemptability of what I had done would be underscored every day by the nobility of their response. I would get my turns in the best hotels; my bags would be delivered. I would be treated like everyone else in every way, except, of course, no one could be expected to hide how they felt about me. That would be too much to ask.

There was one other thing. My name had disappeared from the pool list. The list was alphabetical and kept track of what print reporter would be part of the small group that stuck close to the candidate at each event. But my name was no longer on it. It was clear I would never get near Thomas Crane again.

On my third morning back I was sitting in the lobby when Myra came down wearing black jeans and a Mickey Mouse T-shirt.

"I'm glad to see you haven't lost your sense of style," I said.

It was very early in the morning. I was alone on a couch with the early paper because I hadn't been able to sleep. There were a dozen empty seats but Myra grimaced and sat down beside me.

"I'm glad to see you haven't lost your charm," she said.

"Oh no. Just ask around."

She slumped into the couch. "I've got pool duty this morning, but I've got to write. You wanna take a turn?"

Gratitude swept over me, then fear.

"Are you sure?"

Myra glanced impatiently around the deserted lobby. "Where the hell can you get a cup of coffee in this place? Yeah, why not? It should be your turn anyway."

"They're going to be mad as hell at you."

She smiled. "I know. Fuck them. What's the worst they can do? Give me back my life? It's yours if you want it. But Cliff, just so you know—it's not so nice out there right now."

"I've been watching."

"You haven't seen it up close."

"Then maybe it's time."

She pulled her sunglasses down off her head. "All right, cowboy. Have fun."

An hour later I was standing on a terrace in downtown Lexington. No one had tried to stop me, and I was checked in with the Secret Service and in place, less than thirty feet from the podium. Crane would come out a door behind us eventually, but I didn't want to think about what would happen then. I reveled in this moment, this small sense of return, watching people gather on the plaza below, feeling again the surreal vividness of so many unknown yet always familiar faces. It was amazing, the physical presence of a crowd, how alive it is, how it concentrates and makes tangible the human spirit, the way a bent and tossed forest makes real the wind.

I knew when he came through the door by the way the people spread out below me were suddenly still. I turned to see him marching across the terrace, a poor shivering city councilman pressed into duty by his side. I hadn't been this close to him since returning, and he seemed taller than I remembered, but it was only a reflection of how thin he had grown, how the carefully creased legs of his trousers flapped around his legs. He walked with a stiff-legged gait, as if his knees were locked, his gaze lifted above the crowd, and he seemed curiously absent, as if he had already removed himself from whatever disaster came next. He didn't notice me. I was standing to the side, but I had the feeling I could step in front of him and it would be the same.

The council member, young and fair-haired, managed to drawl a few dozen nervous words before hopping back from the microphone. The sun was still low and most of the crowd, in long rectangular shadows slanting from the buildings around the plaza, milled with uneasy anticipation in the cold.

When Thomas Crane reached the podium, a strange exhalation rose from below, a *huhhh* like when the air has been knocked out of your stomach. There was also applause, of course, thin but feverish, from the true believers near the front of the stage. He seemed to waver in the audible breath as he unfolded the pages held in his suit pocket. I watched his hands and they fumbled but did not shake.

He spoke quietly at first, his voice inflectionless but clear. There was a kind of dignity in it, and I don't know if they were surprised, or if they had to steel themselves, or if perhaps there was some faint stirring of shame in their hearts, the melancholy of the executioner as the doomed man raises his eyes with one last plea for charity, but they let him go for a few minutes.

The chant began in the back, and at first it wasn't too loud: *Crane, Crane, what's her name? Crane, Crane, what's her name?* He bent into the sound and continued. The chant rose steadily and when he hesitated and let his eyes search for the source, it swept forward through part of the crowd and then the dolls began bouncing up and down, wide-eyed and surprised. The bloodred signs appeared, while around them another chant arose: *Ten million dead! Ten million dead!* I'd heard it all before, of course, heard it already in my few days back, but I'd never felt it before, felt the way the words battered against your chest in a blood rush, felt the way they heated the air and filled you with a sense of shame as if you must, must deserve this in some inescapable, final judgment. The choruses crashed against each other and Crane's voice lost momentum and disappeared. On stage the council member took another unconscious step away from him. Crane gripped the edge of the podium so hard I saw his knuckles whiten. His voice rose in the mechanical singsong I remembered from the press conference. He was bent at the waist now, leaning forward as if into a gale.

A crumpled paper cup flew out of the crowd and landed on the steps leading up to the terrace. I saw the Secret Service agents flinch and then heard and felt, as if it were a hand against my chest, the chanting climb a notch. In front near the stage, his supporters were yelling back at the protesters in an antiphonal hysteria. They surged backward and the rest of the crowd surged toward them and I saw a sign come down like an ax, rise and then fall again, the sound lost in the din. Crane stepped back from the podium, holding his hands up in defeat. They should have taken us straight back into the door then, but the campaign was in chaos, and someone in

242

Lexington, who did not understand how things had changed, had planned Crane's exit through the crowd.

The Secret Service led Crane down the steps to a roped-off corridor across the plaza. We descended into a forest of arms and legs and bodies piling up along the edge of the rope as people climbed over each other's backs to reach him. The agents moved ahead of Crane, shouting "Hands out! Hands out!" slapping wildly at hands in pockets. They fell into a tight circle around him, the collars of their shirts going dark with sweat, their eyes darting, heads swinging back and forth. They couldn't keep the crowd back. It pressed in on both sides, stretching the rope line, trampling it down and pressing into the corridor, reaching out, grabbing his hands, his sleeves, his shoulders, faces tumbling into view and then falling, sliding by senseless of where they landed as they tried to catch his eye. They yelled for him to hang in there, yelled for him to remember the veterans, yelled for him to stop for a moment, yelled that they still believed, yelled he was a lying bastard, yelled that God would judge. He moved through them with his arms extended on each side, his hands touching hundreds of hands, never stopping, never slowing down, moving with a measured mechanical pace, seeming somehow still to shrink farther within himself, despite the nodding of his chin, the strangely murmured words he managed out of old habit, *thank you, thank you, need your support, thank you, need your vote,* words that seemed to come breathlessly out of the air somewhere in front of his lips, while fingers tugged at his sleeves, climbed up his arms, and traveling behind him, you moved through the heat and the shifting bodies, seeing a red coat, a shock of blond hair, sea blue eyes, an emaciated hand clenching a soiled letter, a woman in a plastic raincoat falling to her knees, all shifting, turning, clinging to the moment of his passage, and above it, the keening, the hoarse tangle of voices begging to be heard. We were almost through the plaza when we came to the dolls, bobbing like a ghostly drunken chorus. Crane moved like a sleepwalker. The agents' faces were shining with sweat as they pushed hands back and out of the way, shouldered our way forward. The path was coming to an end. You could see the edge of the crowd ahead.

A child with a halo of blond hair floated screaming into the corridor. Disembodied arms held her in the air, a sign hanging from her neck. *Daddy.* Crane stopped and when someone fell against him he stumbled sideways toward the crowd. An agent slid underneath his shoulder, another leaned against his back and they moved him forward. The agent ahead of them reached roughly for the child, but she was pulled back into the wall of bodies. The Secret Service held Crane erect and I followed them through hands that slipped grasping along my shoulders and past a final voice shouting something I could not understand and out of the crowd and around a corner where the limousine was waiting.

They tried to hustle him directly into the car, but he stopped at the door. The head of the detail was swearing violently at a trembling young aide while the agents with Crane clung to their defensive circle. Crane glanced around the car in a panic.

"Where's my wife? My wife, where is she?"

The woman agent who had been guarding his back looked at him curiously.

"She's in the hotel, Senator. She never left."

Crane nodded slowly, all his attention fixed on her, as if she was the most important person in the world, the only one who understood him.

"Of course," he said. "I'm sorry."

He clenched something in his right hand. He saw me and there was a moment of disbelief and then a kind of acknowledgment, as if it was only right that I should be there. Crane glanced at the thing in his fist and handed it to the agent.

"Give this to him," he said and disappeared into the car.

She looked at it and then at me. She held it out to me palm down, so I couldn't tell what it was until it was in my hand.

When I climbed into the pool van, they were quiet until Randall Craig, sitting in back with the CNN camera crew, leaned forward.

"It's been like that for more than a week," he said. "Nice story."

"Fuck you."

I tossed him the thing in my hand. He caught it blindly and held it up, speechless for once. The plastic leg of a doll.

That night on the tarmac I saw Robin walking toward the plane with Duprey and Starke. A handful of reporters followed them, but no one bothered her. Issues didn't matter anymore. They stopped by the stairway at the back of the plane, and she waited to one side, skinny arms hugging her chest against the wind.

I was standing at the edge of the light, alone, and I don't know how she sensed my gaze, but she did. She considered me carefully, minutely, those wide eyes settling on mine without a trace of sympathy. She stared me down until my heart fled, and then she seemed to grow bored with the whole thing and mounted the stairs to the plane.

III.

THEY TOOK Robin off the road the next day. It wasn't fair, but she had been given the one absolutely essential assignment to befall a staff member during the entire campaign, and she had failed spectacularly. They sent her back to Springfield to head the research department, replacing her with a twenty-two-year-old who had to check and get back to you before he could answer the simplest questions. It didn't matter much. The time when Crane's positions were greeted in good faith had slipped away. Everything he said now was open to hard-eyed reinterpretation, attacked by a press that trailed him like a clamorous rabbinical horde, searching each syllable for deviation from past statements, discovering hypocrisy and cant everywhere.

Within the week the *Times*, the *Post*, and the *Wall Street Journal* weighed in with critical assessments of his personal finances, his shift on abortion, his relationships with powerful lobbyists. The stories illustrated one of journalism's unwritten rules: If you don't have the big story when it breaks, you better find *something*. The tabloids had him a bigamist, a wife abuser, and dying tragically of a secret disease. Television reported all of the above without discretion in a state of barely repressed glee. The cumulative effect was to make it very clear that Thomas Crane couldn't be trusted with a position on the local library board, much less the presidency.

Blendin and Duprey were said to be scrambling for a strategy to counter the revelation that started it all. There was talk of an attempt to paint Maureen Barstow as an unstable woman who so desperately wanted a child she had lied to Crane about being on birth control. The idea rose and sank in a day, and I think it was the kind of self-generated rumor that sweeps through the press like a stray virus when reporters are packed together and starved for real news. The next day we heard that there was going to be a public reunion between father and daughter, followed by a joint live press conference. The idea had a luridly mawkish appeal that made it irresistible to television, and it made it onto the air, but in truth, no one seemed to know where Maureen Barstow and Kara were, not even the campaign.

I couldn't imagine the man I had known for almost a year consenting to such public humiliation. I remembered once we had been somewhere deep in Arkansas and the local mayor was also a preacher, a big weepy, white-haired man with a veined nose like W. C. Fields and soft, floury hands like those of a child. He had been going on about poor Lulu Bell, who was only seven and had cancer, and how her family's best hope was the Crane healthcare plan, and how poor Lulu Bell's momma and poppa had never given up hope and still believed that their government, the government of Franklin Roosevelt and John F. Kennedy and Wilbur Mills, wouldn't let them down. Crane was standing off to the side, waiting as the mayor rolled on through great southern swamps of rhetoric, pausing at the muckiest spots with his head cocked, as if listening for applause from heaven, and finally I saw Crane lean toward Duprey and heard his dry, flat whisper: "Poor Lulu Bell's running out of time. It'll be a miracle if she makes it to the end of this speech." The way he seemed to be outside his own carnival at moments like that, watching it from some safe distance with both awe and amusement, had always been one of his saving graces, one of the reasons why so many of us fell for him. I didn't want to believe that that, too, had been a fraud.

But they were spinning spinning spinning in the Crane for President campaign, and what they came up with, and how much of his self-respect he was willing to surrender, became apparent when we swung north and landed in Philadelphia. He was standing with Angela at the base of the stairs leading up to the stage, and no one knows what he said. They only heard her abrupt response.

"Don't treat me like a voter, Tom. Don't try to woo me. Just tell me what you want."

She spoke loudly enough to be heard by everyone behind stage. Crane stood beside her, holding himself erect, trying to smile.

"I am saying they think it might help." His throat was raw from shouting through the protests and there was a rasp to every word.

"Oh Christ, save us from *them*. Forget them and everything they say. What do *you* want me to do?"

"I guess I think it might help. The public loves you."

"The public thinks I'm a windup doll."

"Not at all, Angela. Blendin says the numbers—"

Maybe it was hearing that name, maybe it was the word numbers, as if there was still hope in the shattered crystal of polls, but Angela clutched her shoulders.

"*Stop it*, Tom," she said, loudly enough that the Secret Service agent on the stairs glanced back.

He stood inches away, not touching her, this helpless, misplaced smile stuck on his face like some costume-party prop, and you saw him groping backward into the past for some form of their old understanding, the privately shared cleverness that had always animated their marriage.

"We can't throw out the polls now, Angie," he said hoarsely. "We've already paid for them for the rest of the campaign."

"A doll. Like the ones they wave at you," Angela said. "Only less lifelike. Sit, stand, smile, stare adoringly at my husband. What child? Oh, *that* child? Yes, of *course*, I knew. Of *course*, it was all right. Of *course*, it doesn't matter. Of *course*, I feel the same."

Feeble applause for some unknown speaker washed back from the stage and they stood side by side, facing the opening in the curtain.

"It is not a case, Tom, I would take to court."

He collapsed into himself, staring down at his hands, fingering a palm as if he had never seen it before.

"It might help if you stepped out in front of the public a little more," he said.

Angela's finely boned shoulders sagged.

"That's what you think?"

"You would just introduce me. A wife introducing her husband."

"A wife introducing her husband."

"Yes."

They were speaking softly enough now they could barely be heard. The agent at the top of the stairs looked down at them and an aide gestured it was time. Angela straightened herself, tugging slightly at her dress, running one hand quickly beneath her eyes.

"No one writes a word for me," she said.

Crane nodded, not looking at her. He started toward the stairs but she stepped in front of him.

"Remember you asked me for this," she said. "When they call you a coward."

The next morning a stiff wind blew stray newspapers across the base of a different stage. They skittered and slid, flipping into the air like playful ghosts while the crowd outside the factory huddled against the chill and Angela Crane stood behind the podium on three thick catalogues someone had piled up at the last minute, stood on tiptoes in a blue short-sleeve dress, held her hair out of her face with one hand, and stared into a parking lot full of sullen faces. "I asked to speak today," she said, "because I have listened to too much said about my husband the last two weeks that is untrue, and I thought it was time you heard from the person who knows him the best, who has known him for more than fifteen years. Thomas Crane is not a perfect man, but he is not what you have heard. I want to tell you about the man I know . . ."

She spoke with a precise cadence that reminded one of the measured steps of someone walking into a lion's cage with nothing but the steadiness of her gaze to keep herself from being devoured. For the next few days the world watched hypnotized as she asked for a fair hearing of her husband's virtues, watched from high school football bleachers, union halls, barricaded streets with dead leaves whirling past in the gray air, watched from living rooms and kitchens and department stores and airport bars, watched this tiny woman in Chanel suits and Donna Karan dresses facing down the beast.

Campaigns run on money and faith. The volunteers who stay up all night sorting luggage and stuffing envelopes with no material reward except cold pizza need to believe. Their candidate can be behind, victory unlikely, and they are still okay if he wins the ballot in their hearts. Take that away and the machine loses energy and falls apart. The schedule was changing daily as Crane searched for safe harbors and all would have been chaos anyway, but there was no determination left to make anything work. Luggage ceased to arrive. Meals were forgotten. Rooms went unbooked. At two in the morning in Pittsburgh a bus dropped thirty of us off on a street a mile from our hotel. We watched taillights disappear and started hiking through the city.

We were climbing a hill when a jacked-up Chevy Impala with chrome rims and a Steelers pennant on the whip antenna cruised past. "Hey motherfuckers! You *lost!*"

Myra dropped her bags and shouted back: "Hey motherfuckers! You should see the poor bastard we're following!"

The car slowed and then laughter echoed from the interior and it sped up and over the hill. We resumed our slog, stretched along the sidewalk like a Bedouin caravan.

Stuart's shoulders were bent from the weight of his bags, his thin nose pointing toward the ground. "I'd take Thomas Crane's sorry constipated hypocritical northern ass and kick it halfway up this hill, if I could," he said without warning.

"Now, now, Stuart," Myra said. "Haven't you been listening to Angela? He's badly misunderstood."

"I saw your story. *You've* been understanding. How was it you described him? 'The wounded husband propped up by the love of a good woman— like a bad country western song waiting to be written.'"

"You know what it was?" Myra was panting slightly. "It was when she started talking about their trip to Haiti and those starving children and the tears she saw in his eyes. I probably shouldn't write when I'm throwing up."

"What about you?" Stuart aimed his nose at me. "What do you think? You're the man responsible for this happy state of affairs."

The woman who wrote for the *Dallas Morning News*, a duffel bag slung over her shoulder, was hiking past along the curb.

"Yes. What do you think? You enjoying this hike?"

The caravan was silent, slanted and ghostlike under the moon.

"I think if she waited until she stopped throwing up," I said, "she'd miss her deadlines."

"A practical reporter," Myra said. "His eyes on the essential things."

We crested the hill and part of the city floated below us. Lights, glass, stone, moon, clouds.

Stuart paused and set down the bags, carefully straightening his spine. "They were pretty rough on you last night on *Larry King*," he said more gently.

"I didn't see it."

"One caller kept calling you, 'Clint, this so-called journalist.'"

"Clint?"

"Clint."

"I like it better," Myra said. "You could walk around all squinty-eyed, saying things like, 'When you call me that, smile.'"

"I believe he described you as embodying all the destructive selfishness of the media, or maybe it was the selfish destructiveness of the media. Someone from Grand Forks, North Dakota, named Mike."

I stopped to look at the glowing city. It seemed more beautiful suddenly than anyone could say.

"Good for him," I said.

Stuart swung his bags and his long legs carried him down the hill.

"The public," he said. "It's not that they know nothing, it's that they're so damn proud of it."

There was nobody from the campaign to greet us at the hotel, and we stood in another line and got our keys from a stoop-shouldered clerk who kept apologizing over and over again for something about the water. My room was small with faded pink roses on the walls. I sat on the edge of the bed, so tired I didn't think I could untie my shoes. *What do you think? You're the man responsible for this happy state of affairs.*

I think it is a miracle, every minute of it. I think we are lucky to be here, lucky to bear witness, and if it hurts, if it blisters your feet, if it means you can't eat, if it means you can't sleep, if it means you need a drink at night to close your eyes, it is still a marvel, a moment in history, and it is all part of the truth, every shout, every angry word, every faltering step, every night lost in a place like this. It is worth all the bullshit and all the pain, even this, even this sad limping end to the story, because it is the thing laid bare, and that comes with its own justification. I think it worth everything because it all holds within it the truth, because it is true.

After a while I stood up and unpacked tomorrow's clothes. I looked for my Lands' End bag and realized I had left it downstairs.

The lobby had a single mirrored pillar circled by a cushioned seat. The mirrors were cracked and the cushions stained dark by wear. Steven Duprey sat with his legs splayed, a bottle of Jim Beam in his hand, my bag a few inches from his feet.

"My pal," he said. "My buddy from Montana."

He wasn't slurring his words, but he sounded very tired.

"Have a drink," he said.

"I don't think so."

"Come on, you fuck up my life beyond compare and you won't have a single, solitary drink? My pal."

I sat down beside him and took the bottle.

"Tim wants to kill you," Steven said. "He talks about ripping your head off and carrying it down Pennsylvania Avenue on a pike."

The mirror felt cool against the back of my head.

"Well. It's not an inaugural parade," I said, "but it's something."

Steven swung his head to look at me. "Funny."

I tried to pass the Jim Beam back to him. He considered the bottle gloomily.

"I don't drink," he said.

"It helps. Trust me."

The old man behind the desk stared at us through eyes the color of old window shades.

"Here's what I want to know," Duprey said. "I want to know what happened between you and Robin the night you found out about Crane's daughter."

"Nothing."

He shook his head. "I don't believe it."

The door opened with a brush of wind across our legs. Randall Craig and one of the plane's attendants swept in. He saw us and stopped, startled out of his ironic self-composure for once. I shook my head and he moved on reluctantly.

"Don't fuck her over, Steven," I said. "She was doing a good job."

He took the bottle out of my hand, lifted it and swallowed once, grimacing.

"Got the latest numbers tonight," he said. "In depth."

I waited.

"Nowhere to run, pal," he said. "Nowhere to hide."

He stared at the tile floor as if embarrassed.

"We bet too much on him, on 'Saint Thomas the Pure.' We traded too much on it and we let other things go. We thought we had a natural and all we had to do was put him on stage. In this fucking age, when everybody sleeps with everybody, you wouldn't think it'd make a difference. I mean, Jesus Christ, we know the name of every president's girlfriend for the last thirty years. They go on talk shows, they write books. But you see, old buddy, that's not how they saw him. They thought he was different. That was the whole magic act. Now they don't believe a thing we say."

"They're listening to Angela."

"Oh yeah. That's good for a day or two."

"You could go scorched earth. Bring the other guy down to your level. Like you did in the Texas governor's race."

He squinted at me. "You're offering advice?"

I knew I should go, get up and leave, but we were talking and that was something. "Just thinking out loud."

"Won't work. Just confirms what a hypocrite he is. Besides, you've got to have a candidate who's ready to fight." He took another drink, larger this time. "It's all gone out of him."

He handed me the bottle and I let it sit in my hands. All gone out of him.

"I never thought you'd do something like that," Duprey said. "I thought you had a different standard."

I'd stayed too long. I took a drink.

"You never thought I'd do it," I said, "because you thought I was easy."

He shook his head. "Fair."

"That's just another word for easy in this business, and you know it."

"I thought you saw through all the bullshit to the essential things. That's what fair is."

"Give me your essential things."

"He would have been a good president. That is my essential thing, Cliff."

The old man behind the desk rustled some papers, staring at our bottle with a combination of longing and resentment. We were keeping him awake.

"He lied for eighteen years," I said.

Duprey slammed his head backward against the column.

"Get back to Kansas, Dorothy. Everybody lies every fucking day of their life, and you know it. There are lies and there are lies."

"Is that right?"

"Yes. That's right. That's right. There are lies we have to respect."

"Really."

He turned and smiled.

"You don't think so? Tell me what happened that night between you and Robin."

I handed him the bottle. "Drink, Steven. It can only do you good."

I picked up my bag and took the stuttering elevator back to my room. I was mad and it held me for a while, but later that night, watching a square of light crawl across the wallpaper, listening to the bathroom pipes murmur, I found myself thinking of Robin waiting at my motel in Springfield, waiting for me to disappoint her again. I wondered if she had a premonition I was going to take her down with me. I thought of her pacing back and forth across the parking lot, running through the argument she had to make, and I wondered if she made the essential accommodation then, if she believed in Crane so fiercely and me so little that she prepared herself to say whatever was necessary. I could see her standing there as my car rolled up, arms folded across her chest, bony hip sticking out, hair in her eyes, the way I'd seen her so many times. I wanted to believe she still thought there was a chance I would surprise her, that she could believe in me at least that much. I watched a pale square of illuminated roses drift across the wall, and I could smell her beside me in the car, feel the heat from her, the nervous race of her fingers along the back of the seat. I was sitting beside her again, about to tell her what I had decided, and I willed myself to speak quickly this time, but I was trapped inside a small square of light sliding across the pavement. I was waiting for something, and then it was too late, and I knew I had always been waiting for the softly whispered betrayal I deserved for waiting too long.

The next afternoon in Detroit a heckler interrupted Angela. He was booed down, but the crowd shifted restlessly as she continued. When she got to the part about a man she had known, loved, and trusted for more than a decade, an impatient sigh arose. They'd heard it once too often. I got into my room late that night and turned on the television while I hung the next day's shirt and slacks in the closet. A comedian stood on the stage of *The Tonight Show*.

"You've heard the latest twist in the Baby J case?" he said. "I guess there's some doubt now about paternity . . ."

His rubbery grin curved like a clown's.

"Of course, Thomas Crane immediately issued a statement denying any responsibility."

I kicked the thing off with the toe of my shoe, opened the bottle of scotch I'd bought earlier in the day, and drank without ice or water from a bathroom glass. I fell asleep with the bottle by the bed, and the next day, when they announced that Angela was leaving the campaign, leaving her husband alone, leaving him and going someplace secret, leaving him—we all sensed—perhaps for a long time, it didn't hurt that much at all, and I was very glad to be on the road and holding the truth in the palm of my shaking hand.

IV.

THE LINE OF buses wound down the hill. We were lost and it was long after midnight somewhere in Ohio, in West Virginia, in Pennsylvania. Who knew anymore? We were lost. Rain snapped half-frozen against the windows and slipped between the panes, running down the metal walls and settling in a pool near the bathroom, which reeked from three aimless days on the road. Reporters who used it took a deep breath before entering and shut the door quickly upon exit, but the smell stole farther forward every hour.

The seats in the back were empty. The lights were down but for a single overhead lamp throwing a bull's-eye on the back of Nathan's head. The reassuring clatter of a keyboard could be heard between the grinding of gears as we slid down the curve in the dark. Looking over the seats I saw a pair of taillights floating below us in the rain, reflected on the windshield above the driver's bald head. He had refused to speak to us for two days, disgusted by the filth we left in his bus.

I sat in the last occupied row, three from the back, breathing through my mouth and spying on the hushed metal coffin of our world. Almost everyone was asleep. Three days of wandering from small town to smaller town, stopping at highway junctions and farmsteads, trading on the inbred politeness of rural folk, their awe at the unexpected arrival of this reflection of the television universe, even if the star at its center had fallen, had worn us out. There was little fire left among the press, only a longing to escape.

The bus clattered down a final curve. The door opened and the lights came on. Groans, oaths, and the confused mutter of the sleeping, bags banging against seat frames, shoes scraping the floor. The usual questions: where are we? what place is this? what time is it? Then the rain in the face, sudden wakefulness and awareness of an unmowed hill of brown grass illuminated in razor-sharp shadows and perched on the top, a tilting barn, immense and batlike in the dark. Nothing else.

We stood in the mud, huddling close to the buses, and watched a confused young aide lean into the rain as he hiked toward the barn. He made it halfway up the hill and then slipped on the wet grass and fell, sliding toward us on his stomach before grabbing handfuls of grass and pulling himself into a crouch, only to slip again and slide farther backward, his shirt coming up, his back pelted with rain. When he stood, his pale stomach was smeared with mud and he staggered trying to shake out his shirt. He started up the hill again and we watched, knowing there was no one up there, no crowd, no stage waiting.

The buses had pulled in in a circle and we could dimly make out Crane behind the window in his bus. He sat at a table by himself, a damp smear of white and black, watching his aides stagger about, shouting at each other through the downpour, pointing at the dark shadow of the barn as if it could be made something other than what it was through blind rage, as lost as shipwrecked children. I glanced away and when I looked back he had disappeared. The light out.

We flew through the middle of the night to New York. The city was as still as it gets when we pulled into the Hilton. In Crane's suite that night, Timothy Blendin screamed at Anne Paxton, the chief scheduler: "If we're going to campaign in East-Fucking-Asswipe, Ohio, it might be nice if we knew where it was. The only thing we're still doing in this campaign is facing the people, but we can't do that if we can't *find* the people, can we? We can't do that if we end up at a fucking *barn* at two in the morning, can we? It makes things a little more difficult if we have to campaign in front of *farm* animals, doesn't it? Is that a demographic we've targeted, Anne? The fucking animal vote, the cows and goats and fucking chickens—"

Crane stood up and walked out the door, his Secret Service agents shrugging themselves awake and following him. "We're going for a walk," he said, and when they started to object, he ignored them and continued moving toward the elevator. It was nearly five a.m. and Manhattan was a mausoleum of twentieth-century desire. He walked until he came to the Disney Store, where he stood in his shirt sleeves, his jacket left behind in the hotel, staring at cartoon cells of Mickey and Pluto, shaking his head when one of the agents offered him his coat. He walked on, peering through glass at the Gucci store, the Bill Blass collection, diamonds and rubies, electric trains and bright pastel furniture that looked as if it had been fashioned from beach balls. He pondered televisions small enough to fit in your hand and a telephone inside a pen.

He came, finally, to a wall of televisions, a video display on which a giant bird flapped across all the screens, a thousand different images inside the wings, people, automobiles, fires, riots, basketball games, ballet, buildings, streets, the images changing in a fluid ripple as the wing beat up and down, moving across the screens in one giant image that was the sum of all its parts and much more. He watched it quietly for several minutes, a wrecking ball, a neon sign, a crowd, a church spire, Einstein, Madonna, Hemingway, a broken step, a stained-glass window, a sunrise, a moon, a child dancing in a shower from a broken hydrant.

He stood in front of the window while the agents waited behind him in the pearly light of dawn. Much later they would remember the way he leaned into his reflection on the shimmering glass. "Listen to me," he said.

The next morning Starke stood on a chair in the hotel lobby.

"The visit to the school is off. We're going to a children's hospital."

The room was surgically bright, early sunlight flooding every corner. We had been struggling to shake ourselves free of the previous night, but now a brittle stillness descended on everyone.

"I've got the name here somewhere." Starke fumbled through a handful of crumpled papers. "Oh, of course. The Brooklyn Children's Hospital." He read on in an uninflected voice: "The senator hopes to demonstrate his concern for children suffering from America's healthcare shortage. As you know it's always been a top concern of his and Angela's."

Someone laughed out loud. Myra stood in front of Starke's chair, squinting at him in disbelief. "Jesus, John."

Starke had been battered until his waxed-fruit good health had collapsed into the sheen of a worn seat cushion. But he had become more important to the campaign than ever, his blindness to irony now an irreplaceable asset.

"We'll be visiting with several patients, including a child whose mother is deceased and who suffers from an inoperable brain tumor. I believe we'll also be stopping by another ward later." He coughed and read on. "The problems of America's children are close to the heart of this campaign, and this is a chance for Thomas Crane to talk about the solutions to those problems . . . We'll be leaving in just a couple of minutes."

When he was gone, Myra stood next to Nathan and sipped her coffee, watching steam curl above the cup in a thin ashen wreath.

"This is it," she said. "The thirteenth circle of hell. A photo-op with dying children."

The hospital hallway smelled of the antiseptic cleanser used to cover the odors of blood and urine. The walls were a pale yellow, scarred by gurneys and carts in rubbery black streaks. The dull chant from outside was no more than a murmur. Still, the hospital administrator twitched at the sound, his newly pressed lab coat swishing against his legs.

"Yes, that is correct," the administrator said. "The cost will be well over a million dollars and the family can't pay for any of it."

Crane stood in the middle of the hallway with the cameras running and all of us in a mob behind him. He was the same man whose appearance had been burned into our retinas, the shock of dark hair, the long forehead, the soft, slightly-too-full mouth. He wore the same beautifully cut suits and held his hands together in front of his belt buckle in a way we could all mimic in our sleep. He was the same and yet not the same at all. His neck hung loose in his collar. His knees were awkwardly locked. He seemed to be having trouble concentrating.

"And the aunt and uncle who are caring for her," he said. "I understand they had insurance, but it was canceled when the cost of her care became clear."

"That is correct." The administrator's long face hung heavy with discomfort.

Crane nodded. His gaze wandered down the hall and then swept back over our heads, lingering on the bright yellow frosted glass of the entrance.

"And the uncle has had to . . . quit his job," he said, "so the family would become eligible for Medicaid benefits."

"Yes, sir."

"A situation created by an antiquated healthcare system that . . ."

His left hand moved minutely against his leg, tapping out the rhythm of the muffled chant. *Murderer murderer.*

". . . that doesn't allow families to . . ."

His gaze came down from above our heads and he looked at us as if we were some imponderable embarrassment.

"Maybe you could show us to the girl's room now," he said.

The administrator spun gratefully and led the way down the corridor. Two nurses, who had been standing invisibly against the wall, fell in line. Starke faced the rest of us. "We go to the door of the room and then it's tight pool inside."

The doors to all the rooms were closed, but at each hallway intersection, people waited for a glimpse of Crane—nurses, doctors, children in wheelchairs, patients in shapeless blue smocks. He strode past them and their greetings as if he could not afford a moment's hesitation. The administrator broke into a trot at his side. Boom mikes bobbed like giraffes above their heads as the sound men struggled to keep up. The rest of us trailed in a rush, jostling and clanking along in the narrow space.

Her door was half-open and you could see the girl sitting up in bed, her head shaved, her mouth protruding from sunken cheeks. The cameramen shot forward and Crane approached not only the door but the faint circular reflections of himself in their lenses.

He could have gone in. There is no floor in the cellar of American politics, and we could have fallen straight through the election, slid down and down and down, and no one would have caught us, and this day would have been forgotten in others worse. But he stopped at the doorway.

The girl smiled at him, but she is forever off camera, and there is only his own smile back as his eyes settled on hers and filled with gratitude.

"We're not going to do this," he said.

The administrator halted at the doorway. Starke tried to speak.

"We're not going to do this," Crane said again, more loudly, as if hearing his own voice for the first time. "Not with cameras. Not as a dog-and-pony show." He faced us. "You can wait out here or you can go back to the buses. Nobody is coming inside with me. I'm sorry. We . . . I . . . made a mistake." His old smile appeared like a flame burning through paper. "It's possible it's not my first."

Someone, I believe it was Stuart, started to ask a question and Crane stepped closer, passing in front of a small crowd in an adjoining hall. I remember the caged metal lights above his head, the graying tile beneath his feet, the stained and scarred walls that spoke of parsimonious maintenance budgets eked out month after month.

The woman was waiting at the junction. How she got past security I don't know, but we were in a public hospital with a dozen entrances and the campaign had traveled amid chaos for a long time. She wore a faded print dress with a blue sweater draped over her shoulders. Her hair was stringy, lopped off in featureless bangs that met her eyebrows. She looked like the exhausted mother of a sick child, and when she stepped forward with her right hand extended it took the Secret Service a precious second to realize her left hand held something beneath the sweater.

The agent nearest her tried to block the jar after she threw it, but he only sent it tumbling through the air. Crane watched it turn in slow motion beneath the lights, a glinting mustard brown satellite with a darker heart. He tried, almost absently, to catch it when it was a foot from his chest, but it slipped through his hand. He grabbed once more as it fell, so he was bent over when it shattered on the floor. The preserving fluid spattered him across the chest and along his right cheek.

The fetus emerged as a small, pale thing with discolored veins in its head.

The next moment is lost in a blur, agents pulling him against the wall, the woman's screams cut short by an arm around her throat, guns everywhere, the crowd falling back and then surging forward eagerly, the police, the cameramen stumbling over each other, the random shouts for order.

Crane stood up, lifting the hand of an agent off his shoulder. He stared at the fetus as the puddle leaked toward his feet. He watched it near his shoes; then with a hard, abrupt shake of his head, he stepped over it into the hallway.

"Get someone to take care of that. Handle it decently." He looked at the woman held face-down on the floor by three agents and a policeman. "Be gentle with her."

The hospital administrator had flattened himself against the wall and still stood there as if chained. Crane glanced at him and turned to one of the nurses.

"We'll continue here in five minutes and then we'll go on to the other ward. I need a bathroom to clean up first. What was the child's name, Sally? Please tell Sally I'm sorry but I'll be late."

They were dragging the woman down the hallway behind him. She twisted her mouth free and shouted, "*Murderer!*" but he never looked back. He stood in front of us, wiping his hands on a towel a nurse handed him. He dropped the towel in Starke's arms.

"Send everybody back to the buses. They have their story for today."

The mayor was late that night to a reception at the Helmsley Palace and Crane waited in a room just off the lobby. The press had been shipped off to our hotel for the night, except for the pool. Nathan hung on the outside edge of Crane's circle. The campaign had delayed canceling a visit to the Southern Baptist Convention in Atlanta out of wistfulness about old possibilities. Now it was only two days away and Duprey thought they should travel to the West Coast instead.

"The young Dems at the University of Oregon would love to have us," said Anne Paxton. "The hall is available and they'll handle everything else."

"They've got a great old hall there," Starke said. "Three balconies, brings the crowd in close, great atmosphere."

Crane slumped in a Queen Anne chair, sipping Diet Coke, and he hardly seemed to be listening. Through the doorway, he could see people passing unaware across the lobby, and he watched them intently, as if they held some great secret.

"Well. If they've got three balconies," he said, "then we should certainly fly all the way across the country."

There was a moment of silence.

"We're going to the Baptist convention," Crane said. "If they'll still have us."

"Oh, Christ, they'll have us all right," Duprey said. "For breakfast, lunch and dinner."

Crane crumpled the Coke can between his palms.

"Fine. Let them gnaw on my bones."

He stood up, wavering slightly, picked up his jacket, fumbled with his tie, jerking it into place.

"You're not going to change any minds by showing up," Duprey said. "And it's going to look like shit on television."

"Any worse than it has, Steven? Any worse than it's looked for weeks?"

He started suddenly toward the lobby, Duprey loping at his side.

"It's going to look like hell, Senator."

"I suppose. Your job is to make it look as good as possible."

Duprey stroked his beard and then he started to laugh. They left him behind, standing there with a wild, renewed light in his eyes.

Crane entered the main lobby, crossing the wading pool of pink-and-blue carpet, heading toward the first person he saw, a young woman in a business suit standing with a small leather bag nuzzling her ankle. He approached like an arrow, and she took a step backward before she recognized him. He held out his hand.

"I'm Thomas Crane," he said. "I'm running for president."

He grabbed an overweight businessman next and then a couple who had wandered out of the reception. He stopped a tourist and her daughters and trapped two bellboys. He worked his way across the room with an exhausted, obsessive focus on each hand, each face, each word uttered. When he finished he turned toward the hotel entrance.

"Has anyone seen the mayor yet?"

Starke had been on the cell phone. "He's still five minutes away."

Crane took a deep breath. "Let's go out on the street."

"What?"

"Let's work the street. Right now."

And they went outside. I was ten blocks away in another hotel, watching the rain fall against my window, but I imagine the scene with a particular clarity. A touch of frost in the air. Taxis splashing down Madison Avenue. Pedestrians hurrying past in their blind, end-of-the-day march. A slender man in a gray topcoat steps in front of them, and they glance up reluctantly to see the Democratic candidate for president of the United States. Some greet him warmly. Some turn away. He doesn't seem to notice. He moves on to the next person. Now the rain begins to fall more heavily. The night fills with the hiss of tires and the bleat of traffic. Umbrellas mushroom black and red and yellow. Crane steps back under the hotel marquee, soaking wet, and he is laughing. Water runs down his face, falls off his chin. He stands next to the door and, as people dart in out of the rain, holds out his hand, holds out a politician's hand.

V.

I WAS WORKING on a story and at first I didn't recognize her voice, barely audible through the usual cacophony of keyboards and phones and chatter. When she said my name it took a moment to sift up through my thoughts. I saw myself standing on the other side of a screen door in the sunlight. I saw her considering me like a monster as she shut the door.

The television was in the back of the press room. I had to push my way through a small crowd to get a look. She was sitting on the couch in the studio of the *Today Show*, her daughter at her side. They were both wearing blue dresses with high collars, Kara's a girlish pastel, perched with their knees primly together. They looked as if they had just come from church and would be off after the interview to serve Sunday dinner to the less fortunate.

I didn't hear the question, but Maureen said my name again. "No, I told Mr. O'Connell at the time, I never felt mistreated or ignored."

She spoke in the midwestern accent I remembered and which, I now realized, sounded much like his. She looked her interviewer square in the eye, leaning forward slightly, as if sincerity was a steel bar welding them together.

"You have to understand," she said. "This was as much my choice as his."

Katie Couric asked the essential television question.

"And how do you feel about what's happened to you in this campaign?"

"I don't think it's right the way our privacy has been violated. We didn't ask for a hundred reporters on our lawn. We didn't ask to have to move someplace where we could get some peace. We didn't commit a crime. We didn't do anything wrong. We haven't hurt anybody—"

"But now you've voluntarily come forward," Couric said. "Why?"

Maureen looked into the lens. Her plain, handsome face with its honestly earned lines and its thin, proud mouth had never looked better.

"Because what's being done to Tom is worse. I'm not going to let the man who gave me a daughter I love, and who's done everything since that I've asked, face this alone. He's too good a man . . ."

Cheers erupted in a corner of the room and I turned to see staff gathered around a portable television, slapping each other on the back, stunned, staggering, laughing.

". . . I want people to understand that I don't feel Tom Crane did anything wrong. I don't feel he lied or misled anyone except to protect me and my daughter. I want people to know I'm proud he's Kara's father . . ."

Reporters flew toward tape recorders, notebooks. I walked back to my spot at the table and sat down in front of my computer.

"Hello! Hello! Hello!"

John Starke's cheeks were flushed and his eyes had a mad, midnight glow. The room dropped into astonished silence. He climbed onto a table.

"Transcripts of the *Today Show* interview will be available for anyone who wants them in half an hour. As you heard, the complete interview will appear on *Dateline* tomorrow night. For now, we have this to say, quoting me, not the senator: 'We're glad to see that Maureen Barstow has reaffirmed what we believe the voters already know. Thomas Crane's personal integrity has never been an issue with anyone who knows him well, and it should not be an issue in this campaign."

"What does the senator have to say?" Nathan asked. "Does he have any reaction to this appearance by his daughter and her mother?"

"Thomas Crane is busy with the things that have concerned him this entire campaign. The issues important to American voters, the state of the economy, the condition of our cit—"

"Oh, for Christ's sake, John," Myra said. "*Come on.*"

Starke looked down at her. He raised his thumb to his nose, stuck out his tongue, spun on a heel like a drunken soldier and hopped off the table, skipping once when he landed. The last thing we heard as he disappeared was a high-pitched keening that was widely considered, after some debate, to be the sound of John Starke laughing.

A few moments later an aide stuck his head through the door. "Five minutes. Five minutes."

There were the regular groans and protests that the schedule said an hour at this location. I looked at the half-completed story on my screen: an analysis of Crane's revamped strategy, which was to hold a tier of eastern states presumed more liberal and tolerant than the rest of the nation and then pursue the West Coast. The words seemed to be in some sort of Cyrillic bureaucratese, the dead verbiage of government that infects political coverage: "analysts say . . . indications are . . . reports from local officials suggest . . . grave concerns . . . questions raised . . ."

A modest woman appears on television, says a couple of hundred words, and suddenly everything else is bullshit.

My editor picked up her phone on the first ring.

"We're pulling out early," I said. "I'll get this to you at the next stop."

I could hear voices arguing in the background, phones ringing. Ellen sounded tired.

"Don't worry about it. The story's being bumped back."

"How are things back there?"

"Crazy. You saw the interview? The phones have been ringing off the hook. I've got to go to a war council here in a minute."

"Is there anything you want me to do?"

"No. We're handling it here. Nolan's writing."

"I've got react—"

"It's already on the wire."

We paused awkwardly. I could hear the news editor calling her name in the background.

"Cliff, listen. It was a good story."

"I know."

"We'll talk later. I've got to go."

Nathan was watching me eagerly from across the table as I hung up the phone.

"Trouble?"

You could see the mud-spattered blue of a Peter Pan bus through the

269

window. People were packing up around us. I folded my laptop shut.

"Sooner or later," I said.

Crane went to the Baptist convention that night. They were buzzing about Maureen's television appearance, and he might have seized the moment by confessing his sins and begging forgiveness. It was the right audience for that. But he didn't speak about himself at all. He spoke about what was wrong with the country and what he would try to do about it if elected. He was unrepentant, clinical, a scourged passion ringing through every word. It was the best speech he had given in a long time, but it was not the speech they wanted to hear. He took questions for almost an hour afterward, facing insults, anger, and disappointment with a terribly clear light in his eyes. He looked like someone who has decided very carefully and with grave deliberation that he may have to commit murder.

I don't remember where we were planning to go next. A month earlier a security guard in Miami had accidentally shot twelve-year-old Mayrelle Brown of Liberty City and the city had simmered since on the edge of an explosion. Crane had stayed away, heeding the counsel of Blendin and others who saw nothing but potential disaster in an appearance.

Then, at four-thirty in the afternoon of the day he appeared before the Baptists, a jury decided not to convict guard Harold Williams of manslaughter, and while Crane was speaking, Liberty City and Overtown burned. We arrived at four o'clock the next day, fires still smoldering, oily smoke spreading above the rooftops, a sour yellow sun poking through the haze.

A kid trailing along beside us smiled from beneath his baseball cap.

"Tire fires. Burn forever, man."

Stuart nodded, an overwhelmed look fogging his eyes. We'd flown here without warning, hustled on buses that careened across town in a race to beat sundown.

Myra's earrings, stringers of silver fish, tinkled as she walked. "This is a little nuts. That Thomas Crane—one wild and crazy guy."

Nathan loped alongside her in a T-shirt and a pair of gray UNC sweatpants. His clothes had been lost for the second time in the last week.

"Let's hope it's just him."

270

We passed a corner store with an ad for the Florida Lottery in the grated window, an auto-body shop, rusted fenders in a pile along the curb, a block of houses with small sagging porches. I thought of the Crane family home in Berthold. People emerged from behind barred doors as we passed, eyes appearing in a crack first, then the door swinging open in disbelief. Children broke loose from their mothers and ran beside us. A skinny boy in a candy-cane shirt skipped next to Crane, waving his arms at the television cameras.

Crane led us on, the Reverend Lucas Wain at his side, hurrying as if he saw something waiting at the end of the street that escaped the rest of us. He pulled people down off their porches into his wake and the crowd swelled behind him. When he saw a frail woman in a polka-dot dress hesitate on her front step, he stopped, climbed up, took her hand, and led her into his entourage.

Three young men watched from the next porch with eyes hard as polished coal. Crane took two long strides and was standing in front of them before they could blink.

"Come on. Come see what's happening."

The stucco of the Baptist church was water-stained, blackened. The minister waited in a black suit, standing in the middle of a small crowd on the steps, mostly women in flowered dresses and antique hats. They looked dazed. They'd been up all night, smothering embers blowing into the church from the apartment building across the street, now a charred shell with soot streaking up from its windows in an expression of alarm.

The Secret Service spread out on both sides of us as we reached the church. Four cars of police wearing plainclothes followed Crane's car, which trailed our procession like a tame dog. There would be a shouting match between the head of the security detail and Blendin that night in the hotel, leaked stories the next day about the recklessness of the whole trip.

The minister came down the stairs to shake Crane's hand. I noticed an agent looking backward. The street behind us was filling in, people spilling into the space around the limousine, cutting it off. We'd come without an hour's worth of planning. There were no volunteers with orange rope, no police moving people around in mindless exercises of authority, no preplanned corridors of escape.

Crane stood on the steps, his blue shirt dark with sweat.

"Come on up. Come on up, everybody. I'm only going to ask you to listen to me for a few minutes and then I'll listen to you."

He waited as the crowd drifted forward and the Secret Service backed up in a collapsing circle. "Come up." His voice was hoarse and the veins in his temples stood out below his hair, which needed a trim. "I told you I'm here to listen and I am, so I'll keep this short. The only thing I really want to say to the people of Liberty City is that there is nothing anyone can do to help you if you burn down your own homes . . ."

Somewhere a police siren wailed. I saw the Reverend Wain holding his fear on a tight leash. He'd lived off the anger in places like this for a long time, and he knew it better than anyone.

"I can't stop this," Crane said. "Only you can stop this." The siren blotted out his words, but you could see him straining to be heard, straining so hard his audience strained right back to hear him. The siren faded and Crane was still speaking. ". . . and how do we start? How do we start?"

He was skinny, sweating, pale, as white as any man who'd ever stood on this street. He opened his mouth to continue but his eyes were focused on something at the back of the crowd. He stopped and marched down the steps and through the audience to a young man who stood with his arms crossed, staring through his sunglasses at black cords of smoke coiling into the sky.

"I guess I'm boring you," Crane said.

The young man held his stare, pretending Crane wasn't there.

"You've been looking over there since I started. I don't want to waste your time," Crane said. "I just wondered, is there anything you'd like to ask me? Anything you want to know? Anything you want to talk about?"

Arms crossed, leaning back on his hips so his spine curved in his T-shirt back to his shoulders, the young man was silent. Crane stood in front of him, shirt wrinkled, tie askew, and, unexpectedly, he smiled as if he understood.

"Don't be scared," he said.

The polished chin moved.

"I understand. It's hard with all these people and cameras around. But you don't have to worry about them. You're not scared, are you?"

The glance came down from the sky.

"Don't be scared," Crane said. "You can talk to me."

"*I'm . . . not . . . scared,*" the young man said. But then, of course, he was. He tried to regroup behind his sunglasses.

Crane glanced at the smoke in the distance and shrugged. "Should we let it burn?"

"What?"

"Should we just let it burn? Let the whole thing go down, bring in bull-dozers and knock it down and start from scratch. Is that what we should do?"

The young man pulled his sunglasses down. His eyes were very young.

"No, man. People got their homes here."

"But they're just trash, aren't they? They're not worth anything."

"No, man, they everything they got."

"Then we should try to save them?"

A helicopter diced the air, racing low across the rooftops.

"No, man. Make 'em better."

Crane rocked forward as if he wanted to snatch the words out of the air and pull them to his chest. "All right. That's what I want to do. I need you to tell me how. But first I need one thing."

The young man stared at him over his sunglasses.

"I need you to listen to me for a few minutes. All right?"

A hesitation in young eyes, then a nod and, in the sweating faces gathered too closely around them, relief washing outward in circles, transformed as it spread into an unexpected sense of triumph, one small fire put out.

Crane only spoke for fifteen more minutes, but he had them wrapped around every word. He listened, and when he agreed he told them and when he didn't he argued and a few of them walked away, but others stayed. They talked and the sun began to set and sirens sobbed in the distance and he listened, descending the church steps to be closer to those who were speaking. The stains under his arms spread down the side of his shirt and his voice got worse until it was a ravaged squawk coming from deep in his chest, and I think he would have stayed there all night if the Secret Service hadn't finally convinced Duprey to cut it off.

They drove his car through the crowd to pick him up, and I remember Crane standing by the door, contemplating the people watching him leave, the same light in his eyes that had been there at the Baptist convention, that light that said anything, no matter how hard and how terrible, was possible. I saw that in the right place it held the power of more than his own redemption. He examined the faces watching him very carefully and then nodded and got into the car.

We stayed that night along Biscayne Bay, a mottled black in the moonlight, boats sliding out of the harbor visible by their mast lights, stars that drifted up and over the horizon to join the constellations. The campaign I had known was disappearing like that, slipping over the edge of the known world. Thomas Crane in Liberty City. Who would have guessed?

Robin would have guessed. She saw it in him from the beginning.

I couldn't let myself think about that. It was time to face the future. I ordered a pair of double scotches from room service and turned on the television. The interview on *Dateline* had just started. Maureen, alone this time, sitting on the couch across from Couric.

"In the thirty-eight years I've known him," Maureen said, "I've never known him to break his word or to lie. It's time people took another look at how he cared for his brother after the accident, what kind of son he was to his father—"

"But what people want to know is, what kind of father was he to his daughter?" Couric asked.

Maureen had a cup of coffee in front of her and she lifted it carefully with both hands. I remembered the glass of water she held for me in her living room.

"People have no idea how it was when we first found out I was pregnant," she said. "The midnight telephone calls, the panic. We talked about it for hours and hours before we reached the decision we did."

"You didn't want to get married?" Couric asked. "When you first found out?"

Maureen's smile was rueful, the smile of someone who has made peace with her worst memories. "I was only twenty-two, but I was old enough to know it wouldn't work. I wanted a simple life. My daughter, a house, a husband who came home at night. I couldn't see myself in a place like Washington. Everyone knew that was where Tom was headed."

"Were you in love?"

"Oh God, Katie, we were young. We were kind to each other. I'm sure we thought we were in love."

"Did he—"

She raised a hand. "We weren't meant for each other. The world had plans for him and they weren't my plans. Are you going to ask me if he proposed? I think he might have tried once. I'm not sure. I don't know what I would have said if he'd pressed me. I was confused. But I knew it wasn't right. He didn't leave me at the altar. He didn't *jilt* me. He's helped me out with money for eighteen years. I like him. But she's my daughter. Not his. Mine."

"What did he say when he came back that first time to tell you he was running for the House?"

Her face went soft. "He showed up without calling. It was right after I'd put Kara to bed. God, he was nervous. We talked for an hour. He couldn't stop looking at the pictures of her on the wall. I knew he wanted to ask me if he could go in and look at her, but he didn't. I don't remember what he said. Something about how he had been given a chance 'that could lead to a great deal of personal publicity.'"

Maureen looked down into her cup.

"He never asked me to lie. He asked me if I was comfortable with our arrangement. He asked me if this is how I wanted it to continue—her not knowing. But he never asked me to lie."

"The Senate?"

"He was more relaxed. He called first. He brought Kara some clothes. They were all too small, but it was a nice thought. He brought me flowers. He told me he had a chance to run for the Senate and he knew he wanted to take it, but he needed to be sure I still felt the same way. I remember how confident he sounded. I think he knew he didn't have anything to worry about, but he knew he should ask."

They cut to Couric wearing an expression of sympathy and admiration.

"In his article," she continued, "Clint O'Connell says there was a third visit."

Maureen leaned back on the couch and shook her head with irritation. "Tom was on his way through and he just wanted to talk a little bit, about life, about the way things had turned out for both of us. That's all. Nothing special."

"Did he call you before he ran for president?"

"He didn't have to. He knew what the answer would be."

"What did you think this year when you saw him on television, in all the magazines and all the newspapers?"

"I used to read all the stories and laugh. You made it sound so wonderful. Poor boy makes good. The star athlete, the good school. Walking into Springfield. Oh God, what crap. You know what I remember about Thomas Crane? I remember the way his voice shook in grade school if he didn't know the answer. I remember how he threw up all day before leaving for Saint Aquinas. You know what he wanted to be when he was in grade school? Not president. A teacher. They had the best life he could imagine."

She set down her coffee cup and her dry voice grew passionate.

"When we . . . when I got pregnant, I felt sorry for him. I thought he had less freedom than anyone I'd ever known. That sorry little town had pinned too much on him. You know what the best thing anybody could have done for Tom Crane would have been? Send him back to Europe and tell him not to come back for five years. I was so glad when he found out he actually liked politics. And when he turned out to be good at it. I thought it was the least he deserved. Now all that's gone. Because I had his daughter. Because he gave me the best thing I have in my life. Is that fair—"

I turned the television off and walked to the window. The moon had fallen behind a cloud. A cruise ship moved along the edge of the bay, decks piled up like the layers of a wedding cake, a Fitzgeraldian air of permanent celebration clinging to its slanted smokestacks. I blinked and looked away. We had all traveled like that once. Crane, Robin, all of us. Now we pulled toward shore in an open boat. Now we had only desperate bargains struck with ourselves and others when there was no other choice. Now we felt everything.

VI.

THE NEXT morning Crane was up with the dawn, shaking hands on the street and in the coffee shops of Little Havana before the rest of us were out of bed. There weren't many people on foot, and the befogged members of the pool remember him striding restlessly down the block past windows bright with Spanish advertising outlined in red and blue and orange. His face was palely shaven and stiff as parchment in the early morning, and he spoke in a rasping whisper to the old men in guayabera shirts who took his hand formally, often with a small, unconscious bow, sometimes placing their other hand on his shoulder as they smiled with the comradeship of old soldiers at this man who came of age long after they had lost their country. Their grace seemed to calm him and, after a while, he stopped trying to say much more than his name, nodding to each man, solemnly clasping and holding each weathered palm in his own.

He stopped for breakfast at a greasy spoon and, after working his way through the kitchen to meet the cook and dishwasher and two children busy sweeping and stacking cans even at this hour, he slid into a booth, and the press watched him tuck into a plate of eggs and Cuban pork with an appetite the likes of which they had never seen, sopping up the yolk with a *tostada* while he stopped every second bite to greet those who had heard he was inside, and who waited patiently in a line that grew until it reached through the open door.

As Crane was finishing he caught sight of Stuart sitting in the next booth picking his way disdainfully through a plate of chiles and eggs he had apparently ordered in a case of mistranslation.

"Pretend it's grits, Stuart," Crane said, winking at the confused young woman in a black business suit who stood in front of him. "Just pretend it's grits and cornbread."

They had reordered the schedule the night before, and we hopscotched north and west. It was late September, and spending time in the South made no sense except perhaps as an act of perverse defiance. Still, we stopped in Georgia and took a one-day bus trip across the state. Maureen Barstow was on television for three nights in a row after her first appearance, visiting talk shows and news shows, hitting all the major networks and working her way across the news cable channels. I saw her in rebroadcasts early in the morning, and she was resolutely uncute, implacably dignified. I could see now it was inevitable she would come back to face us. She'd raised a daughter alone in a small town without complaint for seventeen years. There was too much pride in the choices she'd made to think she'd let me or anyone else have the last word.

Still, she couldn't change what had happened. She couldn't erase what people had felt once and how they felt they'd been let down. The crowds that trooped across fields, gathered in courthouse squares, and waited in parks were sullen and suspicious, and the protesters were always there. There was no organization in this haphazard, thrown-together trip to keep them out. But none of it really mattered anymore. Crane spoke through chants and discontented silence. He ignored waving signs and bouncing dolls. In Valdosta, Georgia, he took questions until two in the morning on the steps of the courthouse, and in the end there was no one left but a circle of teenagers, black and white, gathered around a memorial to the soldiers of the Confederacy, which they treated like an old park bench. He came down and sat with them and you couldn't hear his words, but you could see them laughing, and you saw something familiar in the careless way he leaned against the base of the memorial pillar, the way he tilted his head to hear one soft-spoken boy, the flash of a reassuring smile.

The Secret Service was horrified at the way he had worked the crowd that waited to speak to him at the stop before, wading into it until he was surrounded and they could do nothing. They were furious that he had sat down with the teenagers at the end of the night in a position where they could only stand on the edge of the circle. There was a fight about it between the head of the detail and Duprey outside a hotel in Memphis.

"You might as well put him in a fucking shooting gallery," the agent said.

Duprey turned, started to walk away, and then stopped, smiling with the mad light in his eyes.

"You try to talk him out of it," Duprey said. "Go ahead. Tell him to be careful. Tell him to be cautious. Do it. See how far you get."

I had been losing weight since I came back and other members of the press had observed that I did not look well. I told them I thought I might be coming down with something. People on campaigns are always coming down with something and nobody ever remembers to ask if they actually got sick. It was a good answer and it served me well until I found myself leaning over the toilet in a Comfort Inn in Denver, sweat beading on my forehead, the faded fleur-de-lis on the wallpaper swimming through my fever. I threw up and huddled against the wall, laughing. I had come down with something.

The phone rang and I crawled across the carpet to get it. Ellen sounded exhausted.

"Cliff, listen. I have a couple of questions."

"What time is it there?"

Her voice was distracted, impatient. "I don't know . . . About two. Listen. When you interviewed Maureen Barstow, you identified yourself as a reporter with Cannon Newspapers in the beginning, right?"

"Of course."

"And you never sought to speak to her daughter behind her back?"

"What? I've never spoken to her daughter."

"You never went to the high school or tried to grab her after school?"

I leaned against the bathroom doorway. Through the window I could see the Brown Hotel across the street. Crane was over there somewhere in a suite with his wife. Angela had reappeared this morning, emerging from the elevator at his side, her hand discreetly in his, a tight smile on her face as she contemplated our startled throng in the lobby and passed without saying a word. Lights were on up and down the hotel. I wondered if one of them was theirs. In my fever the silhouettes of Thomas and Angela Crane seemed to float in half a dozen squares of waxen light.

"Ellen. You know the answers to all these questions."

"I have one more, Cliff. You did not threaten to interview Maureen's daughter if she would not speak to you on the record."

"I did not threaten Maureen's daughter. What is going on?"

She took a deep breath. "We're getting over a thousand letters a day. It just keeps going up. They wander out of their offices in San Diego and they go to dinner and they hear these things and, of course, because they come from a podiatrist or a lawyer, they believe them, and everything they've been told by their editors and reporters for months becomes suspect, and they call here and talk to Nelson and he talks to me and I talk to you and it's like all of us have never handled a story before in our lives."

There was a ragged edge to her voice I'd never heard before, but she regained control after a moment of silence.

"Listen, Cliff. We don't have a complicated theology. We find out the truth and we tell people so they can make up their own minds. Everything else is just bullshit."

I watched the walls ripple ever so slightly.

"You wrote a good story, Cliff. It's the only thing anyone will remember when this is over."

"Right. Thanks."

"Don't forget that."

"You're a good editor, Ellen."

Her laugh was a bark. "Go to bed. You sound like you might be coming down with something."

I pulled myself over to the couch and closed my eyes again. A thousand letters a day. I could feel the earth tilting beneath my feet.

The fever was gone the next morning. My skin felt like it was made out of tissue paper and my head felt as light as a balloon, but the world held still and thoughts came very clearly and quietly, each word arriving by itself in the middle of a blank sheet of paper. There were mountains floating above Denver, so sharp and blue they hurt my eyes.

Stuart stood at the edge of the press pen reading the *New York Times*.

280

I glimpsed the headline on the op-ed page: "The Press as Misguided Moralists—Why Cannon Newspapers Was Wrong." He realized I was looking over his shoulder and folded the paper shut. His sallow cheeks colored faintly. "You don't want to read that. Baker's always been as sanctimonious as shit."

We were in a downtown plaza of some kind. I thought I should know the name but I couldn't remember it. The press pen was off to one side on the sidewalk. The audience, running down the street next to us, stared enviously at the boxes of donuts and pot of coffee set up for us on a corner of a metal folding table. I helped myself to a cup.

"Don't worry about it," I said. "After you've been called a purveyor of tabloid sensationalism by *People*, you start to develop a healthy perspective on the whole thing."

Stuart looked away. "It's too bad you didn't get her side of the story when you first talked to her," he said. "Might have made for a more complicated piece."

"Sure," I said. "I'll try to do better next time I break the story of the year."

He looked at me, saw Starke crossing in front of the stage behind my shoulder, and seized the chance to escape. I picked the paper up off the table and read: *It seems clear now that Thomas Crane's character is, judged by a realistic standard, more honorable than that of those who have pursued him. As Maureen Barstow has testified repeatedly, the choices he made in his life concerning his daughter were made to satisfy the mother of his child, as they should have been. I confess I was one who originally doubted Thomas Crane's substance. When he burst upon the political scene during the primary season, I feared a pretty boy, a false purveyor of another Camelot. But it's become clear that his life has tested him in a way we had never imagined. Character? Yes, character is and always should be an issue in any presidential campaign. But in the crucible of this last month, we have discovered much about the character of Thomas Crane and of those who have blindly exposed his deepest secrets, and it is not the candidate who has been found wanting—*

I put the paper down. People were pressed up against the edge of the sidewalk, held back only by orange rope. The mayor was speaking and their eyes were on the stage. They looked like the crowds we saw everywhere these days, a strange apprehension on their faces, as if they weren't quite sure what they had come to see, but they expected it to be curious and strange and maybe tragic. They filled the plaza back beyond sight. We hadn't had an audience this size for a while. It left me with a queasy feeling in my stomach.

Myra wandered up. "Have you seen Nathan yet?"

I shook my head.

She smiled. "He's wearing the cutest little outfit. They lost his clothes again. Yes. There he is!"

I followed her finger and saw Nathan hovering uncertainly behind the stage, a pair of jeans rolled up until they looked like balloons around his ankles, a purple jersey hanging down to his knees.

"It's sad, really," Myra said. "Think of all those carefully polished gold cufflinks, those perfectly tailored jackets, sitting somewhere in some dark hotel closet. It's like the lost treasure of the Incas."

I couldn't manage anything in response. She waited and then stared with me into the crowd.

"What did you think about Baker's column today?" I asked.

Myra shrugged. "He's never been able to write."

"Everyone knows that. I mean what he said about Crane's character."

"I think you shouldn't read the editorial pages, cowboy. Not for a while, anyway."

She stood beside me while Crane appeared at the back of the stage. He crossed to the podium, looking out into the audience running down the plaza, and the sight of all of them seemed to fill him with grim satisfaction, as if he would get his chance here. They were silent while he was introduced and they applauded modestly when he took the microphone. I listened and waited for it to begin. The chant started in back, but the breeze seemed to carry it away. You could see the dolls, pale and small, like a child sacrifice in the distance. Yet you could hear Crane and I realized most of the people were listening to him with a curious intensity, as if they had come to see what wisdom could come out of his misadventure.

For the rest of the speech, the chants drifted in and out as the wind rose and fell. But he was able to finish, and as he realized he was going to be able to finish with most of those present listening, hearing what he was saying, his tempo picked up. There was even a moment when he paused, daring to give the protesters the air uncontested, while he surveyed the crowd with the triumphant eye of a battered fighter who realizes he has fought his way to a draw, at least for this round.

When he finished he descended from the front of the stage. They pushed forward along the rope, an old man with long wiry arms and a head of closely cropped white hair throwing his arms around Crane, whispering feverishly into his ear.

"He was never this good before," Myra said. "He's better now than he ever was. He's all here."

She started to slide down the sidewalk toward the edge of the crowd, pen in hand.

"He owes that to you, if nothing else. Gotta go talk to America."

I watched her move down the rope line. Crane was making his way toward me along the edge of the audience, swallowed up and then emerging, leaning forward and letting them have him again, disappearing into a surge of bodies. You could see the yearning for contact in the faces of those waiting ahead as clearly as if it had been cut into glass.

I pulled my cell phone out of my bag and called my editor.

"Listen," I said. "I want to try to talk to Maureen."

There was silence on the other end of the line.

"We're up in Missouri the day after tomorrow and from there I can hop off and drive to Berthold. Mary can fly in. I can catch up with the campaign in Chicago."

Ellen took a long time to speak. "For God's sake, Cliff. Why do you want to do this?"

"We haven't gotten another interview. I think she might speak to me."

"You know her daughter's still staying somewhere else."

"I know. It's her I want to talk to. We haven't gotten an interview since she went public. I think we should try."

My breathing sounded too loud on the phone. I held the receiver away from my mouth.

"This is crazy," Ellen said.

"No. I'm the person she first spoke to about this."

"Cliff! I'm sitting here dealing with rumors that you stalked her daughter through the high school and you want to go back there and show up on her front step. Are you out of your mind?"

Crane was moving along the edge of the crowd, coming closer. I pushed myself back against a building.

"What if it works? What if she gives me another interview? I know more of their story than anyone, Ellen. What if she talks to me?"

She took a deep breath. "No. You can call Nelson, but the whole idea will scare him so shitless he might yank you off the road tomorrow."

"Listen—"

"We have requested a follow-up interview and we have been turned down, Cliff. Mary has made fifteen calls. The answer is no."

VII.

WE TURNED toward the Midwest. We were making every stop we could squeeze in and a giddy feeling overcame the entire campaign, the feeling you have tobogganing down a steep hill late at night, the feeling of gliding into the dark, the air cold and sharp against your skin, trees flying past, the snow spraying your face and the hill becoming a cloud of white through which you fall until everything flies by too fast for comprehension and you descend in a rush of wind and ice and air and night.

We had to make a brief detour into South Dakota to honor a commitment made much earlier, and we arrived at our hotel in Sioux Falls half-drunk with travel and a frozen wind blowing unseasonably from the North. The lobby was tall and badly lit. We poured through the revolving doors in a shivering horde.

"You gotta love this northern climate," Nathan said, pounding his chest, clearly enjoying the noise his gloves made.

Stuart's nose looked as if it had been left outside overnight. He stared down its pale, bloodless ridge in distaste.

"I've always thought winter was one of God's little mistakes."

Myra was wearing a Chicago Bears stocking cap pulled down low. She marched past him to the desk to pick up her keys.

"This isn't winter, Stuart. You'd die in winter up here."

We fell into line at the temporary desk set up in the middle of the lobby. Nathan rocked back and forth on his heels, swinging his arms. A high flush colored his cheeks and his eyes sparkled.

"We've got time for one drink before they close the bar."

Myra nodded. "Something warm. Something with decaf coffee and liquor and whipped cream on top."

"Something with liquor anyway," Stuart said.

"He looked pretty good in there tonight, didn't he?" Nathan said.

"Christ, don't start," Myra said. "We can have a drink if we all agree not to discuss how good he looked, how hard he's campaigning, blah blah fucking blah."

"But he was sharp."

"It's easy to look great when you've got nothing to lose," Stuart said.

"Or it's really hard." Myra pulled down her stocking cap so she was staring out of two eyeholes like someone about to rob a 7-Eleven. "It's one of those two."

"The point is it doesn't matter," Stuart said.

"God, not the point. Anything but the point. The point is I want a coffee drink with whipped cream."

Myra reached the woman with frosted hair waiting behind the table, gave her name and received a manila envelope, room number scrawled across the top in Magic Marker.

"Momma's home," she said.

Half of us got envelopes, the rest were sent to the front desk. The rooms hadn't been right for a month. Nathan waited for us by the elevators, bundled up in two different layers of sweatpants and sweatshirts purchased at hotel gift shops during the last week.

"We'll meet down here in fifteen minutes."

My bags weren't waiting for me at my door as scheduled. I went inside and sat down on the edge of the bed, my head swimming. I'd had three beers on the plane. I couldn't face going back downstairs. I couldn't face the reckless euphoria that had descended on everyone trailing this lost cause. I couldn't face hearing Nathan or anyone rattle on and on. *He looked pretty good out there.* Who? Who looked pretty good out there? Who was he? I sat motionless for fifteen minutes, hearing Maureen Barstow's voice in my head and then a babble of others, until I fell asleep on the edge of the bed in my clothes.

The next day I can't tell you where we stopped or how many times, only that we ended up in Missouri. I stood in the back and looked at the sky, which was bright blue and cloudless all day. In late afternoon I stopped Myra outside the plane.

"I'm going to be gone for the rest of the day," I told her. "Keep an eye on things and call me if anything happens."

She looked confused.

"When is Mary showing up?" she asked.

"I don't know. She might not get here tonight. Just call me if anything happens."

"You're leaving him uncovered?"

"Just for tonight. I'll catch up tomorrow."

"Cowboy," Myra said. "Hoss. Think about this."

"Just don't let him get shot. I'll see you tomorrow."

I rented a car at the airport and drove northeast. I was at least three hours away and it would be dark by the time I reached Phillips. I hoped no one was still staking out her house. If I ended up on camera it was all over. I also knew there was no chance she would come to the door if they were waiting for her outside. I might have to wait until the crews packed up for the night. I saw myself as a ghost waiting down the block and the image was superimposed over Thomas Crane standing in the dark as a young man. He crunched across the frozen streets of Berthold toward the highway rolling past town and I tried to apprehend his disappearing form. *You know what I remember about Thomas Crane? I remember the way his voice shook in grade school if he didn't know the answer. I remember how he threw up all day before leaving for Saint Aquinas . . . I thought he had less freedom than anyone I'd ever known.* I didn't know the person she was talking about, had never met him, didn't want to think he existed. But I could see him standing on the side of the road as well as I had ever been able to see anyone, and I knew him too well. For the first time I understood him.

I drove to Phillips and there was no one outside the house. The lights were out and it was only as I walked up the driveway that I saw how the lawn had been torn up, broken and frozen now in cusps of mud and matted grass. A broken limb hung limply from the apple tree. I knocked on the door and no one answered. I knocked again and waited. The lights came on next door and I saw a face peering through a blind. The night was clear and cold. You could stare up and see the unblinking stars.

I went back to the car and sat there for a while, trying to decide what to do next. There was one more place to go. I pulled back out on the highway and headed toward Berthold.

We have only a few days left now. You know the end of the story as you knew so much of it. You know him and you know me. You don't know Robin, except perhaps as a face on television that stopped you for a moment with its beauty, the sincerity in the nervous rush of words. She always spoke a little too fast on television, as if there wasn't quite enough time to say all that she felt. She always walked a little too fast. She hurried through life as if some part of it was getting away, some chance to change the shape of things.

It is hard to escape a face that shows up at the oddest hours in the box, speaking briefly from Springfield on CNN or ABC. It is hard to escape a voice you hear without warning on a radio or stumble across in the third column of a story. She was never really gone and, if I have not stopped each day or so to record her appearances, it is because of some, probably absurd, sense of pride, a desire to create an impression of final dignity. I waited during my first days back for someone to ask me about her, but we had been more discreet than I realized, and those who suspected—Duprey, Myra, I don't think there were more than that—had their own loyalties and their own codes of behavior. So we were saved by the decency of others, and within a week Robin was back on television, answering questions when others were too tired or defeated. Her banishment came up against her determination and didn't have a chance. So she was never really gone, and while I drive up the highway I want you to think of her as I did that night, bent over a desk somewhere, still trying, still believing that it mattered.

I parked across from the cottage. The lights were on in the back and the thought that he was there made it hard to get out of the car. But I did, and crossed the sagging porch, and knocked and then stomped until the door opened and I saw the pink dome of his forehead and then raised eyes, growing black as they recognized me. He rolled violently forward and yanked the storm door open, and I thought he was going to roll right onto the porch and throw himself at me, but he stopped and I felt the heat escaping around him.

"Can I come in?"

Bill Crane clutched the wheels of his chair, rolled back half an inch, then jerked himself forward.

"I wish I had my legs. I wish I could kick the living shit out of you."

"I need to know some things."

"You need to know some things. You don't know a goddamn thing."

I stood on his porch and his anger seemed not to matter at all.

"Were we all wrong about him?" I said. "I don't mean about his daughter. I mean about everything else."

I could see the television flickering in the room behind him, smell fried potatoes.

"Tell me and I'll go away."

He held the wheels so tightly his shoulders were bunched in a knot. He rolled sideways absently, rolled back. He couldn't keep still. He seemed to be straining to lift himself out of the chair.

"Have you ever seen yourself on television?" Bill Crane said. "Has it ever been you?"

"No."

"I don't think you've spent one day with my brother."

"We used to talk about history," I said. "Ulysses S. Grant."

He stared at me in disbelief. "Ahh, Jesus Christ. Goddamnit." He rolled back from the door and I followed him into the living room. His half-finished dinner was sitting on a corner of the table, hamburger and potatoes. He turned off the television and spun around in the middle of the linoleum floor.

"You see some things. You see how smart he is. You see that he's good with people, has a way of making them feel good, making them feel that he cares. You see these things and you think he must be slick, because everybody who's like that is slick. And maybe he is a little slick, goddamnit, because nobody can be a grown man and a politician and not be a little slick. And you see that he's got some money and he's got himself a good-looking wife, and you figure it must have been easy for him. You think it must have been a cakewalk. That this is how it is. That it's always been like this. And you're all jealous, because you're not there. You don't have it. You're not the one they're all cheering for. And you think you gotta bring him down—"

"No," I said. "That's not it."

"Like hell—"

"No. You have to believe me. That wasn't it. I thought I knew."

His face was beet red. He was breathing hard. He stared at the floor trying to steady himself.

"What did you think you knew?"

"The truth."

He looked at me without comprehension.

"I thought I knew who he was."

There was a light on in the kitchen and nowhere else, a square of yellow falling outward from the kitchen door, long shadows around the table, the rest of the room in darkness. There was no wind but I thought I could hear the cornfield creak in the cold.

"You knew who he was," Bill said.

"I thought so."

He rolled his chair around the table until he was only a few inches from me, his head resting heavily on his shoulders, his thin gray mustache incongruously tidy beneath his uneven nose.

"This is my brother to me. This is what I remembered when I was watching that slide show they put on at the convention. You know, the one where they made our house look like some pretty cottage in Fairyland. I started thinking about when our old man died. Tommy had just been elected to Congress then, and everybody was excited about him. We had the funeral up on the hill and then we came back here. Folks kept coming by all day. One thing about a small town, they show up for your funeral whether they think you were a son of a bitch or not."

He smiled. He wasn't looking at me anymore but out the window and into the outer dark.

"There were all these people coming by. We were sitting here, taking all the food and shit, my sister and me, and I noticed he wasn't around. People would come in and they would look for him, right away. He was the one they really wanted to see. Hell, my sister and me, we were just more folks like them. Old news."

Bill rolled sideways and nodded at one of the doors on the far side of the room.

"He was sitting in the bedroom. I come in to see what's going on, and he's looking out the window and he says, 'I can't do this.' He says, 'I spent half my life hating the son of a bitch for taking so long to die, and now he's dead and I can't forgive him for leaving without straightening anything out. He ran Mom to death, then he left us to get him into a hospital, and then he checked out without even paying his bar tab. And I have to stand out there and hear stories about how he could dig more coal with a hangover than any other poor bastard who crawled down into that tunnel.'

"'Well,' I says, 'that would have made a more interesting speech at the church than the one you gave.'"

Bill stopped, trying to smile, an old, uncomfortable bitterness twisting his mouth.

"We sat there, and after a while I says, 'The old man was better when he was younger. You shoulda seen him before he got so sick. He could pick you up and hold you in the air with one arm. He had a laugh you could hear all the way across the bar.'

"Tommy looked at me. 'And why were you in that bar listening to that laugh?'

"'Mom sent me to haul his ass out of there,' I says.

"'Oh, it sounds like he was a whole lot different, Bill,' he says.

"Tommy's got the flag they gave him for Dad's time in the army, folded up in that little triangle like they do, and he's tossed that on the bed. It's that room where he was born, but I don't know if he's thinking about that. He's just sitting there, looking out the window at the cornfield, and I'm thinking we should get back into the other room, people are wondering what happened to us. But he's just sitting there in his fancy suit. He looked so young back then. Didn't look old enough to drink. Couldn't hold his liquor either."

Bill smiled at that. "He was always more our mother's boy, you know."

The little house hung behind him in the opaque darkness, the two doors to the bedrooms black squares, the posters on the walls indistinct. He was lit in profile by the kitchen and the yellow light defined the seams of his skin, the heavy fold of his jaw, the sharp spiderwebbed corner of his eye.

"So I'm thinking we have to get back to the other room, and then Tommy says to me, 'I've always wondered, Bill, what you thought when you went off that embankment.'

"And I say to him, 'I thought I should've taken the fucking freeway.'

"He looks at me. 'I should have taken the fucking freeway?'

"'That's right,' I say.

"And he starts laughing; pretty soon he's laughing so hard he's crying. We're both laughing. 'I should have taken the fucking freeway,' he says. 'That about says it all.'

"We finally stop laughing and Tommy—Tommy stands up, and he says, 'Let's go. They're waiting for us.' And he marches on out there and he's charming as hell for the rest of the night. They love him. Our old man is dead and they come out of that house smiling. He makes them all feel good. Every one of them."

Bill stopped, still remembering, and then his blue eyes focused on me. He rolled backward slowly, as if trying to get a fix on me, as if I would make some sense if he could just put me in the proper frame. He rolled backward, and his legs and the silver wheels passed out of the square of light from the kitchen and he floated in the shadows, pale and square, his eyes still there, like patches of winter twilight.

"And you knew he liked history," Bill said. "Ulysses S. Fucking Grant. And Diet Coke and baseball and fucking sunflower seeds. And you found out he had a daughter. And then you knew fucking everything. Oh, you had him figured out."

VIII.

I FLEW FROM Springfield to Chicago and caught up with the campaign at McCormick Plaza the next morning. Myra saw me, shook her head, and returned her attention to the stage. I waited until the opening speaker had finished before joining her.

"Your desk has been trying to reach you," she said. "They were calling your name out in the press room a while back."

"Did I miss anything?"

"You know, we've established this quaint tradition on this campaign, cowboy. We try to do our own reporting."

"Come on. Not now. Okay?"

She played with the trinkets on one of her bracelets.

"No. Maybe it went a little better. He finished. They were listening to him at the end. He gave a pretty good speech, really."

"Thanks."

"All right, Cliff. Where'd you go?"

I tried to tell her, but I couldn't.

"I'll tell you later," I said. "I promise."

My cell phone was dead. I walked into the press room, ignoring the surprised glances, and found a phone. I dialed Ellen but the cheerful male voice of another editor answered, a corporate toad who'd arrived shortly before I headed out on the road.

"Let me talk to Ellen."

"She's taking a few days off, Cliff," he said. "I'll be handling the political coverage for a while."

I hadn't slept the night before. I tried to think.

"How long?"

His laugh was so smooth it oozed. "Well, the rest of the campaign. When Ellen comes back, she's going to be handling long-term projects. It's a reward for how hard she's been working, something she can really sink her teeth into, really do some high-altitude, touch-the-readers sort of work."

"Can I talk to her?"

"She's on vacation for a couple of days, Cliff. Maybe a week or two, who knows? She tried to reach you last night. Where the hell were you, by the way?"

I closed my eyes. I didn't want to think about Ellen trying to reach me one last time before they took her job from her. The long-term projects editor slot was internal exile, where you watched over the stories the bureau never finished, the ones that kept reporters a few years from retirement safely toiling away until the end. At least they hadn't fired her. I tried to concentrate.

"There was a mix-up with hotel rooms. I wasn't where I was supposed to be."

"Really? You'd think they'd have that kind of thing all taken care of by now." He paused and shrugged on his new cloak of authority. "Look. I suppose you know we're getting an incredible amount of flak here. The letters and calls just keep coming in. They're worse now than ever. Maybe if Crane had just blown up and gone away. But he keeps trying, that son of a gun."

The phone felt heavy against my ear.

"Bottom line, Cliff. We're taking you off the road. Mary can take it from here. You'll come back to the office. Do some analysis. Some good think pieces."

"Don't take me off the road, Gerald."

"The decision's been made, my friend. Mary's going out to finish up."

"I need to talk to Nelson about this."

"Oh, sure. Absolutely. Give him a call. It was his decision."

I looked around the press room, reporters lolling behind the fold-out tables, watching Crane on television while he spoke right through the open door, a few people writing without enthusiasm, everything so familiar it seemed like all I could remember since the beginning of time.

"When do you want me off?"

He was surprised I gave up so easily. "Well, Mary's finishing up a story and she needs a couple of days. We were thinking Saturday. The wire schedule says you're supposed to be out west. She'll fly out and you can do the switch there."

"Saturday."

"That's right. Don't worry about coming in Monday or Tuesday. Take some time off. Get some rest, all right, buddy? You've earned it."

I walked back into the auditorium and found Myra standing in the same place.

"Is Robin around?"

She fixed me with a fed-up look.

"Why would Robin be around?"

"We're back in Illinois. The headquarters are right down the road."

"I haven't seen her. But most of the staff is back at the hotel."

"Thanks."

"Take it easy, all right, cowboy? Try to relax a little."

I asked at the hotel desk. The campaign had a staff room down the hall off the second-floor ballroom. Robin was sitting around a table with a group of volunteers when I found her. She saw me as I came through the door.

"I'll be right back," she said to the stunned volunteers and met me at the door. We stepped into the deserted ballroom and then, for a long moment, there was nothing we could say to each other.

"You don't look so good," Robin said.

"I want to ask you something."

"Cliff. Now is not the time. I've got—"

I slapped the wall. "Listen to me. I just want to ask you something. Why did you do it?"

"Why did I do what?"

I couldn't say the words. "Why did you say what you did in the car?"

She looked at me in disbelief.

"I thought I knew," I said. "But I thought I knew all kinds of things and I just wanted to hear you say it. It doesn't matter. It can't change anything. Just tell me the truth."

Robin leaned back against the wall, panels of red velvet wallpaper with thin strips of bronzed mirror between them, all beneath a domed ceiling, a false sky. She stared at one of the glittering, tiered chandeliers and blinked.

"Please don't tell me this was just about us. Please don't tell me it was just revenge. Please don't tell me you were just getting even."

"Just tell me."

She stared at the chandelier, her skin pale, her round mouth pursed. I saw her as if I hadn't seen her in years, the tangle of hair, the luminous eyes, the soft hollow at the base of her throat, the long legs and skinny arms. I thought of all the dolls waved at Crane. Our children.

"Is that why you wrote the story? Because you thought I was lying?"

"I wrote the story because I thought it was the truth. Because I thought I would never be sure about anything if I didn't. Not with you, not with him. Not even with myself."

"Oh, Cliff. You were never sure of anything. That's just you."

"That's not true. It's unfair."

"Cliff."

"I was sure about you."

She slumped against the wall in one of the rushes of vulnerability that so often came before her anger.

"How can you say that, when you've just asked me that question?"

She spread her fingers against the wall and pushed herself erect.

"I've made so many mistakes," she said.

"Wait—"

"No, listen. I'm not that good with people. I know that. I expect too much from them. I'm too hard on them. I'm too hard on them when they let me down. I know this, Cliff. I know it." Her hair snapped across her eyes. "I've made so many mistakes. I made a mistake when I left you for the first time. I made a mistake with Danny. Do you *know* how scared I am of making another mistake? I can't screw up again. I have to be careful. I have to be smart. When you started to push, I needed time. I needed to take it one step at a time."

I began to say something and she stopped me by placing a hand against my chest.

"I shouldn't have said it in the car that night. Not then. I was scared to death. I wanted you to stop and *think*. Think about him. Think about what you were doing. Think about us. I did. It's true. I hoped it would help you see."

She touched my cheek with the back of her hand.

"But I never loved anyone like I did you. When I said it I meant it. That's me too, you know. That's the good part of me. You should have known that."

She held her hand against my cheek, looking away when it fell so I couldn't see her eyes. She walked back down the hall to the room where she had been working, passing in broken reflection along the bronze mirrors. I watched her until she shut the door and then I was standing alone in a ballroom, a sea of empty chairs sweeping out to an empty podium, my own reflection the only crowd left.

We made our way east that day, all the way to Buffalo for the American Legion convention, where they listened to Crane, a fellow veteran, with surprising respect. Afterward we turned around and flew back toward Madison, Wisconsin, leaving long after midnight. We were making a short bus trip through the Midwest and then heading toward California and who knew where after that. I wouldn't be along to find out. I had one more plane trip out west and that was it.

It didn't matter. All the things that mattered were finished. I sat in my seat against the bulkhead and tried to pretend it was already over, but I found myself taking everything in. The pennants and cartoons and bad drawings taped up and down the plane. The smell of old food and socks and damp luggage. The peculiar sound of strained voices and tape recorders screeching backward and keyboards clicking like madly chattering clocks, time always running out. I could see Randall Craig in the galley flirting with one of the stewardesses, running his hand through his silver-and-black mane. Nathan was sitting backward in his seat, talking to Kathy Stanton of the *Dallas Morning News*, who leaned against the next row, drinking a beer. Myra had her feet up against the bulkhead in front of her, intently focused on a magazine. I heard a cork pop and Duprey appeared in the doorway of the galley, holding three bottles of wine in each hand.

"Courtesy of the Crane for President campaign," he announced. "Celebrating yet another day in which every thrown object failed to find its mark."

Cheap plastic wineglasses made their way backward. The delirium of the last few days took hold. A paper fight raged in back among the photographers. A correspondent for ABC News moved through the jammed aisle with his camcorder pressed against his eye, taping testimonials to John Starke's sense of humor. "I have heard he finds the antics of small furry animals amusing," someone said. They were trying to sing in harmony in one row, but could hardly be heard. The noise rose everywhere until the plane rang like a cocktail lounge. Stuart stood in the front of the aisle.

"Listen," he said. "Listen, damnit. It's come to me."

He rose in his seat, bottle in hand, speaking in measured cadences, waving the bottle like a conductor's baton.

"A hard time we had of it,
"At the end we preferred to travel all night,
"Sleeping in snatches,
"With the voices singing in our ears, saying
"That this was folly."

They pelted him with napkins. Nathan watched in wonderment. "What was that?"

"Eliot." Stuart swigged from the bottle. "And Stuart Abercrombie."

"Really. Eliot. He writes for the *Examiner*, right?"

All this, all this I found myself pressing into the pages of my mind, trying to hold on to it a little longer.

More than an hour later, most of the plane was asleep when Steven Duprey wandered back and knelt beside my seat, the face behind the beard expressionless.

"He'd like to talk to you for a minute."

"What?"

"He'd like to talk to you. You're a reporter and he is the candidate you are covering and he would like to talk to you."

Crane stood by his seat. He had nicked himself shaving and a spot of dried blood clung to the side of his chin. His eyes were bruised with exhaustion, like my own, but he seemed wide awake. Duprey walked down the aisle to leave us alone. Everyone else was asleep.

"My people are treating you all right?"

The simple courtesy of the question seemed impossible to navigate. I felt like a prisoner who's been in solitary confinement suddenly hauled blinking into the light.

"It's been very professional."

Crane glanced awkwardly at a scratched-out copy of a speech on the table in front of his seat and then into the back of the plane.

"I told them to make sure you were treated properly."

"Thank you."

He nodded formally, a deracinated, empty gesture, one it once would have been impossible to imagine without a playful glint in his eyes.

"My brother said you visited him again."

"Yes."

"If you have a question, maybe you'd like to ask me?"

This was over for me. It didn't matter anymore. I just wanted it to end.

"I have a thousand questions. I don't have one."

Crane nodded again and we stood there.

"There is one thing I would like to tell you," he said. "Off the record."

It was ridiculously long past the time to argue about degrees of candor between the two of us. It was over. I wanted this to be as painless as possible.

"Sure."

"I would like to have known Kara. My daughter. I would like to have known her."

He sipped from his Diet Coke and his face was tired and worn, the cheeks hollow at the end of one long day and the start of another, but he was composed. There seemed to be no anger, but when he looked at me again I saw a sadness I wanted to believe I finally understood.

"I would like to have known her. I made Maureen send me pictures. I asked about her. She seemed like a nice girl."

I couldn't think of anything to say. A nice girl. A pretty girl in a blue dress in a silver frame. A pretty girl with your eyes.

"I don't owe you an explanation, Cliff. I'm not sure I owe one to anybody. Maybe. Maybe I owe the whole country one. But not about her. I don't owe anyone an explanation of how I felt about my daughter. But you're the only one here who has met her, and I thought once we understood each other a little bit. So I wanted you to know."

"I'm sorry. I never really met her. I bumped into her in the doorway once. I only spoke to her mother."

Crane set the Coke can down on the table and stared out the window, as if I had disappointed him.

"That's right. I knew that. All right. Thank you."

I started toward the back of the plane and then I thought of one small mystery that hadn't been answered, and I thought somehow it might make things better if I asked.

"I have one question. Off the record."

He waited.

"The third time you went to see Maureen, what was that for?"

For a moment I thought he was going to dismiss me, wave me to the back of the plane.

"Off the record," he said.

"Yes."

"That was after Angela and I found out we couldn't have children."

I didn't understand and he could tell.

"I wanted to see my daughter. I wanted a chance to look at her, even if it was in the dark, just for one minute. She was the only child I was ever going to have."

The engines thrummed under our feet. The plane flying through the night, streaking above a sleeping country, racing toward the end.

"Now you can, you know," I said.

"I beg your pardon?"

"Now you can get to know her. There's nothing stopping you anymore."

That caught him by surprise. His world had been one way for so long that even when it was broken apart, I guess he assumed it could only be reassembled in its old shape. He blinked, and his hand felt the side of his cheek absently until his eyes settled on mine.

"Maybe. But I would like to have made that decision for myself. Good night, Cliff."

Nathan was awake in the seat next to mine. He felt compelled by some sense of delicacy to wait at least ten seconds after I sat down.

"My God, what was that about?"

"Nothing."

"Jesus, Cliff. Come on!"

"Nothing. Really. He wanted to know if the staff was treating me all right."

He squirmed. "Cliff, really. Come on. Crane wanted to talk to you. You were up there for ten minutes."

I leaned against the bulkhead. The senseless rush of air on the other side was reassuring.

"He wanted to make sure I wasn't being mistreated."

Nathan seemed about to argue and then he slumped in his seat.

"You're a lying bastard. But I don't suppose it matters."

"No. I don't suppose it does."

When Nathan was snoring quietly I sat up. I could see the back of Crane's head through the galley. It was impossible to tell if he was asleep. There was only that dark crown of hair turned toward the window. The scene was so familiar. I had seen him like this so many nights, so many nights I had pondered his thoughts, pondered his life, until I thought I could step inside his memories, his dreams, his fears. But they were always my own. They were mine all along.

IX.

WE DROVE south from Madison, looping into Iowa before turning north. The chill of winter came early that fall, a dreary taste of afternoon light shut down by clouds, a wind rising in the evenings that howled backward out of December, the skittering of leaves, a spattering of rain, a taste of ice upon the tongue. We rode west and north and the people waited for us in small towns where we arrived with the weather.

Thomas Crane wore his collar up and stood on makeshift stages among hay bales and American flags and shouted into the wind, and the people huddled deep in their down jackets, chins tucked into the collars, staring up at him through their eyebrows, their gathered breath rising like the steam of a locomotive.

Watching part of his army weep when forced to retreat at Fredricksburg, Robert E. Lee said, "It is well that war be so terrible, or we should grow too fond of it." I thought of that in Blue Earth, Minnesota, where they lit torches among glacial rocks erupting from the frozen earth. The flames turned the crowd a fiery red, and when Crane spoke they seemed ready to march with him to the ends of the earth.

Myra, who was doing pool duty, remembers he took a particular joy in all the familiar gestures of campaigning that night, the T-shirts handed him, the pictures, the notes, the mothers who held up babies bundled up like logs in their snowsuits.

"If they don't elect me president," he whispered to her, "I'm going to come back here and run for county commissioner."

And I think now that is too simplistic an image, another mistake, a romantic one, as bad in its own way as the others. In Springfield that week they were planning a series of ads questioning the president's honesty. They were working on a strategy to force another debate. They were talking about how to raise and spend millions of dollars through loopholes in the campaign-financing laws. They were back and they were fighting and it was as clouded and murky a route as it always is. Nonetheless, he was out there, facing the country's restless, always shifting desire. He was trying and he was happy again.

I saw Myra when we were waiting to get back on the buses. She wandered up holding a cup of coffee in both hands.

"You never told me where you went that night," she said.

"I went looking for Thomas Hart Crane."

She stared with me into the crowd, tossed her coffee cup toward a trash can and plunged her hands deep in her pockets, glancing up at the gray clouds with a sour look of distaste.

"You know how everybody has their favorite Elvis? Some like the skinny Elvis, some like the *Blue Hawaii* Elvis, some like the TV special Elvis. Well, I always liked the early Vegas Elvis best. You know, before he turned into a blimp, but when he was already wearing the white leather jumpsuits with the fringe. That, to me, is *Elvis*."

I looked at her.

"The thing is, they're all Elvis, every one of them," Myra said. "They're all him. You just pick the picture you put up in your head."

It took a while but I smiled. Myra looked at the rocks.

"This is kind of a beautiful place actually. We have seen some country."

We had seen some country. I thought of my father and his train searching for the coast. I had been there and back a dozen times and if there was nothing else, there would always be that.

"Thanks," I said.

Myra grimaced. "For what? Being dumb enough to stand here with you in the cold? I've got to get to work."

She turned on a chunky black heel and marched toward the buses. I noticed the row of Betty Boop eyes running down the back of her stockings, each startled separate lash clearly outlined on white cotton.

We drove on to Minneapolis and I remember Nathan chattering in the back of the bus. "No, really, he's moved back up here by five."

"So what?" a voice said. "If any state in the Union goes Democratic it would be Minnesota."

"Yeah, but he's closing across the East. He's even in Illinois and Michigan and he's up in New York by a point."

"Really?"

"Yeah. He's gaining on the West Coast too. I tell you he's only down three in Washington—"

"Really?"

"Yeah, listen—"

I sat up that night until the sky turned slate gray, and I thought about Robin and the first days in the snow in New Hampshire and the long glorious ride through the primaries and balloons falling from the ceiling in Manhattan and the night she came to my room in the neon light risen from Times Square and a road that seemed to wrap itself around every bend in the country, course through every city and on into nights lit by a glow along the horizon. I thought about the possibility for happiness I had held in my hands without understanding, and then I couldn't think about it anymore, and I watched the buildings step out of the darkness and straighten themselves against a gray sky.

We rode downtown to the Target Center that morning. The bus clattered to a halt and Myra stood up in the row behind me and grabbed her bag from the overhead bin. She started to reach for mine, saw I wasn't moving, and stopped.

"Aren't you going out?"

"No, I think I'll let this one pass. I'm feeling a little under the weather."

She stood in the aisle looking at me, but the doors were creaking open and the reporters behind her were pressing forward.

"I'll keep an eye on things," she said.

"Thanks."

Bodies filing past, cameras and hips jostling the seat. Then it was me and the driver. He glanced at me in the mirror above his head, and I saw his dark brown eyes floating in a rectangle. Snow fell on the other side of the window. I slid down in my seat, placed my head against a fresh part of the glass. I could feel ice melting against my cheek. When I closed my eyes I heard the idling diesel, a sound like something stirring in the earth.

The bus moved and I opened my eyes. The driver was pulling farther up the curb. The speech was over. The crowd had filled the plaza on both sides of the street, touching Crane's shoulders, reaching for his hands. I thought I saw Robin in the knot of staffers trailing him.

I staggered into the aisle and out the door. The cold hit my face and I took a deep breath. Crane moved slowly, snow falling around him, falling in his hair, his eyelashes. He was smiling. I saw a skinny blond woman again, briefly, and I started to push my way along the sidewalk, grabbing strangers by the shoulder, shoving them aside. It was hard to move, but Crane was going so slowly I was catching up. I saw Robin looking absently into the crowd, holding her hair back against the wind.

Crane stepped into the street, standing in the open, waving. In the confusion the rope line along the other curb had come down and the crowd spilled toward him, calling his name. He turned, and in five long strides he was there, reaching out as if hurrying to an embrace. I never heard the shots. There are some reporters who claim they did, others who say the sound was muffled in the snow and the noise of the crowd. But I know I never heard them. I only saw him stumble backward and saw the Secret Service swing forward like a gate, then the crowd turning, reaching for something black that floated across the collage of bodies for one blurred instant. I saw Thomas Crane stumble. The snow blew sideways and he fell forward, one hand coming up to his chest as if he had just remembered he left something in his breast pocket, a look of mild surprise and then sadness, as if someone had let him down terribly. He fell in a graceful arc, the Secret Service falling toward him to cover his body, so there was this feeling of a house of cards tumbling in on itself, or maybe of a forest all crashing to the same spot. He fell and for a moment he was clear, hanging in the air and you could see his hand on his chest, a half-formed word on his lips, and behind him, his wife, frozen in horror, her hands clenched by her side so hard that later she would be treated for the nail cuts in each palm. He fell past an outflung arm and a bending knee and then he was gone, hidden beneath the body of an agent and the collapsing swirl of other agents crouching, turning, pulling out submachine guns, and the crowd descending on the gunman, the poor, sad man who prayed to God before he pulled the trigger, prayed to God to give him the strength to save us from this Godless man.

He fell as he falls forever, hitting the ground, knees bent, curled on the concrete like an infant, head down, and then all of him buried by the crowd.

You know he died an hour later. You know the doctors tried everything, but the damage to his heart and lungs was too severe. They had him on the table for forty minutes, but he was gone from the moment the second shot hit his heart.

You know the man who shot him was Theodore Roosevelt Gaines, Teddy Gaines to his friends in Jacksonville. He had followed Crane for three days without getting close. That morning he had called his wife, who did not understand what he was doing, and told her he was out of money and would be coming home Friday. Crane was shot on Thursday. You could hear Teddy Gaines screaming about Jesus down the hallway of the Hennepin County Courthouse the day he was arraigned.

So I heard on the radio. I had been sent away by then. When Crane fell I fought my way back to the bus and called my office, like every reporter, and when our bus driver refused to move, Myra, Stuart, and I commandeered a cab and followed the limousine to the hospital, where we didn't have long to wait before the ashen doctor came out and passed on the news. They say Angela was by his side and would not let go of his hand at the end. This is the thing that stares up at me now in the gathering dark. The thought she would not let go.

I stayed with the story and did my job. I wrote two quick takes that flashed out on the wire, one while we waited at the hospital, the other after the doctors pronounced him dead. I did an update an hour later. Work was all I had and I clung to it fiercely, but by early afternoon, Cannon had flown in four reporters, and the company got me as far away from Thomas Crane's death as they could.

So I came back to Washington a day earlier than expected. No one knew quite what to do with me. I sat around the office pretending to work on a retrospective of the campaign until after the funeral. You know the funeral, but I will tell you a secret: I was there. I stood on the corner of Pennsylvania and Ninth and watched the caisson travel toward Arlington Cemetery. I wore sunglasses because the day was bright, but I wasn't trying to hide. No one recognized me. I heard the cannon shots rippling across the Potomac and then I went inside and watched them lay him to rest. We are never together in this country anymore except when we celebrate or mourn. For the next few days I listened to those who had scorned him express their public sorrow, and it brought a faint smile. In the end he held us together as he hoped he would.

I took three weeks' vacation after the funeral and it turned into a year's sabbatical. Cannon Newspapers was only too glad to pay me to disappear. I signed a contract to write a book about how I broke the story that ended a presidential campaign. The publisher said he wanted "something like Woodward and Bernstein." But I have been in Washington long enough to know that Woodward and Bernstein are really Robert Redford and Dustin Hoffman. I have written this instead.

You may have seen Robin in the last month. Since she went to work for the Urban Coalition she shows up on television now and then, and sometimes I catch a glimpse of her. She has a new, shorter haircut, but other than that she looks and sounds the same. She looks good. You can tell she cares.

I don't know what I would have said if I had caught up with her that last morning. I suppose I would have asked her to give me another chance. It was a terrible, impossible price to pay, but I am glad, at least, we were spared that.

When I started the book I drove to New Hampshire to remember what it had been like, and then I found myself traveling to so many of the places we had been on the campaign. I stared at empty fields and deserted halls and vacant parks and tried to fill them with the crowd that still lives in the back of my head. The day of the president's second inaugural, I was in Iowa standing in an unheated barn at the Des Moines fairgrounds, remembering the plaid shirts on the band. I drove through a dozen states, but mostly I drifted west and north in a slow spiral that has finally taken me to the place I was headed all along.

X.

THE LIGHT has fallen now across Berthold and the snow blows only along the ground. Stars race through patchwork clouds. I open the car door and step onto the road, the gravel hard under my feet, the air stinging my lungs. All the familiar ghosts have faded. The cornstalks are the shattered remains of a beaten army. I wade through the dead grass in the ditch out into the field behind the Crane home, stumbling over the frozen ground until I stand across from the small town.

The houses are disappearing in the darkness, their canted roofs cardboard cutouts against the sky. As I stand there yellow squares of light bloom in the darkness and people move within the light. I feel a melted snowflake slide down my back like a single finger running along my spine.

I remember standing outside of Havre in the same quiet, on the same kind of night. I know the stillness, the wind-born smell of wood smoke, the feeling Thomas Crane must have had when he contemplated his hometown in the early morning light.

His life was more of a trap than most, and at times this odd hatful of houses huddled against the cold must have felt heavy around his heart. But I want to believe there was more than that. He must have, in all the days he spent here, once stood where I am standing, must have confronted this town so fragile against the immense emptiness. He must have felt an inescapable tenderness at the stubborn survival of this place, his home, a place he probably already knew he had to leave behind.

I can see him standing in the open and looking back, feeling the weight of an idealized and impossible expectation, but believing he can live with it, persevere, believing he can trim the role to fit himself. Maybe this Thomas Crane is no more real than any of the others, but I hang on to him. I choose to believe he became the man he became out of love. I choose to believe this because if I don't I have nothing.

The town is so small that when I hold my hand out at the end of my arm I can almost erase it; only the cemetery and the moonlit silver grain elevator escape the darkness of my extended fingers. Yet I feel it there, the lonely, longing heartbeat at the center of a continent. The place where the road begins.

ACKNOWLEDGMENTS

For their support and encouragement, I would like to thank Jenny Bent, David Everett, Patty Edmonds, Jim Lipsiea, Betty Karaim, Robert Wilson, and, especially, Karen Brown.

For their close reading and suggestions for improving this manuscript, Adam Goodheart, Laura Sands, Connie McGovern, and Starling Lawrence.

For space and time to work, The Sanskriti Kendra Foundation of New Delhi, India.

For all of the above, Aurelie Sheehan.